COURT OF MIRACLES

COURT OF MIRACLES

A Human Comedy of 17th-Century France

Brigitte Goldstein

Library of Congress Number: 2004090969
ISBN: Hardcover 978-1-4134-4719-4
Softcover 978-1-4134-4718-7

This is a work of fiction. Names, characters, places and incidents either are the product of the author's imagination or are used fictitiously, and any resemblance to any actual persons, living or dead, events, or locales is entirely coincidental.

This book was printed in the United States of America.

To order additional copies of this book, contact:
Xlibris Corporation
1-888-795-4274
www.Xlibris.com
Orders@Xlibris.com
23727

Pygmalion and Galatea

Galatea, whom his furious chisel
From Parian stone had by greed enchanted,
Fulfilled, so they say, Pygmalion's longings:
Stepped from the pedestal on which she stood,
Bare in his bed laid her down, lubricious,
With low responses to his drunken raptures,
Enroyalled his body with her demon blood.

Alas, Pygmalion had so well plotted
The articulation of his woman monster
That schools of eager connoisseurs beset
Her single person with perennial suit;
Whom she (a judgement on the jealous artist)
Admitted rankly to a comprehension
Of themes that crowned her own, not his repute.

Robert Graves

Book One

Chapter 1

Paris, France, Winter 1661, the social season in the Marais is in full swing.

THE MARQUIS DE Valinquette sailed into his wife's boudoir, fell on his knees before her recumbent form arranged in languid repose on the divan, and fervently pressed his lips into the palm of her limply tendered hand.

"You were fabulous, absolutely marvelous! Splendid! Brilliant! Ravishing!" he exclaimed.

"I am happy to see you so pleased, Antoine!" The Marquise suppressed a yawn behind the daintily raised hand he had left free to her. Her resplendent copper curls sparkled like flames, brushed patiently to perfection by the indefatigable hand of the chambermaid. At first glance, the Marquise presented a picture of radiant feminine grace and beauty, enveloped in silk and satin, a woman ready to receive her lover. Yet, from behind this facade shimmered, as through a gossamer veil, a tragic air radiating from doleful violet eyes hinting at secret suffering, passionate yearnings unfulfilled.

The Marquis hardly took note of that aspect of the object of his profuse adoration. He ended his dramatic effusions as abruptly as he had entered into them, rose and without another look at his wife, he launched into a nervous measuring of the room with drawn-out strides, gesticulating fervently while recapitulating the social triumphs of the evening.

"Do you realize, my dear Galatée, the full significance of all this?" he exclaimed as if instructing a child innocent in the ways of the world.

"A visit from the Grande Mademoiselle herself! Her Ladyship graciously assured me before she departed that this will not have been her last visit, that she was completely enchanted with the breeze of freshness and youth your presence has brought to Paris. This means, my dear, we are on our way. Before the season is over, all of Paris will be at your feet. I'm certain of it. Madame de Valinquette's salon will rival the most famous gatherings in the Marais, the grandest nobles will frequent this house. And then, it will be on to the Royal Court! The day is not far off when I shall present you to His Majesty King Louis XIV, the Sun King himself, my treasure."

Antoine's flights of fancy made his usually calm, sonorous voice fairly squealed with excitement.

"This calls for a celebration!" The Marquise, too, now seemed to have caught her husband's fire. "Let's send for some wine and a light supper. We'll celebrate, just the two of us, tête-à-tête. Please, Antoine, just this once!" She pouted when she saw him stiffening though she knew that not even her sweetest allure was likely to move him to accede to her wish.

"You know that is impossible," he said with a suddenly sobering tone. He took her hands into his and spoke to her intensely, half scolding, half soothing like a father to a recalcitrant child afraid of the dark.

"Business is still awaiting me in town, you know that. It is already late and I must go now. You were magnificent." He kissed her on the forehead and straightened himself up.

"Could your business not wait until tomorrow, just this once? You said yourself, this is a special night!" She did what she had sworn she would never do, she begged. "It gets very lonely in this huge bed at night."

"Galatée, don't be unreasonable now." The Marquis wagged an impatient finger at her. "You mustn't listen to gossip, either. But most of all you must get your rest now. Tomorrow is another big day. I feel my Pegasus, I want to get to work in the atelier early. And I want you to be fresh and beautiful."

A listless resignation took hold of her. She did not resist when he lifted her up and carried her to the huge oak-frame bed. He placed her down gently and once more grazed her forehead lightly with his lips, as if he were putting a child to bed.

"Sweet dreams, my darling, my little bird," he whispered. "Dream about all the wonderful things we'll be doing together. This is only the beginning. Soon you will be the most admired woman in the world, I promise."

"If that's what pleases you, Antoine. My wish is only to make you happy."

"There. Good night!"

"Antoine!" she called before he reached the door. "Can I go for a ride in the city tomorrow? Monsieur Dupré has asked me to join him for afternoon tea. He wants my opinion about a piece of music he has written for me, but he says it is not ready for public performance."

A shadow fell over the Marquis' face.

"I have asked you not to accept invitations," he said sternly. "Monsieur Dupré is a gifted musician, I am sure he can do without your advice. When the piece is ready, we'll be glad to have it presented to an audience at one of our soirées."

"Antoine, you are not jealous, are you?"

"Don't be silly. I simply do not want my wife gallivanting around this city. There are too many dangers. The streets are full of riffraff—it is hardly a safe place for a lady."

"Of course! You're right! The riffraff! How could I have forgotten about the riffraff !" she said with a soupçon of vulgarity. But the Marquis was already beyond her reach.

Galatée, the Marquise de Valinquette, the glittering new star on the glittering firmament of Parisian society, pressed her face into the mount of satin pillows to muffle the throbbing of her heart.

The bitter famine that ravaged the Kingdom of France in the winter of 1661 caused not the slightest disturbance in the lavish dissipations of the Parisian social season. As always, the minds of the beau monde were fixed on ceaseless rounds of feasting, the gallantries and intrigues that were part of the game. Much time and energy were devoted to keeping up with the latest trends in fashion and determining which were the desirable social circles of the moment, and attaching oneself to the habitués in order to gain access to this or that society matron's salon.

During this particular season, the "intimate" Thursday evenings at Madame de Valinquette's had become all the rage of Paris. Everybody who was anybody and anybody who aspired to be somebody vied for the honor of being among the select of the inner circle. So completely had the Marquise's salon eclipsed all others that even the venerable Madame de Sablé had to move her reception, a Thursday fixture, to the less desirable Friday evening—although Friday had for three decades been the evening with Mademoiselle de Scudéry—so as not to find herself reduced to accommodating the overflow of Madame de Valinquette's gathering.

Madame de Valinquette was a new face in town that season, but her wit and charm had already become legendary. In fact she had already been favorably compared, by those who remembered ever so dimly, to another legendary hostess of great charm and wit, the inimitable Madame de Rambouillet, who had reigned among the beau monde from her equally legendary blue salon decades earlier and whose passing was still bemoaned by the few survivors of those halcyon years in the reign of King Louis XIII, before the civil war, that in retrospect appeared so idyllic and uncomplicated.

Madame de Valinquette, of course, was much too young to have such memories. Besides she was a foreigner, a noblewoman of ancient Iberian blood, so it was said, an attribute that did its share to enhance her appeal among the legions of her admirers. Youth was in fact Madame de Valinquette's greatest asset, youth and beauty—nature had been kind to her and had spared her from the universally common bouts with smallpox, the scourge that was wreaking havoc with the complexions of the day. She required little of the powder and creams that others massively applied to smooth out the blemishes and fill in the pockmarks, which in some cases were veritable craters.

The most famous salons of the day were presided over by venerated, still venerable relics, like Madame de Sablé or Mademoiselle de Scudéry, of distinguished wit and charm—wit and charm being the qualities most valued, although in the case of Mademoiselle de Scudéry one had to add, of course, her extraordinary literary talent. Her prodigious writings were among the most beloved in circles that prided themselves on a precious literary taste.

During this particular season, these same qualities—wit and charm—were frequently mentioned in connection with the Marquise de Valinquette, who was said to possess an abundance of both. All these attributes, taken together with her stunning, quite obvious beauty and a certain melancholy aura of mystery that attached to her, made her a rising star among the beau monde. So great was her fame that bon mots attributed to her began to circulate, and it became fashionable among the fashionable to sprinkle their conversations with "in the words of Madame de Valinquette," or "as Madame de Valinquette said only the other day." All to convey the impression that one was part of the coveted inner circle.

In reality Madame spoke very little. She rarely ventured an opinion. And she certainly never engaged in controversy. But she was, one might say, all ears. She listened intently while sinking her doleful, violet eyes into the eyes of whoever had garnered her attention at a particular moment. She had the very pleasing and pleasant ability to see the wisdom of almost any viewpoint that was presented to her with coherence and conviction. She showed understanding for somebody who might prefer Racine to Corneille and understood just as well why another might prefer Corneille to Racine. And if a third party expressed displeasure with both dramatists and declared himself in favor of the fabulous Monsieur Molière, she was not remiss in nodding her understanding for that position as well. Sincerity was the attribute she valued most, and within that constraint she was able to accommodate a multitude of perspectives.

Her reputation was enhanced by the great interest she took in furthering aspiring young artists, who frequently dedicated their works to her. Among the côterie of young men she had taken under her wing, her particular favorite was one Alain Dupré, a musician and poet, who wrote several songs in her honor which he was then invited to present at her salon to the illustrious Thursday evening throng.

Since the young man's skill of vocalizing did not match his skill on the clavichord, the Marquise herself graciously consented on one occasion to lend her voice to one of his compositions. To the delight of her guests, she produced such pleasing tones that soon no Thursday evening was complete without a "little musicale" by Madame.

At first, she presented selections from her friends' works to the accompaniment of the clavichord. But as her guests' appetite grew, she would reach for a lute and accompany herself to an ancient ballad born in the Catalan mountainside or to a doleful Andalusian love song. The mellifluous plaint evoked such haunting passion, it pierced the heart of many a lady and gentleman who would grope for their handkerchiefs if not for each other's hands.

One of her most devoted admirers was her husband, the Marquis de Valinquette, who, however, usually kept in the shadows of an alcove from where he observed the scene, content to leave center stage to his wife. A placid smile played around his mouth and eyes, deepening to smug satisfaction as each evening brought greater success and acclaim to the Marquise de Valinquette. The guests hardly took note of his presence since he rarely mingled with them. But the Marquise never forgot who was the grand master, the choreographer, whose will controlled the movements of the crowd, of grandes dames and grands seigneurs, of the poets, musicians, and artists, the renowned and the seekers of fame and fortune, who gathered around her.

Most of all he controlled the woman at the center, the magnet of these gatherings, as by an invisible cord. She was his creation. That was his satisfaction. His work was done during the day when he directed hordes of fashion designers, seamstresses, coiffeurs, chambermaids, and a host of servants to create the exact effect he wished to achieve.

Amidst the most outrageous sartorial creations of satins and silks, brocades and lace, in every color known to the rainbow and beyond, the pearls and diamonds, the fantastically coiffed wigs, the mountains of rouge and powder, wherein the men did not cede anything to the women, amidst the strutting and posturing, the Marquise held court robed in simple elegance of subdued hues, frequently of black and gray velvets, trimmings of white lace or embroidery, only the sleeves slashed with scarlet silk. The Marquis' instinct not to have her wear a wig turned out to be just right, for few ladies were as naturally blessed as the Marquise, whose loose tresses of resplendent henna were covered only with a black mantilla reminiscent of her Iberian homeland. He understood perfectly the effect of understatement, and so her face had to be left untouched except for a soupçon of rouge to heighten the cheeks.

Even her first appearance had created a sensation. Fresh like a rose petal carried by a gentle breeze, the saying went, she had fluttered into an easily bored and jaded world where jadedness and boredom were cardinal sins. The challenge for the Marquis was to keep the image fresh without resorting to outrageous artifice, as a musician is challenged to find infinite variations of a theme without departing too far from the basic melodic phrase. So far, he had proven himself perfectly up to the task.

When the first snow began to fall in early December, the Marquis took stock and found that he had good reason to be satisfied. Everything was going as planned. His fondest dreams had become reality in the three months they had set up house in the rue des Rosiers in the fashionable Marais quarter of Paris. He was confident that they would soon reach his most ardent goal—to be received at the royal court. The time was propitious and all obstacles seemed to fall like a slate of dominoes.

The king's hated minister Mazarin had departed this world. The youthful King Louis XIV had taken over the reins of his kingdom himself. He would need dependable men. The field was open for those with ambition and a willingness to serve their King without seeking to outshine His Majesty. Or so Antoine thought.

The night watchman announced the hour of midnight when Antoine Barca, the Marquis de Valinquette, turned into the rue de Tixanderie. It was a dark, moonless night, but carrying a lantern would draw unwanted attention. But his feet knew every step of the way so well he hardly had need of guideposts in the dark. He had been following the same itinerary every evening for several months, though on this night he was unusually late and therefore in a particular hurry to reach his goal.

He was more vexed at not having heard them coming than frightened when two ragged fellows appeared next to him, seemingly out of nowhere, and blocked his path in the narrow alley. His hand moved instinctively to the hilt of his rapier, but he hesitated to unsheathe it when it became clear that he was not being attacked.

"His Lordship, the Marquis, is in a great hurry tonight!" one of the thugs said softly.

"Clear the way, immediately!" Antoine replied with the imperious tone of the aristocrat. "I shall have you arrested and flogged on the spot if you don't let me pass at once."

"I don't think Your Lordship would want to do that. We are just two well-meaning citizens who have been looking for an opportunity to chat with His Lordship."

"Why would you want to talk to me? What makes you think I want to talk to you? What about?" Seized by a sudden uneasy intimation that he had met these two fellows somewhere before, he added less forcefully, "What is it that you want?"

"Prosper, light the lantern, maybe His Lordship will remember when he sees your face. Who could forget your face?"

With a grunt, the shorter, crooked figure struck a light in a lantern and held it up close to Antoine's face, totally blinding him.

"Your insolence has reached its limit. Clear the way immediately."

"Prosper, now you have aroused the Marquis' anger. Hold the lantern this way so His Lordship can see us. My Lord must forgive my brother, he is a bit of a dimwit. I am Gaston Caillart and this is my brother Prosper. Though it has been a long time, His Lordship cannot have completely forgotten."

Antoine now took a good look at the two wretches. The taller one was broad and stocky with an impertinent grin on his not unappealing face. But he only seemed tall next to the one he said was his brother, who was bent by a hump that made him look like Atlas carrying the weight of the world on his back.

"No, of course, I haven't forgotten," Antoine muttered. "But what is it you want? If it is money, here, take this, it's all I have on me right now. Here, take it all."

He groped for his purse. But Gaston made a clicking sound with his tongue and shook his head while waving an admonishing finger at the Marquis.

"No! no! Your Lordship mustn't think that. We don't want anything from Your Lordship."

"Then why are you waylaying me in the middle of the night?" Antoine asked, suspicious of this display of modesty. A dark premonition told him that he would not be rid of these thugs so easily.

"Well, there is one thing Your Lordship might do. Not for us but for an old woman. She sits in a house at the court of miracles—actually it is more like a hovel, Your Lordship will kindly remember, nothing like the magnificent mansion of Madame the Marquise de Valinquette—well this woman, she is heartbroken, cries her eyes out day and night. All her life she has worked her fingers to the bone, broken her back, now she is almost blind from the strain of sewing and her back is bent from washing laundry. If the Marquise could pay her a visit that would bring much joy and comfort to her pained soul."

"If it is money she needs she shall have it. I don't forget those who have been kind, but a visit from the Marquise? Out of the question!" Antoine was unmoved by the soppy tale that was dished up. He knew these thugs were first-rate comedians and if it suited them, they would sell the very mother for a pistole.

"Why? Is she a prisoner in that beautiful mansion?"

"Of course not!" Antoine suppressed his anger so as not to dignify the fellow's impertinence covered only thinly by obsequiousness.

"The Marquise is said to be the most beautiful woman in Paris, but she is rarely seen in public," Gaston continued.

"You've been spying on my house, you miserable worm!" Antoine was in a mood to tear out the wretch's tongue. "If I see either one of you within a hundred yards of my house, I shall have both of you flogged and thrown into prison."

"No need for alarm. We only wanted to catch a glimpse of her ladyship whose beauty is being praised in all of Paris." Gaston retreated again into a humbler tone. "But His Lordship should not leave such a beautiful woman alone at night."

"So you have been spying on me too!" Antoine made a menacing motion.

"Your Lordship needn't worry, his secret is safe with us. Isn't that so, Prosper?" The hunchback eagerly nodded his head while his brother continued: "All we have in mind, as said before, is some help for the woman in the hovel at the court of miracles, crying her eyes out day and night . . ."

"You need say no more." Antoine cut him off. "Maybe we can meet again at a more convenient time in a less public place. I am sure a small annuity can be arranged-well, enough so she can live comfortably," he added when he saw the cringing the word small evoked.

"I am afraid we have kept him too long already. May we escort His Lordship the rest of the way. The streets are not safe for a man to walk about alone at this time of night."

This fellow has the politeness of a slimy eel, Antoine thought, repressing the queasiness he felt churning his stomach.

"Thank you, but I shall not be in need of your protection. You'd better look out for the night watchmen yourselves, it is long past the hour of curfew."

"When shall we meet then?" Gaston's whispering tone was at once familiar and conspiratorial. "Would Friday afternoon, four o'clock at the tavern of Sainte Geneviève be convenient for Your Lordship?"

"All right! All right! I'll be there. Just be gone now."

Antoine pulled his fur-trimmed cloak tighter and hastened his step, quickly putting a safe distance between himself and the roughnecks, whom he left to shiver in their threadbare tatters. He shrugged off a dark sense of foreboding. What could such sordid scum possibly do to him?

With a sigh of relief he noted the light still aglow in the window at No. 17 rue de Tixanderie. His thoughts turned to how he would explain his tardiness to the fair Manon.

Chapter 2

THE HÔTEL DE Valinquette, in the fashionable Marais quarter of Paris, had fallen into disrepair in the decade it was unoccupied. Unhinged shutters, peeling paint, crumbling plaster, weed stalks stretching their tentacles through the rusted wrought-iron fence surrounding the garden, had been an eyesore in this neighborhood where meticulous attention to masonry and shrubbery was a matter of proud ostentation. It was for this reason alone that the return of the scion of the House of Valinquette was hailed among the Parisian beau monde with a degree of auspiciousness far exceeding customary exuberance or the importance of the event itself.

Mercifully, expectations were not disappointed. When the cream of society flocked from their provincial summer haunts to invade the glittering precincts of seasonal festivities in the autumn of the year 1661, the year King Louis XIV attained his majority and took the reins of his realm into his own hands, they found the erstwhile splendor of the Hôtel de Valinquette restored, rivaling the finest residences of the Marais.

The results of the massive renovation of the mansion were quite impressive—imposing, Italianate columns extending to the garden, once a jumble of virgin flora and now transformed into a sanctuary of geometric lawns, flower beds, and gravel paths lined with sculpted hedges of viburnum, buckthorn, and boule de neige, populated by a host of marble antique gods and goddesses, with nymphs and fauns frolicking near crystalline ponds and spurting fountains. An espalier of pyracantha cast its shade over the path that led to a charming pavilion, nestled among towering cone-shaped myrtle, hydrangea, and germander. A white-washed Doric colonnade had been added to its façade and a huge skylight replaced most of the roof—a Grecian temple illumined by the silvery skies of the Ile de France.

The Marquis de Valinquette had taken a personal hand in designing and supervising the restoration. His fondness for antiquity often got the better of him and the mythological motive was carried through in what some might regard a heavy-handed fashion. The renovation of the pavilion had been especially close to his heart, and after they were settled in their new abode, the Marquis and Marquise passed many of their daytime hours inside this secluded cottage. They continued in this practice even after the arrival of the drafts of winter had made a prolonged stay there less than comfortable.

A veil of secrecy lay over the doings inside the pavilion. Nobody was admitted, not even the servants, except for the personal attendants of the Marquis and Marquise, who were sworn to absolute secrecy. Rumors abounded and speculation was rife among servants and neighbors about sinister scientific or alchemistic experiments, orgiastic pagan rites, dissolute devil's worship—the entire litany of human depravity was cited at one point or other. The Marquis and Marquise were suspected of being adherents of all manner of nefarious heresies.

The imaginings ranged unbounded until an unexpected visitor breached the wall of the garden and the closely guarded little temple and set in motion a series of events that slowly unraveled the secret of the Hôtel de Valinquette.

All was peaceful, however, on the morning after that great social triumph, the visit to Madame de Valinquette's salon by the famed Grande Mademoiselle, Anne Marie Louise d'Orléans, Duchesse de Montpensier and first cousin of the King. The kind words of their illustrious guest still echoed in their minds as Antoine and Galatée wandered arm in arm through their garden, its verdant spaces now covered with a transparent early December frost. They chatted animatedly in high spirits in a language that seemed entirely their own. When they reached the pavilion, or atelier as Antoine liked to call it, they disappeared inside, shutting themselves off from that same outside world of which they desired so much to be a part.

Two charcoal braziers dispensed a pleasing warmth and cast a homey glow over the spacious hall. In the middle was a small table set with breakfast for two. Antoine and Galatée sat down still discussing the details of the events of the night before, each guest's reaction, what it all might mean for their future and their aspirations.

Suddenly Antoine's mood shifted. He seemed to have no mind for the piping hot café au lait and petits pains with confiture de fraise over which he usually lingered in the morning with great relish. With the abrupt adroitness of a cat, he jumped up and in an impetuous gesture, he pulled away the canvas from a huge stone sitting on a workbench cluttered with an assortment of chisels, files, hammers, and other tools. Revealed was a block of pure white alabaster into which had been carved a human form, a woman's body but with individual parts at various stages of completion and perfection.

Antoine let his hands glide over what were the thighs and legs and then again over the rounded form of the lower torso already in a state of near perfection. The cold smoothness of the stone ignited a fierce glow in his eyes, frightful to anyone not familiar with his sudden fits of passion.

"Yes, yes!" he muttered to himself several times with satisfaction. The upper parts of the torso, the arms, and the head were still a rougher, more primal mass, the human feature as yet but a crude, rudimentary hint. Antoine patted the still angular shapes of the breasts, kneading as if they were clay until, with a sigh of despair, he picked up a small chisel and chipped away a rough edge here and there.

Suddenly he seemed to remember his wife and he turned his dark eyes, flaring with excitement, toward her.

"My darling Galatée, I can feel it with every fiber of my being, nothing will hold us back anymore. I have been waiting for thirteen years, thirteen long years, but at long last, my work will find its achievement."

He held up his hands, his fingers bent like the talons of a giant bird. His voice was unearthly in its hoarseness: "These hands shall be the instrument that creates the perfect woman."

"Shall we begin then?" Galatée said listlessly without pretense of enthusiasm. She had been witness to his effusions all too often before.

Demurely, she stepped up on the pedestal placed a few feet opposite the statue. She positioned herself and let her robe glide from her shoulders, exposing the full exquisiteness of her naked form. Antoine moved the braziers closer and then proceeded with grim concentration to arrange her posture. He bent her torso this way and that, moved her arms around, up and down, trying myriad stances and contortions—almost half an hour passed in this exercise, to which she passively surrendered herself, before he was finally satisfied. He retreated behind the block of alabaster and immediately set to attacking it with maddened frenzy, chipping, chiseling vigorously.

The world ceased to exist. Only intermittently did he halt in his activity. Sending up anguished groans, he would walk over to inspect his model. His hands would then trace the shape of the perfect spheres of her breasts with the same intense detachment he expended on the piece of stone. He would then retreat again to his struggle with the lithic matter, undaunted, with dogged determination to fashion a faithful replica of nature's most vibrant, sensuous creation.

Galatée did not resist his bending and shaping of her body. Her supple form was putty in his hands. She responded to his every movement even when, in his search for the perfect pose, he twisted her into such contorted, unnatural shape as to make her writhe in pain. In the end she was transformed into a statue, an immobile figure, frozen in space on her pedestal. Her feet and legs were pressed close together, her upper torso tilted to the side and arched so as to raise the fullness of her shapely breasts; one arm was locked at the nape of her neck while the other hang down loosely holding the seam of her robe that was scattered at her feet.

A visitor happening to enter the atelier at this moment would have been struck with awe, certain to have encountered the reincarnation of a goddess of antiquity, a Venus risen from the sea, fresh as the early morning dew, a thing of breathtaking, timeless beauty—Pygmalion's Galatée infused with the breath of life.

Her immaculate, supple skin reflected the glow of the embers that daubed her in a luminous hue, blending with the russet of her pubic hair, and magnified her long, perfectly carved legs, the voluptuous curves of her hips and buttocks, the luscious roundness of her breasts and shoulders, the elegant curvature of her neck, the inviting arms. Her least perfect part was perhaps her face, which nature's design had sprinkled with a few playful flaws. But even these, a mouth slightly too small and a nose that started out in an elegant curve but was cut off too abruptly, leaving the tip slightly turned up, had a certain charm, especially since the sparkle of the big round violet eyes, which exuded so much life, effaced all shortcomings. The copper mass of corkscrew curls, lightened to an unnatural hue at Antoine's insistence with henna treatments and tamed in a knot twirled up and fastened at the top to leave the long line of her neck exposed, rounded out the picture of a very pretty woman.

Galatée perdured in this tortuous position, and despite considerable discomfort, she even hummed a few of the Spanish tunes Antoine loved so well. She knew singing pleased him and put him into a calmer frame of mind. But nothing seemed to work for him on this morning. His concentration seemed to fail him without apparent cause. At last he flung down his tools and flew into a senseless rage.

"These cursed breasts!" he yelled. "They simply won't take shape. To hell with this blasted stone."

"Antonio! My dear Antonio! You are torturing yourself!" Galatée cooed in Catalan, the tongue of his mother, which usually soothed his temper.

"You shouldn't drive yourself so hard. Let's take a pause. You have not touched your food. How can you concentrate when your stomach is empty?"

But this time he was not appeased.

"Why don't you say it?" he pouted. Whether it was with himself he was angry or just the world at large was, as so often, unclear. "You don't want to model for me anymore—is that it? All right I shall find someone else," he added, defiant like an unreasonable little boy."You know that is not true, Antonio. You know I never said that and I would do anything to please you." She wrapped herself in her cape and put her arm around his stooped shoulders, pulling him down next to her on a velvet-covered bench. "You shouldn't brood so much. Didn't you say yourself that everything was going well? Everything is going the way you planned. This little snag will pass."

When he persisted in his sulking, she playfully ruffled his hair. "Sometimes I really wonder what goes on in that little boy's head of yours."

Without a word he got up, pushing her with such vehemence that she almost toppled over. He strode back to his statue, staring at it. This was the mountain he had set himself to conquer, as if nothing else existed at this moment or mattered in the world besides this piece of stone.

"You frighten me, Antonio. Do I deserve to be treated this way? Please speak to me!" But not even her bitter sobbing made him yield.

"What I don't understand is, if my body is so repugnant to you, why do you want me as your model?" she finally said, resigned that nothing would shake him out of his irrational behavior, not on this morning at least.

"What did you say?" he said, disoriented. "Must you constantly blabber now? Why can't you hold your tongue just for once?"

"I want to know why my body repels you so much," she insisted.

"I, repelled by your body? How can you say that? Yours is the most exquisite feminine form in the world. If anything, I worship your body!" he exclaimed with a sudden ardor as high flown as had been his anger. "It's your tongue I detest."

"Why then, why is it that we have not made love since . . . you know very well since when?" she said softly, almost inaudibly.

"But, this is precisely why . . . because I worship you, because your body is a divine vessel that can only be approached with awe," he stammered, his eyes fixed on the floor. "You are not the cause of all this anguish. It's this rock. It resists my hands, refuses to bend to my will."

"I often wonder what you feel when you stroke my breasts, when you position my arms, my legs with that impenetrable mien of yours. Can you really be so totally detached, feel nothing? Is it all just about this block of stone?" Her voice was still soft, though entreating; the whisper of an anguished prayer.

"I don't know how to explain. I thought you understood. Of course, it is not easy for me either. But consider, if we did make love how could we be sure that nothing would happen that would destroy . . . the immaculate form of your body?"

"Maybe we should never have come back to Paris. We did love each other back home in Catalonia, and we were happy—at least, I thought we were."

"You know very well what happened. Need we really rehash old stories? We were lucky that time. So why chance it again?"

The obstinate irritation in his voice was now transferred to hers.

"You mean we were lucky to lose the child?" she shouted.

"Yes! A thousand times, yes! And didn't we agree then that it was a good thing, that it was a sign from heaven, and that it would be best if we did not chance it happening again? Is that not the way it was? Why must you bring this up again now, for heaven's sake?"

"Yes, we agreed," she said, submitting once again to his irrefutable logic.

"How could I not have?" she muttered under her breath. He had once again carried the argument. Her energy was spent. It was useless to try to make him see. Secretly she reproached herself for having brought up the matter at all. But inside, in the dark labyrinthine chambers of her being, the memory conjured up set off such turmoil, she asked him to be excused. She felt chilled to the bone and a slight indisposition was coming on, she told him.

With obvious relief that she had relented in her interrogation of an unpleasant subject, he urged her to return to her apartment for a rest so she would be fresh for the evening at the theater. All of Paris would be there for the premiere of Corneille's new play and he wanted her to shine. He would stay a while longer in the atelier, later in the afternoon he had business to tend to in town, but he would join her for supper. He politely escorted her to the door. His eyes followed her until she had crossed the garden and had disappeared inside the house.

Chapter 3

THE MARQUISE DE Valinquette languished in hot herbal vapors swirling about her, caressing her body with a soothing, sensuous balm that slowly dissolved the tautness of her limbs and heart. When she finally rose from her bath, she gave herself over to the caring hands of her chambermaid who rubbed her entire body with a thick towel and massaged her immaculate skin with luxuriant oils, fragrant with musk and amber.

"Thank you, Madelon. That'll be all for now," she dismissed the girl when she had been wrapped in a soft velvet robe. The girl fluffed up a pile of satin pillows, stirred the embers in the fireplace into leaping flames, and left her mistress to herself for her early afternoon rest.

Galatée stretched her lithe body sensuously upon the cool satin, sinking with abandon into the luxurious eiderdown. Her eyes closed, a cloud of aromatic warmth held her secure. All was perfect for an afternoon of repose, but her mind found no rest. A rebellious spirit stirred in her against Antoine, her hero, the man to whom she had surrendered her whole being. Obedience to Antoine in everything she did had been her life. Now a darkness had stolen into her heart, it was nagging at her, churning up resentment, at times even hatred—

but the mere thought that she should be capable of hating Antoine chilled her with fear.

Antoine had been for so long the pillar of her existence, the very essence of her life. She had never really questioned the wisdom of the endless demands he placed on her. She had always gone along with his fancies and dreams, as her overriding sense of being beholden to him would not allow her to rebel. But was it merely gratitude she felt? No, she assured herself it was more than gratitude. That's how it was at first until he taught her the ways of the world.

After all, what did she know about the world? Or anything else that went with it? He was the worldly one, possessed of knowledge and experience. He had seen more of the world and experienced more than she ever would.

But if she loved him why that constant sense of dread in his presence? Why did her stomach twist into a knot whenever he was near her? Was it fear of never really being able to measure up? Of never being able to fulfill his expectation no matter how she tried? Why was she always relieved to see him go, happy when he turned his attention elsewhere? Why could she not even muster a twinge of jealousy for the "business" that took him into town almost every night? She had tried a few times to hold him back, to test her power over him, but was every time rebuffed.

She tossed restlessly between the down and satin. Somehow this was not the way it should be. The unspoken fear of something terrible to come, the dull sense of courting disaster, of hurtling toward doom and destruction had held her in its grip from the day they arrived back in Paris.

This crowded city where filth and luxury dwelled in close proximity under a permanently leaden sky oppressed her heart. She longed for the countryside, for the bright Iberian skies and the simple kindness of its people. She dreamed of sunny slopes and vineyards, of shady olive groves, and chestnut trees. There they first had loved. But in her innermost being she knew that this too had been an illusion, a dream that was never real. Nevertheless, it was a dream, a memory she cherished, a place of refuge that gave solace to her anguished heart. Only in rare moments did she admit to herself that this place too had not been the paradise she liked to imagine.

For seven years she had lived in the Barca household, raised with love by Doña Elvira Barca y Alarcon, the Marquise de Valinquette. Like a daughter she had been taken in. Antoine had departed for unknown parts of the world. For long, long years nothing was heard from him. Nobody knew if he was dead or alive. Then one day a letter arrived, followed by others, all brief with little information beyond that he was well. The letters came from places she had never heard of. She memorized the names and tried to imagine what they were like—Lisbon, Casablanca, Sâo Paulo, and again Lisbon, Madras, and who knows where else. To while away the hours of tedious needlework, she engaged in a game with Camila and Gabriela, his sisters, imagining his homecoming, what he would do, what they would do the moment they laid eyes on each other.

She never ceased dreaming of him but had almost given up hope that she would see him again when one day Doña Elvira burst into the girls' French lesson waving a letter.

"He is in Barcelona!" Her eyes were filled with tears and she breathed hard with excitement. "Antonio is in Barcelona! He will be here in a week."

It was the longest week of her life. What would he say? Would he be pleased with her? Everything she had done in those seven years she had done for him, the question would he approve always foremost on her mind. Now that her dream was to become reality, she could not sleep or eat, so plagued was she with doubts and apprehension.

What would he say or think or do? She had studied hard to learn the ways of the world. Would he find her pleasing in manner and conversation? How many hours she had spent mastering this art as well as how to move with grace and dignity. Her days had been rigorously filled with instruction. She learned to read and write. Great emphasis had been placed on Spanish and French elocution. She had lessons in dancing and singing—although she had a naturally beautiful voice, the instructor insisted that it must be refined through proper breathing and projection exercises. She learned to accompany herself on the lute and the clavichord.

Would he like the woman she had become in the seven years since he left her an unformed eleven-year-old waif? She spent almost the entire week of waiting in front of the mirror, scrutinizing her image—first, her face and hair. Would he find her beautiful? From her head to her shoulders tumbled a russet mass of soft curls framing the rosy glow of a complexion that stood out among the dark, olive-skinned, somewhat sallow Barcas. She had noticed for some time that the Barca men gaped at her with devouring eyes, though none would dare come near her. Doña Elvira, who guarded her as a lioness guards her brood, was too formidable a barrier. She was known as "Antonio's girl." And in a way that was true. That's what she was. She even thought of herself that way, though it was hardly in the usual sense.

She examined her face with a critical eye. It was not perfect, but it was fresh and pleasing. Her mouth could be a bit larger, but at least her lips were full. The nose was the part she liked least. Too short and undistinguished. Her cheeks were round like two ripe apples. Her best feature was her eyes, the violet blue that gave her so much life. She was pretty, no doubt. But would she be Antonio's type? What silly thoughts she had then. There was no good reason why he should have any romantic interest in her at all. They had been friends, had helped each other out. But he was His Lordship and she a little girl, a child of no consequence. But what if, in spite of everything?

She remained transfixed on the image in the mirror, almost in a trance. She slowly let her chemise slip from her shoulders, letting it glide down her body until she stood there completely naked. A tremor of awe and delight seized her. Here was a fruit, ripened to perfection, ready to be plucked. It was almost twilight, but she could not tear herself away. Turning from side to side, playfully, swaying sensuously, humming a silly tune, she suddenly let out a shriek.

Like Narcissus she had been entranced by her image. She did not hear the door opening and closing and was unaware of another person's presence until a dark figure suddenly loomed behind her in the mirror. Her startled body still convulsed uncontrollably even after the stranger had identified himself. By the time her gasping died down and she could say "Antonio?" he had carried her to her bed and placed a cover over her. He sat down at the edge of the bed, holding her hand like a doctor attending a sick or dying patient.

"You mustn't be frightened, my little bird," he said gently in French. "But what were you doing? You shouldn't do this with the door unlocked. There's no telling who might surprise you. Fortunately, it was only me," he added mockingly and waved a scolding finger at her.

"Your Lordship isn't cross with me?" Her face glowed with shame, she wanted to hide under the covers. This was not at all the way she had imagined their reunion.

"Of course not. But you needn't have any shame in front of me," he said, reading her thoughts. "You know, I have been to many places and have seen many things, but nowhere in the world, not in Europe, in the Americas, or in the farthest lands of Asia, have I encountered a woman's body as perfect, as exquisite as the one I just saw in this room."

She did not know what to say. The dark eyes that stared at her with such strange seriousness stirred up an unknown jumble of emotions in her. She was not sure whether he was fathoming the bottom of her soul or whether his thoughts were elsewhere and he was just looking at her. Then he suddenly jumped up as if something had struck him.

"Your ears must have been burning constantly these last few days," he declared. "I could not stop thinking about how it would be when we met again. I knew that you had to have changed, grown, that you were no longer the child I had left in the care of my mother. Oh, what plans I was making! But first of all, you need a new name. And I have thought about that very carefully too. You will always be my little Fauvette, but the world shall know you as Galatée, my Galatée!"

It all happened so suddenly. She was overwhelmed that he should have been thinking of her. At first she could hardly grasp the meaning of what he was saying. It seemed like another dream. Was she losing touch with reality? In the end all she was able to say was: "Your Lordship is very kind."

"Very well," he said, self-satisfied, patronizing. "Now you must get dressed. My mother is expecting us for dinner. I told her I would fetch you because I wanted to surprise you."

"That you did, my Lord," she said now in Spanish and in a more self-possessed manner. She even managed a chuckle. "Welcome home. We have all been awaiting your return with greatest anticipation."

Later in the night, when she was in her early sleep, he came back to her room. She hardly knew what was happening. He dispensed cavalierly with formalities of wooing or courting, jumping right into bed with her as if it was his God-given right. Even if she had wanted to, she did not have the strength to fend off the passionate kisses with which he muffled her mouth. When she had become pliable, devoid of any will of her own, she felt his lips move, along her neck down to her taut, virgin breasts. She felt helplessly in his power and knew not what to make of it when, in his growing excitement, he impatiently shredded her chemise. His embrace was not violent but firm and expressed intent on getting what he had come for. Somehow, by some unwritten contract, it was understood that her body was his even before he took possession of it. Although this too was not how she had imagined it would be, she was convinced that she had reached the fulfillment of her destiny.

She was somewhat astonished and not a little disturbed by this bizarre behavior, especially since it gave her very little pleasure. This was not at all like the novels that had nourished her fantasies of lovemaking. Only being in such intimate closeness with him and being the object of his intense attention gave her some gratification. But then again she could not help but wonder whether he was at all aware that the round pieces of flesh he seemed so obsessed with belonged to her. He was getting rather heavy, sprawled as he was on top of her, his face buried between her breasts. He breathed so evenly that she was sure he had fallen asleep. She writhed a little under him to maneuver herself into a more comfortable position. As if stung by some insect, he jumped up with a start. Afraid to move, she watched him move about the room searching for something. Finally he lit the candle stumps on the table and moved them closer to the bed.

"Did I incur Your Lordship's displeasure?" she asked, meek and frightened.

"No, of course not, my little bird," he said as he climbed back into bed. "I just want to see you, feast my eyes on your beautiful body."

Again he pulled her into his arms and touched his mouth to hers, first just grazing her lips, then pushing them apart with his tongue. She was overcome with a pleasurable, dizzying sensation that traveled along her spine to the back of her head where it destroyed any resistance she might have had, and though her stomach felt queasy, she wanted to hold on to it at all cost. She was levitating on a cloud of bliss and could have continued in this ardent exchange forever, but he began moving downward, apparently with a different goal in mind.

The story of Adam and Eve came to her mind and she convinced herself that this is how it must have been in paradise. Her curiosity was aroused when his part, the one the girls only whispered and giggled about, suddenly flashed before her. She observed his grim countenance with growing apprehension. Was she doing something wrong, or was she malformed, unable to give him the ultimate pleasure? A senseless fear gripped her that he would leave her, sure to find more pliable women.

But she knew very little about men and even less about their determination. Without a word, still with ferocious mien, he finally got inside of her like a canon demolishing everything within its range. He moved back and forth three or four times before collapsing onto her, groaning and gasping that struck her as very bizarre indeed.

To her surprise, he immediately fell into a peaceful sleep, remaining on top of her, dead as a sack of potatoes. She did not dare move and lay awake plagued with doubts and pangs that she was not adequate to this awesome task. He did not seem to have taken notice of her reeling in pain under the onslaught nor of the gashing wound he inflicted. Somehow she had to smuggle the soiled bedding to the laundry without letting anybody find out. She pondered for a while the sensations she had experienced during this night of her first lovemaking. But knowing little of the ways of the world, she decided that she was madly in love with Antoine and resigned herself to thinking that for a woman pleasure in love came from giving pleasure to her beloved.

In the weeks that followed Antoine was all over her and she was happy and grateful for the attention he lavished on her. He did not tell her much about his adventures of the past seven years, but she surmised that somehow he had become a wealthy man. On several occasions, he had to go away on business, presumably to Barcelona. The nature of this business he kept vague. He returned every time with expensive presents for all the women in the household, including the servants. No wonder everybody loved Antonio. But she alone was the one he made love to.

He was not entirely happy with the state of her education, especially her French elocution was not what he thought it should be. This became the cause of frequent rows with Doña Elvira, which made her very uncomfortable. She even hated him sometimes for the rudeness with which he berated his mother.

"What is good enough for your sisters is certainly good enough for her!" She overheard one of their disputes while passing the drawing room with the door left ajar. Neither one of them took care to contain the temper or volume. Doña Elvira brimmed with indignation at the suggestion that she should have short-changed the charge he had left to her.

"But I think your infatuation with this girl is getting out of hand, and it is more than a bit ridiculous. Don't misunderstand me. I have raised her like a daughter, and I love her like one of my own. She has given me nothing but joy and she never fails to express her gratitude. I have nothing to reproach her with, but let us remember where she hails from."

"Well, I am pleased, dearest Mother, that you too love her, because then you will be happy to hear that I intend to make her my wife."

"In that case you leave me no choice but to disinherit you!" Doña Elvira's ordinarily shrill voice reached an as yet unscaled pitch of horror. Antoine laughed in a manner that made her skin crawl. How can he be so cruel to his mother, the kindest woman in the world?

"Aren't you forgetting that I am a wealthy man? And as for any other inheritance, I have already lost my birthright due to an old man's cantankerous schemes."

"How dare you speak like that of your father?" Doña Elvira was aghast that her son should not recoil from desecrating the memory of the dead.

"Don't worry! Don't worry!" he said in a more conciliatory tone. "I have every intention of restoring the honor of the Valinquette name. You can rest assured of that. I have made it my mission and I shall not rest until my patrimony is returned and I am recognized by the French Crown as the Marquis de Valinquette. Not even Mazarin will live forever. In fact I hear that he is not well at all."

"Oh, Antonio, such rumors have been around for years. His death has been prophesied many times—yet he seems indestructible, like the devil himself." Doña Elvira quickly made the sign of the cross.

"My time will come, Mother. I shall be lying in wait, when the moment comes I shall be ready to seize it. Meanwhile, dear Mother, I would like your blessing. I know Galatée would not be happy if you withheld your blessing."

At this moment, Galatée entered the hall, and since she did not want to be found eavesdropping she moved on before she heard Doña Elvira's answer.

In the weeks that followed, Galatée waited for Antoine to say something to her about his plans. But those weeks spent in intimate proximity passed without a hint from him. How could she draw him out and not betray that she had overheard his conversation with his mother? Her daily instruction in French elocution and the manners and customs of the French nobility finally gave her a pretext.

"May I ask Your Lordship a question?" she asked him during practice of a fast whirling rigaudon, which she found particularly awkward and difficult to execute.

"I was wondering why it should be so important for a humble woman like me to be accomplished in the manners of the French nobility."

"Why?" he asked genuinely astonished. "Why? Don't you know?"

He took her hands into his and pulled her down to him on a fauteuil.

"My beloved Galatée is going to be the most admired woman of Paris. In due time, of course, it may take some time, a few years even. Also as long as Mazarin is alive and in power our prospects for returning to Paris are not very good. But I have no doubt that I shall reclaim the inheritance of the Valinquettes, and then you will be my Marquise! All the world will grovel at your feet! Meanwhile, though, we have a few rough edges to smooth out. It will all come together with time and patience."

Not knowing what to say, she lowered her face. Should she feel elated, honored, flattered? All she felt was blind fear. Antoine lifted her chin with one finger, forcing her to look him in the eyes.

"You won't disappoint me, will you?" he whispered gently. She shook her head and even tried a smile.

"But when Your Lordship speaks of all the world, he really means Paris."

He nodded.

"I thought we were happy here. Paris frightens me."

"But you must understand, we cannot stay in this provincial backwater—this is not a place where ambitions and dreams are realized. Paris is the center of the universe! We must set our sights high. I am a French aristocrat. I love Catalonia for my mother's sake. But I am a Valinquette, in my veins flows French blood, my destiny lies in France, and so does yours."

Seeing her tremble, he enclosed her in his arms.

"You have nothing to fear. We shall be together. As long as I am with you, nobody will dare do you any harm. Now, be a good girl. We have an arduous path ahead of us, but together we shall reach the summit of our dreams."

Funny how he always spoke of "our dreams." Although she was not persuaded, nor were her fears allayed, she kept her thoughts and feelings from him. Since nothing happened for the time being, she managed to keep her apprehensions locked away in a secret chamber of her heart.

She learned to dance the rigaudon with the same grace she applied to the chaconne and other courtly dances. Antoine was especially fond of the pavane because he could strut with the splendor of a peacock about with measured steps bowing and curtsying to a wailing, solemn melody.

She also learned to recite French poetry with verve and style. The slight Catalan accent colored her diction with a certain charm. Her singing voice was her greatest natural asset. It soared like a lark's through the house and fields, echoing in the vineyards and olive groves along the slopes of the river, warming the hearts of masters and servants. Antoine had shown excellent judgment when he dismissed her vocal instructor who had insisted on harnessing her voice to the yoke of stylized operatic rules.

Her favorite time of day was early morning, when she would go horseback riding with Antoine. They hurtled over the countryside at breakneck speed, trampling everything in their path. It was then and only then that she exhilarated in a sense of boundless freedom.

It was an outing on horseback that brought about the event, though soon forgotten by Antoine, which left a quietly festering wound in her heart. Outwardly nothing changed between them; she lived to please him. Yet in her innermost being the gratitude and adulation she had felt for him died without her knowing. But that was much later.

At the end of their first rapturous summer, Doña Elvira finally relented and gave her blessing to her son's marriage. Antoine and Galatée were united in holy matrimony with pomp and splendor at the Church of the Holy Virgin in Tarragona. She thought herself happy as she descended the steps of the cathedral on Antoine's arm, basking in the adulation of well-wishers. Camila and Gabriela wept and embraced her.

Antoine had made the announcement to her in his usual manner, presenting her with a fait accompli. He did not order her, but told her with the presumption that she would not object. And, of course, she didn't—not even saying something as basic as that he had not asked her if that was what she wanted.

"Preparations are under way! Doña Elvira herself will supervise everything—we shall be married on the fifteenth of September!" He told her one day and that was it.

A week later another surprise. He had just signed the deed to a villa, owned by a local hidalgo who had squandered the family fortune and was forced to sell at a pitiful price, with considerable acreage of vineyards and olive groves and with a magnificent view of the river valley. The thought of leaving the Barca estate, her sisters Camila and Gabriela, and the kindhearted Doña Elvira to live in a big house by herself filled her with dreadful foreboding.

But there was one hope. Antoine might settle down and forget about Paris and his fancy of conquering Parisian society. Alas, she soon realized that acquiring land was an investment of his money, not a way of sinking roots into the place. Once they were married and established in the big house on the hill, Antoine's absences became longer and more frequent. She still had only the vaguest notion of the nature of his business. She surmised that it must be very profitable for she was not wanting for material things. During one of his absences, she undertook a pilgrimage to the shrine at Montserrat. She prayed fervently to the Black Virgin to grant her the blessing of a child in the hope that this would tie Antoine to Catalonia and make him give up all thoughts of Paris.

In November, Antoine returned from a journey to the coast of Africa. He arrived just in time for preparations for the great hunt, an annual event staged by the Barca y Alarcon clan to which all neighboring barons were invited. The Barca women, who had something of a reputation for being Amazons, on this occasion would ride as hard and drink and eat as merrily as any man. Galatée had enjoyed the lusty, unbridled festivities in the past, but that year she had a reason for wanting to remain on the periphery.

She had kept her condition a secret even from Doña Elvira so far, since she wanted Antoine to be first to share her happiness. But the suitable moment seemed to elude her, and then he was away again.

So it was that she never had a chance to warn Antoine. On the night of his return—he had been away for over a month—he came in with that certain look on his face. As soon as they were alone, he started to unfasten her dress and then, as was his habit, he lit the candles next to the bed. That way, he liked to explain, he could feast his eyes on her figure first. She stood before him in the candlelight, in which everything appeared magnified. Never would she forget the horror on his face, the incredulous stare that seemed to pierce her naked body.

"What happened to you?" he shrieked. "You look grotesque. Your waistline is gone, your hips expanded, your belly is protruding, and look at those breasts, my beautiful breasts, sagging like a cow's udder! You're getting fat!"

"I was trying to tell you . . . ," she began but was unable to form the words. It was as if she had been slapped with a force that knocked the breath out of her.

"What were you trying to tell me? How can I take you to Paris looking like this? Your body is your greatest asset. Galatée's beauty was timeless, immutable."

"Galatée is a figure in a story, a statue. She was one man's dream, not a real woman! You told me so yourself," she protested. "What I wanted to tell you, but you gave me no opportunity, is that when people make love there are consequences."

"You mean," he pondered for a moment, "you mean to say you are with child, carrying my child?"

"Yes. Didn't this possibility occur to you?"

"I suppose I was so happy I didn't think of the consequences of our passion. Of course, I should have."

He seemed bewildered like a child who had done something wrong without meaning to and was looking for a way out. She could not help but feel sorry for him.

"Aren't you at least a little bit happy?" she asked cautiously.

"Yes, of course, I'm happy. I'm going to have a son. How could I not be happy? Just give me a few minutes to absorb the news," he said distractedly as if he were grappling with a complex philosophical or scientific concept. Slowly the meaning seemed to sink in. He took her into his arms and begged her forgiveness, calling himself an insensitive peasant clod and a whole litany of self-accusatory epithets.

He assured her again that he really was happy, it was just that the news had come so suddenly, so unexpected. He placed a robe around her shoulders and carried her to the bed and placed her down gently.

He tucked her in with great care as if she was an invalid or a child. He breathed a kiss on her forehead and left. They did not make love that night, nor on any other night thereafter.

"I need some time alone to think about this new circumstance," he said.

Did he contrive to make her lose the child? She would never know. He was almost cheerful when he related to her the results of the doctor's examination after the riding accident during the great hunt. The shock from the fall had ejected the fetus from her womb, expunging it in a stream of blood. He took her into his arms and said a few consoling words, but she felt utterly alone in her grief. Then he went to join the hunting party.

He had been very solicitous in the days following the nocturnal drama of his startling discovery that she was with child. But only once more did he touch on the subject.

"I think it would be better if Doña Elvira did not hear of your condition," he said as he lifted her into the saddle of the magnificent black Andalusian stallion he had presented to her a few days before the hunt.

"Now all you need is a new riding costume. I have sent for the tailor and boot maker. Something a little wider than usual will hide any protrusions and you might even set a new style. I know you will still be the most ravishing woman at the party."

"Do you think it wise for me to participate in the chase? I don't want to be ungrateful, the stallion is beautiful, but a bit impetuous," she said anxiously.

As if to confirm her words, the stallion under her chomped vigorously at the bit and churned the ground with his hoof.

"A more sedate palfrey might be more suitable under the circumstances."

"This beautiful beast is just like you!" he said, laughing off her fears. "Come on, the Barca women have always held their own in the chase and we wouldn't want anybody to think that you don't have the mettle of a Barca."

He gave the horse's behind a good whack and off it went in a cloud, neighing its enthusiastic approval to be thus given free rein.

The stallion took the fields in a wild gallop, over fences and streams. Nothing stood in its way. Antoine tried to keep pace, but his horse had nothing of the recklessness of the Andalusian. After about half an hour of wild racing, its pace slackened just enough for Antoine's horse to catch up to it within a length. But when it saw the other horse coming, the Andalusian raised itself on its hind legs, neighing as it pranced, and ejected its rider from the saddle with a violent jolt.

"Madame! Madame! It is time for Madame's evening toilet. Monsieur has already inquired several times." Madelon's voice brought her back to the mansion in Paris.

"Just tell Monsieur not to worry. I shall be ready in time, as always," she said, rising to inspect her wardrobe.

"Let's see, what shall we wear tonight? Something glittering, something truly gaudy—the way Monsieur likes it. Ah, maybe this one," she said, fingering the gold brocade with inlaid sparkling diamond and ruby studs. "That should do to dazzle them!"

Chapter 4

ANTOINE'S BOOTS CUT a brownish trail through the thick snow that robed the filthy city streets in virginal white. The night was clear and breezy and he inhaled deeply the crisp air. The wind blowing off the river whirled up periodic gusts of snow, slowing his nocturnal perambulations. He steered clear of his customary path the narrow, curving alleys and took a detour along the riverbank instead. Maybe he wanted to delay reaching his goal. The thought flew into his mind. For some time now the beautiful Manon had been losing her allure.

At first he suspected that he was simply tiring of her. But even in the arms of other hospitable women of this city, he did not seem to find what he craved. An indistinct, dark, nameless longing had filled him since the night of his delayed visit to Manon. It was more than pleasure, more than a desire to indulge his sensuous nature. If anything, it was oblivion he sought and oblivion seemed to elude him more and more. Several times, in the heat of passion, he caught himself whispering and pining "Fauvette, my Fauvette."

The image of the nude woman on the pedestal haunted his thoughts.

"What is the matter with you?" he scolded himself. "She is your wife. She is yours already. You behave as if you were in love with some unattainable maiden."

"But that is exactly the point," his other self answered back. "If I love her, if I make love to her I shall destroy her—her beauty will be vanquished forever. No man shall ever touch her pristine form."

"Pristine form! Where did you get such a harebrained notion? You already destroyed her pristineness and now you are neglecting her. You're insane, stark raving mad."

Antoine stood by the river's edge. The moon's rays danced on the icy surface. He spread his cloaked arms like a huge, primordial bird its wings. His scream echoed from the opposite bank.

"Your Lordship should be more careful. The ice is very thin in places." He whipped around.

"Ah, my guardian angels! Can't I ever be alone, anywhere in this city without having the two of you follow me?"

"It is dangerous to be alone in this city, especially at night?" Prosper said.

"Yes, you keep saying that. And you should know since it is scum like you that makes the streets unsafe for decent citizens. I guess I'm lucky to have two thugs like you watching over me!"

"We only have the best interest of Your Lordship in mind." Gaston made an obsequious motion with his head.

"All right, I just gave you a hundred pistoles, she could not possibly have used it all up already. Unless, of course, you gentlemen take a hefty cut for yourself."

"It's not money we want—not now at least," the hunchback explained. "But you must understand a hundred pistoles doesn't last forever."

"When did this fellow learn to talk, I thought he had no tongue?" Antoine wondered aloud. Why did he ever permit himself to become involved with characters like these?

"He's in love," Gaston explained as if the question required an answer. "Love loosens the tongue, especially happy love. Your Lordship surely knows about such matters."

"What is that supposed to mean, you rake?"

"Well, we couldn't help but overhearing Your Lordship calling out over there before."

"What did I call out?" he grabbed Gaston by the throat, threatening to squeeze the wind out of him.

"Nothing terrible," Prosper filled in for his brother who was unable to utter a word. "Only that . . ."

"Only, what?"

"Your Lordship only called out, with some force, I should say—I love her!"

"Her, who?" Antoine insisted.

"It sounded a bit like Fauvette."

"You're sure?"

"Absolutely."

Antoine let go of Gaston. He had to be more careful. It would not be easy to get rid of these pests.

"Madame the Marquise is well, we trust?" Gaston inquired in the polite conversational chatter that made Antoine grit his teeth.

"Madame is splendid. Your interest in her welfare is most touching, but I should prefer not to discuss it. Good evening, or shall I say good morning, gentlemen." Antoine mockingly touched the rim of his hat and prepared to move on.

"Your Lordship!" Prosper called after him. "There is one more thing!"

"And what might that be?" Antoine turned toward the two men and it was only then that he noticed the dark figure of a third man lurking in the shadows. He had apparently been there all this time and had overheard the conversation between these roughnecks and an aspiring peer of the realm. This was most embarrassing. He really must be more careful in his dealings with that riffraff.

"Here's a gentleman who would like to greet Your Lordship," Gaston said with that humility that always had something mocking about it.

"Well, let the gentleman show his face if his business is so urgent that it cannot wait till morning."

The man stepped out into the moonlight, removed his hood and extended both arms: "Antoine! Antoine Maximilien Dupuis, Marquis de Valinquette, Seigneur de Chazeron, also known as Antoine Barca or Antonio Barca. Am I right? I hope I didn't leave anything out?"

"Guibert?" Antoine's face turned wan as the fading moon.

"Close your mouth, Antoine. No, you are not seeing a ghost, even if you wish you did. It's your old friend Guibert, the Count de Mallac, in the flesh, come back from the dead, or shall we say from the living tomb of Pignerol."

"What are you talking about? Of course I am happy to see you . . . alive. Surprised, yes, but also happy. Believe me this is the happiest surprise . . ." Antoine had recovered his composure and quickly enclosed the slightly shorter and stockier man in his arms.

"You're choking me, Antoine!" Guibert said laughing.

"Where have you been all these years, what have you been doing?" Antoine asked breathlessly.

"All this is easily explained," Guibert said. "But not here. Can we meet tomorrow, somewhere undisturbed? Where can we talk?"

"Of course. You will come to my house, I insist that you accept my hospitality. The Marquise will be overjoyed."

"Madame's reputation of graciousness and beauty precedes her, but I would prefer not to be seen in society for the time being. You will understand when I explain. Just now, no questions." Antoine thought he detected a strange weariness in his old friend's familiar face.

"All right. There's a wicket in the rear gate to the garden of the Hôtel de Valinquette; it will be open. I shall await you there at noon tomorrow. There is a pavilion deep inside the garden where we can meet undisturbed. I'm sure these two gentlemen can show you the way," he added with a note of sarcasm.

"I'm sure of that. Until tomorrow then!"

He could still hear Guibert and the two thugs laughing like bandits who had just made off with a purse of gold.

Any thought of Manon had flown from Antoine's mind. He reached the gate of the Hôtel de Valinquette drenched in cold sweat, gasping like a fugitive on the run. Elation at seeing the friend, believed long dead and now so very much alive, alternated with dread and fear of what his sudden reappearance might forebode.

That night the Marquis de Valinquette found no rest. He tossed and turned as he relived the moment he had last seen Guibert, almost ten years before. There were the dark streets near the fortress of Saint Antoine, the two of them battling an overwhelming force. The battle had been won that day, but the hand-to-hand fighting continued into the night. Again and again the memory of Guibert going down surrounded by Royal Musketeers resurfaced. His call for help had echoed in his mind for a long time after.

"But how could I have come to his aid?" he kept mumbling. "I was wounded myself and beset upon by Musketeers. I thought he had been killed. I even was told so later."

With the first rays of dawn, exhaustion from mental anguish finally overwhelmed him, and Antoine fell into a deep, if uneasy sleep.

When he awoke several hours later, he sent word to the Marquise that there would be no atelier session this morning, something had come up, he would explain later. He groomed himself carefully. Guibert should not think him a pauper. Then he withdrew into the solitude of his atelier in the garden. At first he sat and waited. But realizing that it was long before noon, he picked up the chisel and hammer to pass the time. He began chipping away at the hips and legs of his statue but soon the tools dropped from his listless hands. No, not today. He would not make any progress today.

What would Guibert say when he saw him still working on the "cold stone Venus," as he had called it?

Maybe Guibert was right even then. Maybe he was wasting his time. Why did he arrange to meet Guibert here, in his most private realm? Was he deliberately inviting his scorn? Was he expecting Guibert to help him face the truth he had so long avoided, the truth that his talent was limited and that he simply did not have the ability to create the likeness that had haunted his dreams since he was a raw youth. And what did he still need this stone for? He had the most perfect flesh-and-blood model already in his possession. But how could he give up now?

For thirteen years, he kept alive the hope that he would return one day and finish the work he had begun. He remembered well the day—it was the 27th of August 1648—when he left the unfinished block of alabaster in the stonecutter's shed, believing he would return to it within a year's time. Guibert had been the messenger who called him to his duty to be with his family at a time when the Valinquettes were losing their protracted feud with the Crown, that is, Cardinal Mazarin, the unpopular minister who held all power in the Kingdom. Nowhere was that man more deeply hated than among the Parisians.

On the morning of that hot summer day in 1648, a furious populace had barricaded the city's narrow streets with chains, sacks filled with dung, and whatever else came to hand. Throngs of raucous marchers moved back and forth between the Palais de Justice and the Palais-Royal with shouts of "Down with the Mazarins!" and "Release Broussel!" and more shouts of "Broussel! Broussel!" The roar of the restive crowd resounded across the river to where Antoine Barca, as he then liked to be known, awoke from a fitful sleep. He was in a brooding mood and paid scant attention to the noises penetrating his chamber from the usually noisy city streets. He quickly went through the motions of his morning toilet—he tied his stringy black hair at the nape of his neck, donned a wide-sleeved checkered blouse and striped loose breeches, and stepped into open-toed shoes in the fashion of the Parisian artists.

Suddenly he seemed in a hurry, as if pushed by some irresistible force. He left off shaving and on his way down the narrow stairs of the rooming house, he almost collided with his landlady who was hauling a heavy tray loaded with fresh-baked, fresh-brewed breakfast fare up to his room. Huffing from the exertion of the climb to the top floor, she gave off an angry scream, but, mumbling an excuse, he had already disappeared into the street.

He walked briskly, without bothering to inquire about the purpose of the excited multitude. From his lodgings in the rue de l'Echaude, which ran along the compound of the Abbey of Saint Germain des Prés, he raced down the rue de Seine and crossed the Pont Neuf to the Isle de la Cité. On the Cité side of the bridge, he caught his breath in front of a young girl seated on the pavement. She was apparently blind and lame. She sat motionless, a tin cup in her hand into which he tossed a handful of coins. He spoke a few words to her and continued on his way.

Near the Palais de Justice the mob's shouts of "Broussel! Broussel!" intensified. The twisting alleys were clogged with a human mass shouting itself into a near state of hysteria. Antoine elbowed his way through the crowd, determined not to be deterred from his course. Several ruffians suddenly blocked his way with shouts "There goes a Mazarin spy!" An angry horde of mean-looking brutes seemed intent on roughing him up. Luckily their attention was distracted by the parliamentarians of Paris who just then appeared in the street. A procession of dignitaries, robed in red velvet and satin, issued from the Palais de Justice. They stopped briefly, and the head magistrate addressed the crowd before they continued on their solemn march in the direction of the royal residence at the Palais Royal. One of the magistrates held up a long roll of paper and declared: "This is a petition, signed by every magistrate of the city, asking the Regent for the release of Councilor Broussel, whose arrest has caused us all such grief this morning. I am sure Her Majesty will be guided by the will of her people!"

The crowd gave the parliamentarians an enthusiastic send-off, confident that they would accomplish their mission of freeing this popular Broussel.

Antoine had been unaware of the incident that had aroused the ire of the Parisians and was even now not inclined to find out more about it. He quickly seized the opportunity of the diversion created by the parliamentarians and ducked away from the ruffians. Without looking back, he ran as fast as his feet would carry him across the Parvis de Notre Dame and did not stop until he was safe inside the stonecutters' yard behind the cathedral.

The yard was empty. All the masons were apparently at the demonstration. Even the old master stonemason himself, Master Redillon, who was always early at his station, was nowhere to be seen. Antoine moved across the yard to a squat shed, undid the latch and let himself in. Inside he took several determined strides and confronted a huge amorphous shape covered by a canvas. He pulled away the cover and exposed a block of white alabaster. For a while he stood lost in thought, then with caressing hands he traced the rudimentary outline, a rough-hewn form of a nude woman carved into the stone. Suddenly he threw up his hands in despair and muttered: "If I only had the right model!"

How long he stood there contemplating the monolith he could not tell. So absorbed was he by his obsession that he remained unaware of somebody entering the shed until a brash familiar voice exploded near his ear: "Aren't there enough warm, breathing women in Paris? What do you want with a stone Venus?"

"Guibert?" The sardonic tone could not have belonged to anybody else. He turned and faced his friend's characteristic beaming smile.

"Guibert! You devil! What are you doing in Paris?" Antoine was not sure whether he should be delighted or annoyed by the unannounced appearance.

"Suppose you first tell me what you are doing doting on a piece of rock with a gaze so languid as if it were the most ravishing woman."

"You know I came to Paris to become a sculptor," Antoine replied stiffly, not in the mood to be mocked. "When this piece of rock, as you call it, is finished, it will be a representation of the ideal woman, more beautiful than anything—if it turns out as the image in my mind."

"Well, Antoine, I don't know much about the difference between ideal and unideal women, they all seem pretty ideal to me. Any shape or form will do for me, as long as they are soft and warm to the touch."

Guibert drew out the last words with sensuous delight, touching his fingers to his lips in an appreciative gesture of the connoisseur. Antoine realized that it was hopeless to try to impress this clod with the artist's view of the world.

"You haven't changed at all, Guibert!" Antoine said rather pointlessly.

"I'm sorry, I don't mean to mock you, but I'm just a simple fellow. At any rate, you will have to put off playing God for a while. I am here to take you home and without delay—strictest orders from Monsieur the Marquis."

"My father cannot mean this. Not now, when I am so close to the examinations. How can I leave now? He promised . . ."

"Yes, but circumstances have changed. The Sicilian snake apparently means business this time. From the racket in the streets here, I surmise he won't win a prize for popularity in Paris either."

"Burning Mazarin in effigy is a popular pastime among the Parisians. But as long as he is in the Queen's good graces, not even the street mob can topple him."

"Besides, he also commands the allegiance of the royal troops," Guibert added, "and they have been giving us quite a bit of trouble of late. The horses are waiting for us in the Faubourg Saint Marcel. We must leave right away."

"Let me at least take care of a few things. We'll get a fresh start early in the morning. And tonight, my friend," Antoine placed his arm around Guibert's shoulder, "tonight we celebrate—as in the old days. I'd like to see that old animal charm of yours do its trick on the Parisian wenches."

"I'm glad to hear that you have not become completely immune to the pleasures of the flesh!" Guibert proclaimed, all too eager to comply.

Antoine was glad that Guibert was so easily persuaded, for he was in no mood to confide in him the real reason why he was anxious to delay their departure till morning. He placed the canvas over the statue with a resigned "I guess you'll have to await more peaceful times," and they left.

Outside in the yard, where several stonecutters had now returned to work in the August heat, Antoine bade his friend wait while he looked around for Master Redillon. He was just then appearing in front of his lodging, and Antoine met the master stonecutter halfway, bowing respectfully. He handed him a leather coin pouch to cover the rent for the shed and commended the alabaster block to his safekeeping. With the promise to return before the first snowfall to finish his work, he took his leave. Antoine did not know then that thirteen years would elapse before he would make good on his promise.

In the street the two young men became immediately engulfed by a surge of people streaming toward the Palais de Justice. The delegation of parliamentarians was just then returning from their audience at the Palais Royal. The ever-popular Broussel was apparently not among them, for the crowd's shouts for the release of Broussel rose in a renewed crescendo.

"Who the hell is this Broussel anyway that he inspires such passions?" Guibert shouted at Antoine over the heads of a club- and pitchfork-swinging mob that had forced its way between them.

"For God's sake let's get away from here before we get trampled," Antoine yelled, wildly gesticulating like a swimmer battling a raging stream.

Guibert meanwhile reached the fringe and, hugging a wall, was able to withstand the propelling force. He reached out for Antoine's hand and pulled him to safety. Edging along carefully, backs against the houses lining the narrow street, they at last reached safe ground.

Bursting with laughter they raced each other to the banks of the river.

"All right, who is this Broussel who is causing so much trouble?" Guibert demanded to know.

"I don't have the slightest idea," Antoine howled. "Probably a nobody. Let's ask this gentleman, he looks like an informed man of the world."

"Excuse us, dear Sir," Antoine bowed before a passerby, still laughing. "My friend and I are strangers in this town. Might you be able to tell us who this Monsieur Broussel is?"

"Haven't you heard?" the man said, amazed at such ignorance but happy to fill them in. "He is a venerable parliamentarian. He was arrested for opposing the new tax decree imposed by the Queen and her Italian. He has become a hero, a symbol of the people's discontent with the royal regime. They should know better than to stir the ire of the Parisians."

"So Mazarin does not have many friends in Paris," said Guibert.

"He is the most hated man in this town," the man stated ominously and, with a bow, he went on his way.

They crossed the Pont Saint Michel into the Latin Quarter. The area lay almost deserted—the entire student body, usually clustered at the corners, apparently had gone off to demand the release of

Broussel. The friends wandered through the empty streets toward the Mont Sainte Geneviève, chatting and jesting, two young men of roughly the same age, so obviously intimate with each other, like brothers, yet as unlike as any that could be found.

Antoine Barca, whose Iberian blood dominated the Gallic strain in his physical characteristics, was the taller yet the more delicate one of the two. Everything about him, his limbs, his face, and especially his hands, was straight and elongated and suggested a smooth suppleness short of being effeminate. The olive tinge of his skin, the straight, jet black hair, which he usually wore loose on his shoulders in the fashion of the day but which was on that day pulled back because of the heat, the oval of his face complimented by a long, narrow nose and melancholy, charcoal eyes—only the fullness of his sensuous lips, accentuated by a thin moustache, drooping toward the corners of his mouth, disturbed the orderly arrangement of lines and shapes in this visage of a prince of an exotic kingdom.

Guibert de Mallac, the scion of a disinherited Breton noble house, was, by contrast, undeniably the descendant of the Celtic hordes who once had struck fear into the hearts of Roman invaders. His stocky frame breathed the ruggedness of the Breton coastline. His hair undulated freely over his shoulders in a sandy cascade, as if nature had meant to replicate in him the coloring of his ancestral landscape. Most arresting was his face, broad and ruddy, with a pair of watery blue eyes that radiated an earthy lust for life, a rather stubby nose widening into nostrils that were almost always twitching like a pointer picking up a scent, and rosy, full, voluptuous lips framed by a thin moustache. Not even the marks left by the pox of his childhood impaired the irresistible attractiveness with which nature had endowed him. Everything about him exuded life and charm, and yet even so, one could detect etched into his youthful face certain bewildering traces of a debauched coarseness.

"I seem to remember a time, not so long ago, when you relished crossing swords like a true Valinquette," Guibert was saying as they crossed the square at the foot of Mont Sainte Geneviève. He was responding to Antoine's vain attempt to explain that his hands were made to hold a chisel and hammer not a sword.

"But that was long ago. I was young then and bursting with energy that had nowhere else to go," Antoine replied, even though he realized the pointlessness of this exchange.

"And now, at twenty-two, you are old and ready to settle down!" Guibert said mocking.

"Sometimes I wonder how it can be possible that anybody should be as insensitive a clod as you are. You just never seem to grow up. How you used to drive me mad when we were children with your habit of taking everything anybody said at face value and then turning it into something absurd."

Antoine was about to lose his temper, but quickly got a hold of himself, remembering a secret pledge he had made many years ago never to permit Guibert to put him on the defensive. From the day twelve years before when the Marquis de Valinquette had brought the son of his friend and ally Guillaume de Mallac into his household, Antoine had felt challenged by the waif's overbearing manner.

Not infrequently, Guibert's taunts, his twisting of his every word, no matter how trivial, had driven him to tears. His father only laughed off his complaints and suggested he learn from Guibert and emulate him. The one person he could turn to for solace was the Marquise, who with a mother's aversion to the intruder hated him with all her Iberian passion. She would remind her son that he was not only a Valinquette but also of the lineage of the Iberian race of Barca y Alarcon, two ancient noble houses compared to which the Mallacs were nothing but Breton robber barons.

He was, however, not as status conscious as his mother, nor did he share her hatred for the boy, of whom he was at heart rather fond. He resolved to let his tormentor have some of his own medicine. The tactic worked better than expected. For as soon as Guibert, like all bullies, saw that he could not make his intended victim squirm, he began to treat him with something approaching respect.

As they grew older, Antoine came to realize that Guibert, despite his brilliance as a student, simply lacked a certain turn of mind, a certain innate sensibility that would permit him to grasp the subtler meanings of human discourse.

So it was that the two sat in the tavern of Sainte Geneviève on that August day in 1648, still debating the virtues of the life of the artist versus that of the soldier, all the while devouring a kettle of hearty beef stew which they washed down with several pitchers of beer. An episode sprang to Antoine's mind, a telling example of the difference in their temperaments.

The Marquis de Valinquette, who was inordinately fond of his adopted son Guibert, for reasons Antoine only learned later, insisted that he receive the same education as his own son, as befitted a young gentleman of ancient nobility. Although Guibert usually triumphed in fencing, wrestling, riding, and any kind of physical activity, Antoine was by no means physically inept. In fact he was more graceful; further, he was more reticent and was not given to showing off like Guibert.

Guibert also outdid him in memorizing the classical texts, a part of their studies that received great emphasis. He had a prodigious memory, absorbing long passages of Latin from Cicero, Virgil, and Catullus, and even Machiavelli in Italian, which he then recited for the entertainment of the local nobles gathered at Chazeron. Antoine, who was at first overawed, soon realized that Guibert had absolutely no understanding of the meaning of what he was saying although he was able to hide his ignorance from most of the guests with clever platitudes. Antoine always remembered, with a certain tinge of malice, the night when the Duchesse de Chevreuse, friend and confidante to the Queen, wife and mistress of powerful men and one of the most celebrated beauties in the realm—it was rumored that even the granite-hearted Cardinal Richelieu had pined for a favorable glance from her, though his ardor was left unrequited—this extraordinary woman, who was forever spinning intrigues and hatching plots, batted her legendary blue eyes at the fifteen-year-old Guibert when he had finished with a theatrical recitation of Odysseus' homecoming, and said: "What a marvelous performance! A monkey could not have done as well as Monsieur the Count."

Guibert's face turned ember red at first, but like all fops he could not conceive the remark to have been anything but a compliment. For a long time thereafter he would recount how the inestimable Duchesse de Chevreuse had favored him with her attention.

The tutors were more easily duped than the duchess, and in the course of comparisons, which were frequently made, Antoine usually came up short. Where Antoine was inattentive and given to daydreaming, Guibert was ever eager to please, soaking up the teachers' every word and ever prepared to spit back undigested what was placed before him. So it was little wonder that it was Guibert who garnered all the praise and trophies of glory.

"What are you snickering about, Antoine?" Guibert demanded to know.

"Oh, nothing in particular," Antoine replied, quaffing the fresh Sainte Geneviève brew. "It occurred to me that you are still the same old Guibert. Do you remember the summer when we were reading *L'Astrée*? What a marvelous time we had in the peaceful groves and meadows in the Auvergne hills!"

"You haven't changed much yourself, Antoine. You are still the same old romantic fool. I would wager you still dream about falling in love with a shepherdess."

"You never appreciated the incredible sensibility and poetic charm of that story."

"You're right, and I don't deny it. I thought so then and still think so now—that character Astrée is nothing but a scheming female and I will never understand what the fuss over this book is all about. And a man degrading himself for the love of a woman the way this shepherd does deserves not one ounce of my sympathy."

"Do Your Lordships wish to engage the services of the house?" A coquettish female interrupted the friends' exchange just in time, for the stage was set for another heated debate about the merits, or lack thereof, of Honoré d'Urfé's novel about the unhappy love of a shepherd for a shepherdess which was the favored reading of the literate youths of their generation.

"My darling Guillemette!" Antoine exclaimed, gratefully, "please, meet my friend, the Count de Mallac. He is visiting our fair city and I was just assuring him that Parisian women are without compare. But you, my dear child, can probably convince him of that better than I can."

Guillemette, a thin girl of seventeen or eighteen, presented an almost comical admixture of whore and child. Pressing herself against Guibert's side, she searched Antoine's face in mock innocence, as if to say, "Is this what you want me to do?"

Antoine nodded his head slightly while he resisted the advances of a more mature trollop. Despite his outward joviality, he was not in the right frame of mind for amorous games that night. The memories dredged up by Guibert's sudden appearance and the news of the siege of the family estate by Mazarin's troops put him in one of those brooding moods that dampened his desire. He longed to escape Guibert's scornful eye at least until the morning.

Fortunately it did not take much for Guillemette to ensnare Guibert with her wiles. Antoine knew her charms only too well and when the moment was propitious he stole away unnoticed. He returned to his lodging where he tried in vain to find at least a few hours of sleep. Before the crack of dawn, he was up again and began preparations for the journey homeward.

The city was still asleep when he made his way back through the empty streets to the tavern to rouse Guibert. But just as he arrived, Guibert came out of a door on the side of the tavern. He stretched his arms and breathed in deeply the morning air as yet unspoiled by the putrid smell of human and animal excrement that at all other times wafted through the closed-in alleyways. Guibert's rosy face shone with the brilliance of a polished apple and he flashed his broad, virile smile at Antoine.

"A very good morning to you, Antoine!" he exclaimed jumping up and down, bending this way and that, as if he was performing his morning exercises. "For once you were right. Parisian women are exquisite, judging by the two that I have had the pleasure of sampling. But alas, the call of duty compels us to depart from this fair city with the hope for a return in due time."

When Antoine did not deign to answer, Guibert gathered his clothing, pulled on his boots, and without looking back at the tavern where the two young girls appeared at the window, he started down the street. Cautiously he studied Antoine's brooding demeanor.

"I hope I did not offend Your Lordship in anyway?" he said. "You see, the other girl, she was rather hurt at being shunned by your imperial majesty, so I took pity and did my best to console her."

"Oh, why don't you stop your senseless chatter already! Do you really think I care one pistole whether you spend your nights with one whore or two or ten?"

The city was now coming to life. Shutters flung open and they had to cut a zigzag path under the windows to avoid being doused with the content of chamber pots. Street vendors began to intone the shrill chants of their trade. Shops were thrown open and wares and victuals laid out on display. The enticing aroma of fresh-baked bread mingled with the stench of decaying fish and fowl. Antoine was now anxious to put all this behind him, but he still had one more thing on his mind before he could turn his back on the city and its people.

Guibert meanwhile, hobbling a step beside him, continued his chatter. He expressed his approval of Antoine's changed appearance this morning. It was so much more befitting his station, he said, than that artiste garb he had found him in the day before. In fact Antoine had spent a good deal of time this morning transforming himself from an artist into a nobleman. The checkered smock and baggy Turkish ankle breeches had been replaced by a loose-fitting velvet jerkin and knee breeches in gold slashed with black—the gold and black of the Valinquettes. Instead of sandals he wore black top boots, polished to a lustrous shine as intense as his black hair, which had been released from the knot and now draped his shoulders. His broad-rimmed felt hat, similar to Guibert's, was adorned with a huge gray ostrich feather. With a short black cape, a cup-hilt rapier and dagger held in the sash strapped over his broad chest, he was every inch the aristocrat.

With the sartorial transformation came a change in general demeanor and bearing; a stern determined look deepened by a knitted brow had wiped away the languid melancholy expression. Antoine suggested that they pass by his lodgings to pick up a few of his belongings—besides, there was no better breakfast to be had in all of Paris than that prepared by his landlady. He also felt the need to make it up to her for their clash the day before.

With all preparations for their departure completed, Antoine led the way through the maze of streets and alleys, carrying his own baggage since he did not keep a valet. After several turns that took them nearer the heart of the city, Guibert held his friend back, pointing out that he seemed to remember that the Faubourg Saint Marcel, where the men and horses were waiting, was in the opposite direction.

"I'm quite aware of that," Antoine replied. "There's one small matter I need to take care of. Don't worry, we shall be on our way before long."

As they emerged onto the open space near the Pont Neuf, Antoine lengthened his stride and crossed the bridge without regard to whether Guibert was keeping step with him. He scanned the area on the other side, which was beginning to fill with throngs of beggars staking out their little enclaves for the days earnings. Apparently unable to detect what he was looking for, Antoine's face darkened as he muttered to himself: "Why today of all days is she not here? She has never failed me before."

"You are not looking for a woman among those tattered hags?" Guibert remarked as he caught up with him.

"Spare me your comments and keep your mouth shut." Antoine's cutting tone gave Guibert pause. Something told him that he had better hold back. His curiosity was now aroused, of course. He placed himself a few paces away in a position to observe his friend's bizarre conduct unobtrusively. Fortunately, he did not have to wait long for something to happen. It was hard to believe at first, but there was no doubt, it was the appearance of a ragged beggar child, being carried to the foot of the bridge and left to sit on a worn rug by two unsavory-looking characters, that brightened Antoine's countenance.

As soon as the thugs had left, Antoine walked up to the child—Guibert was unable to determine whether it was male or female. He saw his friend bending over and speaking to the wretched waif, but alas too softly for the words to reach Guibert's ears. The child seemed attentive and nodded several times, without looking at him directly and maintaining a vague blank stare even when he placed a small leather pouch into her hand that quickly disappeared under the pile of rags covering the miserable little body.

Guibert had always thought himself forbearing with his friend's eccentricities, but this scene aroused in him more than scorn. This was outright ridiculous. Abruptly he walked up to the pair and waved his hand up and down close to the pauper's face. The child did not flinch.

"What are you doing?" Antoine cried.

"I have heard that most of these cripples are fakes and very cunning at that. When they go home at night, their infirmities have a way of disappearing quite miraculously."

"Well, did you satisfy yourself that this girl is indeed blind? How could a child that age be faking such a dreadful condition? Believe me, I have seen her every day for the past two years. She is absolutely unable to see, nor is she able to walk. You needn't be so skeptical."

Antoine turned his attention back toward the girl.

"You must excuse my friend's rudeness. Before I go will you sing for me? I want to carry your beautiful voice with me until I return."

The girl, who was maybe eight or nine years old—although her thin body, her dirt-encrusted hair and face, her sunken cheeks and expressionless eyes made her look more like a ghostly underworld creature than a living human being—made an obliging gesture. She raised the little sticks of her arms and burst into "Plaisir d'Amour."

Antoine stood transfixed. He closed his eyes and drank in every note of the lilting melody that flowed from the thin, blue lips like a clear, bubbling brook, inundating his whole being. Even Guibert was, for a brief moment, entranced by the voice, coming so haunting and pure from so miserable a body.

The friends were brought back from their separate contemplations by the shuffling feet of an army of artisans marching across the bridge from the Latin Quarter toward the Palais de Justice, brandishing all sorts of makeshift weapons. "We'd better make our exit before the clamor for Broussel gets under way again. It is late already," Guibert urged as the bell from the spire of La Sainte Chapelle rang out eight times.

Antoine bid the girl farewell.

"God bless you and keep you, my Lord," she whispered.

"You sentimental old fool. What was all that about?" Guibert exclaimed, breathlessly trying to keep step with Antoine's brisk stride.

"You wouldn't understand," Antoine replied with a dismissive gesture and doubled his pace.

"You made quite a spectacle of yourself back there, and I think you owe me an explanation. Treating a ragamuffin from the gutter like a lady is not likely to meet with the understanding of Monsieur the Marquis."

Antoine's step faltered as if he had been stabbed in the back. He whipped around with glowering gaze, ready to throw himself at his tormentor.

"You never did have much tact, Guibert. You just can't help being an oaf. I don't owe you anything. This is my business. But if you must know, this girl brings me luck. Her voice has brightened my days for nearly two years. She can always be counted on to be there, at that corner, without fail, in rain or snow, in the dead of winter and the most stifling heat of summer. So how could I leave town without bidding her farewell and making sure she is provided for."

"But why her?" Guibert asked more courteously though Antoine's logic still made no sense to him. "This city is filled with beggars, paupers, cripples. It's impossible to walk a few paces without having to maneuver around tugging hands, bodies rolling in the gutter. The moaning alone is enough to make your skin crawl. Somebody ought to do something about this. Put them to work—but most of them are probably too feeble-minded and lazy to do honest work."

"Do you really believe people like to live like this or that they choose to? Let's face it, it is we who are to blame for the miserable condition of these masses. We deprive them of their livelihood by throwing them off the land and then we don't help them survive in the city."

"If you had your way, we would have schools for the poor too!" Guibert laughed out loud.

"That is exactly what should be done and I would wager that every one of these miserable creatures could be made into a useful member of society."

"My dear Antoine, aren't you forgetting something in your humanitarian fervor? What about differences of breeding, of blood ennobled by centuries of refinement?"

"My dear Guibert, you seem to be talking about horses rather than human beings. It may take time and patience, but I am convinced that any one of these wretches could be transformed into a lady or a gentleman given the proper instruction and care."

Although Antoine had a genuine concern for the poor and felt that society was not living up to its responsibility, at this moment he got carried away with his own rhetoric to state a claim even he, in a more sober moment, would have regarded as an exaggeration.

"But all this is idle talk anyway. We'll never know which one of us is right since neither of us is in a position to do anything about it," he added impatiently, tired of trying to make this pompous bloke of a friend understand something as subtle and complex as human nature.

They had more urgent matters to attend to and were soon on their way south to where the Marquis de Valinquette was urgently awaiting their arrival.

Chapter 5

BERTRAND MARIE AUGUSTE Dupuis, Marquis de Valinquette, stood on the rampart, his eyes fixed on the mass of blue and white banners fluttering above the royal encampment pitched about five leagues to the north. But the royal garrison, which had become a familiar sight for the last four weeks, was not what made him scan the horizon. He had no illusions as to how things stood in this struggle with the crown or his chances of survival against, as he preferred to see it, a rapacious foreigner who was sucking the kingdom dry for his private benefit.

Château Valinquette was enclosed on its northern and eastern approaches by a lake and a forty-foot-wide and twenty-foot-deep moat. To the south and west it leaned against a rugged, almost impenetrable wooded terrain. As it was, the Marquis de Valinquette had his back against the wall. The ultimatum was to expire three days hence, and then, not sooner he was sure, the royal troops would launch their attack. Only a miracle could save the inhabitants of the castle from certain doom. Unless, of course . . . unless he surrendered beforehand. But that, he had sworn never to do. Never would he bow down to that devil in cardinal's purple who parades as a man of God. The odds may be against him, but the Marquis de Valinquette would at least go down fighting for the honor of his ancient lineage. In a way, he even welcomed the confrontation that was to force a resolution of the standoff at long last. He prided himself on being a man ready to die for his principles.

His only wish was to see his wife and daughters escorted to safety. The thought of what their fate will be should they fall into his enemies' hands made him break out in a cold sweat. Powerless to do anything but wait, he kicked the masonry with his boots in frustration.

"Where, the devil, are Antoine and Guibert?" he muttered. They should have been here days ago. Of course, some valuable time would inevitably be lost since they had to make a wide circle around and cut their way through the forest from the southwestern approach to the castle. With royal troops swarming all over the northern route, the direct way was blocked. But they would make it, he was certain. The boys had grown up in this region and knew its terrain inside out.

He stopped his pacing. The eyes behind royal spyglasses, which he knew were trained on the ramparts, should not detect his agitation. Nor did he want his wife to surprise him with his guard down. He had to remain calm. All he needed was a hysteric panic of womenfolk on his hands.

To distract himself, he made the round of his men positioned on the ramparts. He stopped here and there to dispense some good words of encouragement. They were all loyal and proven fighters, able to hold out at least a fortnight. After that, come what may.

He descended into the yard and found himself alone in front of the ancient castle keep. Following an impulse, he entered the massive, ageless relic of unsettled times and began to climb the worn, winding stairs. This venerable square castlekeep withstood the onslaught of Viking invaders and Angevin pretenders. The Marquis' ancestors had stood their ground in this area, the heart of the Limousin province, for centuries. They had their quarrels, but they had always served their kings loyally. But then that was a time when kings were still men, who forged their kingdom shoulder to shoulder with their noble vassals. Would anybody have believed then that, one day, kingdom and king would be squeezed dry by ruthless ministers out for power and personal gain?

Halfway up his breathing became heavy, either from the strain of the climb or from the anger his thoughts provoked in him. He leaned against the wall, gasping.

"I surely am not as young as I used to be," he muttered. But he pushed on, and the view from the top was well worth the exertion. He could let his eyes roam in every direction without being exposed to the view of the hunters. Deep in thought, his heart heavy with foreboding, he settled down to a lone vigil.

After twenty-five years of intrigues, conspiracies, and cabals against evil influences in the Kingdom of France, the Marquis de Valinquette had to concede defeat. He, like many nobles of ancient lineage, had reached the end of his rope. Two fortnights ago the ultimatum had been presented, backed by massing of troops on the plain that stretched north from the chateau. The choice was surrender of all domains or arrest and charge with high treason.

The Sicilian snake, Cardinal Mazarin, minister of the King and, as rumor had it, maybe even paramour of the Queen Mother, held all the trumps in his hands. Valinquette had no doubt that His Eminence could gather ample proof that he conspired against the Crown and have him executed. The times had turned against the old established, feudal nobility. The courts were stacked with "new" men—anybody with money could now buy a noble title and a seat in a Parlement. Blood and breeding counted for little anymore. He would not be judged by his peers but by ambitious office seekers who would twist his every word against him. Who would believe that whatever acts he committed, they were not directed against the Crown but against the corrupting influences of power-hungry men whose titles had very little to do with an ecclesiastical calling?

By sheer luck he had survived the regime of that other man of the cloth, Cardinal Richelieu by name—he was at least a Frenchman. His friend Guillaume, the Count de Mallac, had not been so lucky. He paid with his life at the gallows for his devotion to the Queen. Now this same Queen had her own Cardinal, and if this little Italian wasn't cleverer than his predecessor, he certainly surpassed him in greed.

Anger made Bertrand Dupuis squirm like a trapped animal. A pernicious foreigner was wielding unlimited power in the Kingdom of France and went about dispossessing the oldest French families on whose estates he settled his Italian relatives in grand style! But even if the Valinquettes had to fall, there was still hope that at least France would be saved, there was still the alliance of the great nobles, the princes of the blood, the peers of France cemented together in a bond forged in a common past. The remnant would rally around the Prince de Condé and continue the good fight. His sacrifice would then have been for the greater good.

The Marquis no longer scanned the horizon. His gaze was turned inward and his thoughts spun feverishly in his head. His son and heir would take up the challenge, he would avenge the infamy. But then he was not so sure. Antoine was not at all the kind of son a nobleman would wish for. His son, with his fancy of being an artist! The Marquis spat out an expression of profound contempt.

Were his son a man like Guibert de Mallac, matters would be different. Then he could rest assured. The Marquis blessed the day he took the orphan into his house and raised him as a son—a promise he had made to his father. And into what a man he had grown! Here was a scion of true Gallic blood, who would do his Breton ancestors proud—a man after the Marquis' own heart! Yes, that Guibert could be counted on. Some day he would avenge the defamation and restore the honor of the good name of the Mallacs and the Valinquettes. The day would come when the old nobility would regain its ancient rights and France would once again have a king like Henri Bourbon and Navarre. There still was hope. The present king was but a boy. He might well turn out to be of the same mettle as his famous grandfather.

The Marquis lifted his eyes with a start. The sun was about to set. He had lost track of time. The Marquise would have one of her Iberian outbursts, as he called her easily aroused temper, if he was found missing from the supper table. But he did not hurry on his descent.

"How will Antonio get safely through the royal lines?" Doña Elvira, his Iberian wife, had been asking the same question ten times every day since the Marquis had sent for his son in Paris.

"What if he has fallen into the hands of Mazarin's men?" she wailed.

The Marquis had answered politely, even soothingly. The Valinquettes are skilled in getting out of tight spots, he explained. Antoine would know how to evade the troops and he saw no cause for worry. But after three weeks of waiting, even a man of the Marquis' self-possession finally lost his temper.

"Haven't I told Madame a thousand times, there is nothing to worry about—Paris is far away from here. It takes time. Besides there isn't a man in the service of that sleazy little Italian whom Guibert could not outwit—he knows this area like the inside of his coat."

"Guibert! Guibert!" the Marquise exclaimed with disdain. "All one ever hears around here is Guibert this, Guibert that. Sometimes I think you forget that you have a son and heir of your own."

"Oh no! I haven't forgotten! How could I? But where is my son when the honor and life of the family is at stake? In Paris, following some Iberian fancy, chipping away at pieces of stone. And who is the man who stands beside me, shoulder to shoulder, fighting my enemies—Guibert de Mallac, a true French nobleman. He has never let me down."

Valinquette had talked himself into such a rage that he lost all sense of how his words tore into his wife's heart.

"Do you mean to say that Antonio has let you down?" she snarled like a cat being poked with the point of a rod. "Antonio has fought for France in the Empire and in the Netherlands. He has paid his dues and has earned the right to follow his heart's calling."

"What calling besides bearing arms does a French nobleman have? You and your Antonio! He even calls himself Antoine Barca! As if a good French name was not good enough for the future Marquis de Valinquette. Generations of Valinquettes must be reeling in their graves to see how their once-proud line has degenerated."

"You call your son a degenerate? Your own flesh and blood!"

He had overstepped all bounds, but it was too late to retract. Before his eyes, the Marquise was transformed into an avenging fury. She seemed to expand into the formless shape of a hovering mythical creature, her eyes, smoldering coals of passion and pride, flashing in a more intense shade of black, her voice inhumanly piercing, shrill.

"You should know better than to dare deride the race of the Barcas!" He knew what was coming and he knew his only redemption was to demur, submit to a lecture on the history of the most noble house of Barca y Alarcon, a Catalan race as proud and cantankerous as might be found anywhere in the Kingdom of France. She would remind him that her family was descended in direct line from the Barcas of Carthage, whose most famed offsprings had been Hannibal and Hamilcar, governors of Iberia before the Roman conquest. To raise the objection that a direct lineage through hundreds of generations would be hard to prove was pointless—Valinquette knew from experience the woe that befell those who dared jest or voice the slightest doubt about this most cherished of the Barca family traditions.

Valinquette had always shown respect for the legend in the interest of domestic peace. Only on one point he had stood firm. Every male Barca y Alarcon bore the name Anibal or Hamilcar, if not as first then as second name. His Gallic soul revolted at Antoine Anibal. His son would not be named after a barbaric, prehistoric madman, elephants or no elephants—his son was a scion of a French house of noblest lineage and not the spawn of Catalan mountain chieftains. That, at the same time, he blamed the Spanish blood in his son's veins for his "degenerate proclivities" did not occur to him as a contradiction at all.

Doña Elvira de Barca y Alarcon and Bertrand Dupuis had married for love, and twenty-seven years of an often tempestuous union had not completely erased the passion they had for each other since their earliest youth. From the very moment their eyes had met in the stultifying atmosphere of the Prado in Madrid, they both knew they were meant for each other. They were both only children. She was thirteen years old, a lady in waiting to the Queen of Spain. He was fifteen, a page in the escort of the King's sister, Princess Elisabeth de France, herself only a child come to Madrid to be married to the future Philip IV of Spain.

The Spanish court was assembled in the throne room with all the oppressiveness of its awesome pomp. Elvira stood near the Queen. Bertrand flanked the little princess who walked with tremulous step down the aisle, ready to catch her should she stumble or faint. The procession came to a halt in front of the royal dais, and there she was, looking straight at him. She did not even avert her eyes, as modesty dictated, when he gave his head a slight nod. A refreshing presence in a stuffy atmosphere. Her eyes were as dark and sparkling as her hair. She was not fully grown to womanhood yet, but everything about her presaged a budding beauty.

They managed to arrange several trysts in the course of which they exchanged vows of eternal love and faithfulness. But Bertrand soon had to return to France, and almost five years passed before the lovers were joined in holy matrimony. The delay was largely due to family resistance on both sides. For although both families belonged to the upper nobility, each considered the other not quite up to snuff.

The lovers' persistence finally carried the day. Their connubial bliss was clouded only by the early miscarriages that raised the specter of that most dreaded of a woman's afflictions—barrenness. But Doña Elvira was not one to resign herself to such a harrowing fate without first moving heaven and earth. With stubborn determination, she undertook regular pilgrimages to the Black Madonna at the monastery of Montserrat in Catalonia, until at last her prayers were heard. She conceived and bore a son and heir.

Perhaps it was because she had waited for him so long—a miracle and a gift from heaven—that from the moment of his birth, Antoine became the center of her existence. She still loved Bertrand, but he now had a formidable rival for her passionate hovering.

Doña Elvira was pregnant eight more times. Some were stillborn, others did not survive infancy. But the last two, the daughters Camila and Gabriela, grew into delightful young ladies. The Marquis held them as close to his heart as the Marquise did her son.

The girls, twelve and eleven at the time of the siege, were one reason for the Marquis' feverish anticipation of his son's return. Nobody else could be trusted to take Doña Elvira and his daughters safely across the mountains to the Marquise's homeland.

Bertrand rose from the dinner table. He had forced down a few morsels of food so his wife and daughters would not perceive his troubled state of mind. The girls kissed their father good night with good cheer, apparently oblivious to the seriousness of the situation. But Doña Elvira's keen eye was not so easily fooled. She knew her Bertrand all too well. She too rose and came up behind him, placing her arms around him.

"We don't really have a chance against the King's soldiers, do we Bertrand?" she asked softly.

"The Cardinal's soldiers, Elvira! I have no quarrel with the King of France," he corrected her.

"Yes, I understand that. But they are still royal troops," Elvira snapped back, irritated that in this moment of the greatest crisis of their life, he kept himself aloof.

"There is nothing for you to worry about, my dear." His tone was conciliatory but distant. "Tomorrow, Antoine will be here, I am sure of it. I hope the preparations for your journey are complete."

"If the situation is not critical, as you insist, why do you want us to leave? I would really rather that we see this through together."

"Come what may, I shall rest easier knowing you and my daughters are in safety. The whole thing may blow over very quickly, and then I shall send for you again."

"In that case, will Your Lordship honor me with a visit to my chambers tonight?" Doña Elvira drew closer to him. She was still a beguiling woman. For a moment, the Marquis pulled her toward him and held her firmly in a silent embrace. Then he pushed her abruptly from him.

"Madame honors me with her request. But my responsibilities at this moment are too many and require my full attention," he said with a dry tone.

"As you wish, my Lord." Doña Elvira had almost expected this response. "But since this may be our last night, or our last hours under the same roof, and neither of us is likely to close an eye tonight, we should at least hold this vigil together."

"You are sensible as always, my love." He took her hand and pressed his lips against the palm of her hand. "I shall not be remiss in bidding you good night after I have checked on the sentries. Nights spent in waiting tend to be long, and I shall cherish Madame's company—although I do hope that you will find some rest before the long journey."

The Marquis made the rounds of the sentries, thinking how lucky he was to be loved by a woman like Doña Elvira. How many men could boast of a wife as understanding and loyal, even if she was temperamental and passionately articulate about her likes and dislikes. But then that was part of her charm. No, he had no regrets. She had enriched his life immeasurably, and he was that rare husband among the nobility who had never strayed. It pained him for her sake to think that they might soon be separated forever, that, for all he knew, she might soon be donning the widow's veil.

Valinquette never made it to his wife's chambers that night. It was a mild, moonlit, late summer night. Everything was quiet except for the chirping of the crickets and the intermittent hooting of an owl. About an hour past midnight, the sentry on the western rampart reported a disturbance in the thicket of the forest.

"What kind of disturbance?" Valinquette called up in a muted tone. "Can you make out anything?"

"Nothing except for some definite movement in the underbrush," the sentry replied. "But I can clearly hear rustling and shouts, almost like groaning."

Before he had finished speaking, the Marquis and the captain of the guard were next to him. They peered into the dark shadows of the forest seeking to pierce the density.

"Most likely it is our young master and the Count de Mallac returning," the captain said reassuringly.

"But we cannot be certain that it is not a skirmish."

"There, what was that clanking? There it is again, louder this time!"

"Your Lordship is right," the captain conceded. "It could be a skirmish. But who is holding them off?"

The Marquis ordered a detachment to investigate. But as they were about to leave he called on the captain.

"I shall lead myself," he announced.

Disregarding the captain's objections, the Marquis girded his sword and led his horse at the head of the small band through the wicket of the western gate.

About twenty minutes later they reached the edge of the forest. The clanking, now clearly audible as the clashing of swords, and the shouts became more distinct. The Marquis ordered his men to dismount and they forayed into the woods on foot. The sounds came from deep inside but were clear enough to guide the way.

"I suspect Antoine and Guibert have been ambushed," the Marquis whispered to the captain. "We may be just in time to rescue them."

Suddenly the clanking stopped. A ghastly groan rent the air, followed by uproarious laughter.

"Those devils!" cried the Marquis. "Couldn't they have given us a chance?"

Minutes later, he embraced his son and ruffled Guibert's head.

"Not to alarm you, Sire, but the entire area is crawling with royal garrison," Antoine informed his father. "We practically had to fight our way through step by step—lost several of our men and horses, but we took quite a few of them along."

"And what a pleasure it was cutting up the bastards!" Guibert roared.

"I didn't think they were positioned that far to the West." For a moment the Marquis' brow became heavy with concern. Then turning to Antoine and Guibert, he demanded, "What took you scoundrels so long to get here? Well, at least you are safe and sound. Let's turn back, before Barbizon sends out another patrol."

It was an intrepid crew Doña Elvira went out to greet. They trotted, two horses short, into the courtyard of the Château Valinquette in the small hours of the day. Her son, Antoine, was seated in the saddle behind the Marquis, and Guibert shared a ride with the captain of the guard. Their high spirits did not quite befit the circumstances, but they brought welcome relief to the unbearable tension that had hung over the castle all these weeks.

Doña Elvira herself gave off a shriek of joy as she sank into her son's arms. Then she gave off another shriek, this time of terror and fright.

"Antonio, you are hurt!" She held up the hand that had touched his arm. It was stained with fresh blood.

"It's only a scratch, nothing to worry about." He kissed her on the forehead and wiped her hand with a kerchief. "But I am dead tired. How about you, Guibert?"

"My son," said the Marquis. "Go rest now. Let your mother bandage that scratch or we'll never hear the end of it. It is good to have you home."

"Your Lordship should have sent for me earlier," Antoine said to his father when they met the next morning in the privacy of the Marquis' study. "I was not aware how serious the situation had become."

"We did not take the threats very seriously at first," the Marquis replied. "After all we've heard it all before. But now, the massing of troops and the ultimatum . . . Mazarin is pressing his advantage this time."

"Where are your allies, the companions for whom you have risked your neck many times?"

"There is nobody left. Mazarin plays his clever game of divide and conquer. And Condé, well, Condé has bigger fish to fry. Why should he risk losing the battle before it has begun just to save the patrimony of one landed baron?" The Marquis shook his head. "No, my son, things have changed, the nobility of France is no longer a proud, united confederacy."

Antoine had never seen his father so utterly dejected, so totally without hope.

"Perhaps it is time to accept the changes, to accommodate to the new conditions." Antoine spoke tentatively on what he knew was a sore subject. "All these years of intrigue and rebellion, first against Richelieu, then Mazarin, what did it really accomplish?"

"What did it accomplish?" the Marquis burst forth. "That I have to explain this to my own son is sad indeed. We have preserved the honor of the French nobility no matter what the outcome of the struggle. That's what we accomplished. And if we are forced to succumb in the end, nobody can say we brought dishonor to the first estate of the kingdom!"

"But is the kingdom not the monarch? Is it not the nobility's duty to serve the king? How often have you told the story of the Marquis de Valinquette, your father and my grandfather, may he rest in peace, who died shielding his king from an assassin's assault?"

"Ah, yes! But that king was Henri Bourbon, a king who was the first among nobles, not a minister's puppet. He never genuflected before a man of the cloth. He did not trample the rights of those bearing arms to defend his kingdom."

"But the times have changed and sometimes one has to bend with the times." Antoine recognized his mistake and quickly sought to give the conversation a different turn. "But as for the business at hand, we can probably hold them off for a week or two, and who knows, we may get lucky and the troops will be required on the battlefield in the Netherlands."

"No, my son, I don't think we'll be that lucky. Only a miracle could save us. But we shall keep the wolves from the door until you have led your mother and sisters to safety. Then come what may, let it be God's will."

"You mean you expect me to leave you here alone?" Antoine was genuinely indignant. That he should leave his father while the domain was under siege with only a handful of soldiers to defend it seemed preposterous to him.

"I won't be alone. Guibert will be at my side."

"Guibert will be at your side! Your own flesh and blood is not good enough to defend the honor of our name and family. Wasn't it you who just spoke about honor? Now you want me to do what is dishonorable?"

"Antoine, my son, please understand," the Marquis pleaded. "Let me be frank. We don't stand a chance. You know what will happen should your mother and sisters fall into the hands of the enemy. I cannot let that happen. It matters little what happens to me, but only under your escort can I be certain that they will reach safety. Come back as soon as you can. If the siege is still on, we shall fight side by side. Should everything be over, then join the army of the Prince of Condé and continue the fight for our family name and the restoration of what rightfully belongs to you. You are the last of the Valinquettes and it is your duty to survive, to carry on after I am gone."

Antoine saw the rightness of his father's reasoning. To sacrifice everything would make the enemy's triumph complete. But, of course, there was a way to avert the impending tragedy. Against his better judgment, Antoine pressed one more time.

"Unless," he began hesistantly. "Unless Your Lordship were to make his peace with the royal house."

"Never! Do you understand? Never! Not while this swine of a Cardinal holds the reins of power. Maybe it is better for the house of Valinquette to become extinct, since the last of its descendants seems completely devoid of the mettle that once was the mark of its warriors!"

His father's words pursued him like a flock of screeching, accursed furies, shredding his heart with their ghastly claws. He rode alongside the carriage that shuttled his mother and sisters southward, across the Pyrenees into Catalonia, and still they haunted him day and night. His thoughts circled around the scene in the gray courtyard at dawn. The Marquise's departure had to be kept secret from the enemy at all cost. An artificial air of calm and politeness surrounded the farewell scene, as if the wife and daughters were leaving for a weekend visit with friends. The Marquis showed himself calm and firm. Except for a brief flirtation between the young ladies and Guibert, emotions were kept locked up in the strongbox of the heart. The women obediently entered the carriage. Doña Elvira's dark eyes met her husband's in a last, long glance. She knew then that she would never see him again.

Antoine felt his father's steely look fastened on him for the final few seconds.

"Remember, my son, I am counting on you!" were his only and last words as he embraced him furtively.

Antoine had bowed to his father's will. But he couldn't help being irked by the farewell scene. Guibert standing next to his father, waving goodbye, flashing his broad virile smile at the ladies, his eyes alive with self-assured impudence.

"Don't worry, my friend, we won't let the bastards get the better of us." Guibert embraced him and patted him good-naturedly on the shoulder. Turning back in the saddle, Antoine caught a glimpse of his father's hand resting on Guibert's shoulder. The picture of the two men, standing together on the terrace with the natural intimacy of father and son, would burn in his soul forever.

The fugitives from France were greeted with typical Barca clan ebullience. The simple good cheer of his grandfather, Don Fernando Amilcar de Barca, and his five sons, all answering to Anibal in combination with some other Christian name, for a time lifted the veil of melancholy from Antoine's mind. To be back in the warm nest of his mother's family, the place of fond memories of his early childhood, was a true return home.

Don Fernando asked few questions about the reasons for the unexpected visit. He was sure it had something to do with another one of the harebrained schemes his son-in-law had been hatching for years. He had never been very happy about the marriage of his only daughter to the swaggering Frenchman. His dislike of Bertrand Dupuis came as much from disdain for everything French as from his daughter's being torn from the bosom of the Barca family and transplanted to foreign soil. That she and her children were back was all that mattered now. He was especially delighted to see his grandson, grown into a handsome man.

Antoine, or Antonio, ready to put the French troubles out of his mind, found this not too difficult in the lusty company of his uncles and numerous cousins. The homecoming was celebrated with ceaseless rounds of reveling, drinking, hunting, and gorging on the finest bounty. Antoine got sick with gluttony.

At the end of two weeks, he sobered to severe pangs of conscience. He confessed to the local priest the feelings of jealousy and hatred that had consumed him and the evil thoughts he had harbored against his father and his friend Guibert. His hatred was so intense at times that he wished them both dead. The father confessor promised forgiveness but advised him to return immediately to France, for if all was not yet lost he might still have a chance to redeem himself.

So he bade his mother and sisters farewell and headed back north. Accompanied only by his valet, he rode several horses close to death.

Day and night he rode, driven by fear that he might be too late. When he reached the height from where the Château de Valinquette came into clear view, a black pillar of smoke billowed from its ancient tower.

Antoine stopped at the inn of the village of Valinquette, where he was greeted with subdued joy by the local residents.

"My Lord," the innkeeper, who also functioned as local magistrate, addressed him after some hesitation, "I'm afraid Your Lordship has come too late. There is nothing anybody can do to keep the Italian from seizing Your Lordship's domains. Just tell us that Madame the Marquise and the young ladies are unharmed! We have been praying to God these weeks that he may keep his protecting hand over them."

Antoine turned to his father's tenants who were gathered at the inn. "My good people, I want you to know you needn't worry, the Marquise and my sisters are safe, out of reach of Mazarin and his henchmen. They will be deeply touched to hear of your prayers and good wishes. I know you all are in their prayers as well."

Moved to tears, he grasped the hands reaching for him.

"But you must tell me everything you know of what has happened during my absence."

At first complete silence. No one stirred to answer. The pain in the faces did not bode well. Finally, the innkeeper spoke again.

"My Lord, the fighting lasted no more than a week. After that Mazarin's troops took the fortress by storm. It wasn't lack of courage—His Lordship, the Marquis, and his men fought like lions—but in the end they were outnumbered and had to surrender."

The innkeeper lowered his head.

"What happened then—after the surrender?" Antoine coaxed him to continue.

"Well, the Marquis never really surrendered. His resistance only made them angrier, I guess. They probably thought he would give in when they set the fires, first to the crops and then even to some of the villages. Burnt to the ground. Just ask the villagers of Bouvier—they had to flee for their lives from the rampage."

"I'm afraid, my Lord, the soldiers are not done yet with their work of devastation," said one of the villagers the innkeeper had pointed at.

"Are you from Bouvier?" Antoine asked.

"Yes, my Lord, but I'm afraid not much is left of my house and barn or the crops, nor of anybody else's in the village."

"I am truly sorry for what you had to suffer, and I wish to God it were in my power to make it up to you." Antoine searched for words, knowing full well that words would not spare these peasants from hardship and hunger during the winter that lay ahead.

Some day he would set things right, but at the moment he was himself as destitute as these poor wretches, who had to suffer all because their landlord had gotten himself entangled in a war he could not win.

Antoine almost did not dare ask the question that was most pressing on his mind. "What happened to His Lordship, the Marquis?"

"His Lordship was taken away, shackled." The innkeeper quickly made the sign of the cross. "Nobody here actually saw it. But this is what everybody is saying."

Another peasant who had until then remained silent stepped forward.

"There is one other matter. During the night after the castle was taken, the Count de Mallac knocked on the window of my hut and asked to be let in. He was bleeding and in terrible shape, but he wouldn't stay the night. My wife gave him a bowl of gruel, for which he was very grateful. He then asked for a horse and rode off in a southerly direction."

"So the Count was not captured," Antoine muttered to himself.

"Not as far as is known. Of course, one never knows what might have happened a few leagues down the road. But then again that is where the army of the Prince de Condé is camping out. That's maybe where Monsieur the Count went."

"Thank you all very much, my good . . ." Before Antoine could launch into another benevolent landlord speech, three young peasants bolted into the inn with shouts of "The Royals! The Royals are overrunning the village!"

"My Lord, it would be safer for you and all of us if the soldiers did not find you here," the innkeeper proposed quickly.

"You are absolutely right. A pair of fresh horses and a few provisions will get me on my way. Tell the people that I shall return some day, under different circumstance . . . I promise."

Antoine made an inglorious escape through the kitchen of the inn. It was not until he was far along on the road south, where the revolt of the grand nobles was gathering force, that he felt the profound humiliation to his name.

Thirteen years had passed since then and much had happened.

Chapter 6

ANTOINE'S GAZE WAS riveted on the alabaster sphinx—a habit he had acquired of late in moments when the inner turmoil drove him to search through the rubble of his soul—as if he could somehow coax from her the meaning of the encounter of the previous night. He was still pondering whether Guibert's return had been a dream when the object of his anguish entered the pavilion half an hour before the time they had agreed to meet.

"Still worshiping at the altar of the stone Venus!" Guibert exclaimed predictably. Thirteen years had passed, much had happened, but Guibert was the same. He leaned forward toward the statue with brash curiosity, but Antoine quickly threw a canvas cover over it.

"I see you have made progress. Seems you found your model. I hear the Marquise is one of the most exquisite beauties in all of Paris."

"I am sure you have not come to Paris to discuss the art of stonecutting with me," Antoine said brusquely. Guibert obviously had not changed in all these years—if anything, his sarcasm had become more acerbic. The lines that creased the corners of his mouth betrayed his outward joviality mixed with a well-concealed bitterness. He had aged, but he was still handsome, and the flash of his smile was as bright as ever.

Antoine stirred the braziers and poured claret into two glasses. He could have sworn he felt Guibert scowling at him behind his back, but when he turned toward him he found him lounging comfortably on Galatée's divan with eyes closed, giving the impression that he had fallen asleep.

"If you would like to rest, we can talk later. I'm sorry I didn't notice it right away, but you do look somewhat worn," Antoine said.

"No, I'll be all right." Guibert propped himself up on his elbow but had apparently no intention of giving up the recumbent position. "Just being on the run all the time, hiding, trying to elude your captors, eating and sleeping becomes a haphazard affair."

"Who in heaven's name is chasing after you, Guibert?"

"Don't be so surprised! The whole country is after me, the police, the King's Musketeers. I guess the King himself, although I have not had the honor of an audience with His Majesty. The name Mallac is a curse in the kingdom of France. Haven't you heard? I'm happy to see the same cannot be said of the House of Valinquette. Monsieur the Marquis has done very well for himself. I fully understand that the Count de Mallac could not be received through the front door of so splendid a palace, but had to steal in through a back gate and is received in a shed, a pretty nice shed though," he added and lifted his glass in salute.

"Why the accusing tone, Guibert?" Antoine protested. "Of course you are welcome in this house for as long as you wish. I seem to remember you yourself requested a secret rendezvous. But you must tell me what happened since that moment when we were separated at the battle of Saint Antoine. Believe me, if it had been in my power I would have come to your aid. But I was injured myself and was set upon by a whole troop of royals."

"But you did elude capture, didn't you? That's the difference."

"A stroke of luck, Guibert. I was just lucky. The odds were just as much against me. It just happened that I was able to escape from them by a fortunate intervention. It could easily have been otherwise."

"But it wasn't. Tell me, how did you get away, considering we were practically surrounded? Deus ex machina or maybe . . ."

"No, I did not surrender nor did I make a deal. If you thought for one minute that I could betray you to save myself that would be enough to drive me mad. You are wrong, absolutely wrong to think so. It was war, and the fortunes of war are unpredictable."

"Forgive me, Antoine, I shouldn't accuse you without hearing you out. But all these years in a dungeon, much of the time chained to a wall, make you lose your sanity, the thoughts that swarm around your brain like vultures day and night are worse than the physical discomfort. And then here in Paris, what do I hear? Nothing but stories of the fabulous Marquis de Valinquette and his even more fabulous wife, the toast of Paris. The glittering receptions in one of the most elegant mansions in the Marais, the respect, opulence . . . yes, I must admit, it does make me a bit envious. Especially if you consider that the Marquis' father died a broken man in my arms in a snake pit in the fortress of Vincennes."

"Please, please Guibert! I can well understand your bitter feelings but can we not talk about this calmly, without recriminations? I need to know what happened to my father, but I also want to know exactly what happened to you. The inquiries I made led nowhere. All we—that is the Marquise, my mother—received was an official letter stating that her husband, the Marquis de Valinquette, had passed into eternity. That is what the notice said—'passed into eternity.' Not when or how or where—nothing. But all that was years later."

Antoine looked imploringly at his friend. But Guibert persisted in a grim silence.

"There was no way I could have found confirmation of your fate," Antoine said.

"I wonder if you even tried? Was it not more convenient for you to have me out of the way? Although I never laid the slightest claim to your title or possessions. I served your father with no other thought than to repay him for his kindness toward me and his loyalty toward my family, yet you always regarded me as the intruder, the challenger to your rights and privileges as son and heir." Guibert had gotten on his feet and started pacing.

"I shall tell you what happened from the moment I called to you for help at Saint Antoine—the only time I ever called on you for help, the only time I ever sought anybody's help. Then tell me whether I had cause to feel that I had been betrayed." Guibert stood with his back to his friend as he spoke hastily, pushing out what had been stored inside of him for so long.

Silence engulfed the friends when Guibert came to the end of his story. Antoine was at a loss for words. Was that the way it happened? Was he really to blame for his father's death and Guibert's misfortune? Was it he, and he alone, who let them down? Guibert seemed to think so. But that was not at all what happened. He did not know that his father had been alive still at Vincennes during the battle of Saint Antoine. And what could he have done had he known? He was himself an outcast, a mere soldier in Condé's army. Maybe he should have been with the old Marquis at Vincennes instead of Guibert. What would he not give to have been at his father's side during his final hours? But that is not how fate dealt out the cards. Nor could he have known that Guibert was taken alive. Was not his own life too in the balance for weeks? He was saved only from certain death by the kindness of a street urchin. By the time he had recovered from his injuries, he was himself a fugitive.

He had been lucky, at least luckier than Guibert. That was his greatest transgression. And did he not toil all these years and amass a fortune with the sole purpose of making good on the promise he had made to his father at their parting? In everything, had he not been guided by the single-minded desire to restore the good name and honor of the House of Valinquette? And succeed he did. It may have cost him a small fortune, but that was how things were being done now. True, his father would never have understood the power of money. And he would not likely have approved of what he would have regarded as bribery to regain the family title. This was not his way.

"So you bought back your title and estates from the man who confiscated them illegally in the first place?" Guibert's voice spewed utter disgust.

"Not exactly." Antoine could barely contain his resentment at Guibert's moralizing sneer. Why should he have to justify his actions to this nobody, this worm his father had rescued from the muck? But he went on nevertheless.

"I received my rightful title and estates from the hands of the King of France. Mazarin was dead and gone by then. Never would I have made any concessions to the snake, never! But my father had no quarrel with His Majesty, the King."

Those last words he intoned with haughty defiance, placing undue emphasis on the word "my." Like a flying dart, the utterance struck his adversary and, whether it was intended or not, opened the wound of his family's misfortune.

"But His Majesty had no compunction taking your money for something that had been the Valinquettes' for centuries!" Guibert's ruddy complexion glowed with anger.

"The money was for a commission in the royal army. I'm sure if you petitioned His Majesty, Louis would permit you to clear your name. He is a most magnanimous monarch and free from the pernicious influence of gray eminences."

"He would magnanimously permit me to clear my name, would he? And at what price? At the price of throwing myself at his feet, begging his mercy, since my pockets, alas, are quite empty? No, never! Never would I give a Bourbon that satisfaction. The Mallacs ruled in Brittany long before these upstarts seized control of our province. You also seem to forget that there was another man of the church, the great Cardinal Richelieu and his Bourbon master Louis XIII, who had my father hung in a public square before the very eyes of his eight-year-old son. How can that memory be erased? One day I shall blot out that mark of shame, but not by bowing to the son of my father's murderer."

The admixture of contempt and deep-down affection that had always complicated his feelings for Guibert was getting the better of Antoine. What was the use of harping on the past? Guibert was obviously in trouble and he certainly would not abandon him to the wolves. He owed him this much.

"Why don't we let bygones be bygones and face the present and the future?" Antoine extended his hand. "I hope you will accept my hospitality."

Guibert took Antoine's hand, whether out of desire for reconciliation or sheer need—a drowning man would be a fool to reject a lifeline tossed to him—was impossible to say. What lay behind that Breton joviality nobody needed to know.

The ringing of a silver bell relieved Guibert of the need to give a more definite answer; or perhaps it was Antoine who felt relieved of continuing an exchange in which he seemed constantly to be on the defensive.

A servant brought a billet from the Marquise.

"Madame is expecting us for tea," Antoine announced. "Afternoon tea is the latest fashion among the genteel."

"I'm always willing to be educated in the latest fashions, especially if it gives me an opportunity to meet the famous Marquise de Valinquette," Guibert replied.

From the moment he settled into the Hôtel de Valinquette, Guibert's presence illumined the daily life of the household. Galatée was somewhat surprised to find that Antoine should have a friend so different from him in every way. Also that he should never have spoken of him puzzled her. She welcomed his stay as a break from the boredom of the strict regimen Antoine imposed on her day. She caught herself looking forward to the Breton's company, but that was only natural, she told herself. Antoine permitted her little company outside the formal Thursday circle, and she was starved for conversation that was not always weighed on the scale of social suitability.

After several weeks, Guibert had become so much a part of the household, even the servants could not imagine life without him. With or without Antoine, the Marquise and the Count fell into the habit of spending the morning together in the sunroom overlooking the garden. During these extended breakfasts, the Count was at his most charming and attentive. These daily encounters came to replace the modeling sessions with her husband in the atelier. Antoine did not seem to mind, in fact he suggested that they suspend work on the statue. He pretended to have too much else to take care of. In reality, he feared Guibert's scorn for his artistic endeavors. The work would have to wait until the guest had moved on.

On those few occasions when Guibert was otherwise occupied and could not be at breakfast, her heart was seized with dark intimations that would not leave her until she saw him through the window in the garden returning with fast, short strides. She reproached herself for her silliness, but in time she had to admit that she had come to live for the moments she spent in his company, that her thoughts were constantly filled with anticipation of the hour when they would be together. And that she was utterly unhappy when he was away.

Yet he remained a mystery and a stranger. Maybe it was the aura of inscrutability that intrigued and attracted her. Much of his behavior was puzzling. There was something in his manner she could not fit together into a rounded picture. He was always the perfect, attentive gentleman, but underneath the polished surface, she sensed a restlessness, a constant vigilance like the keen alertness of the hunted animal.

At times she was filled with ominous foreboding. She feared that he may be the harbinger of some catastrophe, some disaster or tragedy.

But all these feelings were fleeting, momentary glimpses that quickly dissipated when his gaze met hers. She found herself strangely stirred by his watchful, gravel eyes that seemed to follow her everywhere. She could not say that she disliked being the object of his attention. His good cheer made her feel giddy. She hadn't had a good laugh for such a long time.

Antoine's decision to suspend work on the statue was only too welcome as far as Galatée was concerned. His stated reasons for doing so—some vague obligations—barely registered with her. She was certain it had something to do with Guibert. Whatever the reason, she did not trouble herself over it since it brought a respite from what had become an odious chore and she was happy to have more time for Guibert. Although she now could no longer avoid her needlework, which she hated but accepted because that was what gentlewomen do, she also had ample time to indulge in more enjoyable activities—her beloved music, reading novels and poetry, and with the coming of spring, walks in the garden.

As Antoine's business in town required more and more of his time, frequently extending into the daytime hours, it fell to her for the most part to entertain their guest. She had never known a man quite like him—solicitous and attentive, just waiting for her to make known her pleasure so he could hasten to fulfill it. He sat and chatted with her while she fussed with her embroidering frame in the morning and, as with everything, he had some very definite ideas about how it should be done.

She never had been adept at needlework; her fingers simply wouldn't do as they were commanded. She was, therefore, filled with wonder to watch Guibert demonstrate how to do a particular stitch that had more than once pushed her patience to the limit. His hands were small and amazingly delicate, his short fingers were nimble and adroit. It was calming, soothing to watch them work. She was almost certain that those hands could perform miracles—heal the sick, even make the dead rise from the grave.

"The secret is concentration, guiding the needle with your eye, before the hand does it," he explained one day, when she was frustrated again and ready to throw it all down.

"Your Lordship seems to be able to do it with eyes closed," she protested. "I simply have no talent for this endeavor."

"Your Ladyship is too impatient," he replied, seizing her hand and guiding the needle and thread in a loop through the fabric. The sudden touch of his hand on hers sent a sensation so strange and pleasant through her body she would have given anything at that moment to have it last forever. But he withdrew his hand quickly when the task was done, seemingly without notice of the stir he had caused.

Her hands were much more skilled at the clavichord or at strumming the lute or guitar. In music he yielded completely to her sovereignty. He would close his eyes, savoring with delight her playing and singing of doleful Spanish melodies.

At other times, they choose books by their favorite authors to read to each other. She appreciated his pathos and fervor in declaiming passages from *L'Astrée*, the story of the poor shepherd hopelessly in love with a cruel shepherdess. His favorite stories and poems all seemed to be about unrequited, unhappy love. Strange that he should select those, she thought, and it made her wonder more about him.

Was he in love with someone, somewhere? Or was he trying to tell her something through these stories? Was there some other meaning in the way he regarded her? But then again, she quickly told herself, most tales and poems were about love and loss and that sort of thing, so it was hard to avoid these subjects.

She pondered the questions she might ask him—had he ever been in love, had he loved and lost—but a fear of the intimacy that his answers might produce between them held her curiosity in check.

Within a short while after Guibert's arrival, Galatée's life had become divided into two separate existences. One was the Marquise of the night, reigning queen of the most glittering salon of Paris, a glamorous and charming fixture of the beau monde. The other was Galatée of the day, a woman of simple tastes and pleasures, devoid of artifice and frivolity, eager to learn, to exchange thoughts, yearning for true friendship. More and more, while in her role of queen of the night, her thoughts would trail off to the morning, to the man whose presence unlocked in her streams of feelings, of unknown sensations that became dear to her. And more and more, the hours without him became unbearable to her.

Guibert was never present at Madame de Valinquette's little Thursday evenings. She remembered Antoine saying something to the effect that he was better not seen or recognized. Whatever his secret was, the thought of what he was doing in the time away from her caused her heart to grow heavy with fear that he might disappear from her life as suddenly as he had entered it. But then, without fail, as soon as she had bid her guests farewell and Antoine had taken his coat for his business in town, Guibert was back at her side, challenging her to a game of checkers or cards until it was time to retire. And all clouds vanished from her horizon.

In early April, just two weeks before the Holy Feast of the Resurrection, Antoine received orders to join his regiment for spring maneuvers near the troubled northern border of the Kingdom. Husband and wife bade each other farewell with the effusive emotive display customary among the beau monde. In her heart, though, Antoine's departure caused her little grief. If anything, she felt a weight lifting from her as he mounted his horse and moved with his small retinue out of the yard toward the gate of Saint Antoine. The words with which he had addressed Guibert as they said good-bye were unintentionally provocative.

"Guibert!" Antoine said in a pompous, somewhat comical tone. "I commend Madame's well-being to your hands. I know she will be in the best of hands with my dear old friend."

That he should use the word "hands" twice struck her as amusing. Funny, she thought, that they both should be almost prisoners at the Hôtel de Valinquette. Guibert would venture out into the city once or twice a week, a few hours at a time and always under cover of night. He too had apparently "business" to tend to. The thought caused a burning sting near her heart, sharper and more disturbing than the dull displeasure she felt at Antoine's nocturnal peregrinations.

"Antoine is such a fool!" Guibert remarked suddenly one evening out of the blue while they sat by the fireside absorbed in a game of chess. She, however, ignored the remark even when it was repeated several times, pretending to ponder her next movement of the pawns on the board so as not to hear him. Only when he persisted did she finally deign to answer.

"Monsieur is speaking of my husband in whose house he is a guest. What, dear Count, would you have me reply to this rather indelicate suggestion?" She spoke softly, a slight tremor in her voice, her head still lowered, her gaze fixed on the board.

"What I am saying is that any man who neglects a beautiful and charming wife, and squanders his time pining at the feet of common courtesans is a damn fool—and that is putting it mildly."

"He has confided in you?"

"Not really, which makes me also doubly suspicious since he has shared every confidence with me since childhood."

"Perhaps the reason why he did not enlighten you on the nature of his business is that it is different from that which Monsieur is inclined to presume."

In vain did she seek to maintain her composure. But no matter how she tried, she felt that she was losing her footing.

"Oh no, there can be no doubt about its nature—I have it from good sources," Guibert replied.

"What sources? Gossip?"

"Not exactly. Just two citizens of this town. His guardian angels, Antoine calls them. They follow him like his shadow."

"Do you know their names?" Galatée looked up, suddenly alarmed.

"Their names are common enough—Gaston and Prosper, one is a hunchback. They are just two thugs, but somehow I suspect they know something our Marquis would prefer to keep a secret. That is, judging from the fact that tidy sums of money regularly grease the thugs' hands."

"You have spoken with those . . . thugs?"

"Well, I had some business dealings with them and they were helpful to me in finding my old friend Antoine when I came to Paris. They always seem to be somewhere in the vicinity of this mansion. I would wager that they are out there in the street right now."

"If you will excuse me, I think I should retire. I am not feeling well. We'll finish the game tomorrow."

She rose. Her face was a white mask. She took a few unsure steps, swayed slightly, and before Guibert could reach her, she sank lifeless to the floor.

When she opened her eyes she was greeted by Guibert's reassuring smile. His breath faintly brushed her cheeks. She realized she was lying on her bed in her evening dress. She tried to smile. It was undeniably pleasant to have him so near.

"What happened?"

"Your Ladyship lost her balance," he whispered.

"How did I get here?" She knew the answer, but something in his look, a dark seriousness, compelled her to struggle at all cost against drifting into silence.

"I took the liberty of carrying Madame to a place where she could rest comfortably." His lips lightly touched her neck, then he moved back. Don't retreat now, a voice within her cried out. She was lying perfectly still, her eyes closed, waiting, waiting for something, she knew not what. She could still feel his presence close to her. Then his breath again touched her ear, she felt his tongue against the opening. She did not move. The voice within her begged him, "Don't stop, please don't stop, just go on, I am all yours."

He didn't stop. She felt his lips touch her closed eyelids, one by one, then they glided gently down her cheeks and came to rest again on her neck. Meanwhile, his hands, those nimble hands that were so adept at the most delicate tasks, proved their nimbleness in unfastening her attire. A few masterful pulls and tugs and she lay completely bare. She opened her eyes. He was hovering above her, smiling. An incredible tenderness shone from his eyes. Even those bitter creases in the corners of his mouth had dissolved. The tips of his fingers were gliding playfully over her skin, slowly, barely touching, igniting her smoldering body into a burst of a thousand flames.

Then she felt his fully clothed body pressing against hers. His lips met hers. Their tongues entwined, clinging, melting. For an instant she thought of Antoine and how much she had savored their first kiss. But the image was quickly blotted from her mind by her one desire to dissolve her being into that of this stranger, to be consumed, ravished, obliterated.

His face was serious, but it glowed with a tenderness she had never seen in a man before. Antoine always looked grim when they made love, his features almost contorted as when he worked on his statue. Her presence in this act seemed incidental. This stranger, by contrast, seemed there only to serve her, elicit pleasures she never knew possible. She relinquished herself completely. He was caressing, wooing, teasing, enticing until she succumbed to a wave of tremors that rippled to the far reaches of her very being.

Their lovemaking lasted until the small hours of the day. Again and again she beckoned to be taken, to become one with him. Insatiably she opened herself to receive him. The birds began their busy chirping outside the window when they finally abandoned themselves to a fathomless, exhausted sleep.

The sun was kind that spring. The snow on the ground melted from one day to the next, and the garden at the Hôtel de Valinquette was transformed into a floral realm bursting with life. Among the servants there was much hushed discussion about the transformation so noticeable in Madame, whose singing voice, though familiar, soared more jubilantly than ever, like a lark rising into a boundless, cloudless sky. Other changes appeared in Madame's habits—she received few people and slept away most mornings. Often she was not seen before the afternoon. As for other doings at the Hôtel de Valinquette, the servants were too discreet and too devoted to their mistress to mention them.

"Sing me a French song!" Guibert begged her suddenly one day. They were sitting in an alcove in the garden, playfully holding hands, the way young lovers do. She was singing softly to him, an ancient Spanish ballad of the ill-starred lovers King Alfonso XIII and his beautiful Jewess Raquel.

"I don't know many French songs," she replied, puzzled by his request. "I am more at home in the music of Iberia."

"Surely you must know one or two French songs," he insisted.

"Well, there is one old song, but it is sad, and I don't want to be sad."

"Your Spanish songs are not exactly cheerful or light-hearted."

Instead of a reply, she burst into "Plaisirs d'Amour," coloring the tale of love and loss with such intensity of feeling that tears welled up in her eyes.

When she finished, he sat in pensive silence. She noticed the furrows of his brow had deepened and worried that she might have done something to incur his displeasure.

"What no applause? You see, now I spoiled our morning," she reproached him when he did not answer.

"I was just trying to remember when it was that I last heard this song," he said. "There was a little girl of about eight or nine, a beggar child, frail and lame and blind, but her voice had the power to move people to tears. I remember Antoine was quite obsessed with her. He thought it would bring him luck if he listened to her sing at least once a day. She sat on the Pont Neuf, I believe, it could have been some other bridge, but it doesn't matter. That was so many years ago. She was so miserable. Who knows whether she is still alive."

Galatée's face was ashen. She had turned away while he spoke, afraid that he might perceive the pounding of her heart. She reached discreetly for her handkerchief and wiped her palms.

"Paris is full of beggars, they are full of tricks, anything to attract attention," she finally said, just to say something.

"Yes, but this one was different, at least as far as Antoine was concerned. He was at that time—it was thirteen years ago—well, he was in a rather sentimental, even maudlin frame of mind. He even made the preposterous proposition—I'm not sure whether we actually made a wager or not—anyway he claimed that given proper upbringing and education any one of the riffraff could be turned into a lady or gentleman!"

She persisted in her silence. She desperately wanted to escape those eyes that studied her face with frank curiosity.

"My God!" he exclaimed suddenly. "He did it. He really did it. Antoine Barca fooled the entire world! Didn't he? What the devil! Who would have thought that he would pull it off?"

"If you tell him you know, he will kill you," she said with sudden calm. "I know him, he won't let anything get in the way of reaching his goal."

"Antoine, capable of murder?" he laughed. "No, I know him quite well myself. I guess I owe him a hundred pistoles."

He rubbed his hands with delight. So taken was he with the idea, he did not try to hold her back when she abruptly stormed through the garden toward the house.

He found her in her drawing room, slumped over a chair, dissolved in pitiful sobs. He lifted her face toward his and tried to kiss away the tears, but she pushed him away, refusing to be consoled.

"But what is so terrible? I think you are the most marvelous woman in the world and I love you. I don't care one bit where you hail from, whether from old Spanish pedigree or good old feisty Parisian stock. Truth to tell, I much prefer the latter."

She laughed a brief sardonic laugh under her tears in spite of herself, but then immediately became serious again.

"How do I know that for you all this is not just a way to get your revenge on Antoine?" There, she had said it, the thought that had haunted her, nagged at her soul when she was alone, when he went away in the evening into the streets, and she was stricken with agonizing fright that he might never come back.

"You must believe me. It is true when I first came here I had thoughts of revenge, and when I first started to court your favor that may have been a secret motive. Though it was never that alone. But that vanished long ago. You must believe me, it is the truth."

He drew her toward him. Their lips touched, and they clung to each other in a desperate embrace. That afternoon the lightheartedness went out of their lovemaking, but their passion was never more ardent.

Later in the evening he cradled her in his arms. She purred the tune of "Plaisirs d'Amour," content as a cat by a warm stove.

"What are we going to do?" she finally asked.

"It will be our secret," he replied. "Let Antoine continue to play his game. I should like nothing better than to see you received at the court of Louis the Magnificent. It will be a glorious moment."

"But I have no desire to be a party to this masquerade. If I ever did, I certainly don't anymore, not now. I meant what are we going to do about us?"

"We could bolt out of here together if that is your pleasure. But be reasonable, where would it get us?"

"I could not do anything to hurt Antoine. Never."

"You see. Then we'll just have to wait and see what happens. But I'm afraid Antoine will insist that you be a party to his game of deception—after all, you *are* the deception."

"Yes, that is certainly true. But this season is almost over and it does not look as if his wish will come true any time soon. A whole summer lies between now and the next season. Oh, I don't know why everything has to be so complicated!" She gave off a helpless sigh.

"For the moment, everything must stay the way it is. Antoine must not know. Since he never sleeps with his wife, the fool, it shouldn't be too difficult to keep our little secret from him."

Galatée was in a state of total confusion. Suddenly she was so plagued with guilt over her betrayal of Antoine that she clung to Guibert's words as if they were the source of her deliverance. She felt she had nowhere to turn, so her only recourse was to subordinate her will to that of the Count de Mallac.

Guibert, however, was so intrigued and impressed with Antoine's espieglèrie, as one might be impressed by an older brother's daredevil feat that he whistled through his teeth with relish and took the whole affair with the lightest of hearts.

"Satisfy my curiosity, mon amour," he coaxed her, "how was a miserable waif, unable to walk or see, transformed into a beautiful woman of exquisite limbs and eyes as bright as the stars?"

"That, my dear, is a secret that belongs to the Court of Miracles."

"The Court of Miracles?"

"The Court of Miracles at Saint-Médard—that's where . . . where the Marquise de Valinquette hails from. It's a realm where, at night, the lame walk and the blind see, it is a miracle that is repeated a hundred times over every day. We do have royalty in the family—kings and princes of thieves, queens of the gutter—preceding generations of beggars, whores, smugglers, cutthroats, pickpockets. Not a bad lineage—goes back centuries, at least as far as any duke's or count's in the Kingdom of France."

She had fallen into the patois of the Paris canaille, but quickly caught herself when she saw his patronizingly amused smile.

"I didn't think I could still do it—Antoine worked so hard to perfect my dic-tion," she laughed. "So what do you think now, my dear Count?"

"I think you are wonderful, and I love you even more."

"Do you really love me? Antoine seems to love only his creation, his Galatée!"

"I told you he is a fool. Galatée!—not very subtle, but he certainly had me duped, or I should say, you had me duped. The role suits you perfectly. No one would ever suspect. You can be certain. Just tell me, what is your real name? I'd rather not call you Galatée—it's too much like him."

"I didn't really have a name. I was the youngest of so many children, my mother forgot to name me. Besides, she was angry with me because I was born at an inconvenient time. When I was a small child, I was very thin, just skin and bones, and some people called me little goat, later they just referred to me, if at all, as the lame one or the blind one, or the lame and blind one—I was so good at pretending to be lame and blind that people thought I really was. Then when they discovered that I had a pleasant singing voice, my mother and sister called me La Fauvette, after the little birds—warblers, you see—that flit about in the gutters of Paris. But you'd better not use that name."

Chapter 7

LUCIEN LEFÈVRE PAUSED in his grim task. He wiped his brow with the back of his hand. Never, in the six months since he had become overseer for the disposal of human bodies washed up by the Seine River, had he been moved to such pity. The young woman could not have been in the water very long. Her body had not yet ballooned. Her face was not yet twisted into a grotesque grimace. She merely rested in peaceful repose as in a deep sleep. Her little chemise, shredded and tangled with algae and debris, could not conceal the slashes around her breasts and thighs and the black marks around her throat, like the maulings from a ferocious, wild animal.

Lucien lifted up the dripping corpse and carried it, carefully as if he were handling a fragile porcelain doll, to the cart on which the day's harvest from the river was heaped up. But he hesitated before placing her down. He was still unable to tear himself away. He knew too well the fate that awaited these bodies. It was his task to transport them to the Cemetery of the Holy Innocents where they would be dumped into a pit of lye. If a priest could be found, he would say a brief prayer for the departed souls. If none was available, the ceremony was dispensed with.

The woman's head had fallen back and her blue eyes stared into the gray January sky. Lucien propped her up. For a moment he thought he perceived a smile on her face. He arranged her on top of the cart, stroked back her hair, smoothing it, and folded her hands, mumbling a tearful prayer. He was unaware of the crowd that was forming around the cart until he heard somebody shout, "Lucien, let her be, she deserved what she got!" He turned in anger and shame. People were craning their necks to see what the fuss was about. Bets were made about the identity of the woman, besides the usual bets on the number of bodies that would be retrieved that day. Coarse jokes were hurled at the gatherer of corpses.

"Hey, Lucien, who is your sleeping beauty?"

"Lucien likes them lifeless, they're easier that way!"

Then someone in the anonymous crowd called out: "It's Guillemette! Guillemette, the harlot from across the river!"

The news that Guillemette had been found dead in the river passed along the streets and alleyways, across squares and bridges like lightning. Lucien seemed to be the only one in Paris who did not know who Guillemette was.

"I don't care if she was a prostitute, she is an angel now," he muttered and made the sign of the cross over the lifeless shell.

Suddenly there was another commotion. A heartrending scream pierced the laughter and chatter of the crowd. Lucien looked around, at first seeing only the mass of the gleeful, dirty faces of the street people, beggars, thieves, peddlers, fishmongers, washerwomen. It seemed the entire riffraff of Paris streamed to the quay in hopes of indulging their taste for a morbid spectacle. Then he saw the girl. She was running a gauntlet of taunts and sneers and was coming directly toward him. She flung herself on the cart, coming to rest on the dead woman's body with shrieks of anguish that made Lucien's blood freeze.

Before he could decide what to do next, two sinister-looking types came racing up to the cart and pulled away the weeping girl, whose frail frame reminded Lucien of a matchstick doll. One of the toughs, a hunchback, picked up the screaming girl and threw her over his shoulder, while the other shouted: "What the hell are you doing? What in devil's name do you think you're doing?"

"It's Guillemette, she is dead!" She pointed at the body, bawling hysterically. For a moment, the man halted, seemingly baffled, then he quickly decided what had to be done.

"Prosper, get them both away from here before anybody notices. I'll take care of this. Maybe this gentleman," he pointed at Lucien, "can tell us what happened."

At this moment another outcry rose from the crowd: "It's a miracle! It's a miracle! The lame can walk and the blind can see. Our patroness Sainte Geneviève still works her wonders!"

"What do you mean?" one of the bystanders demanded.

"Don't you know," answered one who seemed to be sure of the facts, "the blind and lame girl from the Pont Neuf de Notre Dame, she couldn't walk or see and the death of Guillemette has healed her!"

"What nonsense! Guillemette was a harlot, not a saint!" the first one answered. The crowd instantly split into two camps—the believers and the skeptics—and the proponents of each side launched into a boisterous debate that quickly dissolved in a general brawl of fist swinging.

A voice of reason was heard from somewhere. "Let's settle it right now. We'll find out whether she can see and walk!"

A pack of toughs started across the square to where Prosper was standing with the girl slung over his shoulder.

"Prosper, run!" shouted his companion, while he tried to hold back the gang.

Prosper held tight to the feather-light bundle. He hurdled past the thickening crowd, dodging, swerving, ducking, cheered by some and jeered by others, who in turn were jeered by those who cheered, pitting the partisans in a mêlée of rancor in which many a nose was bloodied.

Prosper meanwhile disappeared with the corpus delicti into the back alleys, sprinting over rooftops and soon descending into the murky caverns of the Court of Miracles at Saint-Médard.

Gaston fended off the crowd, giving Lucien a chance to escape with the body of Guillemette, who had caused more of a stir in her death than ever in her life. Together, they disappeared inside the Court of Miracles and the dwelling of the Widow Caillart. Lucien placed the body on the kitchen table in the one-room hut. He looked around the unfamiliar surroundings, uncertain what to do next. The Court of Miracles was a realm ordinary Parisians only mentioned with a whisper, an enclave from which, they said, no Christian soul could escape alive. What Lucien saw was a place of murky, crooked alleys lined by ramshackle dwellings, peopled by the dregs of society. For the second time that day, his heart was filled with aching pity for the misery that existed in the world. There, nearby shouts roused him from his contemplations.

It was Gaston lashing out at the little girl, who cowered sobbing and shivering in the corner where Prosper had dropped her.

"You goddam bitch, what do you think you are doing?" Gaston lifted her up and battered the little body with such force it crashed whimpering into the corner of the kitchen, barely missing the embers in the open pit.

"Leave her alone, Gaston!" The gap-toothed hag who said these words did not look up from her task of washing the body.

"Leave her alone? Do you realize what she's done? Not only did we lose Guillemette, now this one here won't bring anything in anymore either. The whole world knows she's fake."

He pulled the girl up by the wrist. "You'll take Guillemette's place!" he hissed.

"Don't be ridiculous, Gaston," said the hag. "Look at her, nobody will pay a centime for this body. In a few years, maybe, but now she's still too young and too skinny."

"Maman is right," said the hunchback. "Fauvette has to put on a bit more meat, look at her, there are hardly any tits or hips on her."

"So what are we going to do? Are we going to feed her for free?"

"She can do laundering and ironing until she is juicy enough. Meanwhile, you see to it that our dear Guillemette gets a decent burial and then find the beast who did this to her!" Gervaise Caillart sounded a tone her brood knew permitted no protest.

"Besides, you were supposed to watch over your sister. Where were you keeping yourselves last night, you two?" Madame Caillart started paddling her sons over the head with her cooking ladle.

"We had to take care of some business," Prosper ventured meekly.

At this point, Lucien, who was still standing there apparently unnoticed while the battle raged around him, thought it best to quietly slip away and return to his duties. As he was closing the shaky door behind him, he just heard the Widow Caillart warning her sons:

"Smuggling contraband through the city walls at night, that's what you call business! I've told you many times that you'll come to a bad end with that kind of stuff!"

He had heard more than he wanted to know and quickly fled from this underground realm of beggars and thieves.

Inside the Widow Caillart's hut meanwhile Gaston and Prosper took turns assuring their mother that they would find the bastard who did this to her daughter and string him up.

"It won't bring back Guillemette!" she called after them as they were leaving. Tears gleamed in her eyes. The girl they called Fauvette was still crouching in the corner. She had never seen her mother cry. The murderer of Guillemette Caillart was never found.

Gervaise Caillart was not a doting mother. Life among the dregs was too rough and uncertain for sentimentalities. She had survived hunger and disease, had born a dozen children and had seen half of them die before they could walk and lost two more to smallpox without shedding a tear. But to find her daughter, the prettiest and most charming of her brood, her Guillemette, who was always cheerful despite the grim trade she was forced to ply, butchered in the flower of her youth broke her heart.

All that was left to her now, besides her surviving sons, was her youngest daughter, the girl she had forgotten to name when she was born. She had never much cared for this runt of the litter and had left it to Guillemette, who was six years older, to raise her. She would not have known how to put it into words, but the mere sight of her caused her heart to ache. She was a living reminder of that terrible night—the night she gave birth to this scrawny little thing—when she lost her reason for living. The night when, awash in sweat and blood as she was from the labor, she was prevented from rushing to the side of her beloved Achille, who was lying on a tavern floor with a knife in his stomach.

Later, when she realized what an asset the child's singing was, as it seemed to open up people's purses, she called her La Fauvette—not out of affection or because she appreciated her singing, no, but because she felt that she should call her something when she was counting the proceeds from her panhandling.

On the night after Lucien Lefèvre and the two brothers had brought home Guillemette's martyred body, Gervaise had no one to turn to in her pain but the little songbird. They sat together in a long candlelight vigil, at first silently and apart, but gradually, as the night wind blew through the hovel and chilled their bones, they were drawing closer together. The mother placed a blanket around the shivering girl's shoulders and, in an unusual gesture, held her hand in hers. Their eyes rested on the candles flickering behind the waxen body. Gervaise tried to remember a prayer from her childhood, but the words had too long been in disuse to be conjured up readily. Yet, the effort pried open a hoard of memories, sealed and stored away long ago. Suddenly she began to speak. She spoke of her life. Whether she was talking to herself or to her last remaining daughter, trembling at her side, was not clear, but for a woman given more to grunting than to free expression, she waxed amazingly eloquent. It was then that the girl heard of another life her mother once had. Gervaise had not always lived at the Court of Miracles, the forbidding realm of beggars and thieves the dregs and scum of humankind called home. She had not even always lived in Paris. Nor was she destined by her early years to be a washerwoman, to a life of scraping and scouring in a daily struggle for survival.

Gervaise Ardant had been the only child to survive infancy of a mildly prosperous, if not wealthy, velvet weaver and cloth merchant in Amiens. Her mother, of whom she had preserved a picture of elegant frailty, reclining on the sofa with a book in her hand, had died in childbirth when she was five. How the loss affected her at the time she did not remember, but she seemed to have very vivid memories of warmth and comfort, of fine clothes and accessories, of sunshine and kindness, of lavish meals and endless feasts and dances while she was growing up.

La Fauvette hung on her mother's every word as she spoke of a world that was hard for her to picture. As the descriptions became ever more elaborate and fanciful, she tried to imagine the pink dresses of taffetas and lace, studded with gems, of the roast duck, boiled mutton, oysters, and wine, an oak-carved bed with thick piles of luxurious feather pillows, soft and caressing. It seemed to her that it must be pure heaven to sink into such a bed. It was not clear whether her mother had all these things when she was a child or whether she only remembered them from other people. But what did it matter. Her mother's story aroused in her an unaccustomed feeling of warmth, of security, and a vague longing for . . . oh, well, maybe someday.

The first time Gervaise saw Achille Caillart, she was twelve years old. He was sixteen, a filou, her father called him. Her father had caught him breaking into his shop and had tied the thief to a chair. He asked Gervaise to watch him while he went for the gendarme to haul the rake off to jail. She was then too shy to get close to such a dangerous criminal, so she leaned against the wall near the door. Not daring to look at him directly, she observed him out of the corner of her eyes. He certainly did not look like a villain. Against her will she had to admit that there was something appealing, even irresistible about that smudged, impertinent face and those fiery eyes.

"Psst! Psst!," he signaled to her. "If you cut these strings, I'll give you anything you want."

"What could you have that I would want?" she said.

"Well, I don't have much, but someday I'll be rich."

"And I'm supposed to wait that long for my reward?" she asked with a haughty laugh.

"As an advance I can give you a kiss."

Her father's return with the gendarme saved her from giving an answer. Achille was taken away, and when she asked what would happen to him, her father told her that he would probably be put to hard labor that would make a decent man out of him. It's for his own good, he assured her. It'll keep him out of trouble in the future.

"I could not get that boy out of my mind," Gervaise said with a sigh. "None of my suitors—yes, I was young, but believe me, I had a fair number of suitors, serious young men of good families, vying for my hand—not one of them was as appealing as that ragged thief."

"When and how did he come back?" the girl asked, bursting with curiosity.

"Two years later, he escaped from the slate quarries in Picardie," Gervaise replied. "I was fourteen then and already caused many a head to turn in church or on Sunday afternoon when we took our walks on the town promenade."

Carnival season was just then drawing toward its end. After much begging and crying, Gervaise's father had given her permission to attend the big dance of Mardi Gras, the finale in the city to two weeks of uninterrupted carousing and reveling, drinking and dancing, and indulging in all sorts of vices unheard of for good citizens the rest of the year. It was the time of year when many a young girl lost her virtue in the revelry. Gervaise soon eluded her chaperon's watchful eye and lost herself in the mass of costumes and masks, moving from masked dancing partner to masked dancing partner, never knowing who it was who swung her around in his arms. The anonymity of her partners aroused in her the excitement of a forbidden adventure. She did not mind the liberties some of the faceless fellows were taking—it was carnival and such frivolities were all part of the game.

Although she could not see his face, she knew immediately it was Achille when the young man seized her around the waist and planted a kiss on her lips. From that moment she was lost. She would follow him anywhere, and believe all his promises. Although it was to the Court of Miracles in Paris that he led her, giving her nothing but children and grief and poverty, she loved him to the day he died.

The new day was dawning when La Fauvette fell asleep in her mother's lap. The next day, life resumed its course. They buried Guillemette in a simple grave at the Cemetery of the Holy Innocents and returned to their daily drudgery. La Fauvette's head was swirling with questions, but Gervaise Caillart—this is what she called herself, although she and Achille never received the blessing of a priest for their union—after that night seemed more withdrawn than ever. La Fauvette would have liked to hear more about those events that led to her disgrace—her proud, defiant parading of her blown-up belly before a scandalized town, her father's rage and knife attack against his daughter's seducer, his vain threats, their flight to Paris.

Whether it was from the loss of her favorite daughter, or just a decline precipitated by a night of remembering, of breaching the wall that had blocked her mind from the events of twenty-four years before, Gervaise acquired, almost overnight, the heavy, unsteady gait and stooped shoulders of a woman twice her age. She was not yet forty at the time of that nocturnal deathwatch over her favorite child, she was still the way it is with women, but in her heart she was old. Her grunting became even harder to decipher. If it was a dialogue, it was one only between herself and the ghost of Achille.

La Fauvette looked in vain for a weak spot in the circle of silence her mother had drawn around herself. She was too timid, too cowed to dare a break through, not until many years later at least and then under vastly altered circumstances.

Whether time would have wrought a change, whether a time would have come when she would have admitted the girl once again into her confidence, a time when the pain from remembering would have lessened, was never put to the test. A cannon blast from the Fortress of Saint Antoine, set off by forces anonymous and beyond the control of the little people of Paris, changed forever their destiny—or did it bring the fulfillment of her destiny?—and that of the little girl with matchstick arms and a voice as soaring as a lark's.

That morning La Fauvette was crossing the rue Saint Antoine when a mighty explosion flung her birdlike body through the air and landed her on the other side of the street faster than she could have gotten there on her own feet. A few bruises was all she received, but the shock stuck in her bones and riveted her in place. Then suddenly, still numb and before she had a chance to gather her wits about her and seek refuge in an alley, she found herself in the midst of a fierce battle. Packs of soldiers streamed through the gate of Saint Antoine; others advanced from the Hôtel de Ville; the opposing forces clashed at the very spot where she was pinned to the side of a wall. For several days, the words Frondeurs, Royalists, Orléanists, Mazarin, and Condé had been on almost everybody's lips. She had heard talk of the possibility of a breach of the city but without understanding what the words meant. People were placing bets on which side would win. But what did a twelve-year-old child from the Court of Miracles have to do with such things as war?

Nobody paid attention to the trembling girl clinging to the wall as soldiers slashed each other with swords. She saw men on both sides falling to the ground, although she was not sure which side was which. Ghastly moans rose from the throats of the wounded and the dying. The confusion increased with every passing minute, more agonizing screams rent the air, shots rang out mingling with the clanking of swords, the noise shattered the ears.

Into the pandemonium charged a horde of mounted cavalry. La Fauvette, still cowering by the wall, looked up at these latest arrivals on the scene of battle, and there she saw him. She recognized him right away, high on his horse, wielding his sword with fierce mien. Immediately she was overcome with a sense of relief. Her benefactor, her savior had returned at the head of a victorious army, so she imagined. All would be well, she told herself.

Then, realizing that it would nevertheless be better for her to gain safer ground, she managed to climb to a rooftop, from where she was able to observe the battle. Now she had a champion to root for, as though the battle were a spectator sport. She cheered whichever side he was on—it must be the one that had invaded the city, she reasoned—and never took her eyes off him. Then suddenly his horse collapsed under him, she gave off a gasp; he dispatched it quickly with a single pistol shot before he continued to battle on foot.

By late afternoon all the horses had fallen and the ranks of the soldiers had thinned, but none of them were ready to put down their weapons.

Dusk was settling over the city and still the jabbing and slashing continued unabated. Her heart began to race again. Her hero and a small band around him were beset by a large enemy force. Her hero's troop was driven into a narrow alley where one after another fell to the ground. In the end only he and a companion were left. She had witnessed enough tavern brawls to recognize that they were weakening. They would not hold out much longer.

Her hero was limping and straggling backward. His companion shouted something to him, but both were by then completely surrounded and were pushed apart. A bone-chilling groan rent the narrow alleyway. Night was falling. La Fauvette strained not to lose sight of her hero. As her eyes adjusted to the dark, she caught sight of him as he was retreating into a cul-de-sac, five enemy soldiers in close pursuit. It was clear that only a miracle could save him. No time was to be lost. She would have to make the miracle happen.

Fortunately she was on familiar terrain. Even in the dark, she could find her way through every twist and turn of the maze of alleys and passageways. The houses in this quarter had been deserted, its inhabitants had taken refuge in the parish church when the fighting began. This was good. Nobody would get in her way.

So it was that Antoine, staggering with pain and bleeding profusely from wounds to his head and stomach, trapped in a Paris alley, found himself miraculously spirited away, snatched from under the nose of his pursuers and pulled into the shadows by a frail but determined little bird.

For three weeks La Fauvette clung to the side of the stranger who lay partly unconscious, burning with fever, on a pallet of straw in the hovel of the Widow Caillart in the Court of Miracles at Saint-Médard. For three weeks, although she had never learned to pray, she prayed fervently to whoever it was who held power over life and death to preserve this nobleman's life. Never before, except for the night she and her mother had held vigil over her murdered sister's body, had she given much thought to the divine hand that guides human destiny.

Gervaise Caillart had dressed Antoine's wounds herself. Not because she cared to save the life of a stranger, and a nobleman at that, but because he was there, bleeding on her floor, and it would have been inconvenient to let him die. She had a longstanding familiarity with stab wounds, having become quite skilled at ministering to them in the course of all her years with her dear Achille, who was never able to stay out of the way of open blades. Only during the embroilment that was to be his last had she been prevented from rushing to his side. "If only!" she was in the habit of muttering to herself, gnawed at by guilt. "If only I had been there!"

"Have you gone completely out of your mind?" Gervaise had screamed at first in a rare outburst of articulate expression. What a sight! The lifeless willowy corpse of a grown man dragged by a little girl, both splattered with blood. Near exhaustion, she was driven on by an iron will that he should not die. Where she found the strength, God only knows.

"What are we to do with a dying aristo?" Gervaise wrung her hands.

"Keep him from dying!" the girl begged, "please, I don't want him to die."

"Look at the mess! Blood all over! And look at yourself!"

"What does it matter? This is hardly the first time this floor has been soaked with blood. Please, look after him, I'll take care of the rest."

The girl had never spoken this firmly with her mother before, and something persuaded Gervaise that it may not be good to leave this man to die.

"How are we going to explain this to your brothers?" Gervaise said as she kneeled on the floor and began to tear away the man's coat and shirt.

"I'll think of something." Big words for a meek little girl, but there was a fierceness in her eyes that gave the older woman pause.

"All right," Gervaise said, "go, boil some water so we can clean him up."

The Caillart brothers, recognizing the colors of the man's coat as those of the Frondeurs, at first suggested that they sell him to the royal forces. But that plan was made useless when it became clear that the Frondeurs had gained the upper hand and were now in control of the city. So they decided to wait until the lines had become more clearly drawn. They congratulated their sister on "capturing" such an important person. One way or other, they would figure out a way to profit from what they saw as a stroke of luck.

La Fauvette threatened to kill them if they laid a hand on the man. They laughed and teased her with having a crush on an aristocrat.

Antoine's features became more recognizable as his wounds began to heal.

"I remember this fellow!" Gaston exclaimed one day, though the wounded man was still unconscious.

"Don't you remember, Prosper? Several years ago, he came around every day and listened to her sing. He stood there in front of her with a face so solemn, one might have thought he was in church or that the Holy Virgin herself was appearing before him."

"Sure, I remember," nodded Prosper, his words were muffled by chunks of stale bread with which he was stuffing his mouth. "Generous he was, too."

Gaston looked as if he just had a revelation. "How about that little bitch? Maybe it's not a crush she has on him. She probably brought him here so she can milk him for all he's worth!"

La Fauvette was sitting on the dirt floor next to the patient. Gaston yanked her up by the arm, twisting it until she screamed with pain.

"Whatever your game is, little bird, don't do anything underhanded if you don't want every one of your little bones smashed into a thousand pieces." He let go of her with a hard push that sent her crashing against the wall. Gaston fingered the man's coat and breeches that were spread out next to him.

"He doesn't have any money left!" the girl screamed. "Why don't you talk to Maman, she robbed him of everything he had on him the moment he got here."

Gervaise declared that she was entitled to whatever he had. After all, it was she who doctored him and gave him shelter. Without her he would be dead, dead as a mouse. They could hardly object that she made sure she was rewarded for her troubles.

"So you're calling your mother a thief, eh?" Gaston lifted up the wretched little body by the neck with one hand, holding her like a chicken about to have its throat cut, and with the other he slapped her face so hard a gush of blood streamed from her mouth and nose. Even then he did not stop. Prosper washed down his bread with a few swigs from a flask and Gervaise stirred the gruel on the stove. Not one of them made the slightest move to hold Gaston back. He would surely have killed her had not suddenly a hoarse but firm voice from the corner commanded him to let her go.

A request from an aristocrat, even one as helpless and near death as this one, was enough to make Gaston cease immediately. He let the girl drop to the floor like a rag doll.

Once the fever had subsided and he had regained consciousness, Antoine's recovery proceeded with good speed. Within a few days he was sitting up and chatting with his hosts as if they were the most distinguished company. The girl, her face and neck still bruised and swollen, beamed with a wry smile. When he pressed his lips against her hand, thanking her for all she had done, she felt for the first time in her life what it was like to be happy. She hovered over him, supported his first steps, washed and pressed his clothes, and even mended some of the tears with clumsy fingers.

"I don't understand why you should be doing all this for me," he said.

"Your Lordship has been very kind to me in the past. I'm only repaying that kindness with whatever kindness is to be had in this place."

"But this is much more than I ever did. I owe you my life! I shall never be able to thank you enough."

"Who knows?" she just shrugged her shoulders and declared that she had to join her mother at the washing post or she would get another beating and they both would get nothing to eat. But he still held her back with a curious look. She felt his gaze reaching the bottom of her soul.

"You are neither lame nor blind." He made the statement as if he had just come to this conclusion after a long deliberation. "By God, you certainly had me duped!"

"And the rest of the world. I hope Your Lordship is not too angry," she said with a shy grin. "Everybody has to bring in something somehow. That's why they call this the Court of Miracles. Because every night miracles take place here, the lame walk, the blind see, the crooked become straight."

"Of course I'm not angry! How could I be?" he said, pressing her hand. "In fact, if anything I am very happy to see that you have none of these terrible afflictions."

"This doesn't mean that every blind and lame beggar in the city is a fake," she said quickly. "There's a lot of misery among the people here, real misery, and we have our share of it in other ways."

"I know," he said kindly. "And I very much want to do something about it. I can't blow away all the wretchedness and poverty in this world, but I want you at least to have a better life."

The sincerity with which he spoke touched her heart, but then she shook her head. Aristocrats were known for making false promises. She had heard it said all her life that they were selfish and arrogant and could not be trusted.

"I'm sure Your Lordship will soon forget all about me," she said with a nervous laugh. "I really must be gone."

One day, the Caillart brothers came in, trumpeting the news.

"The Fronde is finished!" declared Gaston, the mouthpiece of the inseparable twosome. "The Queen's Italian is back at the Palais Royal. Your Lordship had better leave the city. But all the gates are guarded and they're combing the streets for any straggling Frondeurs."

"You know a way to get him out," La Fauvette reminded Gaston.

"You'd better learn to keep your mouth shut!" Gaston snapped back.

"No need for getting all that angry, please!" Antoine placed his hand on Gaston's shoulder and somehow the thug's anger abated like air escaping a pricked balloon.

"I shall make it worth your while," Antoine added.

"With all due respect, my Lord, but Your Lordship's pockets are empty."

"I still have my sword. The hilt is studded with emeralds and rubies. You fellows ought to know the value of that!"

"Prosper!" Gaston yelled. "Bring His Lordship's sword!"

Prosper reluctantly produced the sword from its hiding place. He had taken custody of it to protect it against theft, he explained. The king of the Court of Miracles, that blackguard Pélégrin, had been snooping around already for some time since the news of the presence of a stranger had leaked out.

"You'll get it back. But we'll have to do a small favor for His Lordship. We may be thieves but we are not dishonorable."

The party of four advanced single file, hugging the shadow of the formidable wall that girded the city of Paris. It was past curfew and pitch dark. Gaston and Prosper, with the agility and keenness of alley cats, the only other living creatures one encountered at this hour, crept along like thieves in the night—which is, of course, what they were.

When they reached a certain point along the wall, Antoine and the girl were told to stay back a little while the brothers lit a lamp and began to examine the masonry a few feet away.

"They seem to know what they're doing," Antoine whispered softly, while huddling with La Fauvette in the shadows.

"Oh, yes they sure do. How do you think all the contraband gets into the city? Surely not through the open gates in broad daylight, and the river is too well guarded."

There was something impersonal and defiant in the girl's tone of voice, a certain devil-may-care, sulking attitude. Antoine tried to search her face, but the darkness obscured her demeanor.

"My little bird is not happy," he said to her.

"Happy?" That's a strange word under the circumstances, she thought. "Tomorrow, Your Lordship will be gone and life will go on as usual. That's nothing to look forward to."

"I promise, I shall come back and make things right for you. But what can I do at this moment?"

"Your Lordship can let me come along, now, tonight."

"But I don't know what it is that awaits me on the other side of this wall," he protested.

"I can tell Your Lordship what awaits me on this side of the wall," she said. She bent down, picked up a few pebbles, and started rolling them around in her hand. "Gaston will send me to the whorehouse, that is, if he doesn't kill me first."

"But you're much too young . . . besides . . ." Antoine was at a loss.

"He can hardly wait for me to fill out a bit more. That's what they did to Guillemette. And then she was murdered. Eighteen years old she was, snuffed out, her throat slashed just like that." She made the gesture across her throat.

"Guillemette?" said Antoine.

"Yes, my sister, only prettier."

Antoine said he once knew a Guillemette at the tavern of Sainte Geneviève. He described her briefly.

"Yes, that's her, my sister. And now she's dead, killed by some drunken fiend probably. We'll never know."

Antoine became pensive for a moment. It was a shame. He liked that Guillemette.

"I want to take you with me," he finally said, "but I don't see how. If I were to fall into the hands of Mazarin's soldiers, what would become of you?"

"We'll just have to make sure this won't happen." And after another pause, "If all goes well, what are you planning to do?"

"Somehow, I don't know how, I must reach the southern border. In Catalonia, at my mother's house, I can gather my strength. But I shall return, that much I promise."

Catalonia! She had not heard of such a place, she had no notion where it was and how long it would take to get there. All she knew was that it must be a haven to yearn for.

"We can go there together," she said urgently. "It must be a wonderful place! I can look after Your Lordship. I can wash and cook and I can learn . . ."

"Wait, wait! I have no money, I may never even get there."

"But we do have a chance if we try together." She reached deep inside her cloak and pulled out a leather pouch. He recognized it as the one he gave her on the day he left Paris to join his father.

"I wanted to wait until we were outside the city to let you know," she whispered as conspirators whisper to each other. She placed the pouch in his hand. "Your Lordship may remember his last farewell."

He reached inside the pouch and counted ten pieces of what he was sure were gold écus.

"You never used any of it?"

"No, I kept it from my brothers and saved it for a special occasion. This occasion is here now. Put it away, quick." She jerked her head in the direction of her brothers, who were removing a block of stone from the wall. "I don't know why, but somehow I always felt that these pieces would bring me luck. How right I was! This should buy us a horse and then off to wherever! To Catalonia, did you say?"

He stuffed the pouch inside his coat and pressed her frail body to his chest. "You are truly marvelous, my little Fauvette! Court of Miracles! What a fitting name for the place from which issues such a wonderous child!"

"Oh, it's a wretched place, and not worth a single look back."

Prosper motioned for them to approach. The brothers protested that they could not let the girl go for nothing. Antoine, not about to relinquish any of the girl's secret treasure, was insistent.

"I've already overpaid you with the sword. It will bring you a handsome sum and that is all you're going to get."

In the end Gaston relented. "Your Lordship's pleasure. She's not worth much anyway. Just another useless mouth."

Antoine and the girl no longer heard his obscenities. They were already inside the tunnel in the wall and on their way to freedom.

"So the other man in the alley was you," Galatée observed when she had finished her story.

"Yes, and to think that you were there, that the three of us were in that alley that day!" Guibert said, pondering the past. "Then you must have seen what happened. You are an eyewitness to what happened! It's almost too fantastic!"

"I did not really see you. I was only aware that there was another man. By then it was dark in the alley and all my attention was directed toward Antoine."

"But you say Antoine was wounded and surrounded?"

"Yes, that's what worried me. Antoine was shouting something to the other man and then I thought that man had been killed. But I didn't actually see it. It was all too confusing . . . and it was so long ago."

There was a sudden heavy silence between them.

"He could not possibly have come to your aid," Galatée finally said with certainty.

Guibert nodded. "I should be satisfied. Why am I not?"

"Because you prefer to see him as a traitor, as a friend who let you down, a villain, so you can be justified in making love to his wife without feeling guilty."

Galatée's accusation was as severe as it was unexpected. She had opened herself up to him as she never had to any human being and suddenly the ground had shifted and she began to stumble. She felt ill-used, betrayed, reduced to an instrument of revenge in the love-hate friendship of these two men. But she had permitted it to happen. Not only had she permitted it, she had been a willing accessory, an equal partner in the crime. She too wanted to have her revenge against Antoine? Did not Guibert have reason to feel just as ill-used and betrayed by her?

Her gaze fell on him sitting there, encased in an immense sadness. He stared at her, forlorn and bewildered, as if he saw her for the first time, as if he did not recognize her. She realized then that she loved him more than anything. But how to bridge the chasm that had opened up between them? All she knew was that she had to reach out to him somehow. This terrible thing, born of guilt and recrimination, could not be left to exist between them. She realized that she had to go on loving him, for without him, without his love, her life would be empty and devoid of meaning.

"My darling Guibert," she began, softly, hesitantly, not knowing how to go on.

"Why would you say such a terrible thing?" he asked. "Why would you destroy everything we had ? As if our love had been nothing but a whim, something merely to spite Antoine."

"If we are honest, we must admit that it was a bit of that, at first at least. Now all is different, of course. Maybe I shouldn't have told you this story. It brought it all back, all that ties me to Antoine, all we went through together. All that I owe him. Please forgive me!" she pleaded. Tears rose in her eyes when he persisted in his silence. "My life is nothing without your love."

These were the words he seemed to have been waiting to hear. He suddenly drew her into his arms and kissed her passionately.

"As long as we believe in each other, everything will work out in the end," he assured her. "But let's not think of ends. Antoine will always be a part of our lives, yours and mine. Like you, I too am tied to him through memories of a friendship that goes back a long time. He is like a brother to me. Neither one of us would want to hurt him, but we cannot permit our love to be destroyed by feelings of guilt, by mutual suspicions and recriminations. You must promise me that."

"I promise! I promise!" she managed to proclaim before his kisses took her breath away.

Chapter 8

THE LOVERS' INTERLUDE of self-castigating was of but fleeting duration. In the end the desires of the flesh triumphed over any moral qualms and stilled all pangs of conscience. Galatée justified her conduct on grounds of being a spurned wife. Guibert needed no justification for indulging in something that gave him the greatest pleasure.

Antoine returned home in time for the Feast of the Resurrection. Galatée was drawn to the window by the sound of hoofs beating the pavement at the front entrance. She saw Antoine dismount, toss the bridles into the waiting hands of the livery, and fly up the curved stairs of the Hôtel de Valinquette two, three steps at a time.

"Good news! Good news, my little bird!" he exclaimed as he entered the foyer. Providentially, he had sent a messenger to announce that he would return two days earlier than originally foreseen. So Galatée was ready to receive her unsuspecting husband with the sweetest allure of the unfaithful wife. But he was oblivious to even that.

"There will be a war this spring!" he seized her by the waist and swung her around, beside himself with joy.

"Now, Antoine, is that something to rejoice in?" she reprimanded him when he finally put her down. "You must have lost your head to be so delirious about the prospect of a war."

"Think of it, my little bird. What an opportunity! I shall distinguish myself on the battlefield! What an opportunity to gain the attention of His Majesty, the King! This campaign is very dear to his heart. Come next season, we shall surely be received at the Royal Court. I can feel it, we shall finally realize our most exalted dreams."

"Why is being received at the Court so important, Antoine? Haven't we achieved enough here in Paris?" she asked. "You gained back your titles, your possessions. You're respected in the highest society, is that not enough?"

"Not the highest my dear. This is only the beginning—I told you so. Mazarin is gone and it is my duty to restore the Valinquette name so that our family will once again be admitted to the Royal Court, as it has been for centuries. At last the disrepute brought about by mere misfortunes in the past and the conniving of evil men will be lifted from the name of Valinquette. And I expect you not to let me down when we are this close."

"You call cabals, intrigues, conspiracies, hatching plots, mere misfortunes?" Guibert came lazily trotting down the curved staircase that was leading from the upper living quarters to the marble entrance hall. Any stranger unfamiliar with the situation would have thought he was the master of the house.

"We are both bearing the consequences of the sins of our fathers. Let's be honest about it. Our fathers conspired against the Crown, in other words, they gambled and lost. And you and I are paying the price."

"You're a fine person, Guibert, to lecture me like this in my own house. I knew I should have left you to the wolves." Antoine flared with anger. "I have a mind to do so yet—send you back to the fortress."

"Please, my Lords," pleaded Galatée. "Let's stop the provocations! My dear Count, I'm surprised at such ill manners toward your host. I think an apology is in order."

"I should prefer to face the wolves, as Monsieur the Marquis puts it so delicately."

"I should be happy to see them swallow Monsieur the Count skin and bones," Antoine retorted.

"This is really ridiculous. You behave like two little boys. Won't you ever grow up? At least we don't need to do this bickering in front of the servants." She shuttled them into the library like a governess exasperated by her charges.

"Now," she continued. "I suggest you both be reasonable and reconcile. Here, shake hands."

The two men complied, each for reasons of his own.

"There," Galatée said, satisfied. "You must forgive me, dear Antoine, but I was a little taken aback by the news that you are planning to leave again so soon. Besides, there is the danger to your life to consider. For now, however: Welcome home!"

"It's very sweet of you to be so concerned about me," he replied gallantly, raising her hand to his lips. "Of course, there is always that risk, but it's a risk worth taking."

"Your father certainly would be proud to see that the old fighting spirit of the Valinquettes is still alive in their last descendant," Guibert struck a flattering tone—whether mock or genuine was not clear.

"Thank you, Guibert. In the old days, you were always the warrior. The day will come, I assure you, when we will relive the glory of Rocroi together."

Mention of the battle of Rocroi, the zenith of glory of the Kingdom of France, when the two raw youths, still in their teens, had first tasted battle together, provoked a rush of nostalgia even in the unsentimental Guibert.

"My God," he moaned. "It seems a lifetime has passed. What a victory! The great Condé . . ."

"Yes, what a victory!" Antoine chimed in.

Galatée interrupted their reminiscing with a more practical matter.

"Enough of this for now. At present we must consider what to do with this house during our absence this summer."

"The house will be cared for," Antoine said. "You needn't worry. While I'm away it will be best if you install yourself for the summer at Chazeron since Valinquette is still in disrepair."

"Actually, I, that is, we, received an invitation from the Duchess de Rochemouton to spend the summer at Beaupré in Anjou. A small group of rather pleasant people will be gathered there and I think we would enjoy their company. Of course, since Monsieur will be otherwise engaged, I shall have to decline the invitation and go to Chazeron."

"But no, not at all! This is marvelous, a wonderful opportunity, you mustn't pass it up!" Antoine seized her by both hands and pressed them to his lips, as he was wont to do in a state of excitement.

"The Rochemoutons are very well connected. The Duchess is very highly placed by birth and by marriage, this could be very advantageous for us. She is said to be close to the Queen Mother, although the latter is said to be ailing and her influence on her son has been waning of late. The Duke de Rochemouton is said to be on almost intimate terms with His Majesty."

"Well, then it is settled." Galatée tried to hide her impatience with her husband's preoccupations. "I shall tell the Duchess that we are happy to accept her gracious invitation, but alas, Monsieur the Marquis regretfully is detained by his duty to King and country."

"Well, not really regretfully," said Antoine.

"Oh yes, of course not. Rather happily. But what about our friend, the Count? He cannot possibly stay in Paris. Of course, nobody would think of looking for him at the estate of the Rochemoutons, would they? Unless he would rather join you in this jolly little war."

"I'm afraid that won't be possible as much as I might be inclined to do so," Guibert said with the briefest laugh.

Antoine was immediately taken with the idea of sending Guibert along to Beaupré. The only qualm he had was that the name de Mallac might conjure up memories in the Duke and Duchess, who had been around long enough and might well remember a certain affair during the reign of King Louis XIII.

"Thank you for the reminder of my family's disgrace," Guibert retorted indignantly. "What means do I have at my disposal to restore the honor of my name?"

"Guibert, we cannot solve this problem this instant. But it wouldn't help to have you returned to the fortress or worse. Ah, I have an idea! You shall accompany Madame the Marquise as her horse master. No family names and no one will have cause to wonder." Antoine was quite taken with the idea, but not so Guibert.

"You mean I'm to present myself as a commoner, some low-born flunky?" Guibert huffed.

"Please, you must calm yourself, dear Count!" Galatée intervened. "Just consider the alternatives over the advantages of traveling incognito."

For a second her eyes, which had been avoiding his during the entire exchange, met his, taming his outrage and even making him feel a bit ashamed to have played the aristocrat like that.

"You're right, Antoine," he said more calmly. "Please forgive me for seeming ungrateful."

"Believe me, nobody understands your feelings better than I do. When this campaign is over and all goes as planned, I shall certainly petition the King to grant you a pardon. After all, you are my brother and I shall never forget the good services you have rendered my family."

"Good services rendered"—words well meant perhaps, but ill chosen. But Antoine was far too euphoric to notice the sting they caused in Guibert's heart.

So it was that a few weeks later, in the beautiful month of May, Antoine Maximilien Dupuis, the Marquis de Valinquette and Seigneur de Chazeron, sallied forth to war, imbued with the singular desire of covering himself with fame and glory. A few days later, the Marquise de Valinquette and her horse master set out for Anjou, imbued with the singular desire of indulging their passion.

The calèche carrying the Marquise de Valinquette, two servants' carriages in train which creaked under the weight of coffers stuffed with clothing, toiletries, and other necessities, entered the domain of

Beaupré long before the château came into view. This luscious terrain of rolling hills capped by dense forests, freshly ploughed fields of rich and fertile black soil, rushing brooks and shimmering lakes, a landscape dotted with clusters of peaceable villages no longer betrayed any signs of the devastation centuries of warfare had once wrought. Human diligence and the regenerative powers of nature had erased all traces of past strife.

Galatée knew nothing of the struggles, the violent clashes between French and English armies, of the blood that once had soaked this soil, nor did she have more than a vague knowledge of the religious conflict that had ravished this land and its people less than a hundred years before. To Galatée this idyllic landscape was paradise. Before she even set foot on this ground, she felt a deep longing never to leave again. Never to have to return to Paris!

Through the open window she saw him riding tall in the saddle alongside the carriage. Her heart rejoiced and she felt secure, protected. He never made demands, he seemed there only to serve and love her. He endured the position of servant with stoic resignation. She loved him all the more for she knew how demeaning it was for him. She closed her eyes, overcome with longing for night to come.

Guibert had taken her off the pedestal to which Antoine had relegated her, next to his piece of alabaster. Guibert loved her as a woman. He had aroused in her the womanly instincts she did not know she possessed, something she was convinced Antoine could never do.

How and where it would all end, she refused to contemplate. This would be the most wonderful summer of her life and beyond that she did not permit her thoughts to wander. No clouds would gather in her firmament. In those rare moments when the voice of reason tried to assert itself, it was quickly put to rest. In fact, during this summer in Anjou, the voice of reason sank into a deep, protracted slumber.

The road rose, scaling a sudden steep incline and the horses, the train of heavy carriages in tow, struggled uphill through a densely forested area. To lighten the load, Galatée and her companions, Alain Chartier and the Abbé Nicolas Fougère, disembarked and walked alongside. Only the elderly Paul Desmoulin, who was plagued with gout, remained inside the carriage. They had walked only a few paces when it became clear that Galatée's fashionable Italian footwear was not suited for wanderings through nature. She stumbled in a most unbecoming manner on the gravel road and would have fallen had not Guibert pulled up next to her and scooped her up with one arm, landing her in the saddle behind him.

"Madame will be more comfortable this way," he said with a servant's humbleness.

"You know I am," she whispered, as she pressed herself close against his back and breathed in deeply the aroma of his body.

At the top of the hill, a panorama of breathtaking beauty opened up. On a vast plateau, in the midst of lush fields and meadows, rose a massive gleaming white structure, a fairy tale jumble of turrets, parapets, and ancient keeps capped with the blue-black slate of the region, the entire structure forbidding and formidable, yet irresistible at the same time.

"Our hostess, the Duchess, promised a retreat from civilization," noted the Abbé Fougère as the passengers reclaimed their seats inside the carriage. "This is indeed a magic castle out of the pages of ancient lore."

"The Abbé fancies magic realms and romantic dreams everywhere," growled Desmoulin, an old libertine whose rational mind scoffed at the flights of fancy many of his contemporaries indulged in. "And a man of the Church at that, you ought to be ashamed of yourself, Abbé. Such swooning may be excusable coming from a young man like Chartier here, after all he is an artist, but an old goat like you!"

"I beg your pardon," replied the Abbé. "The fact that one has passed the first flower of youth does not mean one's senses and sensibilities have become blunted. It does not mean that one has to become insensitive to beauty, one need not be cynical about everything even if life no longer holds many wonders and surprises."

Desmoulin was about to reply when Galatée intervened. She knew the gentlemen well enough and she was determined to forestall one of those acrimonious battles of wits, in which the considerate views of the man of science, the rationalist curmudgeon plagued with gout, who saw absurdity in everything, and those of the worldly man of the cloth, who refused to see evil anywhere in nature, only the benevolent hand of a romantically inclined mover, would be pitted against each other.

"Gentlemen, why the bickering? I say, shame on both of you. What impression would it make on our gracious hostess were we to arrive carrying the scars of verbal battle? Even a man such as you, my dear Desmoulin, cannot deny the beauty of this sunset. Don't tell me you have never been enraptured by the sight of its vermilion splendor."

"How can I contradict Madame, who is as wise as she is beautiful?" Desmoulin replied gallantly. "Of course, I'm not immune to beauty, be it the female of creation or nature. In my time, I have worshiped and sacrificed at the altars of Aphrodite and of Demeter and it has brought me certain pleasures, even if they were of the irrational kind. But they do not compare to the pleasures one derives from exercising the mind, the satisfaction that suffuses the brain in the course of combating superstition and irrationality."

Galatée had developed a special liking for this crusty old philosopher and even derived a certain pleasure from his pompous expositions. He had something of the reputation of a misogynist but did not seem totally immune to the allures of feminine wiles, and from the beginning of their friendship he had taken her under his protective wing. Some residue of a dissolute youth apparently still clung to him. Back then he was a renowned poet and pamphleteer, a wit and gallant, much given to chasing the fair sex. He was said to have been among that august body of men, reputedly legion but nevertheless privileged and envied, who had enjoyed the intimate favors of the reigning queen of the Marais, Ninon Lenclos. Galatée had more than once been tempted to turn the conversation to the great courtesan, but his lips were sealed tenaciously on the subject.

"Madame had better look after this lovelorn youth," said Desmoulin, changing the subject with a nod toward Alain Chartier, who was absorbed with scribbling in a notebook.

"Our friend is mostly devoted to his poetry and music. And whatever affection he may have for me is surely a passing fancy," she whispered.

"He reminds me much of myself as a young man, and I can assure you that his ardor will be fanned when he realizes that Madame has eyes only for her horse master."

Galatée's face turned flaming red. "Is it that obvious?" she finally managed to say.

"Right now, only to those with a keen eye for human foibles. That is the advantage of old age, maybe the only advantage, after all there is not much else to be said for getting old but the pleasure of observing the follies of the young. But you needn't be flustered, my dear," he added. "Understanding and forbearance are also attributes one gains with age. The horse master is a proud and handsome man, not at all servile as would befit his station."

Galatée strained to produce a smile. She glanced at the other companions, but was reassured that they were otherwise preoccupied. The Abbé was leaning out the window, nostrils flared to take in the sunset and the good country air. Alain Chartier was still scribbling and mumbling to himself.

"I think you are quite mistaken where Monsieur Chartier is concerned, my dear Desmoulin," Galatée said, shifting the conservation back to more neutral terrain.

"Here we are!" The Abbé announced as the carriage came to a halt in the circular pathway in front of a colonnaded facade that had been grafted on to various gothic structures, a bricolage of architectural styles collected over centuries as the Duke, their host, would point out with pride on numerous occasions.

The wealth and status of the hosts, the Duke and Duchess de Rochemouton, could immediately be gauged by the army of uniformed liveries and valets who lined the sweeping staircase in espalier formation. The white marble steps were bathed in crimson and orange, a reflection of torchlight mingled with the rays of the declining sun. Under the stately colonnade stood the equally stately and imposing figure of Germaine d'Alembert, the Duchesse de Rochemouton, flanked by her daughter, Hélène d'Alembert, the celebrated La Belle Hélène. Two priestesses officiating at the temple of Aphrodite or Athena, it was not immediately clear which. One would have to see.

Galatée thoroughly relished life in the lap of the boundless luxury that pervaded Beaupré. The Rochemoutons were among the few remaining nobles of ancient lineage whose extravagant lifestyle was actually within their means. Every meal became a sumptuous feast, an occasion for ostentatious display of opulence and decadence. Liveried stewards, one stationed behind each guest's chair, served the pièces de résistance, myriad varieties of roast meats—pheasant, boar, venison, quail, wild duck—that came from the bounty of the daily morning hunt in the forests of the Lord of Beaupré, who repeatedly assured his guests that he himself had never seen the outer edge of his domain.

The Lord of the Manor exercised his ancient rights and privileges, which allowed him to pillage the livestock of his peasants to further load up the Lord's table with beef, mouton, pork, veal, and whatever fowl could be gotten a hold of. The meat was prepared on the spit in the fireplace, turned with monotonous motion by some servant.

For a brief moment, Galatée tried to calculate in her mind how many people at the Court of Miracles could be fed by only one such meal. But she quickly chased away the thought and nibbled on a succulent chicken leg, indifferent to the woes of the world but ever conscious of the shape of her waist. She rather liked the vintage from the Beaupré domain, but when she raised her goblet for the third time to have it filled, a voice whispered near her ear "enough" and the goblet was removed from her hand.

That night Galatée's lovemaking was more passionate than ever. The fantasy of the lady and the stable hand stimulated in her an insatiable appetite and she prodded Guibert to ever more exulted heights of ecstasy.

"Finit," Guibert said at last. He pushed her away rather rudely. "Don't pout. Enough is enough. One man alone can hardly satisfy Madame's voracious appetite."

She looked at him in disbelief, unable to understand why he should be so disgruntled. Didn't they have everything they wanted?

"No, you have everything you want. You seem to revel in this life of aristocratic decadence. Is this what you want? Do you really want to be a sycophant to the rich, like that old goat Desmoulin with his wisecracks he passes off as philosophy? Or that tottering Abbé, who ambles about boudoirs but never sees the inside of a church? And that pathetic, half-baked salivating whelp—calls himself a poet—with his doleful gaze raised to Madame the Marquise? If this is the company you enjoy, why should you need me? So you can be serviced? Any stable hand, I'm sure, would be happy to oblige Madame's desires."

"Why are you so cruel, Guibert? Why do you want to destroy me?" Guibert had exposed a side of him that she had not suspected. There had to be some explanation.

"You're jealous!" she exclaimed.

"As well I might be! But not of your foppish admirers. No, I'm jealous because my rightful place is at the Lord's table, not in the kitchen with the servants. Do you realize how humiliating it is to be treated as if one doesn't even exist?"

"Strangely enough, I can well imagine. Is it not interesting—once an aristocrat, always an aristocrat. What's innate and inbred cannot be erased! We're all products of our heredity."

"Be facetious, sarcastic, it changes nothing—this is how the world operates."

"If it pleases Your Lordship," she said with scorn, "introduce yourself to the Duchess as Count de Mallac, see what she says."

"And risk being arrested. That might please you, little guttersnipe, but I won't fall for your tricks to be rid of me so you're free to play your frivolous parlor games."

"Leave this room at once!" Galatée had risen to her feet, trembling with indignation. "I don't wish to see you again. And I don't give a sou about what happens to you."

She wrapped her satin robe around her quivering body and turned away from him. At the sound of the door closing, she flung herself on the bed, sobbing in profuse despair.

May was a rainy month. The heavens opened and drenched a receptive earth, often for days without end. Galatée stood by the window waiting for Guibert. He had disappeared, gone without a trace, no farewell, no note, nothing. Her face was growing gaunt and wan. She had lost all appetite; her body was drained from crying and lack of sleep. She tried to hide the telltale signs, the pallor of her complexion and the dark rings under her eyes, from her hosts by masking them with thick layers of rouge and powder, and so far she seemed to be succeeding. But Desmoulin's searching eye was often fastened on her, piercing through the mask to the bottom of her soul, so it seemed to her.

What an imbecile she had been! How could she have expected a man as proud as Guibert to bear humiliation without a grudge, even if it was for his own safety? How could she have imagined that being with her was compensation enough for him? What wouldn't she give for an opportunity to make it up to him? She would be his slave for as long as he wanted her, if only he would give her the chance. But the weeks passed, and then a month, and with it all hope.

Meanwhile the merriment among Madame de Rochemouton's houseguests continued unabated indoors. Galatée was grateful for the distraction of endless rounds of masquerades, balls, parlor games, chases through the length and breadth of the château, accompanied by pranks of frequently questionable taste. Card and board games—pitting opponents in fierce battle—raged all night. The stakes, to Galatée's mind, were often astronomical. The players were all high-strung gamblers addicted to the game, and, she was appalled to find, they all cheated.

Life was a game. One of the most ardent pursuits was the game of love. Every lady had a gallant groveling at her feet, some even had rival grovelers, but then again some of the grovelers groveled at more than one pair of feet. The Duchess de Rochemouton herself was the apple of the eye of the Abbé Fougère, whose devotional orisons were more inspired by pagan deities, nymphs and fawns, and their amorous exploits than by the Christian God of mercy whose word he was sworn to disseminate.

Galatée found herself pursued, as if she were a bitch in heat, by two gentlemen whose acquaintance she had made only recently—the Duke de Rochemouton himself, of somewhat large girth and no longer young but nevertheless an inveterate pursuer of the fair sex, and Henri de Varenne, Duke de Chambayard, who had fallen out of the sky with the rain and had declared his undying love for her at first sight.

Alain Chartier, her previous undying lover, had shifted his poetic sensibilities to a woman whose place within the grand scheme of Beaupré was somewhat tenuous. Galatée could not remember hearing her speak. Yet the lady's quiescence graced any company among which she was sitting pretty, and indeed her main function appeared to be that of an ornament. Although Galatée did not see herself in the same category, she wondered whether this was what Antoine had in mind for her. Was this what he sought to create? Later she learned that the woman's name was Angélique Guyon, that she had become a celebrated courtesan by the time she was eighteen, had changed hands with the regularity of a gold coin, and was now the possession of the Duke de Rochemouton, who apparently bought her for a fair price and was determined to hold on to his investment.

La Belle Hélène was the exclusive object of adoration of a certain Count de Launay. He had been wooing her for years, so Galatée was told by that old gossipmonger Desmoulin, and had repeatedly asked for her hand in marriage. Although his love was not unrequited and his lineage unquestionable, he had been rebuffed each time. The reason for this unhappy state of affairs, Desmoulin revealed, was that the gentleman was a Huguenot and therefore was not deemed suitable marriage material

"Why doesn't he simply become a Catholic if he loves her so much?" Galatée asked, naively as she soon found out.

"Customs in Spain must be different, or Madame would not ask such a naive question." She felt stung by the discourteous remark and wondered how much Desmoulin knew about her.

"Isn't it obvious? He comes from a family related to the House of Bourbon. His father is the Duke de Guyenne, a powerful but stubborn old religionist. The son would find himself stripped of his inheritance, his title, his succession, he would be a penniless nobody, which would make him an even less desirable marriage prospect. So the poor man is caught, trapped. At least he is permitted to languish at the feet of his beloved. Life has its compensations. But there is a lesson to be learned here, the pernicious influence of religion in human affairs."

Galatée quickly turned away before she would be subjected to another long lecture about the evil influence of religion. She was beginning to tire of Desmoulin, his maxims, his philosophizing. If all that life amounted to was a dance in circles, a series of aimless pirouettes, why go on, why persevere, what for? This libertine would, of course, deny the possibility of any rewards in the life beyond, even the existence of eternal life he held to be uncertain. His philosophy could be summed up in one sentence: there is nothing to be gained by death, therefore the pleasures of life, every form of dissipation, should be indulged in to the fullest. It made no sense to her. Without Guibert her life had lost all meaning.

And yet she went on with the dance. She graciously received her gallants' elaborate paeans to her incomparable beauty, which she read aloud to the gathering with hilarity and good cheer. At night she was lying awake, alone with the trepidations of her heart. Then the image of Antoine would appear before her. Poor, poor Antoine, what an errant knight he was! Chasing a dream that did not matter. Did she feel guilty? Yes, a little; but no remorse, no. She would do it over again, loving Guibert. And if she were never to see him again, never to rest in his arms again, having loved him was a happiness that would last her a lifetime. Or so she tried to tell herself.

The rainy season finally yielded to the dryness of summer. Amusements could now be sought outdoors. Galatée played a respectable game of lawn tennis and she welcomed the relief from physical inactivity. Just then the Duchess took to her bed with a pernicious case of the vapors. To amuse her in her time of trial, her guests crowded into the ruelle in her bedroom. It was, however, impossible to fit the gaming tables into the narrow aisle and the games of charades were soon getting tiresome.

"Enough of the silly games!" La Belle Hélène declared. "Why don't we gather around and take turns reading out loud from a work of literature. To make it more challenging, let's set up a prize for the best dramatic declamation."

"Bravo! What a splendid idea, my dear Hélène!" The Count de Launay clapped his hands so vigorously the rest of the company was compelled to join in.

"Which book shall be first?" asked the Duke de Chambayard. "Monsieur Desmoulin, have you any suggestions of a literary nature?"

"That depends on the company's pleasure," Desmoulin replied with weighty self-importance, flattered to be consulted as oracle of wisdom and knowledge. "There are the philosophers, ancient and modern, or perhaps a Greek tragedy, it always illumines the spirit. Of course, there is also our own good man Corneille of whom we have every right to be proud. We could take turns or even stage a play for our gracious hostess, Madame the Duchess."

"Don't try to flatter me, you fawning old goat!" the Duchess protested from inside her pillows. "Ladies! I don't think we should leave the choice to the gentlemen. I'm sure they will come up with something drab that will bore us all to death. My dear Marquise, what would you suggest, something diverting and instructive at the same time? After all, we want to stimulate the mind as well as the heart."

"In that case, and since we are in the country, a reading of *L'Astrée* might be instructive as well as entertaining," Galatée suggested after some reflection.

"Excellent, my child!" the Duchess exclaimed. "Hélène, wouldn't you agree? Oh, I'm looking forward to the delicious intrigues of the Marquise's namesake Galathée!"

The Duchess brimmed with such excitement, the pernicious vapors seemed to lift almost in an instant. She made a miraculous recovery and the readings were moved out into the open air.

The story of the shepherd Céladon and his ill-starred love for the shepherdess Astrée, the vicissitudes and trials these lovers endured, was familiar fare to everyone present. But the fact that every move, every scene of love and every quarrel, intrigue, misunderstanding of the fustian narrative could be anticipated made enacting the reading all the more exciting.

As their involvement intensified, the would-be thespians' identities began to merge with the story's characters. They began to pattern their speech after the rustic heroes, even at times when they were engaged in other activities. The fictional characters leaped off the pages, took possession of the bodies of these aristocrats who sauntered and frolicked about sparsely clad in shepherds' attire, flower garlands wound through their hair in pastoral bliss. Love's heady fragrance mingled with the summer heat that almost stifled the air around the domain of Beaupré.

Early one evening the shepherds and shepherdesses, clutching their Astrées, wandered singing in exuberant procession through blooming groves and meadows that sloped gently toward the river's edge, and settled in a round on a group of fallen tree trunks. They took turns delivering their passionate declamations, the pages illumined by torchlight borne by an invisible servant's hand standing in the shadows.

The company had left off the previous reading with the abduction of the shepherd Céladon, the lover of the shepherdess Astrée, by the nymph Galathée, who held him captive at her father's palace at Isoure.

"Céladon is visited by the Druid priest Adamas, who desires to know the shepherd's feelings about living in a palace," explained La Belle Hélène, and turning to Galatée, she asked her, "Madame, since this episode concerns your namesake, though the two of you have only noble birth in common, would you please lead off the reading?"

"With the greatest pleasure," Galatée replied. She arranged herself so the light of the torch held by a servant behind her would fall more clearly on the page. For a brief second, the servant's face emerged from the darkness and like an apparition receded again. Her heart almost skipped a beat, for joy or fear, she knew not which, but there was no doubt it was Guibert.

"Go on," he whispered. "I'm right here."

Reassured that she had not seen a ghost, she began with trembling voice that charmed her listeners for its dramatic effect:

With the intent of gaining some immediate clarity of the state of Céladon's mind, Adamas spoke with him thus in the evening when all the nymphs had retired.

"I believe, Céladon, that you must have been not a little perplexed to find yourself elevated to such good fortune as the one now in your possession. After all, I can assure you, this is completely beyond anything a man like you could have hoped for, having been born that which you are, that is a shepherd raised in the villages. Now you find yourself cherished by nymphs, caressed and waited upon—not by ladies who are used to being commanded but by those who hold absolute reign over this entire region. A good fortune indeed. Truth to tell, this is what the

grandest of men aspire to, but nobody has ever attained that which you have attained. For this you must praise the gods. You must pray that they will continue to guide you in your good fortune."

Adamas spoke to him this way to inveigh him to reveal his true sentiments. It seemed to him that by expressing approval, he would have a better chance of discovering the truth.

The shepherd replied with a deep sigh (here Galatée took a deep breath and let out a doleful sigh): "*My good father, if this is good fortune, then my taste is depraved, because never in my life have I tasted a more vexing absinth than that which you call good fortune since I have been in the state in which you find me here."*

"How can this be?" added the Druid to hide his ploy even further. "Is it possible that you have so little appreciation for your good fortune that you do not recognize to what grandeur this encounter elevates you?"

"Alas," replied Céladon, "it is this which threatens me with an even more precipitous fall."

"What you fear then," said Adamas, "is that this good luck will not last?"

"I fear," said the shepherd, "that it will last longer than I desire. But how is it that lambs get confused and die when they find themselves too long in deep water whereas fish enjoy themselves there and flourish?"

"Because," replied the Druid, "they are in their natural surrounding."

"And do you believe, my dear father," replied the shepherd, "that it would be less against nature for a shepherd to live among such ladies? I was born a shepherd in the villages and nothing that does not accord with my station can please me."

Galatée's voice abruptly fell silent. Her hand, still holding the book, dropped into her lap. She glanced up at the attentive faces fixed on her. Did they see the panic that laid its cold hand around her throat?

"Go on!" they prodded kindly.

"Something gives our dear Marquise pause," said the Duchess. "My child, what are your thoughts?"

"It is only a silly story," she heard it whispered into her ear.

"I was just thinking what it is this simple shepherd is trying to teach us," Galatée finally answered.

"Well, let us hear what the old Druid is saying and we'll see," the Duchess said. Galatée continued.

"But is it not possible," resumed the Druid, "that ambition, which seems an innate human trait, could make you leave your woods or that the pursuit of beauty, whose attraction is so strong in a young heart, could divert you from your original destiny?"

"Ambition, which everybody must have," replied the shepherd, "serves one to do well that which one must do to be the best among those of one's own station. And beauty, which we observe and which attracts us, that is, the one we can love, but not the one which one must revere and regard only with eyes of respect."

"Why?" said the Druid. "How do you explain the existence of greatness among men who are without merit or virtue?"

"Because," replied the shepherd, "all things must be contained within their proper terms, where nature has placed them. Just as a ruby can have only one particular appearance, as pleasing and as beautiful as it may be, it cannot hope to become a diamond. Those who aspire to elevate themselves, or better, those who wish to change nature and make themselves into something they are not, waste their time in a vain effort."

The Druid, amazed by the shepherd's ruminations and at ease to see him so far removed from Galathée's designs, spoke again this way: "My child, praised be the gods that I should find in you so much wisdom. I assure you if you conduct yourself this way, you will give the heavens cause to continue to bestow upon you all manner of happiness. I know other men who, carried away by vanity, have fancied hopes even more vain than those I proposed to you. But what became of them? Nothing, if not after long and incredible pain, great remorse at having disabused themselves of such ideas for so long. You can thank heaven for giving you such knowledge before you had occasion to repent so that it may preserve you for the sweet and tranquil life you have lived until now. But since you do not aspire to this kind of greatness, nor to these beauties, what is it, o Céladon, that keeps you here among them?"

"Alas," replied the shepherd, "it is merely the will of Galathée that makes me a prisoner. It is quite true, if my bad situation were to permit, I would in any case have tried to escape by all means possible, even though I recognize the difficulty of such an undertaking without assistance. And leaving all respect aside, I would use force only to get away. But Galathée keeps me under close watch, and if she is not there, it is the nymphs, or that little Méril, who remain with me. I cannot take a step without them at my side. Every time I try to plead with Galathée, she hurls accusations at me with such anger that, I must admit, I have not had the

courage to speak to her of the matter since. But my stay here has been so vexing that I must blame her for my malady. If you have ever held compassion for an afflicted soul, my father, I implore you by the great gods you serve with such dignity, through your natural goodness and the honored memory of the great Pélion, your father, to have pity on my life and to join your good offices to my desire so that I can leave this oppressive prison, for that is what I call this place."

"This story is getting too ridiculous!" interjected the Duke de Chambayard. "Why wouldn't a shepherd, or a peasant, or any commoner, be happy to be the object of affection of a princess?"

"But Céladon is in love with Astrée!" said the angelic Angélique Guyon. She was quite agitated and apparently surprised that somebody should not understand this.

"Yes, my dear, this is, of course, true." The Duke de Rochemouton patted her hand to calm her sudden transport of emotion. "What the Duke means is something more . . . shall we say, more universal. The relationship between aristocrat and commoner in general. And there I must agree with him. Céladon is a character of the imagination and the author is trying to make a point through this story, to express some universal truth of the order in the world. But in real life, should such a situation occur, that a princess should be stricken with love for a commoner, such a man would surely deem himself the most blessed of mortals."

"Louis, you speak rubbish!" exclaimed his wife, the Duchess, whether out of true conviction or just because of a habit of playing the devil's advocate whenever her husband ventured an opinion.

"You know nothing about the human heart. Human beings cannot be placed in categories this way, it all depends on the individual. Wouldn't you say so, dear Marquise?"

Amid the surge of opinions being uttered all at once, the Marquise was mercifully spared an answer. The exchange threatened to culminate in a round of mutual recriminations and accusations, when Paul Desmoulin made himself heard above the din.

"Ladies and gentlemen! Ladies and gentlemen! Let's be reasonable and examine the author's intent in this parable. For that's what it is, a parable. Céladon is obviously a man who knows his place, a place assigned to him from birth in an eternally fixed world order that mere men do not have the power to alter . . ."

"Please, take me away from here," Galatée whispered to her shadow.

Hand in hand they fled into the woods along the river's edge as fast as their feet would carry them. A bright silver moon illumined their path and they did not slacken their pace until the echo of the dueling voices had faded in the darkness behind them.

A damp warmth rose from the grassy ground. Galatée shivered slightly in the sparse shepherd's tunic that barely covered her knees. Guibert placed her velvet cape around her shoulders. Silently they walked on, farther and farther away from the frivolities of Beaupré.

Finally they came to a willow grove. They settled into the soft mossy cushion and made passionate love. Galatée clung to him like a famished beggar devouring delicacies tossed by a generous hand. She could not help but abandon herself to him, although she knew she should be angry for all the pain and anguish in which he had kept her suspended for six long weeks during which she knew not whether he was dead or alive.

Chapter 9

GALATÉE NEVER FOUND out where Guibert had been keeping himself while she was dying with longing and going mad with fear for his life. He hinted something about the towns of Anger and Rennes and some business that detained him longer than expected. She did not probe further into the nature of this business, maybe because she feared it might be Antoine's kind of business or maybe because she suspected that he was involved in some shady dealings she would rather not know about.

She remembered Guibert's occasional nocturnal outings in Paris, which he had also explained as some type of business. The impression that this business might have some connection, however vague, with Gaston and Prosper had left her with a queasy feeling.

Now that he had returned and most of the summer at Beaupré still stretched before them, she blew all worries into the wind. She refused to let anything, whether thoughts of the future or of Antoine, or Guibert's occasional travels to Anger, cloud her summer of love. She disregarded Desmoulin's warnings and shamelessly paraded her infatuation with the stable hand before her companions.

Even had she attempted to hide it, the very sudden transformation of her disposition from languid melancholy to radiant exuberance, coinciding with the horse master's reappearance, escaped nobody's attention. The change found its echo in the songs with which she entertained her friends. The weeping lilt of haunting Spanish and Catalan ballads to the gentle strokes on the lute no longer fit her mood. She now took up a more spirited repertoire.

Her rendition of one particularly bawdy popular Spanish song, which she accompanied on the chitarra battente, made a great splash among the revelers of Beaupré. The sensual wail of the throbbing vibrato began with a mock dirge, sotto voce at first, then rising with each repetition to an unrestrained climax. The double-entendre of the opening line—Qu'importa que muero se ressuscitan?—was not lost on the audience and the piece became such a favorite that the gathering would not disband at night until Galatée had treated them to a performance.

By the time the days of summer began to wane, the minds of the hosts and guests of Beaupré had become so entangled with rustic romances, with shepherds and shepherdesses, nymphs and druids, the lines between fantasy and reality had become almost completely blurred. It was thought oh so charming that fantasy should extend into real life.

"Our dear Galatée has found her Céladon!" the Duchess would exclaim, enraptured. "But she is more fortunate than her namesake. Her Céladon has only eyes for her, a perfectly willing slave at the feet of his high-born mistress. How altogether charming!"

"Quite charming indeed," the Abbé sighed at the Duchess's feet, in vain hope of fulfillment of his own lofty aspirations.

Galatée would steal a glance at Guibert's darkened face. He usually lingered somewhere near the periphery among the servants. She felt the hurt to his pride that he should be taken for a commoner and she loved him all the more for going along with the deception.

One evening in late August, as the saturnalia at Beaupré were reaching their nightly climax, the atmosphere was heady with wine, love, and song, and the Marquise was just striking the opening chords to the ever popular Spanish song, a stranger mingled with the guests, unnoticed at first. The regulars were clad in rustic tunics, adorned with flowers wound through their hair and around the hips of the ladies, the gentlemen strutted about in the likeness of Roman imperators, crowned with laurel wreaths and brandishing what was supposed to be staffs of victory. Ephemeral couples leaned in languid embrace—the entire scene presented a most peculiar sight to the eyes of someone just entering from the outside world.

The Duke de Rochemouton and Desmoulin were the only ones without partners. Angélique had bound herself for the summer to Alain Chartier, a satyr and naiad sprung from Ovid's tales. They formed a circle around Galatée, who was poised on a table; she was apparently unable to stay off a pedestal. Her shadow rose behind her in the dim hall, magnified by the flickering torchlight. She broke into song and improvised, as she sometimes did when too much wine had dizzied her senses, a few fandango steps, at first in the slow, solemn strut of the pavane, then swaying and whirling gradually into a racy galliard.

She bowed graciously to the applause. But when the general applause died down a single pair of hands kept on clapping with a regular beat. She strained her eyes to make out the figure now emerging from the shadows with shouts of "Brava! Brava!" For a brief moment she thought the visitor had come from the exotic East. His head was wrapped in what looked like a turban, but then she realized that it was a bandage that covered his head and one eye.

"Antoine?" she called out. "Is it you?"

"Yes, it's me, and all in one piece." He opened his arms. She flew toward him and came to rest in his arms. She was genuinely happy to see him.

"What are you saying? You're not all in one piece. What's that on your head? At first I thought you were a Sultan or some Oriental potentate."

"Just a wound from a bullet that grazed my forehead. Nothing serious. More blood than anything else. Main thing is, we won the battle. The soldiers of the King of France gave those Spaniards hell."

Antoine was greeted by the hosts and guests to a hero's welcome. While a late-night supper was being served, the Duke de Rochemouton took the occasion to press the Marquis about the campaign. He especially relished the story of how a small force of Frenchmen, of which Antoine was a part, fell on a massive Spanish cohort and pursued them across the border into Flanders, forcing their surrender. Antoine basked in the glory of the returning hero and was only too pleased to add luster to the story with vivid details for the Duke's benefit. The wine and food conjured up memories of past moments of glory. Rocroi was mentioned again, and as it happened, the Duke too had been present at that site of French glory. For the rest of the night, the two brothers-in-arms, the Duke de Rochemouton and the Marquis de Valinquette, found no end to their reminiscing.

"But tell us about your head wound? Where and how did you receive this mark of distinction?" the Duke insisted, when the Duchess finally broke in with noisy clearing of her throat. Antoine cast an uneasy glance at the liveried Guibert who stood stone-faced behind Galatée's chair, filling her goblet every so often when the level of wine fell below the halfway mark, which seemed to happen with greater regularity than usual that evening.

"Well, a mark of distinction is not exactly the right term," Antoine began, obviously embarrassed. "Actually, the battlefield is a safer place for a man than the streets of some of our towns. While facing the enemy day after day, I never received as much as a scratch, until—please, you must promise not to laugh—until we rode into Amiens. It was there that my forehead intercepted a strafing bullet fired from a window by an irate local citizen."

"This is unbelievable! Scandalous!" declared the Duchess. "A Frenchman shooting at soldiers in the service of His Majesty the King?"

"He was a deranged man, Madame. A local draper. He was immediately arrested, of course, but it was revealed that he had gone mad many years before when his daughter, his only child, had been abducted by a scoundrel and had disappeared without a trace. The man who had brought so much shame on this man's family had apparently been a deserter from the royal army, or so it was said. The townspeople told me that every time a garrison moved into town, the pain of his loss and shame would simply bend his mind and he would temporarily loose his mind. Naturally under such circumstances I considered myself honor-bound to ask the police to spare the poor man. He had obviously suffered enough."

"What a wonderful, noble gesture, my dear Marquis!" raved the Duchess.

"What was the draper's name?" Galatée asked, the seeming irrelevance of this question fastening all eyes upon her.

"I don't know why this should matter, my dear, but if you must know, his name was Ardant, Alphonse Ardant, master draper and otherwise a quite upright citizen and subject of His Majesty."

Galatée had never told Antoine her mother's story. The truth was that she had never thought about it herself until Guibert coaxed it out of her. Antoine preferred to forget about his wife's provenance altogether, so they never spoke of anything concerning her family. Now this incredible, almost providential incident! Could this accidental, violent encounter between her husband and a man who was in all likelihood her grandfather be a sign, an omen? What could be its meaning?

"It's nothing," she heard Guibert muttering as he leaned forward to fill her glass. He always guessed her thoughts. But she was unable to shake a gnawing uneasiness, a sense of impending doom.

If any of those present noticed the pallor of her face and her somber mood, it was not apparent. Attention was centered on Antoine and his heroic exploits. Even those who had only a passing interest in matters martial and honorable, like the poet Alain Chartier and his muse Angélique or La Belle Hélène and her faithful, hopeless lover Aiméry de Launay, had eyes only for each other and did not perceive the anguish she sought to hide. A few times she looked up and met Desmoulin's inquisitive gape from across the table. What did he call himself? A student of human foibles? Well, he must be having a grand old time that night.

After a while she became vaguely aware that her table partner, the Duke de Chambayard, was making love to her. Her unresponsiveness, which he apparently took to be part of the game they had been playing all summer, only aroused him to more gallant transports. He had cooled somewhat in recent weeks, but the appearance of the husband of his object of adoration, in accordance with the rules of the game, fanned the flames of his ardor and inspired him to new heights of amatory oratorical excesses.

Galatée followed the conversation as through an echo chamber, the voices resonated in her head, magnified and distorted. Only a few disparate words and phrases penetrated her consciousness. The Duke said something about the Royal Court and His Majesty the King, devotion to beauty and reward for loyalty. At one point, Antoine raised his glass to her. He smiled, raised his eyebrows and winked, as if signaling something of significance. She raised her glass back to him. Her response was automatic, elicited by years of schooling. Maybe she even managed a smile. It all did not really matter. Her only desire was to be alone with Guibert and her mind worked feverishly how to arrange a secret rendezvous.

The opportunity for a tryst with Guibert did not present itself all week, and she was growing restless to the point of despair. Finally a chance came as the party prepared for the great end-of-season chase. The Rochemoutons loosened all restraints for this crowning event. They unleashed the twin sisters of extravagance and opulence, who held sway over the domain for the entire week of the annual festivities. All of Anjou, the neighboring country squires and barons from miles around, was traditionally invited to the fitting finale to a splendid summer, as the Duchess would say with profound self-satisfaction.

Galatée, whose brush with breakneck chases had made her leery of this type of entertainment, excused herself with a headache, which was diagnosed as a case of the vapors by the Duchess, who added a profusion of advice to that of her daughter. Antoine, on a chase of his own—apparently unable to choose between La Belle Hélène and Angélique, he pursued them both—seemed content not to have his wife get in his way.

"Take care of yourself and get a good rest, my little bird." He gave her an affectionate peck on the cheek, his eyes already roving elsewhere, his face flushed in eager anticipation of the hunt.

In the twilight of dawn, she stood on the landing of the curved marble stairs and watched the boisterous host of hunters, horses, packs of yelping dogs followed by hundreds of beaters on foot, set out for the countryside until they disappeared in a cloud of dust. A deafening silence descended around her as the din faded in the distance. She remained riveted to the spot where she was standing, uncertain where to turn or what to do. A dull pain was lodged in her heart. Guibert was nowhere to be seen that morning.

Still dazed and preoccupied, she suddenly sensed another presence. Light, almost inaudible footsteps on the gravel, like the tread of a cat. No need to turn around. Eyes closed, she sank into the arms that were enfolding her from behind. Deeply she breathed in the intoxicating aroma of the body she worshiped.

"Come," he said, taking her hand.

They raced down the slope toward the river, along the flood plain to the lush bed of moss in the willow grove. Two weeks had passed since they had made love. She received him with the rapturous joy of a city welcoming a liberator after a long siege.

But not even their lovemaking could lift the heaviness hanging over them.

"You are thinking of him?" he said holding her close.

"Of course, how could I not? His sudden appearance! It was just so unexpected."

"If he touches you, I'll kill him."

"You know he won't. That's not what worries me."

"Then what troubles you so, my princess? I have watched you. You have been walking around looking like a ghost all week."

"For some reason, I cannot rid myself of the feeling that something terrible is going to happen. That incident in Amiens weighs constantly on my mind. It's an omen of some sort."

"You mean the fact that the man who shot Antoine in the head is probably your grandfather?" Guibert was greatly amused by this possibility. "A mere coincidence. What did Antoine have to say about it?"

"He doesn't know."

"You mean he doesn't know the story of the draper's daughter and the thief?"

"No, of course not. It does not matter to him. For Antoine I'm what he made of me, nothing else."

"I told you he is a damn fool. But why should that incident upset you so much?"

"I don't really know, it's a presentiment. Or, maybe this isn't it at all. Maybe what really troubles me is that all this is coming to an end, this summer. And I'm frightened that you will leave me, and that I have to return to Paris and have to continue to play an onerous game just to please Antoine. I dare not ask you to stay near me, and besides, I hate to see you in this degraded position."

"There's nothing degrading about serving you, my princess. But what I loathe is this society of frivolous snobs, their shallowness, their pretensions, everything about them revolts me. To think that this is what Antoine aspires to, that this is what he wants you to be! A Madame de Rochemouton!"

"He has been in a state of near delirium since his arrival. The Duke de Rochemouton has made all sorts of promises, he says he will put in a good word for him with the King. Whether he really has the ear of the King, as he claims, I don't know, but Antoine believes that the reception at the Royal Court of the Marquis and Marquise de Valinquette is within reach and the prospect can be furthered through the good offices of the Duke. It's all he lives for, all he ever thinks of, talks about. I'm so tired of it all, especially since he wants me to participate in this farce or whatever it is he wants to prove."

"You'd better look out. King Louis is an infamous lecher, he won't let anything stand in the way of an amorous conquest. I'm sure he will fall for you the moment he lays eyes on you."

"You should be ashamed of yourself, speaking with such disrespect of His Majesty, the King." Galatée waved a mocking indignant finger at him.

Then she lowered her head and whispered, "What will become of us?"

"I wish I knew. I wish I could promise you the world, but I'm not in a position to do that. Believe me I have thought about it, have agonized over it. But for the time being, I see no alternative. You must return to Paris with Antoine, resume your usual life in the Marais, play the gracious hostess. Meanwhile I will tend to some business in Rennes. If all goes well I'll be with you in Paris in two months' time, I promise."

"Two months! What an eternity! Not knowing where you are, what you are doing! Don't misunderstand me, it's not jealousy, but I'm frightened out of my wits sometimes that some harm will come to you."

"You mustn't worry. Nothing will happen to me. Don't you know I'm invulnerable?" he said with a laugh. "Come now, wipe that sadness off your face."

Putting on a happy face was easy in company but not in front of him. For Guibert she could not make any pretense. An uneasy silence curtained them off from each other. The callous hand of fate was pushing them apart, turning them to stone. Galatée wanted to call out, protest. She opened her mouth, but there was no sound. What was happening? Maybe Guibert was trying to speak to her, but could not. She could not let this happen! No, she would not submit to so cruel a fate. She had to break through the barrier. Finally, she placed her hand on his. He did not pull away.

"What happened in Rennes?" she said softly.

"Oh, it's just some business, too difficult to explain. Some day you will know," he said evasively. This was apparently not the question he had expected.

"No, I don't mean now, not what is going on there now. I mean what happened there, years ago, when you were a child?"

"Why would you want to know that now? Don't we have much more important things to worry about? You amaze me. Why on earth would you want to know what happened more than twenty years ago? It's over and done with, passé. Besides, I have forgotten."

"Liar! Something happened in Rennes, something you are still carrying around with you. It may be passé, as you say, but it still dominates your life . . . it's at the bottom of everything you do and who you are. It's there always, even when we make love," she added softly.

"I was not aware that I'm such an open book," he said nervously. "Do you carry the Court of Miracles with you?"

"Yes," she said seriously, "always. The memory is forever imprinted in my heart and soul. Whether we like it or not, we are the products of our origins, the sum of our experiences, however far away and tightly guarded."

"Why did you not ask me this question before?"

"Because I was afraid. I wanted this to be the summer of our forgetfulness. The illusion was beautiful—the games, the pretense, it was all so seductive, so charming. But can one really go on living a sham?"

"Our love, was that a sham, then?"

"No, that will be true forever. But it does not need the trappings of make-believe of this summer in the country. I love you no matter who you are. Even if you really were a stable hand I would love you. Because I love you I want to share your pain as well as your joy. Just a moment ago, I felt a barrier rising between us that threatened to cut us off from each other. You must have felt it too. If you do love me, please promise me—this is the only promise I want from you—promise that you will never let this happen."

He pulled her toward him and held her.

"I promise," he whispered, gently kissing her eyes and forehead. "It may seem a miracle, but Guibert de Mallac is hopelessly and utterly in love. I didn't intend it that way," he went on. "It just happened, against my will. Fate has a way of playing tricks on us hapless humans. For more than twenty years, I have struggled to forget, not to let it interfere in my life, and along comes a woman and tells me that everything I am, everything I have done and still do is determined by this one experience of which I am only vaguely conscious, which is only a blurred and probably distorted memory of an eight-year-old boy. Where did you get that silly notion, that we are the sum of our experiences? Reading too many books like *L'Astrée*?"

A shroud, woven of legends and dreams, spread over Guibert's memories of a childhood spent on his family's estate on the northern coast of Brittany. His memories were infused with a sense of warmth and happiness, though, other than his closeness to his mother, he could not point to anything specific that should have made it so. Of his mother he had preserved a picture of solitary melancholy.

Most prominent in his mind were the long evenings she spent sitting by the window, listening to the howling of the wind whipping the surf against the rocks, waiting. She was always waiting. He would climb on her lap and she would hold him, rock him, sing to him or tell a story, but he felt her sighs, her longing for the return of her husband whose rare stays at home were always brief.

He has important affairs of state to attend, she would say in answer to the little boy's incessant questions.

Since his father was always absent, he remained much longer under the influence of his mother than was customary for a boy of his station. He was never subjected to the rough companionship of fighting men that was part of an aristocratic upbringing from very early years. He had a tutor who taught him the basics, but his education remained rudimentary. He liked it best when his mother told him stories, ancient Breton lore, which she would recite with such vividness that he could see the action taking place in his mind's eye. It was as if she took him by the hand and drew him into a magic world she inhabited. The story that stirred his imagination most—she must have told it hundreds of times, always with slight variation—was the legend of the sunken city of Ys.

In his dreams he set out in search of the city and Princess Dahut, who, so it was said, had brought disaster on the city by her dissoluteness. Some said she was the tool of the devil, who came to her disguised as a handsome suitor and made her open the wall that girded the city against the sea. In other versions it was the god whose wrath had destroyed Sodom and Gomorrah that caused the city to be swallowed by the sea because of what was described as Dahut's lewd consorting. According to the legend, she received her just punishment when her father, good King Gadlon, tossed her into the deep to save his own life.

"I don't like good King Gadlon," Guibert would say. "I think he was bad to the princess."

"But she was a bad person, Guibert," his mother would admonish him, "and bad people deserve to be punished."

Over the years his childish dislike of King Gadlon turned into something bordering on moral condemnation.

"Don't you think it was unjust for this so-called good King Gadlon to kill his own daughter to save his own life?"

"But she was the one who had brought disaster on his kingdom and his people."

"I don't believe that. People only blamed it on her because they are mean and jealous and because she was beautiful and kind."

"How do you know she was beautiful and kind?"

"Because this is how she appears to me. She appears to me at night and calls me to rescue her from the bottom of the sea where she is held captive. Her only sin was being too much in love with an unworthy rogue."

"Guibert, Guibert! Your imagination is taking flights of fancy!" his mother would laugh indulgently. "But if you want her to be beautiful and kind, then that's what she is."

"Please tell me the story the way it should be."

"All right, then. A long, long time ago in a kingdom by the sea, there was a princess who was as beautiful as she was kind. Her beauty was praised in song and legends, and she had many suitors who came from miles around to win her hand. As soon as they beheld her they were stricken with a most severe case of lovesickness. But her father, the king who was mean and greedy and was intent on expanding his kingdom and power, had made a pact with the devil, who, in the disguise of a handsome prince, appeared at the court to ask for her hand. Despite his comely appearance, the princess saw something disturbing in his eyes, in his whole demeanor, that made her recoil from him.

Every time she looked at him, her skin crawled with unspeakable horror. She refused to be his wife. Besides, she had already bound herself to another suitor, a gentle shepherd, who had captured her heart with the sweetness of his song. The spurned demon lover took his revenge by opening the flood gates to the city. He then told the king that he could save his own life if he sacrificed his daughter."

Guibert clapped his hands when she had finished.

"Yes, this is how it really happened. You are wonderful, Maman."

"Well, I'm glad you like it," she said, smiling a melancholy smile. "Now you must go to bed. Tomorrow we'll embellish the story with more details."

She kissed him good night, and he dreamed of rescuing his princess from the bottom of the sea with greater fervor than ever.

Neither of them knew then that there was not going to be a tomorrow, that they would never have a chance to embellish the story. Never again would his mother tell him another story. If she had a premonition of what was to come, she did not tell him about it. But how could she have known about the wave of misfortune, the tragedy that was brewing and was soon to engulf their lives?

There was something else about his mother he remembered distinctly—the proud, defiant glow in her eyes when she spoke of the house of Mallac. She too was a Mallac, a second cousin of his father, Guillaume de Mallac. She was fond of wandering along the craggy shore or over the gorse-covered cliff tops. The Counts of Mallac, she would say, ruled the Emerald Coast centuries before Brittany was joined to France. A Mallac was at the side of Anne de Bretagne when she was forced into marriage to two successive French kings, and another accompanied her daughter Princess Claude to meet François d'Angoulême, the future King François the First of France. But the Mallacs were always Bretons first and in more than a hundred years could not make their peace with their French overlords.

In the religious wars of the previous century, the Mallacs had fought for the Apostolic faith to the very end. Brittany was the last outpost of opposition to Henri Bourbon de Navarre, the heretic who acceded to the throne of France. The Mallacs acquiesced only when the Duke de Mercoeur made his peace, though not without grumbling. From then on their opposition moved from the battlefield to the parlors, combat between armies was replaced by intrigues spun in secret meetings in the shadowy recesses of ancient, remote castles.

The Countess Bérénice de Mallac steadfastly supported her husband's involvement in the endless conspiracies, hatched by a disgruntled nobility against the Crown and its minister Richelieu. She bore her solitude and solicitude with the stoic resolve of the Mallac women, whose fate it had been for centuries to sit and wait for their men to return from the sea or war.

Guibert heard the name Valinquette for the first time on the day his father came tearing into the tranquility of their existence. Even before he dismounted, he ordered the Countess's carriage to be made ready.

"We don't have a minute to lose, Bérénice. Pack a few things, only what's necessary. Those devils are right behind me. They will be here within an hour."

"But won't you at least tell me what is happening?"

"No time for that now. It's Richelieu's men. I'll tell you on the way. I don't want anybody, not even the servants, to find out where we are going."

They packed a few belongings. Guibert looked back at the receding castle from the back of the carriage that hurtled them away from their home. His childhood ended precisely then, in the dust of the speeding carriage. They headed toward Saint-Malo.

"We'll sail tonight on the first ship for any port. We must get away from France and beyond Richelieu's reach. Eventually we'll make it to Barcelona, where the Marquis de Valinquette will await us, he is fleeing with his family south to Catalonia. You can be sure you'll want for nothing once we're there. The Marquise and her family are very hospitable, gracious people."

"But what happened? What brought all this about?"

The Count de Mallac finally filled in his wife with a few details.

"Cinq-Mars has been executed in Lyon and Richelieu is out for more blood."

"I don't know who this Cinq-Mars is or what he did, but why would you and Valinquette be targets of Richelieu's wrath?"

"In fact there are more. Madame de Chevreuse is heading for the Belgian border this very minute. Look, my dear, it was one of those affairs that went awry. Cinq-Mars, also known as Monsieur le Grand, let the King's infatuation with him go to his head. That upstart thought he could outsmart Richelieu—a twenty-year-old fop against the slyest fox in Europe! He made two, well, actually three mistakes. He overestimated his influence with the King, he paraded his affair with a woman who had shunned the Cardinal, and he made a secret agreement with Spain. When the chips were down whose side do you think His Majesty Louis XIII took? The Cardinal's, of course."

"And what has all this, the affairs of this Cinq-Mars, to do with us racing down the road to Saint-Malo in hopes of finding a ship that will take us to a foreign shore?"

"There was one more twist, you see. Gaston d'Orléans, the King's brother, thought the conflict between Cinq-Mars and the Cardinal would provide us with a chance finally to be rid of the hated monster."

"So you all became involved in the secret pact with Spain, the enemy of France. And is Orléans also heading for the border? No, don't answer. I know he wiped his hands clean at the first sign that the scheme might fail. As usual."

Guibert admired the astute grasp his mother had of his father's political intrigues. Her way of chastising his father awed him. His father had always been the embodiment of distant strength and invincibility. Seeing him being scolded by his mother as if he were a schoolboy was very amusing. At this moment he loved his mother more than ever and he despised his father for causing her pain.

They reached Saint-Malo, but no ship was sailing that night. The next day fate caught up with them. Richelieu's men were either tipped off or were smart enough to figure out for themselves that Mallac would try to leave France by sea.

The trial took place at Rennes within a week and lasted only two days. The sentence—death by hanging—was carried out three days later. All possessions, all lands and titles the Mallacs had held in perpetuity for centuries were confiscated by the Crown.

Guibert and his mother followed the train of Richelieu's men who dragged the Count de Mallac to Rennes in shackles and chains. The execution became a big public spectacle, a Sunday afternoon amusement for the townsfolk. They brought out their children not to miss the excitement of a lifetime. Guibert would never forget the cheer that rose from the crowd when his father's body jerked upward and his neck broke with a crunch. The corpse was left to twist for hours, a grotesque sight of a gaping jaw and lifeless eyes bulging in their sockets. Nobody paid attention to the eight-year-old boy who felt as though his guts had been torn out by the pull of the rope.

Later Guibert lived in the streets of Rennes, surviving by begging and stealing. Eventually he found money was to be made from his good looks by doing certain favors for aristocratic gentlemen. He existed this way until one day he heard that a gentleman was asking for him around town.

At this point Galatée spoke up. "This gentleman was the Marquis de Valinquette."

"Yes, Antoine's father, no kinder man could anywhere be found. So you see I too have lived in the gutter, I have felt the pain of poverty, of degradation. You are probably right, we are the sum of our experiences and nothing can ever undo what was in the past. Maybe that is why we were destined to love each other and why we can never be dishonest with each other."

"What happened to your mother?"

"I knew you would want to know. She died shortly after my father was executed. That's all."

"But how and why?" Galatée insisted.

"I don't know—of a broken heart, disappointment, loneliness—whatever it is that kills people."

He was in too agitated a state of mind to go on. She pulled him toward her and pressed his head to her heart.

"Please forgive me, I didn't mean . . . Oh, there is the sound of the horn coming closer. The hunt must be over. They will be back at the castle soon."

They held each other for one more moment. Their lips met, unwilling to part. Then abruptly he pulled her to her feet. They gleaned bits of moss and leaves from each other's hair and clothes, but without the playfulness and gaiety of past encounters in the willow grove. They were both still flushed from sharing emotions he had kept suppressed for so long. She loved him more than ever. But the sounding of the horn was a blaring reminder of reality, of Antoine.

There was one thing she kept from Guibert. A new, unknown feeling took hold of her, a feeling she did not dare confide to Guibert. For the first time she felt herself an adulteress, a cheating wife. What would happen when the fruit of her passion became obvious for everyone to see? Fear of damnation and doom gnawed at her. It was good that Guibert was going away. It was better that she should face Antoine alone.

Chapter 10

PARIS WITHOUT GUIBERT was dreadful. She hardly knew how, but life continued at the most sought-after "little circle" in the Marais as before. She actually looked forward to Thursday evenings, its distraction from the rueful thoughts that haunted her day and night. She gathered around herself young artists, poets, and musicians, who presented their works to an appreciative audience ever in search of the new, the dernier cri. To a never-ending parade of guests hungry for her particular offerings, the hostess served up her incomparable wit and charm with delicate precision. Lavish dinners featured the rarest wines, the choicest viands, the most elaborate hors d'oeuvres and desserts to satisfy the most refined tastes and most gluttonous appetites.

Through the carved oak portals of the Hôtel de Valinquette passed the great minds of Parisian culture along with the glittering stars of society. The venerated Corneille was heard debating the rules of dramatic construction with a young upstart named Racine. Jean-Baptist Poquelin, the King's favorite dramatist, known as Monsieur Molière, dropped by when time permitted. Madame de Sévigné sang the praises of her fabulous daughter to anybody willing to lend an ear. Madame de La Fayette and her consort the Duke de La

Rochefoucault, Mademoiselle de Scudéry and her companion Paul Pelisson, and her literary rival, the Chevalier de La Calprenède, all graced the salon with their presence at one time or other. Even the great Lully, composer to the King whose operatic works entertained the Parisian society with ever new inventions, came to see for himself what the sensational Marquise was about.

If they came as doubters, they left as believers. Her beauty and charm were as plain for everyone to see as was the evidence that the Marquise was very much with child. Habitués of the previous season assured the newcomers that the Marquise never looked more radiant. It must be her blessed condition, they said, that made her glow in such striking resemblance to Italian paintings of the Virgin Mary.

Only Antoine seemed unaware of his wife's condition. He walked about, his head swollen with pride, watching the prominent Parisians come and go, and was ever mindful of the rungs on the ladder still remaining before he would reach the top. He was a regular worshiper at the altar of the beautiful Angélique Guyon, who, though considered demi-monde and not at all in the same class with the Marquise, needed to be cultivated as a protégée of the Duke de Rochemouton, the man on whom Antoine pinned his hopes of gaining entry to the Royal Court.

Since Angélique kept no particular hours or days for visitors and the house in which the Duke had set her up was always open, Antoine was found at almost any time of day or night at the beautiful courtesan's delicate feet, except on Thursdays of course.

Whether the Duke was flattered by the Marquis' fervent attention to his mistress was not clear. Antoine certainly seemed to think so, even when, to his promise of eternal enslavement, the lady responded in a way that was, though unarticulated, clearly not of a platonic nature.

Meanwhile, the Duchess de Rochemouton, who needed only what her eyes told her to put two and two together, decided to take Galatée under her wing, and so, with La Belle Hélène and an entourage of acolytes in tow, she ensconced herself in the Hôtel de Valinquette like a dowager queen.

My dear Galatée, the Duchess would say, a woman in your condition must do this and do that, must rest in the afternoon, must not exert herself, must let herself be pampered, a woman of your breeding, your refinement . . . Galatée realized that the Duchess felt that the presumed blue blood of the fruit of her indiscretion needed special attention so as not to be overwhelmed by the tainted half contributed by the stable hand—a circumstance one might consider charming in the country but which was not as amusing in the city.

"My dear Galatée," the Duchess began again while they were sitting in the drawing room sipping tea and playing a game of backgammon, "am I mistaken or have I not seen your horse master around of late? He seemed particularly competent. In fact I was wondering if you would lend him to us for a while. But I guess he is not for hire."

"No, Madame is not mistaken, the gentleman who was my horse master is away on business somewhere in the provinces."

Then Galatée heard herself say, "Monsieur the Marquis and I expect the Count de Mallac to join us in a few weeks' time." What possessed her she could not tell. Was it pride? defiance? Was it pain at seeing her precious Guibert degraded? She wanted to bite her tongue, but words once spoken, once set free, cannot be retrieved however mortified the speaker might be at having permitted them to slip through. The echo of fatal words, even if spoken softly, hovers in the air, expands, swells to a chorus of infinite repetitions, only to return to haunt and crush the innocent from whose mouth they escaped.

"Mallac . . . Mallac . . ." mused the Duchess, "why does that name sound familiar? Do we know any Mallacs, Hélène?"

"Maybe your Ladyship is thinking of the Counts of Mallac of Brittany, an ancient Breton race," the Abbé Fougère, a Breton himself, ventured when the daughter shrugged her shoulders. "But that house became extinct in the reign of Louis XIII."

"Was there not some infamy, some political intrigue?" Some long-submerged, vague remembrance was apparently struggling to break through the clutter of years of society news and scandal deposited in Madame de Rochemouton's memory.

Why can't you just leave it be? Galatée thought. Why does every name, once mentioned, have to be traced? This name-consciousness was one of the most annoying habits of those aristocrats.

The history-conscious Abbé furnished the missing pieces. "The last Count de Mallac was involved in the Cinq-Mars affairs and was executed at Rennes. All domains and titles fell to the Crown—on order of His Eminence, Cardinal Richelieu, that is. That was more than twenty years ago. Too bad about the Countess. She is said to have been such a lovely woman."

"What happened to her?" Galatée asked, against her better judgment. Was she hoping to learn from gossip what Guibert had been unable to tell her? She felt all along there was something he would or could not tell her. But no sooner had she asked the question than she felt intense shame as if she were spying on her lover. It was too late to retract and the obliging Abbé was happy to indulge her curiosity.

"It's a sad story," he began. A pregnant pause. His face took on the grave expression of a messenger bearing tragic news. "She died a short while after her husband. Tragically too, very tragic and sad."

He shook his head, repeating several times over "very tragic and sad."

"Dear Abbé, don't keep us in suspense," protested Hélène d'Alembert, who had not taken her eyes off Galatée since the conversation had turned to the Mallacs.

"Well, this is what I have heard being told. The common folk in the region still tell this story with hushed awe. It's all hearsay, but you know what they say, there is always a kernel of truth. Well, after her husband's execution, the Countess retreated to the ancient fortress of La Falaise, a Mallac stronghold for centuries. It was, and still is I suppose, situated on an escarpment jutting out to the sea. The Countess is said to have had a special fondness for the sea. When royal troops tried to take the fortress and evict her by order of the Cardinal, she is said to have herself lit the fuse of the cannon, keeping the soldiers at bay for several days. But how long can a woman with only a handful of peasants behind her hold out against the King's army? The fortress was taken in due time. The people in the villages still talk about the terrible humiliation and violation the women in the fortress had to endure. Not even the Countess was spared. In her shame and despair, she hurled herself from the tower guarding the approach from the sea onto the rocky shoals below. Her fractured body was found by her young son. He disappeared in the mêlée and is believed not to have survived."

A reverent silence followed the Abbé's account. Then all eyes turned to Galatée, who was in a state of extreme agitation.

"Your sources were obviously wrong, dear Abbé," said the Duchess, patting Galatée's hand, once again using her powers of observation to deduce the truth, "the son did not perish. He apparently survived and became a stable hand in the service of the Marquis de Valinquette."

"No, that's not at all how it went!" protested Galatée. So much had been said already, too much. Though pained by the Abbé's revelations, she felt compelled at least to set the record straight. "The old Marquis de Valinquette, the father of my husband, raised the young Count like a son. In fact, he raised him together with his own son."

"And now he is showing his gratitude by making a cuckold of the son of his benefactor," the Count de Launay whispered in the ear of his adored Hélène, just loud enough for everybody to hear.

The Duchess sensed that it was time to leave the Marquise alone. "We must be going, my dear Marquise, but we'll see you tonight at the opera. Or is it another play by that irksome Corneille? Whatever, I'm sure it will be a great success. Get some rest, dear Galatée."

She embraced her hostess, touching her lips to one cheek, then to the other, and speaking just above a whisper in her ear, "I'm relieved and gratified that your offspring will be of pure aristocratic blood after all. But you should have introduced the Count to us properly. To think that he was with us all summer and we thought he was a servant! That was very, very naughty of you, my dear, to keep him all to yourself like that. But I'll forgive you this time."

She waved a scolding finger at her, gathered up her rustling taffeta skirts and exited, bosom heaving, her entourage in train. All was well with the world again. That Madame the Marquise was an adulteress put not the slightest crimp in the Duchess's universe.

Antoine discovered his wife's condition one night when he paused long enough in her boudoir to announce that the Duke de Rochemouton had finally made good on his promise and had secured an invitation for them to the grand winter ball at Saint-Germain on New Year's Eve. His Majesty was already aware of the great reputation of the Marquise de Valinquette and was most anxious to have her introduced. So said the Duke, whose only request was to have Angélique accompany the Valinquettes. She had her heart set on the ball, but somehow it did not seem fitting to impose on the Duchess.

Galatée stood in her dressing room in front of the mirror, marveling at the extent of her husband's naiveté. But she patiently heard him out.

"Unfortunately, I shall not be able to attend," she said quietly during a brief lull in his verbal effusion. "Maybe you should just go with Angélique, you make a beautiful pair."

"What did you say? How can I attend such an occasion with a kept woman? Come now, my little bird isn't jealous, is she?"

"Look at me, Antoine!" she shouted suddenly, as if trying to reach him across a great distance. "Look at me! Do you ever look at me?"

"Of course, I do. I'm very proud of my beautiful wife," he assured her, still unable to make heads or tails of this sudden obstinacy. "That's why I want to present her to His Majesty, the King. The others mean nothing to me. They're just part of the game, and Angélique is only a means to an end."

"Life is not a game, Antoine, human beings are not pawns. Things have not gone according to your grand scheme. Use your eyes, acknowledge what all of Paris is shouting from the rooftops: the Marquise de Valinquette is heavy with child!"

She hurled the last words at him with savage aim. If she wanted to wound his heart, she succeeded famously. Only the cry of agony, as of a wounded animal, that rent the air finally brought her to her senses. She collapsed onto a chair and dissolved in tears.

Suddenly there was deadly silence. She looked up through her tears at Antoine. He sat on the sofa, his face in his hands, and made no sound.

"It's Guibert, isn't it?" he said after a while, trying to sound calm.

She nodded, though she was not sure he could see her.

"Oh! What a fool I was! I should have known. I should have known better than to leave the wolf alone with my wife. How could you let him use you this way? No, I don't blame you. It really is my fault. He has always been a thief and always will be. He will stop at nothing to humiliate me, that greedy conniver, that accursed bastard!"

"You're right on one point, Antoine. It is your fault. I was so beholden to you, eternally grateful for all you did for me, I would never have looked at another man if you had only loved me a little bit . . ."

"But I worshiped you. I shared everything with you, my name, everything I own, everything, everything . . ."

"You shared your possessions—but you did not share your heart, your mind, not even your bed."

"Why did you never speak to me? I thought you were happy. Why Guibert, of all people? Why him?" Antoine was talking more to himself than to her. "All of Paris is at your feet, you have more admirers than even the Duchess de Longueville."

"It's all frivolity! Don't you understand? None of these people would waste another thought on me had they only the slightest suspicion about who I really am."

"You are the Marquise de Valinquette!" he stated emphatically.

"I don't think that would impress the Duchess de Rochemouton were she to discover there is not an ounce of blue blood in my veins and that the society I hail from is that of the Court of Miracles."

"Perhaps you are right on that point," he conceded sheepishly. "The whole beau monde is pretentious and degenerate and worse. You are living proof that their world is a sham. That much is indisputable. But if for some reason you thought me remiss in my obligation to you, I still must know, why him? Why Guibert?"

"Because he is kind-hearted and appreciative. He loves and understands me, and he makes me feel like a desirable woman."

"How can you believe this charlatan? Don't you realize he is using you? It's all a subterfuge calculated to hurt me. I know him, this is exactly the way he has always manipulated everybody around him. It's his old rivalry, his envy and jealousy. First he ingratiated himself with my father . . . and now my wife!"

"Both of whom you neglected," she said, but his thoughts were hardly with her. She looked at him. There was something infinitely pathetic about him, the way he sat there with his elbows on his knees, supporting his head with his hands, brooding. She realized that his mortification, his agony had more to do with Guibert than with the fact that his wife had been unfaithful.

Even the matter of her pregnancy seemed, for the moment at least, of little importance. He was still the boy fighting over his turf. She pitied him and wanted to console him, but knew not how. She had never felt a greater attachment to him than at this moment. They had gone through too much together from the time they slipped through the opening in the city wall, the months they spent together roaming the countryside, fleeing south, sleeping in the fields under the stars, surviving on stolen scraps of food when their money had run out the bond they formed then could never be severed, she knew it. But she also knew that she would always love Guibert. Nothing could change that.

Antoine finally rose. He came to stand over her, menacing, glowering.

"You will never see him again! The Count de Mallac is no longer welcome in this house. Any obligation I ever felt toward him because of his service to my family and his devotion to my father is herewith erased, null and void. I shall adopt the child—it will bear my name. There must not be the slightest taint of scandal. Then we will continue our lives as before. Of course, since I cannot trust you any longer, I shall have to place you under guard when I have to be elsewhere. I am too close to my goal to have a whoring wife ruin everything. Otherwise I will have to toss you back into the gutter where you came from."

Galatée made no reply. Any objection, any attempt at justification would only fan his anger.

"I should have known!" He paced about the room, knocking his fist against his forehead. "What a fool I was to think that one can make a lady out of a little beggar! I don't know what possessed me to lift you out of that morass, out of that so-called Court of Miracles. I saved you from a life of prostitution, degradation, poverty. Maybe the Duchess is right after all, blood is obviously stronger than breeding."

That he was completely reversing himself on what he had just said a few minutes before never entered his mind.

"From all I have seen of your polite society, fornicating and adultery is a more common pastime among aristocrats than among the poor, or the dregs, as you like to call those on whose backs you aristocrats have been dancing and feasting for centuries," Galatée said, disdainful but calm. "Your Lordship may recall that it was his nocturnal business in town that left his wife unattended and alone."

He came to a halt in front of her. His face showed utter bewilderment. "But you had your admirers. The greatest minds of France wrote paeans of praise to you, celebrated your beauty in word and song. Did I ever raise the slightest objection? What more could you have wanted?"

"Love." The word rippled through the air hanging between them.

"What kind of love?" he asked, confused.

"The kind that warms a woman's bed at night. The kind that ignites and satisfies a woman's passion. The kind that rips away all pretenses, all make-believe, all charades. The kind that lays bare the inner soul. The kind that appreciates a woman as a creature of flesh and blood. The kind that does not treat a woman as a cold piece of marble, or alabaster, a lifeless statue, a piece of bric-à-brac, a conversation piece. The kind that makes a woman feel alive, wanted, desired."

"I don't understand you," was all he was able to reply. "I respected you as a lady and this is how you despise me!"

"I don't despise you, Antoine," she said gently. "I could never do that. But I do pity you. Do you remember when I was carrying your child? You were beside yourself with happiness at first. Then when I lost the child, never once did you ask how I felt. Never again did you touch me, nor did you wonder how it felt for me never to be touched. Then your infidelities, to which you claim some innate right . . ."

"So that's what this is all about! The base desires of the flesh!" His face was flaming red. She retreated, seeing the dumb rage in his eyes, a look she had never seen before that gripped her heart with ice-cold fear. He came after her.

"Paillarde! You want to wallow in lust? Is that what you want?" He lunged forward. She tried to evade him but he seized her by the hair. He pulled back her head and pressed his mouth brutally against hers, suffocating her screams.

"This is what you want, you little strumpet, isn't it?" She tried to squirm free, but her plumpness made her movements awkward, she was too weak to stem the brunt of his attack. Tearing and pushing aside her dress, he pried her legs apart and entered her with a few powerful thrusts. Within a few seconds, he collapsed on top of her in a welter of sobs and tears.

When Antoine awoke the next morning, he found himself fully dressed on his own bed. He felt hung over, as if he had been drinking all night. Then a sudden recognition came over him of what he had done. He jumped up, splashed his face with a few handfuls of water, and hurried down the corridor to Galatée's apartment. The door was locked. His calling and pounding went unanswered. Even his most contrite entreaties, his promises to make good, his pleas for forgiveness, brought no response. Deadly silence reigned behind the bolted door.

Antoine, out of his wits with fear that she might have done some harm to herself, had the door broken down. He found her slumped on her bed, half-conscious, weakened and pale. When she finally responded and opened her eyes, she let out a horrifying scream. She lifted herself up and with a half-crazed look edged backward on the bed, looking frantically about for an avenue of escape.

"Galatée, please listen to me," he pleaded. "I am sorry, I am truly sorry for what happened. I . . . I don't know what possessed me. Please tell me that you forgive me."

"Forgive you? Forgive you for almost killing my child, another child?"

"But you are fine. You will be fine. I shall call for a doctor to make sure everything is all right."

He went to the door and called his valet.

"François, go get Doctor Morin, quick. But say nothing to anyone."

He gave instructions to the servants to tell all visitors to the Hôtel de Valinquette that the Marquise had departed for the country for a rest made necessary by a sudden indisposition. He returned to Galatée, attended to by her sobbing chambermaid.

"The doctor will be here soon. Everything will be all right. You needn't worry."

Unable to sit still, he went to the window, nervously assessing every carriage that came and went in the street. Those thugs, Gaston and Prosper, were as usual loitering at the corner. He had to do something to get rid of them. What an uncomfortable feeling to be under constant surveillance. God forbid they should find out what had happened inside the Hôtel de Valinquette the night before.

An eternity passed. No doctor. The figure of a well-dressed gentleman at last appeared on the stairs, but Antoine knew this was not the doctor. He recognized the swaggering gait.

He went into the corridor, leaning over the balustrade so as to hear the exchange at the door.

As he had been instructed, the servant informed the gentleman that the Marquis and Marquise had left for the country and the exact day of their return was uncertain due to an indisposition that had befallen the Marquise.

The visitor apparently did not believe the story, or had reason not to believe it. Loud enough so he could be heard inside, he hollered at the servant: "Tell your master, Monsieur the Marquis, the Count de Mallac is here to see him."

Antoine quickly glanced inside Galatée's chambers. She was still faint. With luck he could get rid of Guibert before she became aware of his presence. He closed the door to her chambers and descended the stairs.

Guibert spoke as if he had a right to be informed. "What is this nonsense about the country and some indisposition? Is this any way to greet a friend after a long absence? With excuses and lies?"

"Let's step into the library. The Marquise is resting. Let's not disturb her. She has been suffering from fainting spells lately, probably due to her condition. The doctor should be here any moment. So please calm yourself." Antoine led him inside the library and closed the heavy door.

Now they could speak without their voices echoing through the entire house.

"What do you mean, fainting spells and her condition? I don't know what you did to her, but I demand to see her this instant." Guibert moved toward the door.

"Wait one moment." Antoine planted himself in his way. "You are talking about my wife and you have no right to appear out of nowhere and make demands in my house."

"Your wife? You forfeited that right a long time ago." Guibert ducked around him and opened the door.

A shuffle ensued and Antoine managed to push his opponent back into the library.

"Do you know who and what she is?" Antoine asked.

"I know exactly who she is. I also know that I love her the way you never did and never could. If it's the hundred pistoles you're after, here they are." Guibert reached inside his coat and produced a leather pouch. "You won the bet, there is no doubt about that. Amazing as it may seem, this one time you were right and I'm happy to pay my debt."

"I don't give a damn about your money. But perhaps money is all it takes to be rid of you. Name your price—all I want you to do is leave Paris."

"There is no price. I shall not leave without her."

"Where do you propose to take her?" Antoine cursed himself silently for letting Guibert draw him into a discussion, as if this matter could be negotiated. But it was too late to retract the question. What was said was said.

"To Brittany and freedom from the shackles you have placed on her."

"A life on the run, of rags and disgrace with a penniless Count! Her body soon worn and drained from bearing children. Compare what you have to offer to . . . this." Antoine's hand described a sweeping gesture through the air.

"Do you really think you can buy her with this bogus luxury, seduce her with your ambitions? How little you know about this woman!"

Cold fear that Guibert might be right gripped Antoine. She may very well be ready to toss everything he had given her to the wind to flee with Guibert toward an uncertain future. He had to get Guibert out of the house and out of town before she became aware of his presence. Later he would convince her that Guibert had abandoned her. But it was obvious that Guibert could not be bribed or cajoled into quitting the scene. He had to take a different approach.

"Listen, Guibert, you needn't be concerned. I don't hold anything against you," he said in a mollified tone. "The child will bear my name . . . he will be a Valinquette. Don't you think you owe it to the child to avoid any hint of scandal and just withdraw gracefully?"

"You mean she is with child? She is carrying my child?" Guibert's initial bafflement gave way to resolute elation. "I must see her!"

Again he tried to make his way around Antoine, but his rival stood firm.

"If you didn't know about it, maybe it's not your child after all. It really could be any man present at Beaupré last summer."

"No, it is clear what you are trying to do. If she is with child, it can only be mine. And my child will not bear the name Valinquette. He will be a Breton and he will be a Mallac."

"All these years you acted as if you would like nothing better than be a Valinquette yourself. You wormed your way into the good graces of my father, behaved as if you were his son, tried to usurp my place in every way possible. And when you couldn't reach your goal any other way, you went behind my back and seduced my wife. What a contemptible, cowardly knave you are to use an innocent woman for his schemes."

"When I found myself with a beautiful, neglected woman, of course I tried to press my advantage," Guibert taunted with his mocking smile. "Who wouldn't? I had no greater desire than to even the score with you."

Antoine sputtered in rage. "You bastard! You bloody bastard!" He raised his fist against Guibert, but Guibert blocked the blow and went on, determined to have his say.

"I would do anything to harm you, Monsieur le Marquis. You do not deserve to bear the name Valinquette, you have nothing in common with your father. Just remember who it was who fought side by side with the Marquis in defense of your domain and honor. Who it was who was at the Marquis' side in his last days, in his last hour? Remember in whose arms the Marquis breathed his last. And who spent five years in a dungeon! The man you left to die in the streets of Paris, the man you hoped would die, the much—maligned Count de Mallac. I shall do anything in my power to crush you, destroy this beautiful nest of luxury you have built for yourself on lies and deception. You are nothing but an impostor, you may have been born a Valinquette, but you have more tainted Spanish blood in your veins than that of a French nobleman."

At this Antoine seized his tormentor by the throat. He might have killed Guibert right then had not the voice of Galatée make him desist.

"I hate you both! A curse on both of you, on your arrogance, your conceit, a curse on all the Valinquettes and Mallacs of this world!" Galatée stood screaming in the half-open library door. They knew not how long she had been there. She had in fact heard more than she could bear. Her face was ashen, wan, under her eyes the tears had carved dark rings. Her wildly darting eyes and disheveled hair bespoke madness. Her large belly was clearly visible under the thin, white chemise that sparsely covered her trembling body. Guibert felt his heart ache at seeing her like this.

Behind her appeared the stout figure of the Duchess de Rochemouton, who had apparently made her way in unobserved by the two rivals over the servant's protestation. She placed her arm protectively around Galatée's shoulder, the long-awaited doctor behind her.

"My dear, you must return to your bed. I'm sure the doctor agrees with me. This is all too much to bear for a woman in your condition. You mustn't think of anything but your health and that of your child."

Guibert called out to her, but the Duchess nudged her away, and assisted by the doctor, Galatée slowly ascended the stairs.

"I shall not permit you gentlemen to cause this woman any more distress," the doctor said.

The adversaries faced each other once again.

"I see no point in bickering like washer women," Antoine said. "Let's settle this like men, eye to eye tomorrow at dawn, six o'clock behind the Cemetery of the Innocents. You know the place."

"Just as well," Guibert said. "Blades or pistols?"

"Blades," said Antoine.

The Count de Mallac left the Hôtel de Valinquette with a last, wistful glance up the staircase in the direction of the familiar chambers. There the Duchess stood guard at the railing, like a dragon at the entrance to a cavern sheltering a treasure trove.

Chapter 11

THE DUKE DE Rochemouton was finishing his evening toilet. He was putting a final twirl on his moustache and was ready to depart for his habitual rounds of the Marais, which would eventually terminate at the house of Angélique Guyon, when the unexpected happened. The Duchess, huffing from the exertion of flying up the circular stairs at the Hôtel de Rochemouton—no mean accomplishment for someone of her age and corpulence—blocked his way, bursting with excitement.

"Louis!" she called out—she rarely called him by his first name and when she did it was invariably to scold him or to announce an impending disaster. "Louis! Something terrible is going to happen if you don't do something. You must do something to stop this . . ."

"Please, calm yourself my dear. How can I do something if you don't tell me what this terrible thing is?"

"A duel! Somebody will get killed, if nothing is done. Oh, that poor woman, the pain she has to bear! And in her condition!"

"All right, my dear Germaine, let's start from the beginning." It was even rarer that he should call her by her first name, and when he did it was only to soothe some anxiety that provoked in her a temporary incoherence.

"Now, there, that's better. Who is dueling and who is the poor woman?"

"The Marquise de Valinquette, of course. She is in such a delicate state. And caught between those bloody fools. The Marquis and the Count de Mallac are meeting tomorrow, at dawn, somewhere near the Cemetery of the Holy Innocents."

"Which side of the wall?"

"I couldn't hear that much. But it is definitely near the wall of the cemetery."

"It's a long way around this wall. But calm yourself, my dear. I shall pay a visit to the police prefecture and speak with Monsieur de La Reynie in person. Dueling is against the law in the Kingdom of France and I'm sure he will see to it that no harm will come to either one of these fools. I should have thought this Valinquette had more sense than to engage in such childish behavior. Who did you say was the other man?"

"The Count de Mallac—you know him, her horse master. Only he isn't really a horse master . . . but all that doesn't matter at the moment."

The Duchess felt another case of the vapors coming on and betook herself forthwith to bed while her husband dutifully went out and, forgoing his customary rounds, directed his steps toward the rue Neuves des Capucines.

The police prefecture was a bit out of the way of his usual itinerary but the fear that he would never hear the last of this affair were he to take his wife's concerns lightly warranted the inconvenience. He was in luck. His Majesty's police lieutenant Nicolas Gabriel de La Reynie was just returning to his office and professed himself greatly honored by the visit of a man as illustrious as the Duke de Rochemouton. The newly appointed police lieutenant knew the value of cultivating the good will of someone reputed to be close to the throne. He had already gained a great reputation as a devoted servant to the King and had applied himself vigorously to the task of cleansing the city and ridding its streets of crime and squalor.

"I am most honored by Your Lordship's visit to these humble surroundings. How can I be of service to Your Lordship?" La Reynie bade the Duke have a seat and placed himself opposite his visitor with eager solicitude.

The Duke took the police lieutenant's deferential deportment as a matter of course and made himself comfortable. He took in the man opposite him with a quick glance. One of those bourgeois office chasers the King likes to employ to do his bidding was his prompt assessment. Very eager, very proper, and above all, absolutely incorruptible.

"To get straight to the point, a matter has come to my attention, a matter of great delicacy that requires extreme discretion, since a highborn, or shall we say two gentlemen of noble birth are involved. I trust Monsieur will know to exercise the necessary discretion in this matter."

The Duke cleared his throat a few more times. The police lieutenant was all ears, nodding his understanding though he had so far been given little to understand or be discreet about. Then again, he did not attain his position by rushing the measured statements of noble gentlemen. Not the slightest twitch of facial muscle was visible that might have betrayed impatience on his part.

"Well, as I said, to get straight to the point," the Duke began again, "it has come to my attention that a duel is to take place somewhere near, though I don't know exactly where, but near the Cemetery of the Holy Innocents, early tomorrow morning at dawn, six o'clock or so, could be even earlier."

"Dueling is against the law in the Kingdom of France, as Your Lordship is no doubt aware," La Reynie stated when the Duke paused again. "But usually these are private matters and the police generally does not interfere, especially if the gentlemen involved are of noble birth."

"In this case, I am asking you personally to interfere. In strictest confidence, Madame the Duchess and I would be much aggrieved if any harm came to either the Marquis de Valinquette or to the Count de Mallac for that matter."

"Did I hear Monsieur say the Count de Mallac?" The police lieutenant's demeanor suddenly took on the keenness of a fox on the prowl. "Is this gentleman a friend of yours?"

"Not exactly. The Marquis, of course, is a dear friend, but the Count is very dear to a very dear friend of the Duchess. Why do you ask?"

"As far as we know there is only one Count de Mallac, or one man who calls himself thus since the title had been stripped from all possible surviving descendants of the last Count de Mallac. You see, if you don't mind my saying so, the last Count de Mallac was embroiled in a conspiracy against the Crown and was executed for treason. This was more than twenty years ago. Your Lordship may recall the Cinq-Mars affair, as it was called."

"Yes, yes, of course." The Duke shifted impatiently in his seat. The small favor he was willing to do for his wife in the interest of domestic peace was turning into something rather more irksome. He certainly was not prepared for the police lieutenant's next cannon blast.

"The present Count, or the man who has arrogated the title to himself, is one of the most dangerous criminals in France, a bandit who unfortunately has so far eluded justice."

"But that cannot be!" protested the Duke. "This Mallac fellow, I was told, has been a close friend of the Marquis de Valinquette since childhood."

"Exactly. He fought on the side of the Fronde with his friend Valinquette."

"Well," the Duke cleared his throat with renewed vigor and shifted seemingly uncomfortably in his chair, "you must understand, my dear La Reynie, in those days many who are now the most devoted servants of His Majesty, the King had at one time joined the Frondeurs."

"This is too true. But it is not for having been a Frondeur that this Mallac is sought by the police. As it happened, he was captured during the Battle of Saint Antoine and was condemned to ten years at the fortress of Pignerol. He escaped from the fortress about five years ago. Since then he has surfaced in various parts of the Kingdom in pursuit of a career of crime. He has become notorious. He launches his operations of brigandage from an ancient fortress in Brittany that once belonged to his family but which is now the property of the Crown. This fortress he seized with the help of local peasants, who still harbor some sentimental loyalty to their former masters, the Mallacs. The Bretons have always been an obstreperous race . . . But be that as it may. This so-called Count de Mallac has established a smuggling network that extends all over the northwestern part of the Kingdom, if not further. He has defrauded His Majesty's coffers of millions in revenue. We knew he had contacts in Paris and that he visited the city several times in the past year, but he is sly as a fox and has so far eluded us."

The police lieutenant's revelations caused the Duke such consternation that he knew not what to say. He felt extremely embarrassed and at the same time indignant at what he had heard. To think that this Mallac had used his domain at Beaupré as a hideout in the guise of a horse master. But, of course, he, the Duke, had not the slightest notion of the brigand's identity, and besides, he did not pay much attention to him since he was presented as a servant of the Marquise. In fact he had only the vaguest remembrance of him at all. But these thoughts he kept from the man apparently eager to capture the Count.

"My dear La Reynie," he finally managed to say, "what you say, and I don't doubt one word of it, is quite astounding. It certainly is all news to me. But I am certain that the Marquis de Valinquette is quite uninvolved. I would not hesitate to vouch for the honesty and integrity of this man. Besides, the two men are obviously mortal enemies for whatever reason. I would wager my life and reputation that the Marquis' conduct is above reproach."

"One should not be too quick to put one's life and reputation on the line for anybody, Your Lordship," La Reynie cautioned. "Of course, we have no evidence whatsoever that the Marquis is an accomplice, or that he has any knowledge of his friend's criminal activities, but we must also assume that he did provide him with shelter and that would, of course, implicate him as well. But that is a minor offense, the law is interested in bringing the chief perpetrator to justice. Thanks to Your Lordship, this will at last come to pass. Please be assured of the gratitude of His Majesty's police force."

"We all must do our duty, and I am certain Monsieur will acquit himself splendidly." The Duke rose from his seat, numb and in a daze. How was he going to break this news to the Duchess?

"On which side of the cemetery wall did Your Lordship say this encounter is to take place?"

"Unfortunately, I am unable to say. All I have been told is that they are to meet behind the wall of the Cemetery of the Holy Innocents."

"It's a wide circle all around," the police lieutenant said, more to himself than to the Duke, his mind already immersed in a plan for casting his net wherein he would catch his quarry.

The Duke started for the door. A heavy weight lodged in the pit of his stomach. This was a most unexpected turn of events. He had long made his peace with the Crown after a youthful enthusiasm for the Fronde, and ordinarily it would have given him the greatest pleasure to be of service to his King. He suddenly felt the strain of his age and descended the stairs of the police prefecture with lumbered gait, pensive and filled with ill foreboding. Any desire for the merriments of the Marais had vanished.

After a solitary walk that failed to clear his mind, he finally returned home and related to the Duchess what he had heard. Husband and wife sat together until late that night, talking—an occurrence that was indeed unprecedented.

Another candle burned low in the city that night. At the Châtelet, Nicolas Gabriel de La Reynie conferred with his deputy and a handful of watchmen. They hatched a detailed plan for the capture of the man La Reynie called the most notorious criminal in France. The lieutenant took time to lecture the men on the momentousness of this operation. Here was an opportunity for the new police force of Paris to earn its spurs, to cover itself with glory. The gratitude of the King would be their sweetest reward.

La Reynie was determined not to let anything unforeseen foil his plan. The fewer the people who knew about this, the better were the chances for surprise. One thought that worried him was that the Duke de Rochemouton, or the Duchess, might pass word to Mallac or Valinquette. But Monsieur de La Reynie was not given to agonizing over something beyond his control. He trusted that Rochemouton's loyalty to his King would win out over the strange sympathy he seemed to harbor for the perpetrators involved in this affair.

"We have two disadvantages," La Reynie said to his men. Prominent among them was his deputy, Lucien Lefèvre, whose flashy new uniform gave him a certain authority far removed from the days when he first came to Paris from the provinces and earned a meager living retrieving dead bodies, human and otherwise, from the Seine river.

"We don't know the exact location where the duel will take place. Only the most trusted men can be taken into confidence. This must be kept an absolute secret; the slightest leak could spoil everything. Therefore, you must split up to cover all sides of the cemetery wall. It will be up to you men to move quickly and silently without arousing suspicion. Surprise is our greatest advantage. Is that clear?"

The men nodded while studying a magnified map of the area surrounding the cemetery spread out on the table.

"The second disadvantage," the police lieutenant continued, "is that we have very little information about the criminal."

Here Monsieur de La Reynie took the opportunity to deliver a lecture on his favorite subject, the science of police procedure. And since he himself had thought up many of these ideas, he was wont to go on about them for considerable time.

"A policeman's greatest weapon in his fight to bring a criminal to justice is circumspect application of his knowledge of the criminal's mind, his psyche. This knowledge must be painstakingly assembled. Thus a good policeman must become familiar with the patterns of the objects thought, every little preference or habit, no matter how insignificant it may seem. He must determine the criminal's modus operandi. In other words, the policeman must put himself in the criminal's place, begin to think and feel like him. Unfortunately, in the case of the Count de Mallac, we have little to go by. I have not had the opportunity to study his mind, his reflexes. We know nothing about his weaknesses, all we know is that he is very sly and very cautious. He won't take chances. He has apparently been in Paris several times this past year, but no criminal activity can be linked to those visits—as far as we can tell. Now, we have an opportunity that may never present itself again. Gentlemen, this is our chance to serve our King. Vive le Roi!"

With these words Monsieur de La Reynie sent his men to retire, but the candle on his desk flickered long past midnight. At his side remained Lucien Lefèvre, a man who, like him, was filled with personal ambition he sought to fulfill through zealous service to his King. Men of Lefèvre's dedication and trustworthiness were rare. Monsieur de La Reynie appreciated that.

Lucien Lefèvre was hungry. He had been hungry for years and at last his hunger was to be appeased. He already saw himself being hailed as the most celebrated law-enforcement official in Paris. Years of toil in the gutter, of suffering humiliation and disgrace, finally would be rewarded. He had been the first volunteer when the new police force was formed. He immediately grasped the possibilities of the present situation and was not about to share the glory to be reaped with anybody. His instinct and familiarity with every inch of the terrain around the cemetery would take him to the place where his prey was likely to be found.

Setting out before dawn, Lefèvre and a small troop of assistants came to the cemetery wall. He ordered them to disperse to the other side. His deed would be much more heroic if he put the criminal in shackles single-handedly. Treading lightly, sure-footed as a cat, he passed through the dense drizzle and fog, his hunter's eyes and ears keenly alert. Before long he heard a faint clanking noise and voices. He moved in the direction of the sound, until he came upon the scene of two men crossing swords with wild fury. The verbal dueling—curses, accusations, insults—was even more ferocious.

"In the name of the King, you are under arrest for violation of the royal interdict of private combat!" Lucien Lefèvre had stepped out of the fog into the grove of oaks where the two men were doing battle. They did not so much as pause. He repeated his warning, to no effect. They kept lunging at each other undeterred. Lucien's attention was closely focused on the combatants, so he was only vaguely aware of the presence of two bystanders, who had quickly disappeared behind the trees as he came closer. He hesitated now, as he did not know which one was the infamous Mallac.

"You'd better stay back, Monsieur, or you might get hurt!" warned the taller of the duelists without taking his eyes off his opponent. But

Lucien Lefèvre was imbued with the importance of his mission. He moved closer for a better look at their faces. The one who had spoken had dark, exotic features, but the Count de Mallac was said to be a Breton, and this one did certainly not look like a Breton. The shorter, broad-shouldered one with the bright smile, which did not leave his face even as he gave a most spirited defense and his mouth spouted a litany of curses, was much more likely to be the one he was after.

Lefèvre, certain that nobody would dare oppose an officer of the King's law, swaggered between the warring gentlemen and pointed his drawn pistol at Guibert.

"In the name of the King, Count de Mallac, you are herewith under arrest for treason, robbery of the King's property, and brigandage. You are herewith ordered to surrender yourself to the custody of His Majesty's duly appointed deputies."

Guibert made no reply and remained with sword poised in the air, ready to strike again at his opponent. Antoine demanded that the officer of the King's law step out of the way or suffer the consequences. What Lefèvre had not considered, could not have considered perhaps, was the force of the passion that had brought these two men at this hour to this place behind the wall of the cemetery on a misty November morning. He underestimated the opponents' antagonism and overestimated the weight of his authority. He ignored Antoine, single-mindedly intent on arresting the Count de Mallac. A mêlée ensued. Clashing swords, a gunshot, groans and shouts mingled in the morning air.

In a minute all was over. When the fog lifted from the scene, the Count de Mallac and the two witnesses behind the trees had vanished. The Marquis stood in a daze over the police deputy, who was writhing on the ground seemingly breathing his last.

The gravity of his situation—the possibility of being accused of the murder of the deputy—suddenly dawned on Antoine. He heard rushing footsteps, presumably those of the other police officers alerted by the gunshot. The officer's charges against Guibert came to his mind. He had to get away. Even if he were to be totally forthcoming, explain the sequence of events, plead self-defense, which did not really apply anyway, he could never clear himself of a charge of complicity with a criminal and enemy of the King whom he had harbored in his own house. His only salvation was to gain distance from this place. Galatée would be happy finally to leave this city. They would have to get out before the garrison at the gates was alerted. If all else failed, there was still the route through the wall they had taken some thirteen years before. He had to move quickly. No time was to be lost.

The shouts "Halt in the name of the King!" flew over his head as he plunged into the tangle of streets and alleys that were just beginning to bustle with activity. Almost too easily, Antoine managed to shake off his pursuers. Perhaps they were more interested in hauling in the Count de Mallac. That Guibert should have embarked on a career of crime did not surprise him. But he blamed himself for not having suspected something sooner. Guibert's story of his recent escape from captivity he now knew was a fabrication. How could he have been so trusting?

And then there was Guibert's association with those thugs, Gaston and Prosper. That should have been a clear signal. This morning Guibert even had the nerve to bring the two—Antoine shuddered to think of them as his brothers-in-law—along as "witnesses." Now they had all disappeared together, presumably into the Court of Miracles, where no police officer would set foot. Be that as it may, he had other things to worry about at this moment. Galatée in her present condition would slow their movement, but he could not possibly leave her behind. There was no telling what they might do to her!

Such were the thoughts that spun around in Antoine's head. He lost all measure of how fantastic, how removed from reality, were his ruminations and plans of escape with his wife. Even after all that had happened, he had no doubt that Galatée would be there, waiting for him. The police would surely apprehend Guibert and she would see what a knave he was.

He burst into the Hôtel de Valinquette calling her name. He scaled the stairs to her dressing room with a few swift strides, fully expecting to find her there. Even when the maid wailed that Madame was nowhere to be found this morning, he still believed she was merely hiding to punish him. He searched every room, every corner, every closet. He called out for her, begging her to relent. But there was no response.

He stormed through the garden, searching behind every tree and bush, in every niche. Absurdly, his eye roved behind statues and inside shrubbery, as though she could be holed up in a crack or under branches dripping with dew. He reached the pavilion, his atelier. If she was anywhere, this is where she would seek refuge. A dank smell of neglect and decay met him as he broke open the door. His steps echoed in the dusky cavern. In the middle, on the platform, stood, as he had left it, the shrouded, lifeless alabaster shape, alone and silent.

He tore back the canvas and shrunk back in horror. The bare skull was sending down a ghastly gaze from the hollow sockets. The torso, hideous and mutilated, was a mockery of his ideal of feminine beauty. With both hands he seized a hammer. A dreadful outcry accompanied his pounding, crushing, smashing of the block of stone that had so long resisted him, driven him to the brink of insanity. Forgotten was his wife, forgotten time and place, forgotten the threat from the police closing in. Again and again, the hammer swung through the air and landed on its victim until it was reduced to rubble, a shattered remnant strewn over the floor. Even then he persisted in his orgy of destruction. Grunting almost inhumanly, he stamped on the shards in a frenzied dance. The sharp edges pierced his boots, cut through to the soles of his feet—he hardly felt the pain.

His rage did not end with the demolition of the statue. Next he picked up the rocky fragments and flung them at the long glass windows that had been specially designed for filtering the light, in just the right amount, at just the right angle. The panes came crashing down, drawing in a gust of cold wind that finally cooled his senses.

Antoine sank to his knees, and there amongst the rubble, covered with dust and blood, he wept. It was not regret for what he had done. No, on the contrary, he felt good. A strange sense of equanimity came over him. He had finally exorcized the demon that had possessed him. The demon that had driven him to pursue a chimera, to strive for an illusory ideal. More than anything he had wanted success, recognition. But for what? And at what price? He had the most beautiful wife. He had been right only once; that was when he thought that a beggar waif could be made into a lady. She was a more gracious lady than any of those of blue bloods, those born to rank and station. Yet he neglected the woman in her and drove her into the arms of his enemy. What a fool he had been! Now she was gone and he knew not where to find her. Perhaps she had gone to find refuge with the Duchess de Rochemouton. That was likely, she was a well-meaning friend. Or had Guibert reached the house before him and lured her away? Had she heard what he really was, and would she follow him even so? Guibert was running for his life—would he take the risk of her slowing him down? Could she really love him? The thought broke his heart.

Sitting among the rubble, trying to make sense of his life, Antoine was unaware that he was not alone until the voice was almost next to him: "In the name of the King, Antoine Maximilien Dupuis, Marquis de Valinquette, you are under arrest for the murder of an officer of His Majesty's police."

Monsieur de La Reynie had come in person to take the nobleman into custody. It was a courtesy, he felt he owed a man of the Marquis' station.

Antoine did not resist. He acquiesced in his fate as just punishment for his transgressions. He got to his feet, brushed the dust off his clothes with his hands as best he could, and extended both arms with a wry smile: "Monsieur, I'm at your disposal."

Once it became clear that Lucien Lefèvre would survive his brush with death, though for about a week his life hung in the balance, the charge was changed to attempted murder and leaving the scene of a crime. Monsieur de La Reynie conducted the investigation at the conclusion of which was added a charge of conspiracy against the Crown for giving succor and shelter to a notorious criminal and enemy of the King.

Antoine realized that something more was at stake here and that his conviction had apparently been ordained in advance. He protested that the Count de Mallac could not be quite so notorious, since he had never before this time heard of his criminal activities. These words only confirmed the inspector's suspicions that the Marquis may be attempting to protect the Count.

Antoine was incarcerated at the Concièrgerie while he awaited trial. Meanwhile La Reynie made the round of the Marais in search of witnesses who would testify to the Marquis' good character. The police inspector was a fair man. Although he would not tell Antoine so, he thought of him as an unwitting victim of unfortunate circumstances; he was in fact not eager to see him sent to a fortress or worse. The prize he was after was the Count de Mallac. What he hoped for was that the Marquis could be persuaded to help in the Count's capture.

The police lieutenant's search brought to light a curious fact—curious at least to a man of La Reynie's character, whose belief in an orderly universe and the immutability of such virtues as constancy, integrity, honesty, forthrightness, and loyalty, was severely rattled. His appeal to the Marquis' peers in a matter where a man's life was at stake turned up nobody, absolutely nobody, who was willing to testify on behalf of the man whose house they had frequented, on whose food they had gorged themselves, whose wine they had guzzled. The entire beau monde, whose habitués once had been ready to kill to gain entry into the Marquise's famous—now the word used more often was "infamous"—literary salon, a salon that had rivaled even the Hôtel de Nevers and had challenged the latter's claim as successor to the fabled Hôtel de Rambouillet of legendary memory.

Most puzzling was the total about-face of the Duke de Rochemouton, who had spoken with such warmth and affection about the Marquis and Marquise during the interview at the police prefecture only a few days before.

"And my wife, Madame the Marquise?" Antoine asked when La Reynie informed him that he had been unable to find anyone willing to speak for him. "Have you heard anything of where she might have gone? Is she staying with friends?"

"I am sorry, my dear Marquis," La Reynie answered dolefully, "so far we have not been able to find a trace of Madame."

Antoine lowered his head and gave himself over to utter despair.

"But how could she just vanish? And in her condition," he muttered.

"The police is doing everything to find her." La Reynie tried to sound reassuring. "But it might help if Monsieur could give us some hint about Madame's habits, her close friends—obviously the Rochemoutons are not among them. Anything at all. I know Madame is a foreigner so she may not be familiar with this city and its perils."

Oh, she knows! She knows the perils of this city only too well, Antoine thought to himself. A terrible premonition took hold of his mind. What if? Fragments of the scene of that terrible night before the duel flashed before him. He tried to sort things out, to put them into sequence. But his anger had so clouded his perception, he only half-remembered what was said or done by either of them on that night.

After Guibert had left the Hôtel de Valinquette, Antoine had gone upstairs to speak to her. He wanted her to understand his feelings—at least this is what he thought he was doing. He had knocked on her door, softly at first, then pounding. To no avail. She would not answer. He had remained crouched in front of that door half the night. He only wanted her to know that he would take care of her, the way he always had. If she would only promise . . . no, she really needn't promise anything, just stay with him, that was all he was asking.

It then occurred to him that she had more reason to be angry at Guibert than at him. It must finally have become clear to her how he had used her. The way he had always used everybody. Maybe she was ashamed to face her husband after all that had happened. But she needn't be. He would forgive her, forgive her anything. They needn't even stay in Paris. He had come to realize what a sham it all was. They would live in the country quietly, at Chazeron or Valinquette. Or they could even go to back to Catalonia, if she preferred, anywhere far, far away from this world of pretense.

All this he wanted to tell her, but she never gave him a chance. At dawn he went out to meet his destiny. There was nothing left for him to live for. He was ready to die, and in his deepest soul he wished that a fatal stab from Guibert's blade would pierce his heart. The thought of death comforted him, even goaded him on during that early morning walk through deserted streets shrouded in fog.

But then when he arrived at the appointed spot behind the northern wall of the Cemetery of the Holy Innocents, anger overwhelmed him again. Guibert was there, smiling. He wore a thick fur overcoat. He remembered wondering how a dispossessed nobody could afford such a magnificent coat. But his anger was aroused by something else. Guibert was not alone. He was in the company of Gaston and Prosper, and the three of them seemed in splendid good spirits.

"What is the canaille doing here? We were to meet alone!" he grunted.

"Any proper duel has witnesses, and these two gentlemen have graciously consented to make sure that everything is done according to the rules," Guibert replied in that mocking tone that had a way of driving Antoine to the brink.

"A duel is to be seconded by one's peers, not by scum from the gutter," Antoine replied, biting his lips. "But let's get on with it. What does it matter!"

"You shouldn't be so discourteous to these fine gentlemen, Antoine, they are after all your family."

"Stop lecturing me about what I should and should not do!" Antoine tore his sword from its scabbard, ready to start attacking his opponent before he'd even had a chance to draw himself.

"Monsieur the Marquis!" Gaston interjected. "With all due respect to Your Lordship, even in the underworld there are rules that fighting men must stick to."

"All right, I'll wait for him to draw his sword." Antoine was eager to get this whole affair over and done with, and he swallowed this last humiliation of having been put in his place by the likes of this thug.

Guibert slipped off his coat, folded it neatly, and placed it on a tree stump. Every move was calculated, Antoine was certain, to raise his ire further. Finally Guibert drew his sword, and they touched blades. They plunged into the duel with a ferocity only love turned to hate can inspire. As swordsmen, they were fairly equally matched, but looking back, Antoine was sure that their dispute would have been decided right then had it not been for the interference of that officer of the law.

Antoine's thoughts returned to Galatée, and from Galatée back to Guibert, and to the man who had foiled it all by getting between them, whose life he almost snuffed out and who might yet die. His thoughts went round and round, over every detail of the events as he remembered them. Some things were very clear and others seemed lost in a haze. One puzzle, especially, he was unable to solve. How did the police know about the duel and the identity of the opponents? Who had tipped them off? Could it have been Galatée, and if so, whose life was she trying to save? His or Guibert's?

But it really did not matter who the informant was, whether Galatée or someone else. No matter what the outcome of the trial, his life was irreparably ruined, and the one who was responsible for all his calamities was still at large.

La Reynie came to see him one day in his cell.

"Perhaps we can come to an agreement, Monsieur the Marquis, an agreement that would be of mutual benefit to us. His Majesty, the King, is a very gracious and generous ruler. I am sure that His Majesty would not hesitate to pardon a man of Your Lordship's character, if Your Lordship were to give proof of his loyalty and devotion to His Majesty."

"What did you have in mind, Monsieur?" Antoine asked, his patience tested by the man's circumlocutions and obsequious tone.

"If His Lordship would consent to aid the King's police in the capture of the notorious criminal Guibert de Mallac, His Majesty surely would show himself not to be ungrateful."

"What would you have me do? If you want me to infiltrate his organization, I'm afraid he would never believe that I came in friendship. As you must realize, I'm not exactly on cordial terms with the gentleman."

"Yes, of course. But nothing of the sort would be required. What I had in mind was Monsieur's help in sketching a portrait of the Count's mind, as it were. Your Lordship is the person most closely familiar with the Count. So far we do not know what kind of personality we are dealing with. We do not know the patterns of his thinking, his habits, his reaction in certain situations. His strengths and his weaknesses. Do you understand what I mean? Every human being has a peculiar pattern of thought which nobody else shares. Knowledge of these peculiarities can be very useful in bringing a criminal to justice. The Count de Mallac is still a blank page in the registers of the police. You, Monsieur, can help me fill in the blanks, you can help me bring him to life, to help me draw a picture of flesh and blood, as it were."

"I'm afraid he is a very unpredictable character," Antoine said evasively. The police lieutenant's ideas of the unique nature of the individual intrigued him. He had never thought of the practical application of such ideas in capturing offenders of the law. No wonder the King put his trust in this man.

"Unpredictable perhaps, but even the Count's thinking runs along certain mental tracks from which he will not depart. He holds certain preferences, intense dislikes, superstitions, attractions, a weakness for the fair sex, perhaps—the latter has been the undoing of many who thought they could play a game of cat and mouse with the police and get away with murder. I like to think of my work as a science that can be approached through systematic penetration of the human mind. No mystery remains a mystery for long if the key is found that will unlock it. I think my method is the key and has universal application."

La Reynie spoke with considerable pride. He took full advantage of his captive noble audience to expound his theories. Antoine was not averse to listening, as it distracted him from his woes.

Antoine took up the thread: "You endeavor, then, with a sketch in hand of the pursued criminal's mind, to predict his behavior. If you can predict his behavior, you can set a trap into which he will inevitably fall."

"Exactly, my dear Marquis!" La Reynie was overjoyed to have found so astute an interlocutor. All too often he had been ridiculed for advancing ideas that, he was told, must have sprung from a drunken state of mind—and this despite the fact that he, Monsieur de La Reynie, never touched alcohol, not even at dinner. He had successfully propounded his theories once before, in conversation with the King, who had listened carefully and approvingly. La Reynie's jurisdiction was limited to the city of Paris, but he had made it his goal to capture the Count de Mallac wherever he might surface. He was sure of the King's good graces. Once he brought in the big catch, there would be no squabbling about whose waters he had been fishing in.

"Well, my Lordship, what do you say?" La Reynie was in a cheerful mood, certain to have found a collaborator.

Antoine had fallen into a ponderous silence. Here was a chance for vengeance, a way to be rid of Guibert forever. He himself would obtain a pardon and be restored to good graces. He would have liked to kill the knave himself. But was this the way? He wanted to confront him one on one, face to face, on equal, matched terms. A conspiracy, a hunt—that was another matter altogether. This policeman was a dedicated servant of the King, but he was also a man of personal ambition with a mind toward furthering his career. Why should he, Antoine, become this man's accomplice?

Of course, compliance would spare him the humiliation and suffering of years of incarceration. Guibert had been condemned to the dungeon for ten years. Never mind that he had escaped after five—he was there because he had defended the name of Valinquette. Could Antoine besmirch the memory of his father, who would never have betrayed a friend? Besides, was not the Crown the cause for the wretched, dispossessed state of the last descendant of the House of Mallac? Had anybody connected with the throne shown the slightest concern for the fate of the young boy whose father was executed in a public square at Rennes, whose family's possessions and estates, the Mallacs had held for centuries, were confiscated by the Crown, who was left to become a wretched street urchin surviving only by his wits?

"Well, Monsieur?" the police lieutenant pressed.

"Monsieur de La Reynie, three days ago I had no greater desire than to see the Count de Mallac dead. I was so overcome with hatred and anger that one of us would surely have died, had your deputy not intervened. But you must understand that the feud between the Count and me is an intensely personal matter. It is a rivalry between two brothers, and though I would kill him with my own hands even now, given the chance, I could not betray a brother. Please do not demand any more of me."

"Monsieur, do you realize the consequences of your decision for yourself? You leave me no choice but . . ."

"Yes, yes, of course," Antoine said, "and I'm grateful to you for your kindness. You are an upright and honorable man. The King is well served by a man of your caliber and integrity. But please, do not ask me to do something that would make it impossible for me to live with myself."

"Believe me, I deeply respect Your Lordship's decision," the police lieutenant replied dolefully. "I am awed by it. May God be with you and have mercy on you."

La Reynie rose. He extended his hand and warmly pressed that of his prisoner.

Book Two

Chapter 1

AT THE VERY hour when the two rivals battled it out behind the cemetery wall, a woman wrapped in a black velvet cloak passed through the wicket gate in the rear of the garden of the Hôtel de Valinquette and quickly closed it behind her. She cast a hasty glance up and down the street, inhaled deeply, then pulled her hood around her face and plunged into the morning mist. She seemed eager to put a distance between her and this city quarter of grandiose mansions and glittering palaces.

Near the bank of the river, her pace slowed. For a moment, she leaned against a tree, panting and catching her breath, but despite being obviously heavy with child she did not permit herself to tarry. She wandered along a circuitous path that took her ever farther from the dwellings of the beau monde and ever deeper into the heart of the city, into the quarters of the "little" people of Paris. Heedless of the taunts and stares, the shaking of heads and occasional raised fists she provoked as she steered through the gathering crowd, brushing against hucksters, street criers, mountebanks, beggars, washerwomen, and all manner of rabble that clogged the streets even on a cold, gray day, she seemed to know where she was going without going anywhere in particular.

Whether by conscious design or because she was compelled by an inexorable fate, after hours of meandering she found herself in the neighborhood of Saint-Médard and at the entrance to the Court of Miracles. Breathing in deeply, she entered the open gate and disappeared into the murky realm of crooked lanes and narrow passageways, lined by ramshackle huts and tenements. Squalor and feculence met her every step. She waded through mud and excrement that coated the unpaved ground. A putrid stench rose into her nostrils, a stench she had forgotten could exist. Now it was all coming back, all too familiar. But, undeterred, she pushed on deeper and deeper into the realm of cutthroats and thieves. There was no turning back from her descent into the lowest, most debased region of human existence.

The sight of a certain rickety hovel, squeezed in between other hovels that leaned against each other as if this were the only way they could remain erect, put a knot in her stomach and made her heart pound. It was even shabbier than she remembered.

As she came closer, loud men's voices made her pause. Besides the Parisian argot, there was another, more refined, strangely familiar pattern of speech. She leaned against the side of the structure and peeked through the window. Her heart beat rose into her throat. There they were, gathered around a rough-hewn table in the middle of the room, Gaston and Prosper and with them Guibert. He was flashing his smile, his feet comfortably stretched out on a chair as if he belonged to her mother's house.

Gervaise was missing from her fixed place near the stove. She hadn't thought of the possibility before, but could it be that her mother was no longer alive?

An overwhelming desire for comfort, a desperate hope of finding care and protection, had driven Galatée to seek out her mother at the Court of Miracles. That Gervaise Caillart might have passed away had not occurred to her, and the possibility now caused her the greatest anguish. But even if she was alive, what made her think that she would take her in? She, the daughter, had never once sought out her mother while she was living the glittering life of the Marais. Now that her world had collapsed, she had come, a beggar at her mother's door. Maybe it's a mistake, she thought. But where else could she have turned in her distress?

And now, here was the man for whom she had risked everything, the man who had used her love in the vilest way—hadn't she heard him say so himself?—the man she hoped never to see again, seemingly at home at her mother's table, hatching who knows what plots with her no-good brothers. What did she know about this man whom she had trusted, had loved with wild abandon, for whom she had become an adulteress and a traitor? Could she really say she knew him other than in a carnal sense? Did he ever answer her questions about what he did when he was not with her?

The sudden swelling of the voices inside made her listen more intently. Maybe here was at last an opportunity to learn who Guibert de Mallac really was. She almost did not dare breathe as she strained to hear what was spoken. Since she had talked herself into believing that he was of the basest sort, what she now heard was almost impossible to comprehend.

"I still give the orders around here and I shall not leave the city until I'm ready to do so!" she heard him bellow. Guibert had gotten up and was standing with his back to the window so she could not see his face. They were separated only by a thin mud wall. He was so close his breath was audible, and her resolve to stay hidden weakened.

"But Your Lordship must consider his own safety and that of the operation. The police lieutenant is probably combing the entire city with his hounds. He will leave no stone unturned to find Your Lordship," Gaston objected. "It is likely that Lucien Lefèvre recognized us. In that case he will surely lead the police directly to this place."

"They are not here now, are they?" Guibert replied with a scornful smile. "For all we know, Lefèvre is dead. Our dear friend the Marquis did us a great favor. You saw it yourself, he ran the man through clean. What is much more likely is that the police are busy at this very moment charging him with the murder of Lucien Lefèvre. The poor devil shouldn't have meddled. But at least the officers of the law will have their hands full. This will afford me an opportunity for a quiet visit to the Hôtel de Valinquette."

"What if the house is surrounded with guardsmen?"

"Then we shall have to devise some scheme to lure the Marquise to a place of rendezvous outside, and you, gentlemen, will make the arrangements."

"Is any woman worth that much?" Prosper interjected meekly.

"Of course not any woman, Prosper," Guibert replied condescendingly as if he were explaining some difficult concept to a child, "but the Marquise is not any woman. Well, whether you understand this or not, is really unimportant. Just get it through your thick skulls, you two, that I'm not leaving the city before I have spoken to the Marquise. So let's not lose any more time."

At this moment, Gervaise emerged from somewhere in the back. Galatée felt overjoyed to see her. She was moved to leave her hiding place and throw herself at her mother's feet. But she quickly caught herself. It was more prudent to remain undetected a little while longer. Besides, she wanted to find out why Guibert was so adamant about seeing her.

"May I inquire why His Lordship is so intent on seeing my daughter? She still is my daughter, you know."

"I'm fully aware, Madame, of the circumstances. I'm a friend, and I must urgently clear up an unfortunate misunderstanding that has come to mar the high esteem in which we hold each other."

"What kind of friend are you to her?" Gervaise asked, suspicion in her tone.

"A close friend, a friend who loves your daughter more than life." Guibert had turned slightly and Galatée could see him in profile. Though she could not see his eyes, the smile had vanished from his face and he looked uncharacteristically somber.

"Oh, one of those!" Gervaise was all scorn. "In that case, it seems to me all the more urgent that you leave this town before they come and hang you. Gaston! Prosper! Guide His Lordship through the wall while there is still time."

"Madame, I shall not go. I refuse."

"My dear Count, face it: you are a wanted criminal. This is no judgment on my part, only a statement of fact. If you are caught in the company of my daughter, the Marquise, you will endanger her life as well as yours. So, Godspeed, and may we meet again in quieter times. Be gone now!"

Galatée's heart was overflowing with love and gratitude for both Gervaise and Guibert. At the very moment that she felt most alone, unloved and unwanted, as she had when she was a child, she had received proof that those she cared most about still loved her. Although she felt tempted to rush into the arms of her lover, she held back. Gervaise was right. If Guibert saw her now, he would delay his getaway. She could not risk becoming the cause of his capture. She had to let him go for now. The certainty that he loved her after all was solace enough.

She hugged the shadows as the three men filed out of the hut. The edge of Guibert's fur coat brushed lightly against the hem of her velvet cloak grazing the gutter. Here was a last opportunity before he would disappear from her life. But the separation would only be temporary, she assured herself. She couldn't weaken now and endanger his life. She was still wavering, clawing at the crumbling wall to keep herself erect. She held on and waited. The men's steps faded in the distance. They were gone.

Galatée pulled herself up with just enough strength to drag herself inside the hovel that was her mother's home. Before she could say anything to the startled woman, she fainted and collapsed onto the floor.

When Galatée regained consciousness, she found herself bedded on a pallet of straw. Gervaise Caillart's eyes were fixed on her, curiously grim, almost hostile, but otherwise inscrutable. How could she have thought that this woman would welcome her return?

"So you have finally come back," Gervaise said. Her voice was hoarse with drink. Nothing in the mother's demeanor betrayed any of the affection for her daughter she had expressed in her exchange with Guibert just a short while before. "Why did you come?"

"I need your help, Maman." Galatée again felt like the little girl who, faking blindness and lameness, won the sympathy of strangers but never received a kind word from her mother.

"You've been in Paris for more than two years, cavorting with your aristocratic friends. Never once did you come to see your mother then. Why now?"

"I wanted to come, but he wouldn't let me. He kept me a prisoner in that mansion."

"Who?"

"The Marquis. I asked him many times to let me visit, but to no avail. I was too afraid to go against his will."

"Well, at least he's been kind to us, your Marquis. Always paid on time. Not as much as he should've, considering, but it was something."

"That's because he was afraid you might cause a scandal, tell people who I really am. He was afraid that if it leaked out that his wife came from the Court of Miracles, he would be done for."

"Then why did he have to marry you? He could've had you without, I'm sure."

"He had a plan, a wild idea. He got some sick pleasure from duping the aristocrats who believe that everything is in the blood, that people of common birth could never rise to the refinement and culture of the aristocracy, that one's origins will always show. Well, he proved them wrong, but he would have ruined his chances of being presented at the Royal Court had the truth about his wife become known."

"So you lived in a prison of luxury. Not bad, considering. I guess that's all over now. Whose child is this?" Gervaise added in a rough tone.

"The Count de Mallac's," Galatée said softly. She ducked her head as if she expected a slap from her mother's hand.

"Just as I thought!" Gervaise grunted. "What is it with the women of this family? Here you have a devoted husband, even if he kept a close watch on you—not close enough obviously—but he gives you everything, keeps you in brocade and gems, and you have to go and throw everything to the wind for a scoundrel, a bandit, a thief. That's why they were going at each other, weren't they?"

Gervaise made a rare display of indignation. What she regarded as her daughter's stupidity was just too much for her to comprehend.

"I knew one like that once, charming, sweet-talking, best lover in the world . . ." For a brief moment a sweet melancholy softened Gervaise's gruff voice, reminding Galatée of the night of their vigil over her sister's body. But then it was gone again.

"Look where it's gotten me! Makes no difference that yours is a Count, he's a dispossessed Count and he has a price on his head, just like your father had."

Galatée was too drained to answer. Her thoughts swirled around Guibert. That he should be a criminal was hard to believe. If it was true, he certainly was not to blame. He was driven to a life of crime by evil, conniving people. She yearned to be at his side, to fight his battle with him. What could anyone do to them, if they were together? She had to get to Brittany, somehow she had to get to Brittany and find him. Her thoughts trailed off into a land she had never seen, but of which she had formed a clear picture in her imagination.

"You must leave now! Your brothers will be back soon."

"But where should I go? I have nowhere to go." Galatée choked with tears. "Please don't send me away. You can't abandon me now."

"How can you stay here? With all the riffraff around? And in your condition? Go back to your fancy mansion."

"Please let me stay until my time has come. I need you, please help me have this child. I could not bear it if something were to happen to it."

Gervaise assessed her with a keen eye. "You have at least two months to go. What are we going to tell the pack of thieves out there? What am I saying—thieves! That would be the least. How do you suppose we can keep their hands off you, your clothes. And then there is the king. I don't mean His Majesty, King Louis, no, the beggar king, that mean brute. He'll want to be paid, and handsomely, for letting you to stay here."

"But I belong here. This is my home, I was born here."

There was something comical about the protest of this woman in velvet and silk, who even in the degraded condition in which she now found herself exuded an aura of nobility and breeding.

"Did you bring anything? Jewelry, money, anything of value?"

"No. I didn't think. I just wanted to get away from that mansion, as far and as quickly as possible."

"Don't you aristos have any practical sense? What did you think you would live off?"

"Maybe Gaston and Prosper can go back and get some of my belongings?"

"Break into the Hôtel de Valinquette?"

"Why not? I'm sure this is not an unaccustomed task for my brothers. Besides, I can tell them exactly where to find my jewels, and they can bring me some of my clothes as well. They won't have to waste time searching."

The lethargy that had dampened her spirits was suddenly lifted. Planning a burglary at the Hôtel de Valinquette invigorated her. She rose from the pallet and began pacing about the dirt floor. She bubbled with excitement. Gervaise was not even given a chance to object.

Galatée was still enumerating items to be removed from the Hôtel when Gaston and Prosper burst through the door.

"Is he safe? Did he get away?" Galatée showered her brothers with questions without greeting or introduction, as if it had been ten days rather than ten years since she and Antoine had escaped through the same hole in the wall.

"Yes, your Count is safe. Nothing to worry about there," Gaston replied gruffly. Then, turning to Gervaise: "What is she doing here? What does she want? She'll put the police on our trail."

"My dear brother," Galatée said to Prosper, the hunchback, the more susceptible, soft-hearted of the two, "I am here with a proposition that should benefit us all. And don't worry about the police, nobody will suspect where I am."

"Since when is it dear brother? For years we didn't even exist. We were kept like beggars outside the mansion, chased from the front door and the back door, allowed not even a glimpse inside. And now the Marquise has suddenly discovered her love for her family."

Gaston edged up close to her.

"How about a kiss, little sister? Uh, you smell good, and what soft and smooth skin!"

"Leave her alone, Gaston!" Gervaise commanded. There was no doubt as to who gave orders in this household. "You benefited nicely from your sister's connection, we all did. Now she is back and she needs our help."

"If she hadn't screwed around with the Count, everything would still be fine," Prosper remarked.

"Watch your language when you speak about your sister! She is a lady, not some scum like you." Gervaise landed a big hand behind Prosper's ears.

"Come on, let's all sit down now and hear what La Fauvette has to say. But keep it low please, remember the walls of the Court of Miracles have ears."

The foursome gathered around the wobbly table in the Widow Caillart's kitchen, putting their heads together like conspirators. Galatée described in great detail the interior layout of the Hôtel de Valinquette. Downstairs was the spacious parlor, the famous emerald salon of the Marquise de Valinquette, abutted by the library and several other, more intimate drawing rooms. From the vestibule rose the curved staircase leading to the private quarters on the upper level. She advised her brothers that her own apartments were best reached by an interior staircase from the garden. They were already familiar with the wicket gate in the rear wall.

She then enumerated the items, clothing, undergarments, outerwear, footwear, jewelry, silverware, even bedding and books that were essential for her comfort. The list grew longer the more she thought about accessories and appurtenances that had become absolute necessities in her everyday living.

"Do you have all this straight?" she asked. "Let's go over it once more."

Gaston and Prosper repeated back to her the way they would enter the compound through the gate in the rear of the garden—the wicket could be forced, if need be—then to the Marquise's private apartment via the interior staircase. They repeated her instructions once more about all the items they were to remove. How they would carry the loot through the streets of Paris without drawing attention to themselves the Marquise left to them.

What the conspirators did not consider was that the Hôtel de Valinquette was kept under close guard by Monsieur de La Reynie's agents. On the night of the heist, Galatée and Gervaise waited in vain for the return of the thieves and their loot. Gaston and Prosper walked straight into a police ambush as they left the mansion laden with goods and were immediately taken to the police prefecture for interrogation.

No word from the emissaries reached the hut at the Court of Miracles where the mood grew dimmer with every passing day and night. In this murky underground realm, Galatée soon began to feel the depths of her isolation from the world. But there was no turning back. At first she was inclined to go and find out for herself what had happened to her brothers, but she had to concede that in her condition she was not suited for such a venture. She lay on the pile of straw that served as her mother's bed, her thoughts turning on what she felt was her brothers' betrayal. What else could have happened? They must have run off with the jewelry and were probably hawking it somewhere.

"You don't know them," Gervaise protested, "they may be thieves and a lot else besides, but turning against family, their mother or sister, no, never. You must understand, when you left you were still a child and you may not have noticed then, or you may have forgotten in all those years away, family is a matter of honor among us. We look out for each other, believe me."

Galatée was humbled by this simple speech, and she began to feel a bond that tied her to these people, crude and uncouth as they were, the bond of blood, a bond nothing could sever. The aristocrats talk a lot about blood, she thought. Maybe they are right, certain traits are inbred in the course of centuries. They are always talking of how this or that goes back to time immemorial. But common people weren't born yesterday either. They too had their honor, loyalty, duty, traditions—ties that span the generations.

She wanted to lift herself from her prone position and embrace her mother, but sank back. Demonstrations of affection were not needed here, nor would they be appreciated. Besides, Gervaise had already turned to other things. Where her mother's mind was, Galatée could never tell. She watched her for a while as she labored over her ironing with dull, impenetrable mien. She looked old. How much longer could she go on with this drudgery? But maybe she didn't expect more from life. Galatée caught herself as soon as the thought crossed her mind. That was the aristocrats' way of thinking, she told herself. That's exactly what they like to believe about the common people—that the people have no greater expectations, that they don't know any better and are content therefore with their backbreaking lot, meager returns, and sparse food and comfort.

It was hard to imagine that this crooked shape with gnarled arms and hands, a tangled mop of ashen hair above a furrowed brow and features made repulsive by bitterness and the mere pain of living, was once a desirable, vivacious young woman. Passion and love had brought her to this state, Galatée thought, an impetuous love of a rake for which she never stopped paying. Would she too have to pay for the rest of her life for loving a rake?

But Guibert de Mallac was not Achille Caillart. He was a gentleman. Even if he really was a thief, he was of noble birth and ancient lineage. Did that really make a difference? Besides, what did she really know about Achille Caillart, her father? Where did he come from, who were his parents? Did Gervaise know any more about him than what he was when her father caught him plundering his shop? Did she ever find out why he was driven to thievery? She would have liked to ask, but did not dare broach the subject for fear of causing her mother more pain.

Galatée's thoughts wandered back to the night of the vigil over her sister's dead body, the night her mother had spoken to her for the first and only time about the man for whom she had given up her family and exchanged a secure bourgeois existence for a life of poverty and misery, of disappointment and heartache. Yet, despite everything, she did not seem to harbor regrets about having followed her heart. He must have been quite a man, that Achille Caillart, who died in a tavern brawl on the night his youngest child, the daughter who remained unnamed, was born.

Now she was nameless once again. Antoine had given her the name Galatée, but she had never been properly christened. And what a stupid name, Galatée, sprung from a man's fantasy so he could mold her in his image, into something she now realized she was not and would never be. The arrogance! The audacity! Did he expect her to grovel at his feet in gratitude? For what? For being used in his petty game of revenge for the punishment his father received for plotting against the Crown, his harebrained scheme of deception to mock a society that had slighted him but from which he craved recognition? She never figured as anything more in his schemes than an object, a pawn.

It was then that she felt a deep hatred for Antoine de Valinquette, a hatred she was sure would never be extinguished as long as she lived. Never, ever would she forgive him the humiliations he had inflicted on her, the assault on her body and spirit. Never, ever would she forgive him for having caused the loss of their child, nor the attack against the fruit of her love she still carried. Never, ever would she forgive him for seeking to control her mind and body, both of which he thought he could bend and shape without regard for her feelings, her desires.

Her hatred for Antoine grew with every passing day that she lay on the pallet of straw in her mother's hut at the Court of Miracles. She even hated him for having taken her away from there, for the life of luxury he had shown her and which she now realized had become a necessity for her, an addiction, yet there was no turning back, no place left to go back to.

And Guibert? Did not he too use her as a pawn in his game of revenge? Did he not exploit her loneliness and longing to be loved for his own scheme to even the score with Antoine? Two little boys still squabbling over the same toys! May they both go to hell! But then the life inside her battered her with a barrage of kicks and reminded her of the passion in which it had been conceived, a passion all-consuming, beyond all measure. She tried to remember the softness of his lips, the warmth of his body fusing with hers in passionate embrace, the impatient longing that held her when they were apart, her insatiable desire for being close to him. She strained to recapture the tremor that ran through her at the mere sight of him. But now her body remained numb and stiff. She dredged the bottom of her soul but came up empty. Could it all be gone, forgotten, all that only a short while ago was the center of her being? Even his beloved roguish face was but a blur, a fading smudge.

All that was left now was this growing life inside her, the token of what once was. So even before it emerged into the light of the world, she turned to the child in her womb. It became the center of her existence, the object of her all-consuming love.

Thinking of the child invigorated her. She surveyed the squalor around her. Is this where she wanted her child to grow up, did she want to bring it up to be a thief, and if it was a girl, a whore? These were the only careers open at the Court of Miracles, besides begging while faking some deformity. Her preoccupation narrowed around the child's future, which gradually grew into an obsession to the exclusion of all else. Somehow there must be a way out, she muttered to herself.

At first, she hardly touched the food, if that's what it could be called, Gervaise urged on her. But when she was reminded that she had to feed the child or it would be born weak or even sickly, she forced down the thick gruel against a strong urge to retch.

One day she told Gervaise that she wanted to see the king.

"His Majesty, King Louis?" Gervaise asked, playing dumb.

"No, of course not. The king, whatever his name is, the man who calls himself king of the underworld, of the Court of Miracles."

"Oh, you mean King Menelaus, his real name is Pélégrin but he likes to call himself Menelaus for some fancy reason," Gervaise explained. "What do you want with him? He'll probably send for you anyway as soon as he hears about you. I'm surprised the neighbors have left us in peace so far."

"I want to make a deal with him," Galatée stated.

"A deal? What makes you think you can make a deal with Menelaus? He's the only one who makes deals around here, but never with a woman."

"That'll have to change then. A lot of things will have to change," she added, giving herself a firm, reassured tone when she saw her mother's skeptical demeanor. "Please pass the word that I wish to see him. And don't worry, everything will be all right, even better than before."

While Gervaise was gone, Galatée got up. She fixed herself up as well as she could. Since she was totally without any of her toiletries, she had to make do with smoothing her dress and hair with her hands and splashing her face with some water Gervaise had drawn that morning. She reproached herself for having fled without a thought of even the most basic feminine necessities—a comb, rouge, powder, perfume. But that couldn't be helped now, so she concentrated on how she would get this king, who was no doubt a rapacious cutthroat, to enter into a bargain with her despite the fact that she had very little to offer in the way of tribute. Well, she still had the string of pearls and some precious rings and gold bracelets she was wearing the day she arrived, a meager reserve, but her plan aimed in a very different direction and the pieces of jewelry would only serve to put him in a receptive frame of mind for the proposal she planned to put before him.

She had barely seated herself at that rickety table where all major transactions in the house of the Widow Caillart were conducted, when a great commotion arose outside in the street. Gervaise entered the hut ahead of a troop of about six blackguards who flanked a rather ridiculous figure of a man, decked out in a gaudy yellow and red checkered suit with wide sleeves and baggy pants. The seams of the entire outfit were tacked with bells so that with every step he took there was a jingling that announced his approach, prompting demonstrations of adulation and subservience along his path.

Galatée was bemused and fascinated by so much pretension, especially the red turban that crowned his head, which made his effeminate, smallish face even smaller. If he did not exactly resemble an Oriental despot, he could certainly be taken for a jester at a sultan's court.

The scene that then unfolded had something so unreal about it, so farcical—though hardly more fantastic than the pastoral games at the summer idyll at Beaupré—that Galatée was hard pressed to resist the urge to burst into laughter. But she knew it would be most unwise, even dangerous, were she not to play along. To incur King Menelaus's displeasure was not what she needed at that moment.

"Your Majesty is too kind to honor us with a visit to these humble surroundings!" Galatée rose to perform a cumbersome curtsy.

"Please, my dear Marquise, you mustn't exert yourself! The honor is entirely mine." This self-styled king approached her with studied grace and good cheer that betrayed a certain resemblance to the manners of his illustrious royal counterpart, Louis XIV, the most gracious, beloved King of France. His eyes danced about, meeting her only briefly. It was obvious from the moment he opened his mouth that he was utterly cracked. But Galatée also assessed his character as totally unpredictable, humorless, and ruthless. This man was a killer. She certainly would have to take care never to be caught in his presence with her back turned.

"I was just scolding the Widow Caillart for having kept Your Ladyship so long from us. Now that we are at last acquainted, I am most charmed indeed." He lifted her hand to his moist lips, nuzzling her finger with the oiliness of the lecher. "I can see it was well worth the wait. I hope you will feel at home at my court—greater miracles happen here than at the Tuileries. I'm Your Ladyship's ever so most humble servant."

As he straightened himself up, his sugary smile changed in an instant to a predatory, grotesque grimace, his tone went from the purring of a cat to the menacing growl of a jackal.

"What tribute have you brought for your king?" he demanded to know.

"The tribute I have for Your Majesty is worth much more than idle trinkets of gold or silver, gems or silk. Such things give you enjoyment only for the moment. I have come to offer you much more—namely, my mind. The way I see it, if we put our brains together we can conquer the world and get rich in the bargain."

The offer was apparently so unexpected and so unusual, Pélégrin's jaw dropped. His face took on a pained look as he struggled to decide what he should make of this proposition. When he had recovered enough from the shock, he burst into uncontrollable laughter that was promptly aped by the myrmidons around him.

"My dear Marquise," he began, "you must be speaking in jest. If this is a clever ruse to getting around paying the proper respect to your king, I must warn you, the punishment is death by . . ." With the flat of his hand he described a motion across his throat accompanied by a croaking sound. "I would hate to see such a beautiful, elegant neck cracked in half."

He had moved so close to her, his rancid breath almost made her faint. He began fingering the string of pearls she still wore, moving it slowly up and down her neck.

"What makes you think I make deals with just anybody intruding on my court? You must think I can be made the laughing stock of Paris, suggesting that I listen to the advice of a woman." He pulled the necklace tight around her neck, making her gasp.

"If jewels and gold are all Your Majesty desires, please, take this necklace, it's yours. Here take these rings too," she said, still gasping for air. She pulled the rings from her fingers and held them out to him. The glittering objects proffered made him release his grip on the necklace.

"Maybe we can talk of business some other time, when I shall have proven myself worthy of Your Majesty's trust," she added with as much dignity as she could muster.

Pélégrin gathered what he thought were paltry offerings. Galatée quickly assured him that there would be more as soon as her brothers returned from a foray to her former residence in the Marais. There would be a hoard of precious gifts for His Majesty. Unfortunately and inexplicably, they had so far not returned.

"I'm sure Your Majesty's network of connections is extensive, and nothing happens in this city that Your Majesty isn't privy to. Now, if I may be so bold as to suggest that your Graciousness seek to obtain news of my brothers' whereabouts, we could both reap great benefits."

"Of course," he replied, extending his chest so far the bells began to jingle. "I could mobilize my contacts around the city, which are, as Madame observes correctly, extensive, but if these cutpurses should have turned traitor then you, my dear Marquise, will hang. A pity, such a beautiful throat."

He let the back of his hand glide slowly up and down her neck. She suffered the humiliation with a shudder but did not budge. Nor did she avert her eyes from his piercing glance.

"It's the law! And the law is the law! I'll have no lawlessness around here!" Galatée did not doubt for a moment that he would carry out his threat.

"Your Majesty is perfectly justified in demanding obeisance to the law. After all, the king is the law. I realize that my life is in your hands," she called out quickly as he was readying to leave. "If I may ask Your Majesty's immense, magnanimous indulgence just one moment longer. I beg Your Majesty to lend your ear, just for a moment, to the proposition I spoke of earlier."

He turned back toward her with measured steps. Slowly he let himself down on a chair, his eyes piercing hers with the look of someone who believes himself to have triumphed in a high-stakes game.

"All right," he said. "Let it not be said that the king of the Court of Miracles has no heart or that he turns a deaf ear to the pleas of a doomed woman."

Chapter 2

GALATÉE WAS FLOATING on a sea of happiness. The rise and ebb of the travail that had engulfed her, had tossed her about like a boat without mooring, had ceased. An immense calm had come over her as she held the wrinkled, rosy little creature that had emerged from her and was bawling with elemental force.

It's a miracle, it's a true miracle, she whispered, a greater wonder than the Court of Miracles could ever bring forth. Here was the most glorious moment of her life, the moment when she discovered the true meaning of love. Yes, she had loved Guibert, but Guibert was not tied to her, not completely dependent on her, as was this creature. This was a different kind of love.

Her life went on without him. The memory of their summer of passion had already begun to wane. So much of what had been then, the people, the feasts, even their lovemaking was becoming blurred, indistinct, a distant memory, pleasant, but almost ludicrous, from another life in another world. Even at this most exhilarating moment when she held his child, she had no great desire to have him near. It was her child and hers alone.

Her thoughts were disturbed by Gervaise's not too gentle ministrations. She applied herself to scrubbing the blood off daughter's inner thighs with grim determination. Galatée had forgotten where she was, that she was still sprawled on the kitchen table in her mother's hut at the Court of Miracles where this greatest of all miracles had taken place. The labor and birth had taken only a few hours in all. A good amount of time for a first, the midwife had said. Bertrande, the midwife, had been hovering over her all the while. How this woman became the midwife nobody knew. Her qualifications came most likely from being with child and giving birth more often than anybody—she herself had lost count of the exact number—so that she knew a few things about this business. It seemed only natural then that whenever a woman's hour was drawing nigh that she should be called in to assist. In the course of time, she had acquired a competence and her calm presence alone brought comfort to the women of the Court of Miracles in their hour of anguish. Sturdy and squat, she had firm yet nimble hands that seemed to have been fashioned specifically by God for extracting even the most recalcitrant fetus from the womb.

Like most of the women of the Court of Miracles, Bertrande was more given to grunting than to availing herself of human speech. She spoke only three times during the labor and delivery. The first time was when she commanded Galatée to push, a word she then repeated with the droning monotony of a taskmaster. The second time was when she expressed herself satisfied with the smoothness of the delivery. The third time was when she placed the infant in the mother's arms and uttered with a great sigh: "It's a girl!"

Gervaise was typically blunt. "You have to take them as they come, but, I tell you, you'd been better off, much better off with a boy—boys are much easier."

Galatée did not answer. She would not let her mother's gloomy spirit spoil her happiness. Bertrande took the infant, cleaned and swaddled it.

Galatée thought again of her own arrival in this world as her mother had described it. Gervaise's love for a drunken thief that made her so despise the innocent, helpless child born to her that she would not even give it a name, maybe feeling somewhere in her inner being that a person without a name does not exist.

"I shall christen her Chantal—she will sing like a lark, soar like a lark right out of this hole!" Galatée proclaimed.

"There is nobody around to christen her," Gervaise said. "No priest has ever set foot in here."

"No matter," Galatée replied, intent on making her point to her mother. "Her name is Chantal, Chantal Dupuis. Later I shall have her christened at the parish of Saint-Sévérin, and have her name inscribed in the baptismal register, so her birth will be properly recorded."

Whether Gervaise grasped the meaning was not clear, but in the days that followed, Galatée saw a change come over her mother that was as remarkable as it was gratifying. And she quietly forgave her in her heart for not comprehending the hurt she had caused her. There was a mellowing, a softness that had shone through only once before on the night of their vigil over Guillemette's martyred body. Now it was directed toward the child, her grandchild, on whom she shed a fondness, even reverence as on a delicate gift from heaven.

Life at the Court of Miracles was communal. Privacy did not exist in this closed universe of ramshackle huts. Its ragtag denizens, thrown together by the common lot of penury, shared in the most intimate experiences of life. When the word spread that the Marquise—this is how she was known among them—was in labor, columns of women began to form around the Widow Caillart's hut. The moment Bertrande emerged in the door, signaling the completion of her task, a ghastly mob of hags pushed inside. Everybody wanted to catch at least a glimpse of the little aristocrat, if not touch it, who had been born in their midst. Nobody, not even the oldest residents, remembered anything like this happening at the Court of Miracles. It was a sensation.

Galatée, with the help of Bertrande and Gervaise, had been transferred from the kitchen table to a rather comfortable-looking feather bed that had replaced the common sack of straw. All around, the place showed a remarkable improvement, even a certain tidiness. It was still a shack of poverty and far from resembling the palace in the rue des Rosiers, but the musty air of neglect and apathy had been swept out by a fresh energy. An invigorating spirit had entered, a spirit that did not passively suffer any trick a capricious fate liked to play.

So on the very day she gave birth to a daughter, the Marquise held court. Enthroned in her featherbed, she received rows of women passing by as if it were a queen's ruelle. Though most came empty-handed, having nothing of their own to give, they freely dispensed treasures of wisdom gained from spawning the undesirables of this world. The women were especially generous with advice on how to suckle and swaddle a screaming infant into contented sleep. The Marquise, though suffering the strain of maintaining a radiant smile, accepted all graciously and with good humor.

After most of the visitors had filed out again, a small flock of women lingered, helping out with various chores that still needed to be done. Their chattering and jesting, their display of affection made clear that they were on a more intimate footing with the Marquise than the rest of the denizens of the Court of Miracles. In fact, they were all young, some barely more than fifteen or sixteen, and scantily clad. Their coquettish manner, even without men around, and their heavily powdered and rouged faces left no doubt that these were the angels of the Patron Saint Mary Magdalene, members of that ubiquitous species, the common Parisian whore.

Several months had passed since Galatée had abdicated her social throne at the Hôtel de Valinquette in the fashionable Marais and had exchanged the luxury and frivolity of the highborn and wealthy for the squalor and misery among the great unwashed of the Court of Miracles at Saint-Médard. Her survival in this underground kingdom of beggars and thieves came to depend on outwitting the wily Pélégrin, who called himself King Menelaus. So she was justly proud of an ingenuous deal she managed to coax him into and through which she had him soon eating out of her hand.

A few days after Pélégrin had first called on her at the Widow Caillart's, Galatée reciprocated the visit. With a handful of diamond studs she had gleaned from the bodice of her gown, she called on the "royal palace," a dismal, vaulted cellar in a tavern. Despite her considerable girth and a fluttering heart, she descended the worn steps into this hellish domain with a firm stride. She had come to match wits with a madman, fully aware that any sign of weakness, the slightest faltering on her part could mean her death.

"Ah, Madame, my dear Marquise, what a pleasure indeed!" Pélégrin greeted her from behind mountains of delicacies, meats and breads piled on platters set on the floor, the likes of which she had seen only at the tables of the wealthy. "What a pleasure to welcome you to my humble abode!"

He staggered up from the floor, quite obviously drunk. The aura of unreality that attached to this king spread to his surroundings and entourage, a nightmarish realm peopled by grotesque, hardly human figures. Through the shadows Galatée perceived a most bizarre apparition. On an animal skin, complete with horned head, of some indeterminate species was the recumbent figure of a woman, enveloped in purple tulle and scarlet taffeta, holding a silver goblet from which she took small, dainty sips with a look of utter boredom. Oh, God!—the thought flashed through her mind—the scarlet whore of Babylon! Had she walked into a lunatic asylum? Were the hellish surroundings affecting her senses?

"Bring a pillow for the Marquise!" Pélégrin bellowed at one of his blackguards lounging around lazily on the floor.

Spotting something dark with a long tail scurrying across the floor, Galatée described a helpless gesture toward her belly. "I'm afraid . . ."

"Yes, of course! How thoughtless of me! Bring the Marquise a chair, one of our best."

Finally, Galatée took a seat in a comfortable, upholstered chair, though she began to doubt the wisdom of ever having come to this place. Everything about it and its inhabitants was so revolting she had to suppress the urge to vomit. What a despicable lunatic, living indulgently with his whore and thugs off tribute extorted from the poorest of the poor! Yet, she knew she had no choice. She had to strike an alliance with him and the first order of business was to play along with this mock gentility under which lurked his violent, uncouth nature ready to break through at any moment. Could this man have issued from the womb of a woman?

The scarlet whore got up lazily from the horned animal skin. She ambled over and leaned against the king's arm, sizing up Galatée's rotund shape with a condescending sneer.

"You are neglecting me!" she pouted like a spoiled child unwilling to be pushed to the side. Galatée knew she had gained the woman's enmity just by being there. An unforeseen obstacle to overcome, she thought.

"Marquise, may I present my beloved consort, Ondine!" said Pélégrin, still maintaining a fake gentility. Galatée mumbled something about being charmed, while the other woman muttered something unrepeatable under her breath.

Although the thought was outrageous to Galatée, it was clear that Ondine saw her as a rival who coveted her place in the king's bed. She had to arrange a conference with this so-called king without Ondine present if she was to succeed with her business proposition. While she was still pondering how to go about this, Pélégrin himself, as if he had read her thoughts, despite his drunken state or maybe because of it, came to her aid.

"My dear Marquise, what precious gifts have you brought for my precious consort? Surely, you have not forgotten to show your appreciation for my queen."

"Why, of course. How could I have forgotten?" Galatée replied, even though she had been unaware until then of the woman's existence. She presented the diamond studs and several bracelets she had been wearing at the time of her flight from the mansion. She noticed with some dismay that the pearls she had given to the king the previous day were already adorning the Babylonian whore's skinny neck.

Ondine did not wait to be presented with the gifts. She lunged forward and swiped the pouch containing the items from Galatée's hand, then she retreated quickly, jealously hunching over it like a wild beast over its prey. Galatée had to act before she came back for more. She was sure this woman would not be satisfied once she realized how sparse the offerings really were.

"Your Majesty, there is still the matter of my proposals, which, I am sure, you will find quite agreeable and profitable."

"Yes, your proposal," he repeated distractedly, moving closer. As before, his absinthe breath made her recoil. Now his hands began to roam freely over her body.

"You got yourself nicely knocked up there," he mumbled.

"I meant a business proposal," Galatée pushed away his roving hands, determined not to seem intimidated.

"How many horses do you have running for you?" she asked.

He looked up perplexed.

"What do you mean?"

"I mean how many whores do you have working the streets?"

"Are you from the police?"

"Of course not. My proposal has to do with getting greater profits out of them. But I need to know how many we can depend on."

"Who knows exactly? The competition tries to lure them away all the time. Right now, maybe fifteen or twenty. They rob me blind and then they run off. It's a tough world, no loyalty, and certainly no gratitude."

"I know, business is tough. But tell me, how fast can you get them all together and bring them to the Widow Caillart's place?"

Ondine suddenly appeared next to them.

"What are you two plotting?"

"This is business. You wouldn't understand. Go eat something so you put on some meat," Pélégrin snapped at her. "Continue, dear Marquise, I'm all ears."

"The fact is," Galatée went on, "if you want to make money, you must offer something people want to buy. Your product has to be better than that of the competition and you have to treat them better than the competition so they won't run away. This is where you need me, making your ladies more alluring to the customers. If your whores are more attractive than those of the competition, where do you think the good citizens of Paris will take their business? Think about it."

Pélégrin thought hard, squinting his eyes and furrowing his forehead, although he was not quite sure what it was he was supposed to think about. One thing he was sure of was that this Marquise was a clever woman and if he handled her right, she could be very useful to him.

"I'll have them at the Widow Caillart's this afternoon." They concluded the deal with a handshake, and she prepared to go.

As she was about to ascend the stairs, she turned back once more.

"By the way, a small initial investment will be required. But don't fret, the return will be thousandfold."

There goes a woman, thought the king of beggars and thieves, the likes of which one didn't see very often at the Court of Miracles. She had a stir of excitement about her that intrigued him. Things would not long remain the same around here, he was sure. He immediately set about giving orders to his men to round up the whores. As for Ondine, he had no time for her that day, or that night.

The women who were being herded across the Widow Caillart's threshold that afternoon made Galatée's heart ache, so pitiful was their appearance. Unkempt and unwashed, they carried with them a body odor so foul it stung the nostrils. From their haggard bodies hung rags so tattered and torn, they barely afforded any protection from the elements. Some were so young they had not even developed breasts and buttocks. The lack of proper food may well have stunted their growth.

Others appeared worn and shriveled, though they may not have been older than Galatée herself. A lifetime of spreading their legs to violent abuse had twisted their bodies into the withered shapes of desiccated, wind-battered, barren trees. Galatée stared at them in horror. A terrifying chill gripped her heart. These creatures, hardly human, with bad teeth or none at all, thin strands of hair and dull, hollow eyes deep in their sockets struck her as the living dead. Did she recognize herself, her true self, as she might have been, should have been?

"These must be retired," she said to Pélégrin, pointing to several worn hags. "Surely your Majesty can find something else for them to do to earn their keep."

"I see your point, dear Marquise," he said obligingly. "They don't bring in much anyway. None of them bring in enough. If I had to depend on them, I would starve to death. I frankly don't understand your interest in these heaps of trash. I should have sold the sluts a long time ago. But I'm a sentimental fool. I'm often told that I have a heart of gold."

"Of course they don't bring in much!" Galatée raised her voice indignantly, forgetting all caution. "Just look at them! How can they bring in anything in such condition? If you don't feed them, clothe them, clean them, who would want them but the dregs who have nothing to spend?"

"The Marquise is very temperamental!" he said with a nervous laugh, while Ondine hung on his arm, her eyes trained on Galatée.

"I don't know what her game is," Ondine whispered in her gallant's ear, "but you'd better watch out, she is too clever."

"You keep your mouth shut. I don't need a woman's advice and this one I'll have eating out of my hands before long."

Galatée meanwhile went on to suggest that maybe he should invite the women to eat right then. "From what I saw before, you have enough to feed an army. Once the ladies are well-fed, then we'll get to the next stage of my plan. Remember, it's all a matter of an investment sure to bring great returns for both of us."

In the week that followed, the Court of Miracles buzzed with activity as never before. The news spread with the speed of the Spanish disease: the Marquise was cleaning up the whores and the king was fattening them so they would rake in a better price on the market.

Galatée felt as if she was in the cattle business, leading young calves to slaughter. But in the end, they would all benefit. She cringed at the girls' manner of speaking and tried to clean up their language as well as their bodies. In rare quiet moments, between hours of instructing the girls in personal hygiene, applying powder and rouge, arranging their hair, and supervising the seamstresses to fit them for more attractive attire, doubts about what she was doing would creep in. Her conscience was assuaged somewhat by the thought that these girls would be in the street anyway, only in worse condition, neglected and wretched, as had been her sister, the martyred Guillemette.

But whom was she fooling? It wasn't a charitable impulse that made her care for these creatures. She did it for profit, to save herself from having to sell her own body. It was all for her own gain and the gain of that parasite Pélégrin. This so-called king still held the power of life and death over her and the child in her womb. So this was a compromise she had to make with her conscience.

By the end of the second week, she had convinced herself that she was performing a great public service. Prostitution in Paris was a vice that would go on no matter what she did. She came to see herself as the benefactress of fallen women, promoting their welfare and improving their condition. She knew it was still they, and not she, who had to go out and face the night alone. It was they who had to fend for themselves on the front line. Alone they had to bear the brunt of violence and abuse, of degradation and humiliation. What she could do was instill in them some dignity, a will to resist the worst, and a sense of their worth in a human as well as a pecuniary sense.

Gervaise took a jaundiced view of the constant traffic, of prostitutes traipsing through her house. Too many painful memories attached to their sight. The image of her favorite daughter's mutilated body was again haunting her. Galatée's assurances that what she was doing would somehow redeem Guillemette's death did not make much sense to her. What she was able to grasp was that there was money to be reaped, so she gave in and let her house become the headquarters for the fallen women of the Court of Miracles.

Besides, she really had no say in the matter anyway. Since the return of this prodigal daughter of hers, that songbird without a name, her dwelling was hardly her own anymore. The best she could do was lend a hand in her disgruntled way.

One day, as Galatée was curling the hair of one of the girls, in keeping with the fashion among the beau monde that season, a shriek from her mother made her look up. There in the doorway, with a down featherbed slung over his shoulder, was Prosper.

"Where the devil have you been?" Galatée shouted.

"I brought you your bed," was all Prosper said as he threw it down. His head turned in all directions in amazement at the strange activity in his mother's hut, which apparently had been transformed into a boudoir in the two weeks since he had set off with Gaston for the Hôtel de Valinquette.

"Where are my other belongings? And where on earth is Gaston?"

"At the Châtelet."

"What? Gaston or my belongings?"

"Both."

"You mean to say you were caught by the police?"

"Monsieur de La Reynie, the police lieutenant, wants to speak to you."

"What for? These are my belongings. He can hardly say that I was stealing from myself."

"If he wants to speak to me, let him come here. I'm in no condition to wander about the city streets." Her defiant stance hid a sudden sinking feeling.

A curious crowd, attracted by the sight of Prosper coming down the alley with a featherbed over his shoulder, had by now assembled at the Widow Caillart's door. To hear the Marquise talk about the police coming to the court caused a considerable stir.

"Don't worry!" Gervaise assured them. "My daughter does not know the laws of this court. But she will learn. No policeman will set a foot in here."

Turning to Galatée, she said, "No officer of the law has ever entered the domain of the Court of Miracles. It's an unwritten law that goes way back to a time before anybody remembers, but it's the law."

Galatée conceded she had spoken without thinking. She promised she would do nothing that would violate the laws of the Court of Miracles.

"Why does he want to speak to me?" she turned back to Prosper.

"He said something about a deal. A bargain, that was the word he used. He sends you the featherbed as a token of his good will. But Gaston has to stay until you come."

What kind of deal could the police lieutenant possibly want to make with her? After some thought, she decided to send a message through Prosper instead of going herself.

"Would you carry a message to the police lieutenant for me?" she asked Prosper. He nodded. She debated whether she should write or have Prosper deliver the message orally. The decision was made for her since no writing utensils or parchment were to be had anywhere. So at the risk of having her message garbled, she instructed Prosper very carefully what to say and made him repeat it to her until he finally got it fairly right.

"First you must tell Monsieur de La Reynie how immensely, be sure to use the word immensely, how immensely flattered the Marquise de Valinquette is—don't forget the title, these people are very keen on titles—that a man as busy and important as the police lieutenant should want to take the time to meet with her. Unfortunately the Marquise has fallen on some hard times and has nothing to wear befitting such an occasion. No, forget that. Just say that the Marquise would appreciate receiving the rest of her belongings so that she can appear . . . No, forget that too. Simple is best. Would he be kind enough to release her belongings so that she can prepare herself in a manner befitting the occasion."

"Couldn't I just say you need your stuff to do yourself up to meet him?" Prosper ventured.

"All right, put it any way you want, but get me the things that belong to me—everything you took from the mansion, dresses, accessories, especially the jewelry, the whole lot."

Prosper returned the next day, not with much, but enough for Galatée to transform herself once again into a lady of beauty and fashion, ingeniously arranging the loops and ties and laces of her garments to accommodate her round belly. Such finery was a shell that could be put on and taken off at will. Who was she really? She thought as she stared into a cracked looking glass in her mother's kitchen. For the moment, that was a question she herself was unable to answer.

"Monsieur de La Reynie says he is keeping the jewelry. He wants to hand it all over to you in person," Prosper explained when she rummaged feverishly through the bag but couldn't find what she needed most.

In the midst of preparations for her foray into the city, the king of beggars and thieves and the scarlet Babylonian whore suddenly breezed into the Widow Caillart's hut. They were disquieted by gossip that Galatée was going to make some deal with the police lieutenant, who had already gained a reputation for being the enemy of the little people of Paris. His vow to clean up city did not bode well. Among the wretched denizens of the Court of Miracles, the conviction had quickly taken hold that the deal the Marquise was about to make with the police lieutenant had something to do with this clean up business.

Galatée assured Pélégrin that she was only going to the police to see what she could do about Gaston's release. But it was not easy to allay the thug's suspicions, especially with the leery Ondine clinging to his arm like a vine. Galatée sensed that this woman placed her in a precarious situation once again. At last an idea came to her and she chided herself for not thinking of right away.

"There are certain objects of not inconsiderable value that have fallen into the police lieutenant's hands," she explained. "If we play it right, the profit could be substantial for all of us."

Words like "substantial" and "profit" never failed to ignite the spark of greed in Pélégrin's eyes.

"Well, you mustn't keep the gentleman waiting, then. And besides, a summons from a powerful, distinguished man like the police lieutenant cannot be ignored. Who knows, we may be able to gain a friend. I'm sure he will succumb to Madame's charms entirely. Be sure to commend me to his good graces. Don't let us detain you any further. Be gone now! Shoosh!" he added with a limp flap of the wrist. Ever the king of fools.

The passage through the gate of the Court of Miracles into the streets of Paris was a journey from darkness into light. Even the poorer quarters of the city had an air of brightness absent in the troglodyte realm she now called home. But she had no time to bemoan the misery of the world. She was not out to better the world, only to assure her survival and that of her child. And for that she would do anything—almost anything.

Prosper and Galatée slowly walked along in silence. A strange pair, the hunchback and the pregnant lady. She felt he was a decent sort, simple-minded but decent. She wondered what kind of a man he might have become had fate lifted him from the Court of Miracles and dropped him in a place where he would have been raised as a young nobleman. But these were idle thoughts to keep her mind from brooding over what it was that had gone wrong at the Hôtel de Valinquette. She would find out soon enough.

At the police prefecture, Monsieur de La Reynie received her at the door, eager and polite. Prosper was asked to wait in the hallway while the police lieutenant graciously led Madame the Marquise into his office, apologizing for the spartan furnishings. He assured her of the immense pleasure her kind visit gave him. The Marquise sank exhausted, and not all too ladylike, into a fauteuil.

A long silence ensued. The police lieutenant positioned himself opposite her on the edge of his desk. He studied her face with unconcealed curiosity. Then he cleared his throat a few times and came straight to the point.

He was sure, he explained, that she was aware that Monsieur the Marquis de Valinquette was a prisoner at the Concièrgerie, charged with assaulting an officer of the King's law. The charge against him was attempted murder, but might well still change to murder—the victim was not actually dead, but was hovering between life and death, and one feared the worst, one always did in such cases. Whether his deputy, Lucien Lefèvre, survived his ordeal or, God save his soul, was destined to succumb to the grievous wound Monsieur the Marquis' blade inflicted on him and be called into eternity, the punishment for assailing an officer of the King was incarceration at a fortress or—here he paused a moment to magnify the ominous nature of what he had to say—a minimum of ten years of service on His Majesty's galleys.

A silence laden with doom hung in the air when he had finished. He searched her face for the appropriate reaction. Galatée had only a faint notion of what it meant to be condemned to toil on the galleys. To work like a galley slave was a common enough expression, but what life was like on His Majesty's ships she could not picture. Nevertheless, the police lieutenant obviously expected her to be awed by his pronouncement. So her eyes opened wide, struck with horror, and a fearful gasp escaped her lips.

Satisfied, Monsieur de La Reynie slid off his desk and soothingly took her hand in his, patted it in a fatherly fashion, and assured her that as grim as matters looked right now, all was not lost. In fact it was she who held the key, it was in her hands to save her husband, the Marquis, from a fate worse than death.

"There is a very small matter Madame can do. And Madame will be serving her King at the same time." She looked eager enough to hear him out. But he chose his words and tone very carefully to make it seem that what he was asking was but a trifle.

"All Madame has to do is write a letter, an invitation so to speak, to a certain person known to Madame, requesting him to come to Paris."

"And who is this person?" she asked in as innocent a tone as she could muster.

"The Count de Mallac."

Outwardly a slight, almost imperceptible twitch went through her body. But inside a storm rattled every cell of her being.

"And if I were to agree, and the Count were to accept my invitation?" she asked calmly after a brief consideration.

"The Count is a dangerous criminal, Madame, a man wanted in the entire Kingdom of France. No doubt his punishment would be severe. I can assure you, Madame, His Majesty, Louis XIV, will show himself most generously disposed toward those who assist in the capture of this enemy of the Crown."

"The gallows, then," she said. He nodded.

"With your help," he tried again, "your husband will go free. The Crown has no quarrel with the House de Valinquette. You may resume your life in the society of the Marais. No need to hide out in this thieves' nest, the Court of Miracles, so unworthy an abode for a woman of Madame's station."

Galatée was barely able to contain herself. This man was making a lot of assumptions. Whatever Gaston and Prosper had told him, he obviously thought her stay at the Court of Miracles was involuntary. But what did she care what he thought, the fact was that he placed before her an impossible choice: Guibert's life for Antoine's freedom. And this wretched little bureaucrat thinks he can use me as bait, cast me in the role of Brutus and Judas in one, the angel of death of the father of her child, it raged inside her.

Did she owe anything to Antoine? Not really. She had saved his life and he had saved hers. They had used each other to mutual advantage. She played the role he assigned to her masterfully. They were even on every score except one, and that she would never forgive him, never.

If Guibert was really the criminal this bureaucrat made him out to be, she understood better than anybody how he had been pushed toward such a career. To serve the King—a king who had never done anything for her or her people—she should betray the man she loved?

"And if I refuse?" she said softly.

This was apparently not the answer the police lieutenant had expected.

"But Madame . . . I don't understand. How could you even . . . think . . . of refusing?"

"I refuse for the very simple reason that you are asking me to betray the father of my child."

She rose, tossing her head back in defiance.

"Good day, good Sir."

"Not so hasty, Madame."

La Reynie had quickly recovered from the shock of this unforeseen turn. Obviously he had misjudged this woman, but he was not one to give up so easily. She had confirmed his hunch that she was the bait that would hook the Count de Mallac, and one way or another he would succeed.

"Monsieur the Marquis has no other bargaining chip. If you won't come to his aid, there is nothing anybody can do to prevent his utter doom."

"Monsieur the Marquis will have to fend for himself then, won't he?" she replied coldly.

She realized that she had made an implacable enemy. But how could she possibly yield to his demand? Certainly she did not want to see Antoine suffer. Any other request she would have considered, on any other matter she would have been accommodating. But the choice was Guibert for Antoine, which to her was no choice at all.

The stage was set for a duel with this police lieutenant, a dogged battle of wits. The opponents glowered at each other; the mask of gentility had dropped, and all trappings of politeness stripped away.

"Then there is also the matter of the burglary at the Hôtel de Valinquette in which Madame is implicated." La Reynie played this next trump card with calculated nerve. "I could have you arrested for complicity and have you and your accomplices locked up for a long time."

"Since it was my own house from which the two gentlemen removed certain items at my request, this can hardly be construed as a burglary," she replied in an acid tone. "I should also appreciate receiving the rest of my belongings which Monsieur saw fit to use to lure me to this interview."

"I am sure the Marquis de Valinquette will see the matter differently. But we shall find out about that later. Meanwhile, there is also the small matter of solicitation . . ."

"What do you mean? In my condition? Don't make me laugh!"

"I don't mean Madame herself. But the King's law also forbids the promotion of vice among others. The law condemns those who profit from such transactions as much as the perpetrators, perhaps even more."

This man seemed to have spies everywhere. The only course open to her was to ignore his implied accusation. Never admit anything to a police officer unless the truth can be to your advantage, that was the lesson she learned right then and elevated it to a maxim. This exchange was obviously ending in a draw. Neither party was getting what it wanted, neither yielded an inch. She realized she was not likely to get her jewels, but he would not get his letter either. There was nothing further to be gained here. She turned toward the door.

They looked at each other one more time, both infuriated and eager to be done with the interview. The verbal battle had weakened Galatée's physical condition. She staggered. La Reynie, fearful of the possibility of having a mess on his hands, quickly sent her on her way.

Bent by defeat and dismay, Galatée leaned more heavily on Prosper during the arduous march back to the thieves' lair. She had remained unyielding, yet she felt crushed on almost every count. She had also failed to gain the release of either Gaston or her jewels.

And this was not the end of her troubles. How would she face Pélégrin empty-handed? How would she allay his suspicions that she had struck a deal with the police lieutenant that might undermine him, the king of the Court of Miracles?

Chapter 3

MONSIEUR DE LA Reynie was not a man lacking in compassion, but he was adamant in not letting personal feelings interfere with the discharge of the duties of his office. He was foremost a man of staunch devotion to public order and to upholding the King's laws. In fact, to Monsieur de La Reynie's mind the law was the King and the King was the law. His loyalty and allegiance belonged to one as much as to the other.

In the case of Antoine Maximilien Barca Dupuis, Marquis de Valinquette, Seigneur de Chazeron, his compassionate strain had at first inclined him to search for extenuating circumstances. He had taken a bourgeois' liking to a man of noble birth, who had fallen on hard times because of—Monsieur de La Reynie was convinced of it—the treachery of a perfidious friend and a dissolute wife. La Reynie did not take lightly the defeat the Marquise had dealt him in the matter of the Count de Mallac. A desire now burned in him for restitution. He was not a vengeful man, but a humiliation such as this could not be left to stand. Somehow he had to get even, someday the Count de Mallac would be his prized captive.

Meanwhile, the mills of the King's justice ground on. The Marquis de Valinquette was brought before a tribunal of magistrates and charged with attempted murder, dueling, deadly assault on an officer of the King, and leaving the scene of a crime; that the assailed man was alive and recovering from his wounds counted for little in these proceedings. The trial lasted less than a day. The verdict was a foregone guilty.

Monsieur de La Reynie found himself in the peculiar position of being the one to present the charges and of introducing a witness whose testimony mitigated the circumstances. Gaston Caillart attested to the Marquis' kindness and generosity. He described the events of that fateful gray morning as an unwitting entanglement, an adventitious embroilment. These were not the exact words of the witness but rather those of the court clerk's report, which summarized a bit less colorfully the gist of Gaston's testimony. Let it not be said that the magistrates were unmoved by such a vivid, honest testimonial to the Marquis' character. As a result, the statutory sentence of ten years on His Majesty's galleys was reduced to seven.

Monsieur de La Reynie was pleased with himself. At least he had been able to spared the poor devil—for this is what this flower of the French nobility had now become in his eyes—a few years in the pit of His Majesty's galleys. He was therefore in a splendid mood, whistling a jolly tune when he entered the Marquis' cell at the Concièrgerie to bid him adieu.

"Have you any news of my wife?" were Antoine's first words.

"My dear Marquis," the police lieutenant said in a solicitous, fatherly tone. "It may be in your own best interest to put Madame out of your mind."

"You have seen her? Tell me, how is she? Is she well? Oh, God! What will become of her now?"

The man's abject despondency over a woman who would not do a small gesture to save him gnawed on Monsieur de La Reynie's upright heart.

"This is not an easy task for me, good Sir," he began, "but, believe me, you had better realize that the Marquise . . . well, Madame the Marquise has returned to her own kind. And she did so apparently of her own will and without regret."

"What do you mean? That's impossible!" Antoine's demeanor went in a flash from puzzlement to illumination. "Oh, my God, what have I done? What have I done? She will never forgive me now!"

"Oh, no! You mustn't reproach yourself!" It was La Reynie's turn to be deeply puzzled. "What you must realize is, she is quite comfortable, not at all distressed. You see, Monsieur, you did a wonderful thing for this young woman, made her a lady, gave her everything a woman could want. Oh, yes, I know, I know the human heart, I am a connoisseur in such matters, so to speak, one has to be, in my position. Oil and water do not mix, but water will always run to water, a river will always beat its path to the sea, nothing can hold it back. It's where its destiny lies. So it is with human beings, they too will seek their own kind, seek out those among whom they are most at home."

"What are you saying?" "Monsieur, as you know, I had occasion to make the acquaintance of the brothers Caillart, one of whom spoke so warmly for Monsieur, as well he should. But they are still thugs. They were arrested for breaking into the Hôtel de Valinquette. As it turns out, the burglary had been instigated by Madame herself. No, there can be no doubt, she told me so herself. I realize how upsetting all this must be to you. They were to bring her clothing and jewelry, various personal items, and a featherbed. So obviously she plans to stay at the Court of Miracles . . . in her condition no less. But you mustn't worry, all personal items were released to her, including the featherbed. The jewelry will be kept in a police safe until Monsieur's return when he may claim what . . ."

"Why? What right do you have to confiscate Madame's jewelry?" Antoine was in a mood to wring this little bureaucrat's neck.

"Actually, I made Madame an offer, I was willing to strike a deal with her. Had she accepted, the jewels would have been restored to her. But, alas, she refused the offer," the bureaucrat defended himself.

"What kind of deal was that?"

"A very small favor indeed in exchange for Monsieur's freedom and the jewelry. But she was quite adamant. In fact, if I recall her words correctly, she said, Monsieur the Marquis will have to fend for himself."

La Reynie stopped to see the effect of his words. But Antoine seemed unshaken by this revelation of his wife's presumed treachery. What he wanted to know was what that small favor was.

"A very small favor, indeed, and we all would be better off today. But Madame was most obdurate. It would have spared us all a lot of pain." Seeing Antoine glowering at him, he quickly added: "I beseeched Madame for assistance in bringing the Count de Mallac to Paris and to justice."

Silence. Antoine stared at the little man with dull, vacuous eyes. It was impossible to tell whether he was looking at him or through him. Unable to predict what the prisoner might do next, La Reynie edged toward the door. At last, Antoine sank onto the cot and buried his face in his hands.

"You must try to forget her," La Reynie felt called upon to console him.

"Forget her? Monsieur, you don't understand." Antoine straightened himself up. "You must get the jewelry to her, or she is lost. You don't seem to know the customs of the Court of Miracles. Do you have any idea what they will do to her, this rabble, if she is unable to satisfy their greed? Maybe they have killed her already. Not to present the monster presiding over that miserable realm with gifts is an offense punishable by death. Believe me, these thugs think nothing of stringing up a man or a woman."

"Monsieur seems quite familiar with the barbaric customs and proclivities of this underworld."

"She saved my life. Twice she saved my life. First she nursed me back to life from the wounds I received at the Battle of Saint Antoine—yes, Monsieur, it was a long time ago—and then she helped me escape the rapacious claws of the king of this so-called Court of Miracles. She was only a child then, a pitiable child with a heart of gold . . ." Antoine's voice trailed off into a world of memories, where Monsieur La Reynie could not follow.

The hollow tread of soldiers' boots on the rough stone in the hall outside announced that the time for Antoine's departure had come.

"You must get the jewelry to her. You must promise, Monsieur, as a last request from a doomed man who has lost all reason for living. Believe me, it is a matter of life and death."

Monsieur de La Reynie wanted to tell him that Madame had accommodated herself quite comfortably to this realm of the canaille that she even seemed to have made a profitable pact with the king of pimps, cutpurses, and cutthroats by entering the pimping business herself. But he held back and promised to do what he could. The man suffered enough, holy fool that he was.

As much as the Marquis' request went against his grain, the police lieutenant was a man of his word. He handed the cache of jewels over to Gaston and sent him on his way with the admonition to relate to the Marquise her husband's predicament. He should be sure to convey to her that his, Gaston's, testimony had shortened by a few years the severe penalty imposed on the Marquis. And not least, he should explain that the jewels were being restored to her at the request of the Marquis, whose kindness and good will toward her was apparently boundless in spite of everything.

Monsieur de La Reynie was tempted to embellish the story a bit, paint the great remorse the Marquis felt for whatever it was that he had done, but since he was not given a mandate to interfere in the private affairs of this most peculiar couple, nor was he privy to the details of what had transpired between them, he decided against it. His sixth sense told him that the whole affair had resulted from human passions and it would be a thankless job for a third, in this case fourth, party to become entangled. He contented himself with urging Gaston to impress the Marquise with her husband's undying devotion.

Gaston was determined to add his own bit, he assured him. He might be a lowborn hustler, but he was not without a sense of honor and loyalty, and besides, he genuinely liked the Marquis.

"Fauvette is mad to run after that bandit Mallac," he muttered to himself. "Somebody ought to beat some sense into the wench."

Well, it was too late for that now. But she should at least know of her husband's suffering for her sake.

Galatée never did hear any of the paeans of praise to her husband, neither from the police lieutenant nor from Gaston. Nor did her jewels ever reach her hands.

Gaston was a decent sort, no worse and perhaps even better than most petty thieves in Paris. He faithfully held to a thief's code of honor and was loyal to his family and devoted to his mother. Unfortunately, he had inherited his father's penchant for carousing and gambling. Weeks behind bars, without the possibility of putting his hands on either dice or drink, had stirred his hunger for a little action. And what harm could there be if he dropped in at a tavern on the way back to the Court of Miracles for a few rounds?

A man whose hands and pockets contain only a few sous runs no more than the usual risk of getting his throat cut, but a courier with a leather pouch bulging with precious stones attracts the dogs like a bitch in heat.

Dice and drink had sealed the fate of Achille Caillart on the night his wife lay in labor. Dice and drink also sealed the fate of Gaston Caillart. No witnesses were ever found among the roughnecks who packed the tavern where he made a last stop. Like Achille's, Gaston's death remained unredeemed. The police did not investigate. Why should they? Lives like his were snuffed out, crushed under callous blows, every minute in every part of the city. A brawl, a robbery, a vendetta, an accident, a duel, a murder, whatever the cause of death, life was cheap among the little people. Only the killing of people of status and means warranted retribution. Among the poor, only mothers and wives bore the sorrow.

A ghastly moan rose from Gervaise's throat, her horrifying lament rent the air and lingered there for an agonizing moment. Then she sank back into her world of silent suffering, dull, languid, acquiescent in an incomprehensible, unkind fate. She left it to the last two of her children to tend to the bludgeoned body left at her doorstep by unknown hands. Fate had beaten her down one time too often. She no longer had the strength to go through the motions of the funerary rites that were meant to alleviate the pain.

Galatée applied herself to the task of washing and dressing the body as best she could. Instead of prayers, a stream of curses flowed from her lips, she knew not how and from where. Her face was grim and hard, but she had no tears. Prosper clung to her side, whining pitiable little sobs like a pup that had lost its master.

By some ominous trick of fate—or was it a human drama eternally reenacted on the stage of life—the scene of the night of her birth was repeated and pursued her like a malediction. Maybe she had been too hasty, too precipitate in giving up the comfort of the Hôtel de Valinquette. There was nothing in this primordial cave for her but pain and misery. But then what was it she expected to find? A mother's consoling love? She should have known better. Now it was too late. Antoine had been taken away and the house and garden had been sealed by the King's agents.

La Reynie had given her a chance to get out of this hell and she had rebuffed his offer without a moment's thought. How stupid, how incredibly stupid you are, she told herself. What for? For a man who pretended to love you, who insinuated himself into your heart and bed, just so he could get his revenge for some childish quarrel?

And Antoine? Don't you have any feelings for Antoine? It was in your power to save him and you refused. So what if he hurt your pride? Yes, it was rape. But you had it coming to you. He is your husband and you, you are an adulteress.

Galatée mopped the sweat from her forehead, furiously trying to wipe away the thoughts that swarmed around her, stinging her over and over. She had to turn her mind away from the past, away from Antoine, away from Guibert, to the present, however unpleasant this present might be. She had to put all her energy into one thing: surviving. She would not stay in this pit forever. From now on, she would live only for her child.

"Prosper," she said resolutely, "do you know how to pray? The least we can do is pray for his soul, if we can't get a priest to come and sprinkle holy water and light the incense—that's what they do in Christian society. Somehow it helps, so I'm told."

"I don't know," Prosper sniffled. "There is a fellow who had been taken in by monks as a child—maybe he knows something."

"Well, can you get him? I'd like this to be a solemn funeral, for your mother's sake." Why could she not bring herself to say "our" mother?

Galatée was contemplating Gaston's features while waiting for Prosper's return. She noted his strong chin that gave him the appearance of a solid character. She suddenly pictured him as a gentleman; yes, he too could have been a gentleman had he been raised in a different environment. Why not? Then she reproached herself for her flights of fancy when the door flew open without a bang. A young woman rushed in, moaning and clucking, completely beside herself. She gave off an anguished shriek when her eyes fell on the body on the table. She flung herself on the corpse, sobbing, quaking, and covering it with wild kisses as if that could bring it back to life. Her tears soaked the stiff face.

So there was another woman who mourned this miscreant. Galatée realized how little she knew about her brothers. It never occurred to her what lives they might have beyond standing around street corners, picking pockets, and smuggling the occasional contraband into the city.

"You are not welcome here, Fabrisse!" Gervaise's voice rang out shrill and hard. "Get out of my house!"

The woman addressed as Fabrisse slid off the corpse. She walked up to the old woman, threw herself on the floor in front of her, and seized the hem of her skirt, looking up at her from this humbling position with imploring, crazed eyes.

"Please, let me at least help you bury him. I don't ask anything else," she pleaded.

"What else could you be asking? What else could you take that you haven't taken already?"

"All I did was love him. I made him happy. Is that so bad?"

"Love, happiness!"Gervaise disdainfully spit on the floor, just missing the woman. "How many children did all this love get you? Five? All going hungry, all wallowing in dirt, and they will all end up just like him."

Gervaise turned away from the woman and lumbered toward the stove, her refuge from the world's unbearable woes.

"And you, you will end up like me," she muttered.

A long silence. Fabrisse wept and Galatée weighed whether she should put in a good word for the woman. At last Gervaise, without turning her back, threw her hands up in the air and grunted, "Let her help you, Fauvette. She is Gaston's paillarde."

But there was nothing more to do for the moment, except hold a vigil. Galatée took the woman's hand in hers and together they waited.

Prosper returned soon with a scarecrow of a man. You should have stayed at the monastery, you'd surely be fatter then, Galatée thought. At least he seemed to know some Latin, useful for the occasion. They were joined by a handful of sinister figures who lent Prosper a hand in sewing the body into a sackcloth. Then they lifted it onto their shoulders and marched down the alley to the graveyard, the place where all miracles came to an end.

The scarecrow chanted something that might have been a *Te Deum* or a *Dies Irae*, though it sounded more like mumbo jumbo—but then who in there knew the difference? Galatée trotted along with Gervaise, Fabrisse followed with her brood. Along the way the procession swelled with more mourners. Gaston had been a popular fellow. The king and his consort were nowhere to be seen. Pélégrin was said to frown upon sad ceremonies.

Later, when they were alone, Galatée asked Prosper about Fabrisse. He kept his voice low, shielding his mouth to make sure they were not overheard. Gervaise had opposed all of Gaston's women. She did not want him to have children, was the reason she gave him. The world was too miserable a place for children, she would say.

"Do you have a woman?" Galatée asked him.

"Oh, no!" Prosper chuckled with a nod at his hump. "They don't like a cripple like me."

"I can't believe that," protested Galatée. "You mean you have never . . . ?"

"Only with the whores. For free, they know I can't pay."

They laughed together, the carefree laughter of children. For a moment she felt carried back to a childhood she never had. Putting their heads together, exchanging secrets like two conspirators—such simple, pleasant warmth they had never known.

Life at the Court of Miracles was never carefree, not for children or for adults. Galatée took care of her "girls," fixed their hair and made up their faces to create the illusion of beauty. They were allowed to go out into the street only after passing inspection, which concluded with the collection of a hefty portion of their earnings. Galatée made sure Pélégrin would get his share at the exact time each week. Some of it though went to the women and toward paying the seamstresses who were kept busy with mending the flock's wardrobe. Galatée's cut was spread thinner with the addition of Fabrisse and her brood to the household. Prosper without Gaston was a lost soul, and with the Breton connection in limbo, the smuggling business had ground to a halt.

As Galatée's time was approaching, Fabrisse did more and more of the work around the house. She had grown so big that the women predicted twins. But she knew better. It was just one rambunctious Breton rascal. She was so convinced that it would be a boy, she never even thought of a girl. The surprise only heightened her joy.

Some time after the birth of her child, Galatée paid her weekly homage at the court of the so-called king of Saint-Médard, which meant she delivered the requisite tribute. She descended the steep stairs into the cellar. One of the blackguards told her to wait, the king was in conference and could not be disturbed. The place knotted her stomach with intense queasiness as always. The Babylonian whore sat idly on the horned hide. Galatée paid no attention to her. She was nothing more to her than the rest of the ghoulish furnishings of the place, a worthless piece of bric-à-brac. However, as she looked around for a place to sit down, she noticed an intense glitter about the woman, more than usual. The sparks radiating from her head and neck were of such brilliance, Galatée overcame her repugnance and drew closer.

"You like my jewels, eh?" Ondine intoned.

"I certainly do," Galatée replied. From the woman's neck sparkled an array of rubies and emeralds she had not seen on her before. They were set in a fashion not common among European craftsmen. There could be no mistaking, the necklace was exactly like one of the pieces Antoine had brought back for her from his travels in the New World. In fact, she was convinced that the Babylonian whore was decked out in her most cherished gems.

Chapter 4

LIFE UNDER THE Iberian sun and later in the comfort of the Hôtel de Valinquette had blurred her memory of what winters could be like at the Court of Miracles. The rambling walks in the snow, the sleigh rides snug inside thick furs and wool blankets, warm meals, resplendent fireplaces, those were her still vivid memories of winters past. But the misery of drafty huts and threadbare clothing that afforded little protection had long faded.

The winter following her return to her mother's house was among the bitterest in living memory, or so the people said, as they huddled in their draft-swept tenements, chilled to the bones, no warmth to be found anywhere. Present miseries always wipe out the miseries of times past, the present always appears more distressing, more devastating than anything that had gone before. For the inhabitants of the Court of Miracles, the present was all that mattered and it was always the worst of times—past and future had no existence.

In Galatée's mind, the very notion of opulence and comfort had begun to fade like the once-brilliant colors of a garment that had been scrubbed and left out in the sun too long. How to get from today to tomorrow, she and her child, was the goal toward which all her energy and guile was now being funneled.

The transformation was gradual, imperceptible at first. Then one day she noticed she had gotten into the habit of thinking of herself as La Fauvette. Gervaise and Fabrisse called her by this improvised name and so did everybody else around her, except for those who referred to her as La Marquise—but that was more mockery than respect. The name Galatée, at any rate, had lost its meaning and was certainly out of place.

And so it happened that the encasement around her began to rupture, as if disturbed by a force stirring inside. Cracks and fissures began to appear and finally it crumbled like the shell of an egg being hatched. And she felt free. Free like the little bird for which she had been named, the bird that twittered in the gutter and had never been captured by anyone.

In the world of the Court of Miracles, of course, freedom only existed as an illusion or a mad dream. Only a bloodsucker like Pélégrin could afford to ape the gallantry and flattery of the beau monde. What she learned very quickly during her first winter was that the daily struggle to keep from succumbing to hunger and disease, of finding ways not to be eaten by frostbite or fall victim to the treachery of fellow travelers in this abject universe of uncertainties, was no less restricting than the rites and regimens governing the world of aristocratic glamor. Were she given the choice to return to her former life, she would again choose the illusion of freedom at the Court of Miracles.

This is what she told herself during the long nights when she lay awake, ever defiant and proud, curled up with her child pressed against her heart inside the one piece of luxury left to her from her former life, her featherbed that was beginning to get lumpy but was still luxury to her. Privation would not break her spirit.

But privation took its toll nevertheless. The weeks and months dragged on in relentless monotony, and by the time a few sparse rays of spring licked the glum alleys of the Court of Miracles, the transmutation of Galatée, on the surface as well, was complete. She was no longer an outsider, but a daughter come home. There would be other winters, other seasons as the years passed, each one a challenge to face and overcome.

In time it fell to her to preside over the Caillart household, which had more than doubled with the addition of Fabrisse and her five. Gervaise had wilted even more since the murder of her favorite son. She withdrew almost totally into her grunts by the stove. On rare occasions one might catch a flare of warmth animating the frozen features, but such moments were reserved for her granddaughter Chantal and sometimes for the smaller of Gaston's offspring. Most of the time she was bent over the wood stove, stirring a pasty gruel or a turnip soup, the main staples of the family meals.

All practical matters were left to La Fauvette. It may have been beyond Gervaise Caillart's comprehension to fathom why it was that this prodigal daughter had returned, why she had given up all she had; at least she had acquired a certain horse sense while she was out in the world that served them all well in their daily struggle. She no longer grumbled about La Fauvette's insistence on taking in Fabrisse and her flock, making the already cramped quarters even tighter. After all, the children were blood of her blood and flesh of her flesh. Kindred blood was still a stronger bond than enmity between two women.

La Fauvette had given up trying to engage her mother in any but the most perfunctory conversation. The longing for another heart-to-heart talk as on the night of Guillemette's death remained unfulfilled. Although nothing could change Gervaise's lack of emotive expression, one change did occur to everybody's surprise.

Gervaise suddenly seemed to have turned to religion. Not that she had been an irreligious person before; she had simply preferred to wrestle with her God one on one, without the intercession of priests and monks. Nobody knew at first that she was going to church when she left the Court of Miracles three times, sometimes four times, a week and returned with pieces of dry bread and cheese. On one occasion she pulled a string of chitterlings from her apron. She proceeded carefully to slice them up so that each salivating mouth around the table got an equal share. Even if the Church dispensed little balm for her embittered soul, it was no sin to help the fat-bellied priests gain points in heaven by accepting their charity, she explained.

As all things, good and bad, must come to an end, and season follows inexorably upon season, the time came when the harshness of winter gave way to the clement air of spring. Life at the Court of Miracles was never easy, the struggle for survival never ceased entirely, and each season had its woes. But with the warmer weather the streetwalking business picked up again. The whores did not forget La Fauvette's kindness toward them in meager times nor her courage in standing up to the king of beggars, thieves, and pimps, for whom cold winds, ice, and snow were no reasons to slow the traffic in flesh.

It was also time to pay another visit at the king's lair. After an unusually long wait, during which La Fauvette and Ondine eyed each other like two cats, Pélégrin appeared.

"How comforting to see your Majesty looking so absolutely splendid!" she exclaimed with such sweetness she got nauseated.

"My dear Marquise, you are too kind!" protested Pélégrin, who had not the slightest inkling that his leg was being pulled. "You look quite marvelous yourself," he added, his gaze drawn to the leather pouch she held out to him.

"How do I know you are not cheating me?" His tone changed suddenly to a vulgar squeak as he opened the bag to count the proceeds.

"You don't really. You just have to trust me as I trust you to take care of the girls," she said with a sarcasm that pricked his ears.

"How do you mean?" he asked, puzzled and alarmed.

"I mean that three girls have died, two starved to death and one was murdered. In addition, one has gone mad and has been hauled off to La Salpêtrière for putting the torch to a nobleman's house, who she insisted was her father. Most of the others are infested with vermin and disease they catch from their customers. It's a wonder they bring in anything at all."

"What would you have me do? It was a harsh winter for all of us. But things will get better," he said, trying to squirm out of this with commonplace references to the weather. But she was not yet done with him.

"It was a harsh winter for *some* of us," she said, her gaze fastened on the diamond diadem sparkling atop the Babylonian whore's stringy hair. She had given the matter of her jewelry nary a thought in the past months. Now she was intrigued by the mystery of how her finest bijouterie came to adorn this slut. Could she be the police lieutenant's mistress? Men's tastes in women were often difficult to fathom, but surely a man like Monsieur de La Reynie would not keep company with such scum. Or could it be that Gaston had withheld a few pieces from the police and sold them later?

But when would Gaston have had the opportunity? And what was it Gervaise always said? Her boys may be thieves, but they don't steal from the family. And she certainly wouldn't get anything out of those two low lives in front of her. Any way she looked at it, the mystery deepened and there was only one man who could shed some light on it. It was time to pay another visit to the rue Neuves des Capucines.

That visit, however, had to be postponed, and when it finally did take place it was under drastically altered circumstances. What she failed to sense, on her way home from her visit to Pélégrin's lair, were the fateful clouds gathering overhead. She could not know that at the very moment she was struggling to understand what in God's name the king's police lieutenant could have to do with maggots like Pélégrin and Ondine, that same police lieutenant was presiding over a council plotting the doom of the underground kingdom of Saint-Médard.

But all this was still in the future. The surprise awaiting her at her mother's house literally swept her off her feet and effaced all her earthly concerns about jewelry and the daily drudgery of existence at the Court of Miracles.

La Fauvette flew toward him, kissed his face with abandon, eagerly breathed in the sweet, beloved aroma of his body, and died in his embrace. But the moment of reckless exhilaration quickly gave way to more rational consideration. She pulled away and held Guibert at arms length.

"Have you completely lost your mind?" she cried, still a bit breathless from the first flush of excitement. "Do you know the danger you are in if you are seen in Paris?"

"For you my beloved, I'll brave any danger. I'll stake my life."

"I'm ready to faint," she said, leading him to sit at the table.

It was an odd scene. Gervaise grunted over her pots by the stove. Fabrisse rocked one child and watched the flock at play on the floor. In another corner, arranged as the "boudoir," a group of women fussed over each other's hair and makeup. At the table in the middle of the cramped quarters sat La Fauvette, haggard in her faded, dusty dress, her dark-ringed eyes trained on the well-dressed gentleman whose handsome, flushed face and bright eyes lit up the gray surroundings.

"Did Antoine do this to you?" he demanded to know.

"Do what to me?" she replied, genuinely confused as to his meaning.

"Toss you back into this pit. Is this how he finally got his revenge?"

"You may let go of that notion and all that talk of revenge," she said brusquely. She no longer had any tolerance for poses. Something was rising between them at this moment, separating them, something chilling and insurmountable.

"Antoine did not toss me into this pit, as you put it. I left him and that whole make-believe world of the Marais of my own will. I left because this is where I belong and because I had enough of the games you aristocrats play. I was sickened by the artifice, the pretensions, the hypocrisy, the fawning, the decadence, the debauchery, all at the expense of the people, of course. Look at these people around here, they are more dead than alive because they have nothing to eat. For each morsel they put into their mouth, they have to degrade themselves."

"Are you accusing me? I thought we understood each other better than that." He looked estranged and furious.

"You are one of them," she insisted. "How are you different? Just because you lost your patrimony? Is it not your all-consuming goal to regain what had been your family's privilege for centuries? Aren't you using every means at your disposal, even robbing and stealing? You now have the distinction of being the most infamous criminal in the Kingdom of France! If Monsieur de La Reynie gets a whiff of your presence in Paris, and he has an excellent nose, your life is over and done with."

She had talked herself into such a rage, the others present in the room did not dare raise their heads. Guibert looked at her aghast. Who was this woman speaking like this? He felt he had never seen her before.

"This is a fine welcome!" he finally said, jumping to his feet. "All this time I had only one thought, one longing—to be with the woman I love. Finally, I can no longer bear it, I come here—and now this, recriminations, reproaches, accusations, insinuations. I don't recognize you. Next you will hand me over to the police lieutenant yourself, maybe the two of you even plotted to set a trap to capture the Count de Mallac. You seem such good friends."

"He's no friend of mine. But be assured that he has no greater ambition than to bring the Breton bandit to justice, as he puts it." She did not dare look at him. Suddenly she felt very self-conscious about her appearance and she wished that he would not look at her. "Just go away, go back where you came from. Go where it is safe."

"I'm not going without you. I have come too far to go away empty-handed. It is cold at night in that fortress by the sea. The reason why I want to get it all back is to present it to you, without you there is no purpose in anything I do."

No! No! a voice screamed inside her. She couldn't let him do this to her. It was all a lie. She would not permit him to touch her soul with the sweet allure of his lies. She felt the ground shifting under her and she was choking with fear of losing control over her destiny. Then suddenly something occurred to her. Something puzzled her and helped her regain her presence of mind.

"How is it that you came looking for me in this place? How did you know where to find me?"

"Gaston told me."

"Gaston told you? When and how did he do that?"

"Maybe it was the hunchback, whatever his name is. What difference does it make?"

"The difference is that Gaston is dead and Prosper never told you anything. I think you had no idea you would find me here, you came with the sole intent of starting up your smuggling operation again. All this talk of your career of crime being for me—you expect me to believe that? Your feud with the Crown is your private affair, leave me out of it. And now go away."

"I won't go until I obtain the answers to some questions. First, why you are behaving in such a hostile manner? Why do you make me out to be a liar? Even if I did not know of your presence here at the Court of Miracles, I came to Paris to see you. I risked my life to see you, not for some business matter. What have I done to deserve this treatment? If I have wronged you, I want to know. I'll beg your forgiveness right here on my knees."

She closed her eyes tight, banging her fist wildly on the table, as if to drown out his words. Leave me alone with your sweet contriteness, she begged him silently. I'll tear my heart out before I give in.

"Excuse me for saying so, but you don't look well," he said when she finally calmed herself a bit. "Living in this hell must have twisted your mind, you are not yourself."

"I'm quite myself, Guibert. This is me, this is who I am, and this is where I come from and where I belong. This is my family, my mother, my brother, my sister-in-law, Gaston's widow and her children, my nephews and nieces, these prostitutes are my friends, and I am ever so much happier here than I was in the company of dukes and duchesses."

"And which one is our child?" he said suddenly.

"What does it matter?" she averted. How foolish of her to think he had forgotten about the child.

Before she was able to turn away, he took her face into both hands and forced her to look him in the eyes. "Now tell me again it does not matter which one is my child. I can easily find out for myself. But I want you to tell me."

She stared at him, her lips pressed together defiantly.

"Why are you doing this to us?" he whispered.

"Because I want you to leave Paris and forget about all this. I don't want you to die." He let go of her and she turned away.

"Chantal, come here and say hello to Monsieur the Count," she said, after another tearful silence.

She raised her hands to her eyes to blot out the sight of Guibert holding the little girl. She could not bear to see him beaming at the child. She could not bear the child's delighted chatter. But what she refused to let her eyes see, she knew in her heart. Nobody can resist Guibert's charm, his bright smile. Oh, God, what was she doing! She could not permit herself to succumb, not now, not anymore, never again. She owed nothing to anybody. She had risen once before from poverty and she would do it again, and this time alone, through her own will, her own hard work. She had been convinced that she did not need a man—and now this. She felt her blood seethe with maddening longing and desire. She wanted him to go away and she wanted him never to leave again. She wanted him to leave her alone and never be alone again.

When at last she allowed herself to look at him again, she knew that he was not leaving. Eagerly she awaited the night and yet dreaded it.

Privacy did not exist in the Widow Caillart's abode. A small area in the shape of an alcove, although such a description would have been too fancy for the corner where her featherbed was stowed, was her private quarter. Nobody questioned the propriety that the Count should be sharing her bed. It was the best accommodation in the house and a man of his status could hardly be expected to sleep on a sack of straw on the floor. Chantal was transferred to her grandmother's berth so she would not run the risk of being crushed by the two lovers whom only an act of God could have torn asunder.

In more sober moments, La Fauvette continued to urge him to leave Paris. La Reynie had his spies everywhere, as she had learned, and he might already be informed. Though it was not likely that the police would violate the unwritten law, sanctified by centuries of custom, that no officer of the law would set foot inside this precinct, a real danger lurked right inside the court, and that danger was Pélégrin.

"I should be afraid of such a lizard?" Guibert laughed. "I deal with scum of that sort everyday. You really needn't worry yourself."

"But you are intruding on his domain. He is an unpredictable madman. He can't be trusted."

"I certainly don't intend to trust him, but I do intend to intrude on his domain. His way of interfering in my business has long been a great irritant to me."

"You will end up like Gaston and I won't shed a tear," she sulked like a child.

"I don't believe that either. But tell me what happened to Gaston."

"He was murdered, we don't know how it happened. But I do have a hunch that Pélégrin had something to do with it. And maybe even La Reynie, despite his reputed integrity."

She related the story of the bungled burglary at the Hôtel de Valinquette, her brothers' arrest, La Reynie's confiscation of her jewelry, and her subsequent interview with him, though she left out his attempt to blackmail her into luring him, Guibert, to Paris and her refusal to comply.

"The question is how did the pieces get from the police lieutenant's desk to the neck of Pélégrin's whore? It would not surprise me to find that Pélégrin is a police spy. I cannot shake the feeling that Gaston was somehow involved. He must have been released from prison right after Antoine's conviction."

"That may be so," Guibert replied pensively. "The jewels were probably stolen. The question is how and where. I think your hunch is right, it must have something to do with Gaston's death."

Guibert knitted his brow and tapped his fingers; something was storming through his brain. There was a side of him she had not yet discovered, perhaps the real Guibert, the thoughtful, serious Guibert, a side he liked to hide under a frivolous mask of charm and sarcasm. She had caught a glimpse of it on the night Antoine came back from the war, but that had been a fleeting moment.

"Here's what I think happened," Guibert said after a long pause. "While Antoine is held prisoner, La Reynie talks to him, out of courtesy—aristocrats do get special consideration as you know—or to make a deal with him. Probably both. Antoine will help him capture the notorious Count de Mallac and in return he will go free. After all, the murder charges are really trumped up since there is no real murder—the victim is recovering nicely. But Antoine refuses. He wants me dead, but that is his affair, he would not betray an old friend to the police. La Reynie tells him of the treachery of his wife, the break-in she instigated at his mansion. The police have secured the contraband and are holding it for him. Antoine is outraged and orders the items restored to his wife, the rightful owner. La Reynie, a man of integrity himself, respects nothing more than magnanimity. Antoine is shipped off to the galleys and the police lieutenant releases Gaston and makes him the courier of the jewels."

"You are giving both Antoine and La Reynie, two men who do not wish you well, a great deal of credit," La Fauvette said. His story made no sense to her. "And why would Antoine, of all people, give a centime about whether I live or die?"

"I know him better than anybody, better obviously than you." He took her hands into his and made an impassioned plea for the honor of the man who had wanted him dead for the sake of the woman whose hands he was holding. "Consider it for a moment: Antoine may be a coward, a fool, a coxcomb, and a preening fop, but he is not treacherous or dishonorable."

"You didn't think his conduct so honorable at the battle of Saint Antoine. Why else would you harbor a grudge against him for all those years?"

"That is true, but I was wrong. You convinced me of it yourself. God knows I should have known better. Passion has a way of clouding a man's vision."

"So, let's presume you are right. Antoine is this honorable man who not only goes to the galleys rather than betray a friend but who still looks out for the welfare of an unfaithful wife. Where do we go from here?"

"There is nothing we can do for Antoine, at least not for now. And Gaston is dead. But you can go to Monsieur de La Reynie, charm him, try to find out what you can, whether my hunch is right. If yes, you demand your jewels back. The police must arrest Pélégrin for murder and robbery. Simple, isn't it?"

"Not so simple, my dear Guibert," she rejoined. "I don't think La Reynie will fall for what you call my charm. Our previous encounter did not exactly end on a cordial note. And besides, why should the police waste time worrying about the death of one Gaston

Caillart? Dogs like him die in the gutter with their throats slashed everyday in this city. No policeman will set foot in this place to make an arrest in any case."

"If you are correct, then we have no recourse but to forget the whole affair." The anger in his eyes made her shudder. "Since there is nothing left for me to do here, I shall leave for Brittany tomorrow. My horses are at the inn La Vieille Forge at Neuilly. I shall wait there for you and the child for three days."

"You are ordering me to come with you?"

"No, I'm not ordering you, I'm merely saying that I shall wait for you for three days. The rest is up to you. You are free to take or leave the offer."

That night, their last night together, Guibert was distant and lost in thought. They did not make love. But she did not mind, she was too happy, for she was now certain of his love. Yes, she would join him at Neuilly and never leave him again, come what may. As she sank into a deep sleep, the image of a picturesque, ancient fortress on a rocky coast mingled with visions of eternal bliss and lovemaking.

Yet as she lay awake later during the night, more realistic considerations entered her thoughts. Guibert's view of Antoine, in spite of everything, intrigued her. What about herself? Did she make Antoine out to be a demon to assuage her own guilt? The bitter taste of shame collected in her mouth, and she tried to force her thoughts onto a different path, to Gervaise and Prosper, Fabrisse and the children, to Arlette and all the filles de joie in her care. She rehearsed the words she would use to say good-bye. Strange, it would not be easy to leave them. But she owed it to her child to take her to a better place.

Then more doubts. Was it really a better place? What would life be like as the consort of the Kingdom's most notorious bandit? Would she ever cease fearing for his life? Would she be condemned to sit by the window, staring out to sea, waiting, holding endless vigils year in, year out, as had been the lot of the Mallac women for centuries?

Images and questions bombarded her brain like shooting stars in the night, only to dissipate just as quickly. She was too happy to give herself over to brooding.

In three days, perhaps even sooner, she promised as they bade each other adieu. Neuilly, Auberge de la Vieille Forge, she would not forget, she would be there. Only a few things needed to be taken care of. What could possibly come between them now except an act of God?

Was it an act of God, the hand of divine providence, or a caprice of fate? La Fauvette had no time to ponder the question in the upheaval that shook the Court of Miracles like a seismic tremor. She had made all the arrangements for her departure. Gervaise suffered her embrace in stony silence. Fabrisse and Arlette held on to each other, weeping as if their friend had been condemned to the stake. They promised to follow exactly what she told them to do in all matters.

And then there was Prosper. She wanted to take him with her, but who would be there for Gervaise? Not that he did much good. His mother had never expressed anything but contempt for this misshapen soul. Some day she would come back and take them all away, she promised herself, although in her heart she knew she was just indulging in fantasy to still her own anguish.

All the good-byes and tears, the good wishes, the admonitions, last-minute advice, embraces in the end proved premature. At the hour she was to set out for the rendezvous at Neuilly, the tocsin rang out at the Court of Miracles with elemental force, jolting the inhabitants from their uneasy slumber in their squalid huts, and catapulted every man, woman, and child out into the streets. Only a fire or an imminent invasion of the city could have occasioned such ear-shattering peals.

La Fauvette's first thought was that a blaze must be sweeping through the court, and she feared becoming trapped in the labyrinthine tangle of alleyways. She grabbed Chantal and with Fabrisse herded the children out into the street. Gervaise and Prosper followed behind, carrying a few belongings. Outside they saw Arlette beating a path toward them through a churning human mass.

"Stay close together!" La Fauvette called out. "Everybody take the hand of a child."

The human wave swept relentlessly toward the entrance gate, only to surge back in a sudden shift of the tide. There was such howling and roaring, La Fauvette strained in vain to catch a snippet of information. It was clear that the turmoil was not caused by a fire, for there was no smell of smoke and the pitchforks, brooms, and sundry clubs with which the riffraff was suddenly arming itself signaled a different sort of danger entirely. The tide rolled once again toward the front gate.

"Hug the sides of the houses so you won't get trampled!" La Fauvette shouted to Fabrisse. "I'll go and see what is causing all this commotion."

She boxed her way through to the front where a determined rabble was pressing against the bolted gate, shaking their makeshift weapons, and emitting bloodcurdling cries. The object of their threats was apparently a formation of several squadrons of armed troops—Swiss sappers, soldiers from the Maréchaussée, Royal Musketeers, men from the town watch, and policemen—training cannons, muskets, arquebus, blunderbuss, a whole arsenal of weaponry, at the gate.

At the head of this formidable force stood none other than Nicolas de La Reynie, gesticulating, raising his voice above the frightful din in a vain effort to quiet the raging animals trapped inside the cage. At last, La Reynie ordered a series of salvos fired into the air. With the fading of the explosions a tense, anxious silence descended. Monsieur de La Reynie, flanked by officer Lucien Lefèvre, who looked as good as new though he limped slightly, stepped up to the gate, so close they might easily have intercepted a swipe from a pitchfork.

The police lieutenant spoke in a calm, fatherly manner. His Majesty, King Louis, wants only the best for all of his beloved subjects, he declared. Nobody would be hurt if everybody did exactly as told. On order of His Majesty the King, from this day forward, the Court of Miracles would cease to exist, he proclaimed.

"As you can see," Monsieur de La Reynie declared, "you are surrounded, resistance will only provoke a bloodbath. My men will blow a hole into the sides of the wall that surrounds your court. You then have thirty minutes to clear the area before it is razed to the ground. The last fifteen stragglers who are caught inside will be shot on sight."

La Fauvette had heard enough. She weaved her way back through the crowd. The blasts that cracked the mud walls of the Court of Miracles sent her into a panic. In an instant a terrible stampede would break loose. Fortunately, Fabrisse had done exactly as she had been told and everybody stood pressed against the buildings, their hands locked in an iron chain.

"Stay where you are and don't move!" she cried, folding her arms around Gervaise, who was holding Chantal, to shield them against the tearing, thundering herd in search of an escape route. Within a few minutes it was all over, the alleys and shacks lay deserted.

The brood of the Widow Caillart looked dazed and perplexed like the sole survivors of a terrible disaster.

"What are we going to do?" wailed Arlette.

"We are going to leave through the front gate. We won't flee through a hole in the wall like thieves in the night. I won't play Monsieur de La Reynie's game. Let him dare fire a shot!"

They had gone a few paces when their attention was attracted by whimpering nearby. A woman, tattered and torn, crouched in the mud, sobbing uncontrollably.

"You cannot stay here," La Fauvette told her, "the soldiers and police will be here any moment. They will shoot anybody they find within the compound."

"I don't care. I'd rather die." The woman lifted a smudged face toward La Fauvette. Blood streamed from her brow. She obviously had been beaten.

"Oh, my God!" La Fauvette cried. "It's Ondine, the king's scarlet whore of Babylon!"

No words were necessary, nor was there time for explanations. She could well imagine what had happened. King Menelaus had probably been the first to flee through the wall, if he did not clear out earlier that night.

"He took everything from me, every piece of jewelry," Ondine lamented.

"What do you expect from such a louse?" La Fauvette replied. "You'd better join us now if you don't want to get shot."

Outside in the square near the gate of what was the Court of Miracles of Saint-Médard, the last kingdom of beggars and thieves and worse, Lucien Lefèvre reported to Monsieur de La Reynie that the area had been cleared and was ready to be razed.

"They disappeared so fast through the wall, we couldn't even pick up any stragglers," he laughed.

"That's just as well," La Reynie said, self-satisfied. "We didn't really want to shoot these miserable creatures. Now let's remove this gate and burn down the dwellings. I'd rather not know what disease and vermin are breeding in there."

One fusillade demolished the iron gate. But when the dust cleared, a sight presented itself that those who witnessed it at first took for a mirage, a phantasmagoria. Out of the rubble staggered a tattered band of women and children and a hunchback. They grimaced as though they were emerging from a lifetime in an underground cavern into the unaccustomed blaze of sunlight.

It did not take Monsieur de La Reynie long to ascertain the identity of the woman who was marching at the head of the band, a child in her arms and a featherbed slung over her shoulders. He recognized the unmistakable, defiant gait of the Marquise de Valinquette. But as she came toward him, his mouth fell open, so aghast was he at the sight she presented—a once charming woman now in torn and patched rags, disheveled and unkempt, strains of knotted hair falling over a haggard, dirt-encrusted face.

"Monsieur de La Reynie, what an immense pleasure!" The voice was still the same, the same mellifluousness sprinkled with a dash of sarcasm so one never quite knew whether one was being flattered or ridiculed. "You really shouldn't have! To think Monsieur went to all that trouble to arrange this long-overdue rendezvous!"

"Madame, I promised that I shall make an example of all stragglers and have them executed on the spot."

"Aren't you now in a real quandary? You will have to shoot women and children so that the world won't doubt that Monsieur de La Reynie is a man of his word. I certainly would not want to be in your shoes, Monsieur."

"You will be spared on condition that you reveal the place where the Count de Mallac is hiding. We know of his visit, but unfortunately we were not ready for this action in time to catch him in the sweep. But we know he is somewhere on the outskirts of Paris and I am sure Madame can lead us directly to him."

La Fauvette remained perfectly stiff. Nothing in her demeanor betrayed the firestorm his words were igniting in her. She always knew that this La Reynie had spies at the Court of Miracles, but the information he had could only have been obtained from someone very close to her. She cast a glance around over the small horde, resting on each one probingly.

"No, you needn't worry, my informant is not in this party."

"You know very well my answer to this preposterous demand," she said coldly.

"Madame seems unaware of the utter debasement of her position."

"On the contrary, I am fully aware of it," she replied. "You see, Monsieur, I have nothing to lose. You have seen to that. If it will enhance your reputation, kill me and those near me, if you must."

"Madame's game is quite transparent, but I am not about to take the bait. And besides, what have I to do with your situation? That, Madame brought on herself with her obstinacy."

"Monsieur de La Reynie only poses as the friend of the people," she said, turning from La Reynie to Lucien Lefèvre, "but he is really in cahoots with that bloodsucker Pélégrin who calls himself King Menelaus and who, of course, made off with a fortune last night. He apparently knew well in advance what was going to happen today at the Court of Miracles."

Monsieur de La Reynie's face flared burning red, his neck swelled visibly; he resembled a truculent bull.

"May God forgive me, but this insolent woman has asked for her punishment. I shall have you chained and whipped. Nobody, but nobody casts aspersions on the honesty and integrity of Monsieur de La Reynie, the servant of the King of France!"

Bristling with indignation, he called for his horse.

"Sappers!" he thundered as he mounted. "Begin your work! Erase this hell hole from the face of this city, the face of the earth! Monsieur Lefèvre, get this riffraff out of here! To La Salpêtrière with the whole devil's brood and God have mercy on that guttersnipe should she ever cross my path again!"

The Marquise followed him with her eyes as he sped away. I must have touched a raw nerve of truth, she thought with a satisfied smile.

Chapter 5

"THE COURT OF Miracles is burning!" "The Court of Miracles is burning!"

From the entrails of the city the cry whirled up, surged along the banks of the river, spread its wings over the faubourgs, and swooped down again to meander through the outlying villages. Along the way, people nodded, praised the Almighty and his deputy, the most upright of men, His Majesty's lieutenant of the police. Let him root out the devil's brood, they said, the nest of thieves, the lair of vice and depravity so honest folk can rest peacefully in their beds at night.

"The Court of Miracles is burning!" Delirious excitement swept through the populace far and wide. Artisans put down their tools, shopkeepers closed shop, the people took to the streets and celebrated. Monsieur de La Reynie was the hero of the hour, hailed liberator and protector of all good people. The festering boil, the scum of the earth had finally been excised, eradicated, from the city.

Jubilation rippled beyond the walls of the city and soon engulfed the entire Ile de France. Thousands gathered on the hillsides around the city. They stood entranced as they watched the pillars of fire and smoke blacken the sky as if they witnessed the hand of God at work over Sodom and Gomorrah. Few considered that what they saw going up in smoke was only the notorious enclave, which few had ever entered, with its miserable huts and taverns. The denizens of this foul underworld kingdom—the riffraff, ruffians, thugs, blackguards, cutthroats, thieves and robbers, beggars and whores, the decrepit and the maimed—were now dispersed over the rest of the city and would carry on as before their eternal struggle to scrape out a livelihood.

But there was one man who gazed on the billowing spectacle in horror. From the heights of Neuilly, outside the Auberge de la Vieille Forge, Guibert de Mallac stood and watched, paralyzed by indecision. Should he plunge back into the city no matter what. What was his life worth should he lose her?

"We've already stayed in this place too long," objected his companion, one Jacques Brunat, a notorious bandit from Poitou who went by the name "Coupe-Cheveux" for his habit of helping himself to locks of hair from those he robbed on the highways. He had come from an "expedition" through Picardie, having split off from a band of looters to accompany the notorious Count de Mallac to Saint-Malo and a secret council of the kingdom's leading crime lords.

"First it was three days," Coupe-Cheveux grumbled, "now it's already five days and now Monsieur the Count even wants to go back into the city?"

Coupe-Cheveux made up with excited hand movements what he lacked in verbal agility. Quite obviously his was a subordinate position to Guibert's in the hierarchy of thieves, and he knew his place.

"Let me at least go with you," he pleaded when he saw Guibert determined not to leave before he found out what had happened to his lady love.

"And get us both hanged?" Guibert replied. "What are the chances of your mug being spotted?"

"Probably not as great as yours, since I've never been seen in these parts."

"Well, in that case, you might even prove useful."

At the moment when the two companions were making their way from the heights of Neuilly toward the city, Monsieur de La Reynie was receiving Lucien Lefèvre's final report concerning the evacuation and eradication of the Court of Miracles at Saint-Médard.

"And the Marquise?" said La Reynie when his subordinate had finished. "She is well?"

"As Monsieur ordered, she and her family have been quartered at La Salpêtrière."

"Lefèvre, you are the man best acquainted with this peculiar case. I'm putting you in charge of keeping a close watch on the Marquise. I don't want any harm to come to her. Also make sure word of where she can be found gets around. Something tells me the fox is not far and will come back for her."

He punctuated this last statement by waving a pointer at Lucien as if to impress him with his impeccable bloodhound's instinct.

"Mark my word, the Count de Mallac will come back, and when he does we shall be ready. He'll walk right into our trap."

Lucien Lefèvre did not presume to contradict his superior though the lieutenant's smugness evoked his repugnance. He stared straight ahead in the best manner of the obedient soldier. Privately he wondered about this model of a public servant who never referred to members of the nobility without their titles even if a nobleman was a wanted criminal like the Count de Mallac or even in the case of the Marquise de Valinquette, a noblewoman of some dubious pedigree. Maybe this was what it took to make the perfect public servant, a sense of propriety and unerring respect for one's "betters," which, of course, in this particular case was stretching it a bit far.

In a flash, Lucien Lefèvre saw his own future before him and was unable to fend off a shiver of distress. For the first time he felt that the life of a policeman was not enough to still the hunger that had driven him from the boredom of provincial life to the capital where he had started his career as the King's retriever of corpses from the river. As he descended the steps of the Châtelet, where the police prefecture was housed, with some difficulty—the Marquis de Valinquette's rapier had left him with a permanent pain that caused him to limp—he was possessed of a sudden desire to take stock of his life.

He had the distinction of being the only public official who had ever set foot inside the Court of Miracles. The beautiful face of the mutilated body he had placed on the kitchen table in the Widow Caillart's hut had never ceased to haunt his dreams. It had been on that day too that he had first become aware that the blind and lame girl from the Pont Neuf was neither blind nor lame. By what bizarre stroke of fate this wretched waif became years later the beautiful Marquise de Valinquette, whose husband was now sentenced to the galleys as a consequence of a bloody encounter with a rival in the early morning fog of a baleful November day that had left him, Lucien, crippled was almost too much for him to contemplate. But somehow, he concluded, fate had seen fit to intertwine his life with that of this odd clan.

He maneuvered his way through the familiar streets as best he could. A sudden urgency to reach the women's hospice at La Salpêtrière goaded him on, a sense of destiny perhaps.

July had never been more oppressive. A sweltering chunk of stagnant air held the city in a stranglehold, squeezing the last drop of energy from the pores of the languid Parisians. Lucien arrived at the fortress-like compound of La Salpêtrière, just outside the city's ramparts in the Faubourg Saint-Marcel, dripping sweat and panting from exertion. Still puzzled by what it was that propelled him forward with such irresistible force, almost beyond his control, he passed through the gate of the graceless structure. As an officer of the King's police, he was admitted without delay by the gatekeepers. By order of His Most Christian Majesty, King Louis XIV of France, the gunpowder factory and arsenal had been converted into a domicile for women of the great unwashed, whose sight outside in the open air was an affront to proper society. Into the jumble of all those already packed into this den of despair—the beggars and prostitutes, mendicants and thieves, paupers, foundlings, and orphans, cripples of every description, epileptics, the insane, the malformed, the blind and the lame, those afflicted with scurvy, venereal disease, and the king's evil—was tossed the scum from the Court of Miracles.

Lucien lumbered through the narrow aisles, holding a kerchief over his nose to fend off the sting of the pestilential stench that permeated the air. His lungs revolted against the assault from the putrefaction created by the bodily excretions of hundreds of moldering women. The admixture of excrement, piss, and menstrual flow commingling with the saltpeter that still stuck to the dank walls produced a stench, unalleviated by any sort of ventilation, potent enough to reek to the high heavens; but, alas, there was no sign that the heavens were stirred by this human cesspool.

Gradually his eyes adjusted to the murk of the cavernous hall, dimly lit by a few stray rays of sunlight that squeezed through the narrow crenellations in the walls. His eyes wandered up and down the rows and rows of bunks populated with the refuse of humanity. He was ready to despair of ever finding the object of his search in the chaos that reigned in the crowded, narrow aisles. Gaining her attention by calling out her name was impossible since he did not have enough lung power to rise above the deafening din of the unearthly cacophony of bawling and shrieking, wailing and moaning, insane laughter and cackling, squabbling and bickering. But just then, a fortunate coincidence came to his aid in the form of a cloud of down feathers gliding through the air to the squealing delight of filthy, half-naked children chasing after them.

When he finally had overcome the last obstacle, a gauntlet of snatching, greedy claws lunging at him, claws he had to unhook from his skin and clothing, he came upon a spectacle that was as droll as it was bizarre. There on the floor sat the Marquise de Valinquette, looking as if she had been tarred and feathered and uttering the most vulgar curses even as she wailed piteously. The curses were apparently directed at a bunch of toothless crones, perched on a canopy like cackling hens, holding up fingernails as long as a griffin's talons. They peered down on their victim, licking their chops and squealing at the Marquise's vain endeavor to stuff the feathers back into their casing.

"Thinks she can play the fine lady around here, this trollop with her featherbed!" This remark was apparently directed at the visitor, but Lucien was in no mood to humor the demented crones. He gave them a good poke with his club whereupon they quickly fluttered up and beat their retreat.

"That was very gallant of you, Monsieur Lefèvre." The Marquise's voice had regained some of its more ingratiating quality though she was still seated on the floor flanked by Fabrisse and Arlette who, just a moment ago, had been hovering over her, trying to sooth her spirits and lending a hand in the daunting task of feather gathering. Nearby sat Gervaise, with vacuous eyes, and Ondine, with a face marked by dark rivulets and eddies of tears.

"But quite unnecessary," she added.

"We are perfectly capable of taking care of ourselves without hollow gestures of pity from the police," the Marquise stated imperiously.

She rose from the floor, proud as a queen. If she was aware of the ridiculous sight she presented at this moment, covered as she was from head to toe with little feathers that clung to her tenaciously and resisted her repeated attempts to wipe them off her face and clothing, she betrayed no sign of it.

"What business brings you to us?" she continued at her haughtiest. "A message perhaps from that most august and illustrious personage, the hero of Paris and the entire Kingdom of France, Monsieur de La Reynie?"

"As a matter of fact, Monsieur de La Reynie has expressed his particular concern for the welfare of Madame and her family and has instructed me to see to it that nothing is wanted." Lucien had rehearsed the words a dozen times along the way, but the delivery was not totally convincing. The storm they provoked was, therefore, not a complete surprise.

"You mean to say," the Marquise began slowly, heaving a deep breath as she geared up for the onslaught, "you mean to say that Monsieur de La Reynie steals what is mine so I'm reduced to poverty, then drives us into the street, burns down our home, puts us into this living hell, this stinking snake pit, this . . . this devil's hole crawling with vermin and muck, packs us in with imbeciles and lepers, and who knows what, and now this same Monsieur de La Reynie sends you to make sure we want for nothing?"

Her voice cracked as it reached the upper registers of indignation. Her hands on her hips, her gaze bored into him like daggers. If looks could kill, poor Lucien Lefèvre would have dropped dead right at her feet.

A tiny plea arose nearby. "But he's only following his orders. You mustn't blame him."

"You stay out of this, Fabrisse!" the Marquise hissed without taking her eyes off the officer of the law.

"But you're being unfair!" Fabrisse insisted, this time more forcefully.

The Marquise decided to ignore this challenge to her authority for the time being while she was still coaxing Lefèvre into an answer.

"I don't understand what Madame means by the accusation that Monsieur de La Reynie stole her possessions." Lucien seemed genuinely dumbfound.

"I guess there is no reason why he should have taken you into his confidence," she said in a more conciliatory tone. She recognized that maybe it would be better not to kill the messenger but rather to draw this man over to her side. He seemed well enough disposed and could be a potential ally.

"I see you have not heard the story of Madame de Valinquette's gems, some of them very valuable, mind you. Monsieur de La Reynie confiscated them, but somehow they ended up adorning this creature over there, who was not always as pitiable as you see her now. She has a quite glorious past as the consort of the king of beggars and thieves, one accursed snake named Pélégrin. I'm sure you must know about him. Somehow the jewelry passed from Monsieur de La Reynie's hands into Pélégrin's and on to her neck. By some strange coincidence, this king disappeared and the jewelry with him, leaving this wretch bleeding in the gutter. The snake disappeared on the night before Monsieur de La Reynie's brilliant attack on the defenseless fortress of the Court of Miracles. What do you make of this, Monsieur Lefèvre?"

"I really don't know anything about this. I know him to be a very upright man, Monsieur de La Reynie, and above reproach as servant of the King of France," Lucien stuttered, confused and flustered. He knew La Reynie to be a tyrant, but a thief?

"I have no reason to believe that he had anything in mind but your welfare when he dispatched me to this place."

La Fauvette moved slowly toward him and placed her face so close to his that the feathers on her nose tickled his face and her anything but sweet breath fanned his cheeks. As if divulging a secret, she whispered: "I'll tell you what he had in mind. I know exactly what he wants. He wants the Count de Mallac. And the fool still deludes himself into thinking that he can use me as bait. Isn't that what he wants? Am I not right?"

She took a few steps backward with regal abruptness as if she had just scored a great victory, but still kept him impaled on the daggers of her gaze. Perhaps she had bedeviled, bewitched, or hypnotized him, or perhaps she had simply precipitated his moment of facing the truth, the decision he had wrestled with all along; or it could have been that he was moved by the meek voice that had come to his defense, or perhaps it was all of this together, that induced Lucien Lefèvre simply to nod his head. His fate, which bound him to these women, was sealed right then and there.

The Marquise relaxed her stare and beamed her most beguiling smile at him. Fabrisse, watching the exchange, seemed to understand the momentous step he had just taken, held her hand out to him. Suddenly he saw Gaston's widow in a different light, or rather, it was the first time he had seen her in any light at all. She is actually rather pretty, he thought, considering the life she has led with her five children.

It had never occurred to him to attach himself to a woman. The landladies, washerwomen, and whores of Paris had always been sufficient to meet his modest needs, and he never felt the urge to seek more intimate female companionship. But in the course of what turned out to be a peculiarly jovial interlude in the dreary atmosphere of La Salpêtrière, a seed was planted in his mind and heart that was destined to grow with time.

Madame the Marquise obliged the company with a little song to which Arlette and the children danced by hopping up and down in the narrow space, what La Fauvette liked to call her "ruelle." Even Ondine awoke from her stupor and joined Fabrisse in clapping her hands in rhythm.

The merriment ended abruptly though when Fabrisse burst into tears and gave herself over to what seemed to Lucien the most inconsolable sobs he ever saw take hold of a woman. The Marquise and Arlette—Ondine had already retired into her shell at the first sign of sadness—took turns trying to learn the reason for Fabrisse's sudden distress. But only when Lucien spoke to her did she tell of her anguish for her two older sons, who had been taken with Prosper to the men's hospice of Bicêtre.

Lucien promised to do what he could to find the boys and assured her that there was nothing for her to worry about. The idea of being able to do her a favor filled him with a warm sense of satisfaction. It gave him a certain air of authority and indispensability and, above all, an excuse to return. He had already resolved that she could under no circumstances remain in this hole and that he had to get them all out of there as soon as possible.

A plan was forming in his mind. His position as an officer of the law would be helpful. The question was how to go about it without arousing his superior's suspicions. But he would find a way. He cringed at the thought that what he contemplated might be construed as treason, which he didn't think was at all the case.

They parted with mutual assurances of good will. He promised Fabrisse, who had returned to collecting the feathers, once again that he would find her sons and their uncle.

As for the mystery of the gems, the Marquise could rest assured that he would try to sound out Monsieur de La Reynie, though he would have to proceed with the utmost caution in such a delicate matter. In his heart, he still believed that there had to be a simple explanation. The whole affair was so totally out of character for the man whom he had known only as obsessed with upholding the law and persecuting relentlessly those who would break it.

Whistling his pleasure about himself and the turn events had taken—his new-found role of protector of this luckless band of women suited him splendidl y—he passed through the gate and walked straight into a scuffle between the guardsmen and two strangers.

"Ah, Monsieur Lefèvre!" one of the watchmen cried, turning to him in obvious despair. "These two gentlemen claim to be officers in the service of the King's police with urgent business, so they say, and demand to be admitted to the compound. If they are who they say they are, then you would surely know them, wouldn't you?"

"Well, let's see what we have here. It's hard to recognize a face in the dusk." Lucien held up a lantern to one of the strangers and came face to face with the unmistakable rogue's smile of the Count de Mallac.

"Good evening, Monsieur!" Guibert said with good cheer. "Be kind enough to tell these apes to get their hands off us."

"Yes, of course!" Lucien replied nervously. He turned to the watchmen and assured them he would handle the matter.

"How good of you to come!" the policeman said to rogue. He had now recovered his composure. "But, the gentlemen have come such a long way for naught. The matter in question has already been taken care of. There is no need for you to disturb the residents at this hour. Let us find a more convenient place where I can apprise you of the state of the matter."

With the last words he pushed the men to a spot out of sight and earshot of the watchmen.

"Monsieur the Count is endangering his life, appearing as he does in the exact place where the lieutenant of the police is expecting to find him. Monsieur de La Reynie is not a man to be toyed with. His greatest ambition is to bring the most wanted man in France to justice. He says so often."

"So I'm told," Guibert replied, distinctly unworried.

Guibert's companion was much less confident. "I told Your Lordship we shouldn't have come. Your Lordship's face is too well known in this town."

"Isn't it your duty to arrest me or shoot me on sight?" said Guibert to Lucien.

"Yes, sir."

"But you haven't done so."

"No, sir. There's two of you against one."

"But back there, at the gate, the odds were much more in your favor."

"That depends how you look at it."

"You mean you don't want to arrest me? Think of the fame and fortune that await you!"

"Take my advice, leave town and never come back here. And we'll leave it at that."

"Your Lordship heard what the gentleman said," the companion urged. "For God's sake, let's get out of here!"

"I have come with a specific purpose and I don't intend to leave until I get at least some information. But let's get out of the street. There's a tavern just around the corner."

As soon as the three had hustled into the nearby establishment and taken a seat, Guibert besieged Lucien with questions.

"How is she? Have you seen her? Why is she being held in that ghastly place?"

"She is fine under the circumstances." Lucien swallowed hard. "But there really is nothing Monsieur the Count can do right now."

"What do you mean by circumstances?"

"I mean . . . La Salpêtrière is no luxury accommodation. It isn't a mansion in the Marais. But it is better than the street. And Madame has remarkable spunk and spirit."

"I'm sure of that, but I still want to see her. I intend to take her out of there tonight."

"I'm afraid that is impossible, for the moment at least. The police lieutenant is not likely to give up his best trump card in his battle with the Count de Mallac."

"I don't seek a feud with the police lieutenant, but I certainly won't ask his permission."

"Can't you see that you are endangering the lives of everybody, including your own? I beseech you to heed my advice and leave. I should not even be sitting here with you, let alone give you advice on how to evade the arm of the law. But if you do as I say, I promise to do my best to get them all out as soon as arrangements for more suitable quarters can be made. But I shall be of no good to you or to anybody if Monsieur de La Reynie learns of this entretien."

Guibert looked up. The man's honest, troubled face stirred something in him. The brashness he was in the habit of upholding to the world like a shield to deflect the arrows being hurled at him began to soften. As he scrutinized the policeman's face, he wondered why indeed he had not arrested him immediately. Whatever his reasons, he seemed honest and was obviously a man of compassion. He was probably right that he could be much more useful if La Reynie did not suspect him of having been remiss in his duty.

"All right, I shall do as you wish," he said after some reflection. "But you must promise me one thing. Take a message to the Marquise and while I'm gone look after her and the child. If any harm comes to them, you will regret the day you were born."

It was Lucien's deeply imbued sense of his destiny that made him swallow without protest the insolence of this aristocrat, who still did not seem to grasp which one of them was holding the upper hand or that even now he, Lucien, could turn the tables on him. Guibert was about to order paper and ink from the tavern keeper, but here Lucien asserted his authority and better judgment. He would convey a verbal message only. Written messages often had a way of ending up in the wrong hands.

Chapter 6

GUIBERT DE MALLAC'S thoughts wandered far from the raucous council of the kingdom's most notorious thieves and smugglers over which he presided. He hardly had time to wash off the dust—something he was always very particular about—from the breakneck ride through the French countryside, mostly under cover of night and over less-traveled roads, with many a diversionary turn, just in case they should be followed by the gendarmes of the intrepid Monsieur de La Reynie.

Guibert and Coupe-Cheveux had reached this tavern in the woods ten leagues from the port city of Saint-Malo just in the nick of time. A revolt was brewing among the horde of criminals who had been assembled there for several weeks.

Upon his arrival, Guibert had quickly gained control through a few deft maneuvers of divide and conquer; but he knew his hold over this volatile lot could only be maintained if he convinced them of his willingness to use brute force and if he sweetened it by delivering the goods.

In this instance, the "goods" was a haul from His Majesty's merchant fleet, expected to sail into the port of Saint-Malo from the West Indies within days. The operation was one of his most audacious schemes and, if brought to fruition, would be one of the most brilliant coups in the annals of brigandage in France.

The plan had ripened in Guibert's mind for several years and had been nursed through months of preparation, negotiation, persuasion, subterfuge, scheming, conniving, coordinating, and arm twisting. He had traveled to the four corners of the kingdom, had called on every hideout of every brigand, bandit, and cutthroat, always himself hiding, always on the run. He had met challenges and taunts, had escaped with his life more than once by the skin of his teeth, had emerged victorious from many a bout, had bent and compromised, made promises and uttered threats, had cajoled and coaxed, and had at last forged the most sinister criminals of France into a compliant fellowship.

Now that he had these wild-eyed hotheads in his hand, united on his own turf in Brittany, now that he stood on the brink of his ultimate triumph in the brilliant coup he had dreamed of for so many years, now that his supreme revenge for the injustice the Mallacs had suffered at the hands of the French Crown was at long last within reach, he found little satisfaction in any of it.

The excitement, the élan, the energy that had propelled him had ebbed and a singular lethargy had spread over him. The adrenaline that had fueled his spirit in the act of conceiving and devising the great master plan had drained from him. One thought and one thought alone obsessed him. One all-consuming desire burnt in his heart: to rescue the woman left behind at La Salpêtrière.

He had left Paris with great reluctance and only after he had convinced himself that Lucien Lefèvre was a man he could trust to keep his word. So what if Lucien's promise would conflict with his duty as a police officer of the king. That was not his concern. Guibert had no love for any of the Louis Bourbons, be it the thirteenth, the fourteenth, or the sixty-sixth. Without probing what might be Lucien's deeper reasons for risking treason, he was pleased to have found a trusted servant of the police lieutenant and the King secretly on his side. He might be a bit naive, this Lucien, but any man who would apologize for having been the cause of an aristocrat being sent to the galleys certainly was a rare soul.

A strange exchange it had been at the tavern in the Faubourg Saint-Marcel. Guibert had finally agreed to leave Paris without making further attempts at seeing the woman he loved. Lucien had obviously been elated, presumably for having been relieved of the duty of arresting him. In the rush of good cheer that had followed, Lucien confessed his great regret for having been the cause of the misfortune that had befallen the Marquis and Marquise de Valinquette. Guibert protested that this was by no means so, the officer certainly bore no blame and had only done his duty when he became the unfortunate recipient of a thrust from the Marquis' rapier.

"But Monsieur the Count is probably glad to have the Marquis out of the way," Lucien said with a sly grin. "I probably did Monsieur a favor then."

"No, no, I wouldn't describe it that way," Guibert protested, unsure whether the fellow was getting impertinent or was simply fawning. It annoyed him to be on familiar terms with this commoner, but somehow he felt compelled to set things straight. "I never meant any harm to come to the Marquis, although I might have killed him had it not been for your intervention. Then again he might have killed me, which he certainly was intent on doing."

True, he never wished Antoine dead. Never wanted him out of the way in such a manner. It was Antoine who hated him, who had always regarded him as the intruder. Despite years of rankling and rivalry, what he wanted more than anything was Antoine's love and respect. But all his striving, his devotion, his service to the Valinquettes, especially to the elder Marquis, earned him nothing but scorn and hatred from the son.

His defense was that all his life he had felt compelled to prove that he had one up on Antoine. True he stole his father's love and seduced his wife into loving him. But was it not Antoine with his follies who had left the coop unguarded for the fox to enter? He practically invited him in. Those who have the hubris to aspire to be god must bear the consequences. How fatuous of Antoine to call her Galatée! As if she were a piece of marble he could place on a pedestal, there to rest for his aesthetic pleasure, a woman in form only, an object denied all feeling and all longing to be truly loved.

The thought of La Fauvette deepened his melancholy. Here was one of life's great ironies. In the masquerade world of the cream of Parisian society, she appeared to him so vulnerable. An easy conquest, a great opportunity for making Antoine a cuckold. How he had relished the thought, reveled with delight as he went about laying his snares, beguiling his lonely prey with thoughtful attention and charm. But then the unexpected happened.

What he found was an all too willing accomplice. The hunter became the prey. In the end, it was not clear who was ensnaring whom, who was using whom to get revenge on poor, oblivious Antoine. But in the course of all this deceiving and scheming, Antoine receded almost completely from their minds. In the self-absorbed, self-contained world of their all-consuming passion, Antoine became immaterial, nonexistent, as did the whole world, the beau monde, the demimonde, the nouveau monde, everything and anything, only their love, their mad, rapturous love mattered.

Dancing at the edge of the universe, they threw all caution, all regard for seemliness and decorum, to the wind. But the world, if not the gods, begrudges such exclusive self-absorption, such self-indulgent passion. They gave no thought to tomorrow and so the morrow struck them down with jealous rage. But all was not completely lost; there still was a chance and time to make good, to mend. In spite of everything, he at least had the certainty of her abiding love.

Guibert was of a mind to drop all schemes, all intrigues. What good was it to take on the power of the King, the most powerful monarch in Europe? His squabble with the Royal House of France suddenly appeared petty and trivial to him. Even family honor rang hollow, a mere striving for wind. But he was too deeply enmeshed to extricate himself now. There was a price on his head. The only friends, if one could call them that, were these unruly, carousing, boisterous criminals who would not hesitate to cut his throat should they smell betrayal.

He looked around the tavern table. How had he ever put himself in the company of a pack of gallows birds such as these? There was the triumvirate of brigands from the southwest of the kingdom,

Quintère of Condomois, Caprais the Agenais, and Thérou the Béarnais. All three had spent a lifetime burning châteaux, a regional tradition going back generations, but whose original purpose, justice for the exploited peasants, had long been lost in the mists of time. These three actually constituted the moderate wing of this thugs' convention, in criminal history as well as general comportment. Of a fiercer disposition and more volatile temperament was the famed Alayric le Roux of Poitou. He had been sentenced to death five times and stood under the gallows at least twice, but still lived to make honest, ordinary citizens uneasy in their beds at night. Of similar caliber were the one-eyed Marboutin and the one-armed Bourousse, two brothers who hailed from the Nivernais region. Gontran the Savoyard was as wild as the mountains from which he swept down to assault hapless travelers. Armou and Marcou, two pockmarked, scar-faced pieces of work, twin brothers of Narbonnais, were wanted for murder in three provinces. They had the nasty habit of finding pleasure, if they weren't slitting people's throats, in disemboweling cats and dogs or other luckless animals that happened to cross their path.

Then there was Mathurin the Auvergnais, a flamboyant philosopher among cutthroats, a former Huguenot preacher who had abjured all religion. He was a giant among giants with flowing black hair and beard and darting eyes, glowing embers from which sparked the madness of a holy man. Crime to him was a vocation, a profession he practiced with the consummate devotion of the true believer imbued with a mission to redeem the world. His greatest virtue for Guibert, besides his absolute dependability, was his hold over these superstitious peasant criminals. They stood in awe of this simmering volcano who was ceaselessly spouting fire and brimstone against injustice and poverty, against exploitation, degradation, and abuse of the peasant masses. Unlike the others, who were accompanied by a slew of battle-scarred, bearded myrmidons who would set any respectable citizen crossing their path on a dark night to trembling in their boots, Mathurin was unescorted. For years he had stalked the countryside on a lonely crusade against an evil world, invariably leaving a trail of murder, arson, robbery, and incitement.

A sudden racket drew Guibert's attention to the far corner of the tavern. Through the blur of dusk, he made out a giant unkempt character cajoling and swinging his fist at a target that was blocked from Guibert's view by the bulk of the attacker. Flanking him were five or six equally sinister characters who gave a raucous cheer every time he landed a blow.

Guibert was well aware of the dangers of having such an unruly horde lie idle for too long. Allaying the flaring tempers of these hotheads while they waited for the fleet to sail in required the skills of a general and a diplomat in one. Were the Royal Musketeers to get a whiff of France's most prominent criminals concentrated in a forest tavern in the vicinity of Saint-Malo, the whole enterprise would blow sky high.

Guibert decided he had better investigate the disturbance. He rose and pushed his way through the rabble. His surprise at discovering the object of the bullies' sneers quickly changed to anger. There, crouched on the floor, bawling and whining, and bleeding profusely from the nose, was none other than that despicable wretch Pélégrin, the one who used to call himself King Menelaus of the Court of Miracles at Saint-Médard.

Guibert seized the sniveling wretch by the collar and held him up to his face.

"What do we have here?" he marveled. "I don't remember inviting this louse to our gathering."

Still holding him up for all to see, he announced: "Gentlemen! May I present to you the king, or shall we say, the dethroned king, of the Court of Miracles at Saint-Médard! How he wormed his way into our company, we'll have to see. He certainly neglected to present his credentials. I hear he has a good friend at the Châtelet in Paris, the King's lieutenant of police, the very illustrious Monsieur de La Reynie himself. For all we know this renegade may be a spy for His Majesty, King Louis!"

Guibert raised his free hand to calm the threats and hold back the knives that were being brandished as he spoke. "For the moment at least, he may be more useful to us alive than dead. Let's entrust this wretch to the pastoral care of the Reverend Mathurin, who knows how to deal with penitent sinners, presuming he is such. If not, he'd better be, for our preacher has little patience with recalcitrants. As for the rest of you, you'd better send out scouts to scour the area for any traces of royals or militia."

"Here, my good friend," he said, turning to Mathurin, "take good care of this wretch. Guard him as you would a festering boil. But let no harm come to him, at least not yet."

Pélégrin's whining protestations drowned in the commotion. Mathurin showed obvious delight at being entrusted with such an important task and scowled more ferociously than ever. He took custody of the wilted midget, shielded him with his corpulent mass against assaults and taunts and treated him like the apple of his eye.

The next morning, Guibert and Coupe-Cheveux descended on Saint-Malo on a scouting expedition. According to their information, calculation, and a basic hunch, the royal fleet should already have reached port, but then the vicissitudes of sea voyages made predictions of this sort less than a science.

Their inquiries, discreetly placed, for nothing aroused the suspicions of the local merchants and dock workers more than a pair of strangers asking questions, yielded little. Everybody seemed to be as much in the dark as they were. They kept themselves among the mass of transients who regularly flocked into town in hope of work. Word of the approach of the fleet from the West Indies had apparently spread beyond the province. Myriad regional accents were heard from potential hands milling about in the heat of summer along the docks and town squares and subsisting on handouts from ecclesiastical charities and the kindness of their betters.

Guibert observed with some disquiet the prominence of the garrison. Its presence was visible at every corner. But such reinforcement was common whenever a large fleet was expected. He remembered the excitement he felt when his mother took him to Saint-Malo to distribute food among the poor and to watch His Majesty's galleons sail in from the New World. He was a child of five or six. What dreams the sight of soldiers and sailors inspired then! He too would gain fame and fortune, become a great hero fighting for the honor and glory of the King of France. He saw himself elevated to prominence among His Majesty's loyal subjects.

A child's naïveté! Guibert chased the thought, spitting scornfully on the ground. He had more urgent things to do than dwell on nostalgic fantasies. The garrison would be a problem, but nothing that could not be overcome. This is what he told himself without a notion as yet what to do. We'll improvise, we'll deal with obstacles as they arise, he assured the leery Coupe-Cheveux. It was uncharacteristic of him to make light of a grave situation, and Coupe-Cheveux remained unappeased.

The melancholy that had held him enthralled since Paris still weighed on him, slowing his natural energies to an unusual sluggishness. A frightful vision had come to haunt his thoughts. He saw himself strapped to a treadmill of his own making, condemned to keep it in motion because the forces driving the mechanism had slipped from his control and now ruled him and his contraption. No longer master of his fate, he had become the slave of his own invention. No, no, absolutely no, he told himself, he cannot permit himself to become paralyzed by such absurd thoughts.

On their third day at Saint-Malo—Guibert was sitting on the dock scanning the horizon, yearning for something, almost anything, to happen that would relieve his mind of obsessive brooding—he suddenly jumped up with a start. He called to Coupe-Cheveux and pointed out to sea with a degree of excitement more effusive than was prudent. Soon other fingers were pointing, eyes and telescopes were being trained on the horizon. And a great collective sigh went forth from the populace. Far out at sea a single sail gleamed in the sun. The agitation gave way to puzzlement as the throng on the dock tried in vain to make out other sails alongside or behind. Even when it had come into clear focus no sister ships became visible.

And when it became apparent that the lone vessel lumbering arduously through the waves toward the harbor was in bad shape, conjectures, speculation, rumors sprang up like grass in a spring rain—the fleet had been attacked and pillaged on the high seas by Spanish pirates, English privateers, or French corsairs, or even a mutinous crew, and now most of its cargo was likely to be at the bottom of the Atlantic or was already hauled off.

Guibert and Coupe-Cheveux turned away with hundreds of disheartened drifters, though downcast for different reasons. The one factor he had failed to take into account was the limit of the power of the King of France. Though boundless within the kingdom, it extended neither over the elements nor over incursions of high-seas bandits.

But at the very moment that gloom began to settle on the town, someone called out: "Its *Le Vert Galant*! It's a ship from the King's galley! She's leaning in the water!"

The King's galleys were coast-hugging vessels mainly used for the transport of goods between French ports along the Atlantic and the Mediterranean. Their main means of propulsion came from oars powered by the muscles of convicts, supplemented by one rigging. So the vessel that was now approaching could not be part of the high-seas fleet.

A damaged ship would under ordinary circumstances hardly have called forth a cheer as elated as the one that went up from the dockside that day at Saint-Malo. But on that day the mood that greeted *Le Vert Galant* as she limped into the harbor could almost be described as one of wild exuberance, if only for the distraction it provided.

The two would-be robbers disengaged themselves from the cheering crowd and returned to the inn where they had put up. There was nothing to do but wait and see what the next day would bring. Meanwhile a good meal and restful sleep would do them both much good.

Guibert awoke in the middle of the night. His heart was pounding. He was sure he had heard someone call his name. Then he realized it must have been his dream that had stirred him from his sleep. There again was the image of the treadmill to which he was strapped. Sweat drenched his exhausted body, but he could not stop running in place. The treadmill powered a giant wheel, like a millwheel, strangely set up in the middle of an expansive, fallow field, and although there was no stream or pond nearby, the buckets attached to the wheel filled with liquid as they went round and round, irrigating the soil. Suddenly he realized that the liquid was blood and the naked body of a man was tied to the wheel. He wanted to stop but could not. The body went round and round while he kept running in place and the bucket kept on filling with blood.

Then all of a sudden the picture shifted. He had switched places with the man, and it was he who was tied to the wheel and the man ran in place on the treadmill. This went on for a while until they switched places again, and then again. At last from the blood-drenched ground grew a woman, sprouting like a tree, and the wheel stopped turning. He strained but could not make out the woman's face. But the other man's face became clear, it was unmistakably Antoine. He seemed to recognize Guibert in turn, for he called out to him. His speech had the hollow gurgle of someone trying to speak under water: "Guibert! Guibert! Why did you forsake me?"

How had he come to the sunken city of Ys? Guibert thought. And then he awoke.

What a ridiculous dream! Guibert said to himself as he sat up in his bunk. He was used to sleeping soundly and rarely dreamed at all. Never had he been haunted by nightmares. Antoine was the one with the nightmares. He remembered well how he would rouse him in the middle of the night and crawl into bed with him, seeking comfort. They would hug and kiss and rest in each other's arms. But that was long ago.

Sleep was no longer possible on this night. He rose and walked to the window. It would soon be dawning. But for now the town was still illumined by bright moonlight.

Did I forsake Antoine? he muttered to himself. It was the other way around. If anybody was left in the lurch it was I. It was Antoine who left me to die. Or maybe we are both to blame.

A peculiar sight arrested his gaze. In the distance, but clearly visible in the moonlight, a queue of ragged, downcast individuals shuffled single file onto the landing at the dock. One by one they collapsed on the pavement. A chain tied at the ankles linked them to each other and another wrapped around the chest. Some were totally lifeless and were dragged along by those who had strength enough to set their feet on the ground.

Galley slaves from *Le Vert Galant*! Guibert thought. The next moment he was out in the street, hugging the shadows to elude the night watchman.

He detected him almost immediately. He was the only one among the wretches who remained upright as the taskmasters removed the chains. He stood, his naked torso gleaming in the light of the moon. It was unmistakable—that stance of pride and defiance which Guibert used to liken to that of an Iberian bullfighter or even the ancient warrior Hannibal, who had challenged the power of Rome. The man's gaze was fixed on some point in the distance, far, far away. The lashes pelting his already streaked back, intended to make him get down, bounced off his leathery hide.

So you think I have forsaken you, Antoine de Valinquette? Guibert never talked as much to himself as he did on this most fantastic of nights. Maybe the moonlight and the damp heat, mitigated only by soft breezes from the sea, caused his mind to play tricks on him and all this was nothing but a hallucination. It had to be anything but reality. But when he looked up, the man with the Hannibal stance was still there, still unbent by the knout.

He knew he had to act immediately. Coupe-Cheveux was not at the inn, but he knew where to find him. He moved among the shadows, easy and noiseless like a cat on the prowl. He felt the adrenaline flowing, energy was returning to his body. Without disturbing the harlots, he plucked Coupe-Cheveux from their midst. No time for protests or explanations. Later. Later. The new day would dawn soon. They had to move, use the element of surprise. Coupe-Cheveux was just the right man for such an undertaking.

There was only one guard. Apparently they did not expect any of the wretches to have enough life left in them to attempt a breakout. Nevertheless, the guard kept his eyes fixed on Antoine. No matter. There was only one chance and it had to be seized now.

Coupe-Cheveux tossed a handful of pebbles onto the pavement. The guard fell for this oldest of tricks and abandoned his watch over the recalcitrant prisoner to investigate. Antoine turned his head in the direction of a hissing noise behind him. His eyes were dull, devoid of expression. He does not seem to comprehend, Guibert thought, maybe he has gone mad and does not even know where he is. But he was not going to give up, not now, so close. With one leap he was behind Antoine, placing his hand over his mouth and pulling him down and into the shadows. Antoine struggled and thrashed about wildly. A single, well-aimed blow to his head from Coupe-Cheveux's deft hand put him out, and together they dragged him away just in time.

When the sun came up, the three men were resting, exhausted but safely out of sight, in a room at the local brothel.

The arrival of the fleet from the West Indies at noon on the next day set off a flurry of festivities in the town. Throngs of dancing, swilling folk blocked the streets and squares. Nobody had a mind to answer questions about an escaped convict. The guards who attempted a house-to-house search were by turns laughed at and heckled for being a nuisance.

Guibert could not have wished for a more propitious intervention. Never would he have imagined that His Majesty's merchant fleet, which had been the focal point of his preoccupations for so long, would become the deus ex machina in the hour of his greatest need for help.

For as it turned out Antoine was in bad shape. His torso was strong and muscular, but his legs were weak from disuse, and most of all, his mind seemed deranged. He alternated between states of lucidity, when he seemed fully aware where he was and that it was Guibert who was with him, and states of darkness, when he sat sunken in stupor. It would take weeks, maybe months, of patience before he would recover, if ever. The question was how long his presence among the prostitutes could be concealed.

"What about the plan?" Coupe-Cheveux asked impatiently when it seemed that Guibert had forgotten the purpose of their foray into Saint-Malo. "The merchandise is being unloaded from the ships. We have to move while it is still on the docks."

"Oh, yes, you're quite right," Guibert replied distractedly. "Maybe you should go back to the tavern and tell the crew to make their move. Everybody knows exactly what to do. I'm really not needed."

"In that case, Your Lordship will forgive me if I take more drastic steps!" The truculence of Coupe-Cheveux's tone made Guibert look up and come eye to eye with the barrel of a cocked pistol.

"Are you out of your mind?" Guibert hissed, but he refrained from turning his back on him as he might have done in earlier days. Something in Coupe-Cheveux's demeanor told him to take heed. "All right, what is it you want me to do?"

"Your Lordship knows as well as I do that if I return alone to the tavern, I'm liable to get my throat cut. These fellows will immediately suspect some sort of treachery. An explanation that the Count de Mallac is detained because he has to take care of a wretched galley slave won't hold much water. I'm not such a fool as to walk into that kind of trouble. So if Monsieur the Count pleases, shall we go together, now?"

He waved the pistol in the direction of the door. His determination was crystal clear. Guibert readied to follow. The ladies were better at nurturing a sick man than he was anyway. With sudden, newfound fervor, Guibert implored God to watch over his languishing friend during his absence.

Whatever God's ways may have been, he did not shine his mercy on the godless bunch of criminals Guibert had left behind ten days before at the tavern in the forest ten leagues from Saint-Malo. As soon as Guibert and Coupe-Cheveux entered the forest, their nostrils were stung by the ashen smell of smoldering embers. An eerie silence pervaded the air; not even a bird was heard to twitter. Something foul was going on. They dismounted and plunged into the thick underbrush on foot. Cautiously they felt their way, advancing on their bellies like snakes in the grass. They had not penetrated very far when a soft birdcall caught their attention. They veered in the direction of the sound and found none other than Mathurin hugging the ground under a cover of leaves.

"They're all dead. The Musketeers killed them all and burned down the tavern," he croaked. "A veritable bloodbath."

He was shaking with fright, but the fire of madness had left his eyes and he seemed quite rational. "Don't go any further. It's a trap. The Musketeers are waiting for you. That little rat, if I get my hands on that skinny neck of his, I'll squeeze the living daylights out of him."

Guibert did not have to ask of whom Mathurin was speaking. "You were sworn to guard him with your life."

"I know, I know," the big man wailed, beating the ground with his fist. "He tricked me, and then ran off and alerted the soldiers, that little . . ."

"Put the knife away, Coupe-Cheveux, and let's get out of here," Guibert said.

"What about him?" Coupe-Cheveux pointed his knife at Mathurin's throat. "I'm in the mood to make mincemeat of this useless piece of flesh."

"Not now. Pélégrin knows our plans so we cannot risk going back into town. We need Mathurin to get the Marquis out of there."

"And then what do we do?"

"Trust me, I know this area, no Musketeer will catch the Count de Mallac, not on his home turf."

Mathurin showered the Count with effusions of gratitude for having spared his life and assured him he would redeem himself if given a chance. He wanted nothing better than to remain in the service of his gracious Lordship.

When they reached the heights above Saint-Malo, Guibert's prediction proved more accurate than was comfortable. The sky-blue uniforms of the Royal Musketeers and other royal troops were swarming in the squares, near the docks, everywhere. Guibert repeated his instructions to Mathurin with a stern warning not to return without the Marquis or Coupe-Cheveux would still get his wish to operate on his throat.

"How do we know he won't go straight to the royals?" Coupe-Cheveux asked as they headed for the shining cliffs of the Emerald Coast.

"Not Mathurin," Guibert assured him. "That Pélégrin got away was a most unfortunate slip, but never would Mathurin himself go to the authorities. He has a passionate hatred of all authority, for the aristocracy and their servants—remember they are the parasites of society, the exploiters of the people. No, Mathurin will keep his promise. What worries me is that something might have happened to the Marquis in the meantime."

Coupe-Cheveux was not convinced. "But you are an aristocrat yourself. Why should he regard you differently?" Guibert's confidence in this preacher turned scourge of God seemed ridiculous to him.

"But I'm a dispossessed aristocrat. I don't exploit the people. I'm a victim of aristocratic intrigue. Don't you see the difference?"

Coupe-Cheveux grunted his assent. He pulled a blanket from the horse's saddle and hunkered down in the crevice of a rock for whatever sleep he could find.

Guibert made sure the horses could not be seen from the top of the cliff. He stooped in the shadows of the cliffs, away from the water's edge where they might be spotted from afar. How long it had been since he had found leisure to indulge his love of the sea! After an absence of almost a lifetime, he had returned an outlaw, had taken possession of the fortress the Mallacs had inhabited for centuries, but which now belonged, rightfully so it was claimed, to the King of France.

Among the Breton peasants, who had never been very fond of the Bourbon dynasty, he found the memory of the Mallacs still alive. Good memories they were and the people had flocked to him, had offered their services and their lives, and had formed a garrison to man the fortress.

Luck had been on his side, and perhaps it was all for the better that the scheme to rob the fleet had aborted. It was an ambitious enterprise, but too many uncertainties, too many questionable characters had been involved. Although to some extent he was responsible for the disaster in the forest, he could not find it in his heart to mourn the passing of this gang of blackguards. He saw his quarrel with the King as of a different nature, a higher order. It was a struggle over the question of legitimacy, of the ancient rights of the nobility. He was not a common bandit out to plunder the rich. He was not even particularly interested in giving to the poor. He was not a crusader for social justice.

Day followed night with excruciating slowness. The sun was drowning in the sea for the third time and Mathurin was still nowhere to be seen. He had given him two days, and it would require the cover of night to steal out of town. The search for the escaped convict was not likely to have been abandoned and might even have intensified. He thought of Antoine and the fate that had torn open the hull of the galley and brought him ashore at the moment when he, Guibert, was there to receive him.

Immersed in his thoughts, he must have dozed off for some time, for the moon had moved off center stage and was yielding to the graying dawn when he was roused by the dull thump of horseshoes on the sandy beach.

My God, the devil even found a horse! Guibert's heartbeat reverberated in his throat when the flowing mane of the Auvergnais on a Percheron came into view. Then fear knotted his stomach. Where was Antoine? But as the horse came closer a second rider became visible in the saddle behind Mathurin's bulky frame.

"I had to pummel him a little," Mathurin panted as he pulled the lifeless Antoine off the saddle. "Wasn't easy to persuade him to follow along with me. But the bloodhounds were beginning to close in on the hostelry and we got away by the skin of our teeth. I hope no harm will come to those most charitable, charming ladies. At any rate, I came straight here. I had no time to place any diversions to throw anybody who might be following off the track. We'd better be off without delay."

"You did very well, Mathurin. You will find me not ungrateful," Guibert said as he mounted his horse and pulled the still dazed Antoine into the saddle behind him. "En avant! We shall be at our destination within two hours' time if we ride hard."

Meanwhile Coupe-Cheveux had been roused and with unconcealed disgust he made room on his steed for the fire-spitting preacher. The Percheron had been ridden too hard to be of any further use.

Chapter 7

THE LORD OF Mallac stood on the ramparts of the fortress La Falaise near the Breton town of Mallac, looking out over the expanse of a wind swept heath. That troops under the royal banner were massing in the distance did not seem to affect his good cheer. For once he was rightful master of his own domain and he would defend it to the end. Next to him stood Antoine de Valinquette, whose domain he once defended with his life. Together they had fought many a battle and together they would repel this threat.

"This is like old times!" proclaimed Guibert, rubbing his hands together in anticipation of a good fight.

"Yes, just like the old days," grumbled Antoine. "Only this time the odds are even worse."

"Don't be a pessimist, Antoine!" Guibert laughed. "These walls have never been breached, not in four hundred years. Well, maybe once during the religious wars, but that was not a real breach, more of a premature surrender."

Antoine furrowed his brow and shook his head. He still found it hard to believe that his mind was not playing tricks on him. That he should be standing next to his friend—if he really was his friend, even of that he wasn't sure—still seemed some absurd phantasmagoria, a trick played on him by his feverish mind.

He had only a sketchy memory of what had happened at Saint-Malo and how he had gotten to the safety, if it could be called that, of this fortress. Once there, he had recovered his senses and the strength of his body fairly quickly with Guibert's eager help. While he was still suspended between a febrile state and the twilight of recovery, he saw Guibert's beaming smile shining on him whenever he opened his eyes. The friend was at his side during his first tentative walks on the ramparts and, once the former prisoner's legs had regained enough strength, the two lords set out for daily runs along the beach. Few words were exchanged between them at first. All effort went into Antoine's physical recovery.

Once he asked Guibert why he was doing all this for him. Didn't he want to see him dead?

"Dead?" Guibert protested. "But you are my brother, my only brother."

His astonishment increased even more when one evening the two thugs who were keeping them company, Mathurin and Coupe-Cheveux, told him the story of the debacle at Saint-Malo, how all that planning of the greatest plunderage that was to make them all rich and the King of France just a little bit poorer had gone to waste and how the cream of France's underworld perished due to the betrayal of a miserable rat named Pélégrin. Mathurin was writhing uneasily in his chair, preferring not to be reminded of that particular episode.

"Actually, with all due respect, it was all Your Lordship's fault," Coupe-Cheveux said to Antoine with a chuckle, only half in jest.

"Coupe-Cheveux, the story is already too long," Guibert said. But Antoine insisted on hearing what he meant.

"Well, if Monsieur the Count's attention hadn't become so totally attracted by the sight of a prisoner standing there on the dock in the moonlight among those miserable wretches from the galley, it all might have turned out differently."

"How would it have turned out differently?"

"He wouldn't have become so distracted from what he had set out to do, you see. What I mean is, that once Monsieur the Count recognized Your Lordship standing there on the dock, he no longer had a mind for the operation. He could think of nothing but how to get Your Lordship out of there."

"Coupe-Cheveux, your tale is getting very fanciful and tiresome," Guibert interjected. "The operation failed because a traitor had infiltrated our ranks. And we were lucky that we didn't get killed too."

Guibert rose and walked away, but Coupe-Cheveux continued to address the Marquis. He explained that although what the Count was saying is true, he also had never seen him so worried about anybody and willing to risk everything when they were hiding in the whorehouse—except maybe for that woman at La Salpêtrière, he certainly was willing to risk his life for her.

Coupe-Cheveux's words stayed with Antoine in the days that followed. He had no reason to believe that the man was distorting the truth. As he stood with Guibert on the rampart, the words came back to him.

"Was Coupe Cheveux speaking the truth the other night?" he asked suddenly.

"Well, we did snatch you from under the noses of those jailers, didn't we?" Guibert said, equivocating. "The fact is we are here together and out there is our common enemy. We had better concentrate our efforts on the situation at hand."

"But you just said the walls could not be breached. So what's there to worry about?" Antoine said, not without sarcasm.

During the years on the galley, he had nurtured a hatred for this knave with every oar stroke. Hunched over in that dark pit, the bowels of the galley ship, heaving back and forth, back and forth, ceaselessly, without respite, he had sworn some day he would get out and get his revenge. Some day. The thought had kept him alive, had pushed him to go on. And now, this was not all how he had imagined it. Here he was nursed back to health, fed and clothed by this same knave. Should he be grateful? Should he resent the unsolicited intervention? A few weeks ago he had been a prisoner who endured with stoic pride the punishment for a crime he never denied having committed.

There was something bizarre, unreal about this present situation. Thanks to Guibert, he was now an escaped convict on the run from the law in the company of a bunch of cutthroat criminals, one of whom was a madman goaded by voices from beyond and the other a bandit who robbed people not only of their money and jewels but of the hair off their heads.

Could he really trust Guibert? Maybe this was all part of some scheme to destroy him once and for all. Had they not met in mortal combat, each intent on killing the other? Their business had been left unfinished back then due to the interference of an officer of the police. But what choice did he have to reject or accept a gift of life he had not asked for? Once again Guibert had taken charge of his life. And it left him profoundly uneasy.

And who was the woman at La Salpêtrière Coupe-Cheveux was talking about? And what of the object of their dispute? Guibert never mentioned her name. He seemed more interested in conjuring up old memories of their youthful fighting days, the storming of Rocroi, the battlefields of Flanders, and the rebellion of the grand nobility of France, in what was called La Fronde, led by the hero of Rocroi, the great, immortal Prince de Condé.

"Where is she?" Antoine dropped the question one day softly but with the effect of a bomb.

"She's at La Salpêtrière."

"What did you say?" cried Antoine since Guibert's answer had drowned in a sudden cannon blast that ripped through the air with ear-shattering force.

"Ah, they're trying to signal their presence! As if we didn't know that they are out there!" Guibert shouted indignantly. "Let's give them a return salute!"

"Have you gone mad? You can't fight the might of the King of France with a handful of peasants!" Antoine held him back by the sleeve from ordering his peasants, who had just exchanged their pitchforks for muskets, to fire back, a move that could only end in disaster.

"We certainly won't surrender without a fight!"

"Do you want to pay back the loyalty of these people by sacrificing their lives? For what cause? For a quarrel with the Crown that has long lost its purpose?"

"All right. We'll wait for their next move. The blast may have been accidental, or perhaps it was simply a warning. They are certainly too far off, the blast could not have been meant seriously."

Guibert descended the rampart to mingle with his men. He reassured them that the cannon embanked in the tower would wreak havoc among any army advancing on the fortress. Apparently the royals were aware of this themselves, for they stayed clear out of range. At any rate, he did not expect them to attack without a formal ultimatum and declaration from the commander of the royal army. It was the protocol.Antoine followed Guibert on his tour of what he called his troops and together they returned to their lookout post.

"Tell me, what was your answer to my question before the blast?"

"She is, or rather was, I hope, at La Salpêtrière," Guibert said, trying to give himself an air of nonchalance. "Lucien Lefèvre is a good man, he has promised to get them all out of there."

"Lucien Lefèvre? What are you trying to say? I should have thought him dead or maimed."

"Look, I was going to tell you the whole story, but it had to be the right moment."

"Well, I think the right moment has come—now."

"Then let's go some place quiet."

The two men went down a steep flight of worn stone steps and passed through the rear gate out to the rocky shore. They climbed down the escarpment of the cliffs and after a few paces settled among the rocks and the seagulls. The solitary tranquility of the seascape made them forget for a moment the gathering threat up on the heath.

Guibert broke the silence. "The knave looks well stitched together, only limps a little. I had the opportunity not too long ago to assure myself with my own eyes of his good health. Besides, he's back in the service of our good friend Monsieur de La Reynie."

"You saw him in Paris?""Yes, we discussed many a matter over a mug of beer. He seemed most distraught that Your Lordship had been convicted on his account. The man is the most decent soul who ever crossed my path. How many men, after getting run through with a rapier, would then bemoan the fate of their attacker? A true Christian that Lucien . . ."

Antoine interrupted petulantly, "I guess it was also Christian charity that prevented him from arresting you?"

"Whatever," Guibert replied with a smug grin and without letting Antoine's surliness disturb his good humor. "He certainly had the opportunity. And since he's a man of proven honor, I have no doubt that he will keep the promise he made to me, namely that he would get them all out of La Salpêtrière. It may take some ingenuity on his part but he will do it, rest assured."

Guibert had carefully avoided pronouncing the name of the woman who was uppermost in both their minds. But Antoine pressed to know who "all of them" were. Guibert listed the members of the household of the Widow Caillart. Some were, of course, unknown to Antoine, and he had very little desire to learn the life story of each one. Only the mention of someone described as "Gaston's widow" peaked his interest. The news of Gaston's death touched him more than he would have expected. It was a cruel twist of fate that the only man who had stood by him at the time of his trial should have been killed a short time later in a tavern brawl.

"One thing I still don't understand," Antoine said after he had heard Guibert out, "why the devil are they confined at La Salpêtrière?"

"Confined, indeed, or even better condemned by our old friend Monsieur de La Reynie. On orders from His Most Catholic Majesty, King Louis of France—so it is said—Monsieur burnt down the Court of Miracles at Saint-Médard, in a sweep to clean up the city. Of course, the riffraff is now out in the streets without roof or shelter, except for those who were hauled to the Hôpital Général at La Salpêtrière and Bicêtre. But thanks to Monsieur de La Reynie the streets of Paris are now even lined with brightly lit lanterns at night so the good citizens of Paris can amble about without fear of assault, or having their fat purses stolen or their throats cut."

"Never mind about all that! What are the Caillarts doing at La Salpêtrière?"

"Monsieur de La Reynie had them confined there because Madame the Marquise would not be intimidated by him. It must have been quite a scene. Lucien had tears in his eyes when he recalled the confrontation with La Reynie on the day they tore down the Court of Miracles. She walked proudly through the front gate, refusing to steal away through a hole in the side of the wall like the rest of the canaille. She wouldn't bow to him, so to humiliate her, he sent her and the whole family to La Salpêtrière."

Guibert left out the main reason for the police lieutenant's special interest in the Marquise and what it was that irked him so much about her. It would hardly be tactful to mention that he wanted to use her as bait for the capture of her lover.

While Guibert was speaking, Antoine had begun to move about, as if it would somehow help his desperate attempt to make sense of what had been put before him. He walked to the edge of the water and stomped around in the emerald brine. Something in this account was wrong. Why was she still at the Court of Miracles after all this time? Why did she not take lodging somewhere else? Why would she punish herself like that? Did La Reynie break his promise?

"She didn't have the means to leave that thieves nest, even if she had wanted to," Guibert explained. "Besides, that fiend Pélégrin robbed her blind just for the privilege of not breaking her neck."

Antoine's fury competed with the pounding surf. "How dare you speak like that of the Marquise de Valinquette?"

"It's not always possible to observe the rules of decorum, Antoine. When you're dealing with the likes of Pélégrin, niceties simply don't apply. If you ever get your feet on the ground, you'll realize that most of life is a bloody mess. Most people have neither the luxury nor the time to give careful consideration to how they express themselves before the next blow comes crushing down on them. Never mind where the justice is in all that."

"Don't talk to me about injustice!" Antoine shouted, his black eyes flaring. "I've received my share, and more than my share. I've had my feet not only on the ground, I've been mired in muck up to my neck. But I still will not permit the Marquise de Valinquette to be spoken of in terms that are insulting to her dignity."

"I would never insult her," Guibert said calmly. "Never would I think of insulting a woman as courageous, as spirited, as undaunted, as resourceful and compassionate."

Antoine turned away.

"She's a woman, Antoine! Not a statue!" Guibert shouted into the gathering wind. "No Marquise of the blood can hold a candle to her! Marquise de Valinquette! What an empty epithet! She doesn't need a title of nobility!"

Antoine had climbed onto a rock jutting out into the sea. There he sat down, heedless of the wind and the screaming surf. He pressed his face against his knees and began to sob helplessly. His long black hair was threaded with silver, and what had he come to in his life?

Guibert shook his head. What a fool! But then he too was a fool. He matched Antoine inch for inch in folly. The thought frightened him and he tried to shrug it off. But once conceived, it became lodged in his mind. They were a matched pair, he and Antoine, total opposites but complementary. Fate had decreed it that way. And in one of fate's more capricious moments, it had decreed that they should both love the same woman.

And we are both the victims of the sins of our fathers, Guibert muttered, knowing that his words could not reach Antoine's ear. Perhaps it would be best if they died together, fighting the last pitched battle of the Valinquettes and Mallacs against the absolutist royal power. Even if there was no chance for victory, they would at least go down heroically, honorably, paragons of their race in the tradition of medieval knighthood.

Oh, balderdash! My brain must be softening! Guibert scolded himself. There's nothing heroic or even honorable about such a fight. What great cause was it their fathers died for? Petty squabbles, drawing-room intrigues that grew out of all proportion, cabals devised by relics of the past, anachronistic remnants who wanted at all cost to hang on to privileges and traditions that had been shattered by the progress of time. Now, years later, the sons were facing the royal power on a Breton heath, one an escaped convict, the other a common bandit. What noble cause could rally under their banner?

Even Mathurin, the mad preacher, had a cause to boast of that was worthier than theirs.

Guibert had sunk into such a state of gloom he failed to notice that Antoine had risen and was edging closer to the billowing sea.

When Guibert looked up his heart skipped a beat. An awful feeling of impending disaster lodged in the pit of his stomach. For a moment he stood inert, unable to move forward. Then he raced out onto the rock, clasped the taller man in his arms, and wrestled him back to the sand.

"What are you doing?" cried Antoine.

"I thought . . . you were . . ." Guibert was unable to finish the sentence, so breathless was he.

"You thought I was going to hurl myself into the surf?" Antoine laughed nervously. "Actually, I was in the mood to do so, but it would be too dangerous in this high tide. The salt spray felt good. It made me feel rejuvenated. I think it cleared my head."

Antoine was unusually garrulous as they struggled back to the higher cliffs.

"You know what I was thinking?"

Guibert did not answer. He was still panting and could not believe the sudden cheerfulness of this bastard who had him worried to death.

"I was thinking about the galley," Antoine continued. "As I stroked the sea with the oars, they seemed to become extensions of my arms. Hour upon hour—time had no real meaning—I would stroke the surface of the sea, blindly. I could feel it, got to know every ripple on the water's surface, the minutest agitation reverberated through my entire body, but I was never permitted to lay eyes on it. Mostly it felt smooth and soft like the skin of a woman. Sometimes I imagined that I had died and that I had been condemned for all eternity to caress the body of a woman I could not see. And I prayed—how I prayed!—that I might be granted just one glimpse of her, just one glimpse would be eternal bliss. Then I could rest. This is why the sight of the sea exhilarates me like nothing else. It fills me with a desire to embrace the waves, to melt into them. And I have you, Guibert, to thank for this moment, for being able to see the waves with my eyes!"

There was no stopping Antoine's effusions. Guibert had never seen such exuberance. All he could do was listen.

"You see these hands?" Antoine held up his leathery palms. "Completely calloused. After a while they become fused with the oars, you no longer feel where the flesh ends and the wood begins, it's all one. You become a monster with long flapping arms. Of course, your hands are not the only ones crafted to the oar. There are six to a bench, coiled together, all beating with one heart. They thought they could break me, those taskmasters. But they had not counted on the will of Antoine Maximilien de Valinquette in whose veins flows the ancient blood of the Barcas, the descendants of Hannibal who had crossed the Alps with elephants and inflicted defeat on mighty Rome at Cannae. But do you know what really gave me strength to bear their taunts, their lashes, even their scorn? It was the image of Galatée and the hope that some day I would see her again, some day I would have the opportunity to beg her forgiveness. Yes, I told myself, they can crucify me, but they cannot destroy my spirit as long as I have this hope."

Guibert had grown more and more uncertain of how to react to Antoine's ravings. Should he say anything? But what could he possibly say? Antoine seemed totally oblivious of who it was he was addressing and of the storm of emotion his story provoked in his listener. Perhaps by some fantastic trick of self-delusion, he had wiped from his memory everything that had happened—the adulterous affair, the child that issued from the illicit union, the duel in the early morning fog. He spoke to him, Guibert, not as the Marquise's lover but as to a mere bystander he chanced to meet and lend a willing ear, or not even that, as to somebody he met years later and to whom he felt compelled to divulge the tragic story of his love for his wife. No accusation of treachery. No bitterness except against the anonymous power of a cruel fate.

Antoine was still going on when, Guibert's discomfort had become almost unbearable, Coupe-Cheveux, blessed messenger from heaven, appeared and announced a delegation of Royal Musketeers was waiting at the fortress gate requesting to see the Count de Mallac.

The alacrity with which Guibert responded to the call, as to a propitious act of divine intervention, was not at all in keeping with the gravity of the situation it portended.

In keeping with custom and the traditions of siege warfare, the delegates delivered a parchment, addressed to the Count de Mallac, in which was spelled out, in the name of His Majesty, the King of France, an ultimatum and conditions for surrender within forty-eight hours of the fortress and his person and that of the Marquis de Valinquette into the hands of the royal commander. Guibert assured the gentlemen that the message would be taken under careful advisement and bid them a safe journey back to their camp. Outlaw though he might be, the Count de Mallac was ever punctilious in interacting with his peers.

Forty-eight hours gave at least some breathing space. The inhabitants of the fortress, who had anxiously observed the emplacement of the royal field cannons on the plain within close range, no longer had to fear a surprise attack. Guibert made the rounds of his garrison of peasants turned soldiers, exhorting them, despite their trepidation, to remain steadfast.

The cannon embanked in the tower would hold off the onslaught for a while. But how long could they withstand the might of the King's army? they asked. They could hold out as long as the supply of powder and munitions lasted, unless the food supply ran out first.

Unlike his royal adversaries, Guibert had no hope of reinforcements, nor did he have supply lines at his disposal. Depending on the fury of the attack, they might hold off the enemy for ten to twelve days, he estimated, and that would require considerable luck. One way or another, he would face death, either on the battlefield or on the gallows. He was slowly coming to grips with the inevitable. Nor would Antoine find much leniency under the King's law.

But surrender without a fight? The blood of his Breton ancestors flowing in his veins was as proud as that of the Barcas, and it rebelled against any such consideration. Would death in battle not be the more honorable choice? The lusty race of the Mallacs, who had ranged over this rugged coast for a thousand years, was becoming extinct. It was not in his power to halt the inexorable march of fate. But he, the last scion, would not besmirch the memory of his forebears. He would not go down ingloriously.

"Who says we have to go down at all?" Antoine asked, responding to Guibert's proposition that they both seek death in battle for the glory of their ancestors, the medieval knights, who had never capitulated under siege—neither Viking nor Saracen invaders, and certainly not upstart, decadent Bourbons had brought them to their knees.

"What other way is there? It's surrender and the gallows or death with honor." Guibert was beginning to warm to the idea of a hero's death and found it hard to see why Antoine objected to it under the circumstances.

As the time of battle approached, the friends sat down to a lavish repast in the company of Coupe-Cheveux and Mathurin, a last supper as it were. A bountiful board was laid out before them, the very best a country gentleman's larder had to offer. Antoine, as though redressing the wrongs his digestive system had suffered on the galley, carved for himself hefty portions of the roast viands and fowl. Guibert watched from the corner of his eyes with some astonishment the Marquis devouring chunks of venison, roast beef, roast pork, and smoked ham which he downed with mugs of beer and cider.

"I'm happy to see your appetite returned," Guibert said, "but at this rate we will run out of food before we run out of ammunition."

"It will not come to that. Don't you see? The choice is not between fighting and dying and surrendering and dying. Trust me, I have a plan." Suddenly it was Antoine who took charge. He had a plan. "Think of the woman who needs us alive. Neither one of us is any good to her dead."

This last consideration was enough to turn Guibert's mind from his heroic fantasies and make him more amenable to listen to the plan Antoine laid out before them.

A goodly supply of candles had been consumed and the sun began to send out its early morning rays when the conspirators—

Coupe-Cheveux and Mathurin were assigned an important part in the drama—keeled over into a contented sleep right at the banquet table.

Forty-eight hours after the ultimatum had been delivered and no formal surrender was received, the royal artillery sounded the opening salvos of attack. The bombardment lasted for about an hour. But the cannon in the tower of the fortress, which by then could have easily decimated the front line of the advancing infantry, remained silent. Instead of cannon smoke, a lily-white flag fluttered in the wind on top of the garret. The bewildered royal commander, spying this sign of surrender, stormed at the head of his troops across the drawbridge, which had been left down. They passed through the massive gate, left unbolted, into the courtyard where a ghostly silence received them.

Fearing a trap, the commander exhorted his soldiers to caution while they searched the interior. But the soldiers returned one by one with reports that they had been unable to detect the slightest trace of a living soul. The attackers found themselves in full control of the fortress. A hollow victory it was, for the commander had to concede that his prey had slipped through his fingers.

Book Three

Chapter 1

THE DUKE DE Rochemouton peered at his wife over the rim of his spectacles from behind his morning gazette. He cleared his throat several times to capture the Duchess's attention. Unaware of her husband's desire to break a thirty-year tradition of silent partaking of their late-morning repast, the Duchess for her part was so engrossed in the gustatory oblations before her that she remained blissfully unmindful of the signals issuing from the opposite end of the table.

"If it pleases Madame!" the Duke finally uttered, his voice thin and almost two octaves above his natural bass.

Her eyebrows raised, the Duchess twittered, "Yes, dear? You wish?" The pastry she was about to consume remained suspended in her hand halfway between the plate and her mouth and she was obviously annoyed by the distraction from the pleasures it promised.

"I should like your opinion on a certain matter, my dear, a peculiar matter," the Duke began tentatively.

"Oh, dear, you haven't been keeping company with those—what do you call them?—astromancers again, have you?"

"No, nothing of the sort," the Duke replied, now nettled for his part. "No, it is an altogether different matter. It concerns a mendicant, a woman, I have been observing for some time on the Pont Neuf. For some reason, I have not been able to put this rather wretched creature out of my mind."

"This is hardly anything new, is it? Monsieur is incapable of putting most women in Paris out of his mind." The Duchess, ever obliging in their habitual trading of witty insults, assumed an expression of pique in the best manner of the game. Then, thinking again, it occurred to her that there was something strange about the way he broached this subject and a mendicant at that. It was not at all in keeping with the usual opening to one of his confessions of infatuation with some courtesan. Such occasional effusions of honesty he deemed good for keeping the spunk in their marriage; but, as she knew too well, his surreptitious intent was to elicit from her the name of whoever was her lover of the moment. But a mendicant? That was certainly out of character and style.

"Paris is full of mendicants and so is the Pont Neuf," she remarked. "One can hardly get about a few paces without having one's sleeve pulled or a grimy hand shoved in one's way. It is a disgrace, and all the valiant efforts of our good police lieutenant have been to no effect in eradicating this blot on our city."

"Yes, yes, the plight of the poor is a festering sore." The Duke could not conceal his irritation at the Duchess's interminable complaints and abstract dissertations about the problem of pauperism in the Kingdom of France.

"But the topic I wish to discuss concerns neither pauperism nor mendicancy. I am speaking of one woman, a blind woman, who sits at the end of the Cité side of the bridge in the company of a child of about five and a miserable hunchback who collects the coins the good people of Paris throw to her. And . . . " he inserted a pregnant pause, "she sings! From the moment I heard that voice some irresistible force drew me to her. There is something familiar, eerily familiar, I should say, about that voice."

"Perhaps in better days she was a fille de joie and had the honor of entertaining Monsieur the Duke one night."

"Germaine! Be serious, just for once." The Duke's equanimity was rarely disturbed, but when he addressed her by her Christian name, the Duchess knew to take heed.

"I beg Monsieur's forgiveness," she said in a more subdued tone. "If it pleases Monsieur to come to the point."

"It is the voice that is so remarkable and familiar, a voice so pure, so haunting and beautiful, only one voice in the world that I have ever heard had all these qualities. There could be only one voice with the power to stir the soul, a voice that can ignite passions and lift men to a higher plane of being."

"You are exaggerating, as usual, but I presume you are speaking of the Marquise de Valinquette," the Duchess concluded.

"Yes," he said. "I have been passing by this blind woman daily several times. Could there be two voices like this in the world? It is quite possible, of course, that more than one voice should be capable of casting a spell over those who hear it, but could there be two identical voices?"

"My dear, dear Louis," intoned the Duchess patronizingly as if she were speaking to someone susceptible to hallucinations. "It has been years. Memory can play nasty tricks. How should the mind be able to retain for so long the exact timbre, the exact tonal quality, of a woman's voice?"

"Some things are unforgettable. And I shall never forget the Marquise de Valinquette's voice," the Duke insisted obstinately. "Did we ever find out what happened to the poor woman, after her husband disgraced himself in this terrible duel? Always was a hothead, that Marquis de Valinquette."

"Ah, here your memory is not so reliable, my dear." The Duchess could not resist taking the opportunity to gain the upper hand again. "You are forgetting that Madame was hardly blameless in her conduct prior to that fateful encounter. Since she vanished without a trace and we never found out what really happened, it seems safe to assume that she returned to her native Spain, or wherever it was she hailed from, leaving her husband, the poor cuckold, to the galleys."

"I seem to recall, however," retorted the Duke, now assuming the triumphant air of one who has trapped his opponent in a fatal move, "in fact I recall most vividly, that it was Madame the Duchess who advised against testifying on behalf of the poor cuckold, lest the House of Rochemouton become entangled, as she put it, in the sordid affair and earn the contempt of the Royal Court."

The Duchess's face glowed red. "No need now to dredge up bygones. What does all this have to do with a blind beggar woman on the Pont Neuf? It could not possibly be the Marquise as you seem to think. Maybe she has a twin who has somehow fallen on hard times. She may not even be blind, many of these people are very skilled in the art of dissimulation."

"No, not this woman. I have stopped in front of her everyday, I have studied her closely, her eyes are dull and empty, she could not see a hand before her eyes."

"I hope you have at least been generous to the pitiable creature while you were making a fool of yourself hovering about her like that. What if somebody should see you?"

"What do I care what anybody thinks. I want you to go to the Pont Neuf and see for yourself."

"Why, the preposterous suggestion! Expecting a woman of my station to lower herself and cavort about in the squalor of the gutter. May God spare me from coming back as a pauper in my next life!"

"Take your daughter with you. I'm sure she would regard such a foray into the lower world as an adventure."

"Take your daughter where? And what adventure?" The question came from the direction of the door where La Belle Hélène was just making her appearance.

Hélène was quickly filled in about her father's remarkable preoccupation. And although it took her some time to sort out the conflicting bits and pieces with which she was bombarded from opposite directions, in the end she did pronounce herself excited at the prospect of an expedition down into the dregs of Paris, which she usually glimpsed only fleetingly from her speeding carriage.

However, later that day, when mother and daughter alighted near the spot the Duke had described, no singing blind woman was to be found anywhere near the Pont Neuf. They returned the next day, and the next, and so for a week, but the Duke's blind woman with the haunting voice had disappeared.

La Fauvette returned to the place they now called home with sluggish, burdened gait. She toted a basket of washing on her hip while struggling to keep pace with a little girl skipping ahead of her.

"Chantal, you're going too fast," she protested out of breath. "Be patient. We'll be home soon enough."

"But I'm hungry, Maman," the child replied, "and Grand-mère is waiting with supper."

"Run ahead then! I'll be with you in a moment."

The child quickly disappeared from La Fauvette's sight into the twisted maze of narrow alleyways that formed the quarter of Saint-Honoré in the heart of the city. She set down the heavy basket and paused for a moment, leaning against the side of a crooked thatch-roofed structure kept upright only by means of similar structures on both sides of it, like cripples lending each other support on an uncertain course. The years of poverty and toil had not been kind to the Marquise de Valinquette. Hardly a trace of the effulgence that once dazzled the beau monde of the Marais was discernible in the prematurely furrowed face. But her eyes were still able to cast their passionate spell when opportune, those violet eyes whose beam she could set ablaze or extinguish at will, so that they might spark a fire or project a dull, expressionless blind stare on the world.

But the years of struggle among the lowest of the low, in a world where one was never sure what the next moment would bring, where the food for the next meal would come from, this life of ducking and hustling had also sharpened her senses. Her acute perception of any unusual movement, any occurrence out of the ordinary within a considerable radius, set her ready to pounce or to flee.

On that evening, as she rested in the alleyway on her way to the rue Saint Honoré where the noble Lucien had quartered the Widow Caillart's clan, out of the corner of her eye she detected the approach of a stout, richly attired gentleman. Instinctively, she gathered her basket and with head bent she started on her way. Though slowed by the weight of the basket, she deftly navigated the obstacles in her way. But the man was keeping pace. To make sure it was she he was pursuing, she turned several corners in quick succession, but his breath remained audible behind her. Her hope that his pursuit might be frustrated by the clusters of people who obstructed the narrow alley went unfulfilled since the good citizens of Paris obediently made way for the illustrious gentleman who somehow had found his way into their destitute precinct.

At last she halted. The best way to brave a danger from which there was no escape was to face up to it, the more defiant and resolute the better. Balancing the basket on her hip as a barrier between herself and her pursuer, she turned and came face to face with the man whose daily visits to the Pont Neuf had made her abandon that station and take up laundering to rake in a few sous.

The Duke de Rochemouton attempted a smile, but she kept her eyes cast downward, as was appropriate for the servile in the presence of the august; in fact she only meant to evade his scrutinizing gaze.

"You are not blind after all!" He seemed pleased with the observation. "You certainly did fool me."

"I'm afraid Monsieur must be taking me for somebody else," she muttered.

"Oh, no, I am quite certain that you and a certain person with an enthralling voice I had the opportunity to observe several weeks ago on the Pont Neuf are one and the same."

"Since Monsieur is so kind and seems to have taken a special interest in the fate of this wretched woman, maybe he can also find it in his heart to understand that the poor often have to resort to ruses and deception to stay alive and feed their children."

"Very well spoken. A most astounding eloquence for a woman of your station!"

"If Monsieur only wanted to convince himself of the identity of the beggar woman from the Pont Neuf, may I request his kind permission to move on. There are pressing tasks that await my attention."

"Unfortunately, I cannot let you go so soon, now that I have found you. I must confess I was quite distraught when the blind woman disappeared from the bridge. But then the hand of providence made our paths cross again."

"What possible purpose could Monsieur have with a humble woman like me?" La Fauvette had stopped playing the part of the lowly beggar. The despair that rang in her plea was quite genuine as she struggled to come up with a way to disengage herself from this most inopportune situation.

"What is your name?" the Duke continued his investigation.

"My mother calls me La Fauvette," she replied.

"How beautiful and fitting! Like the little singing bird from the gutter!"

She felt the Duke's inquisitive glance moving from her face to her entire person with the unabashed frankness of a nobleman. She retreated slightly under his penetrating gaze. Suddenly he leaned close to her ear and said softly: "Qu'importa que muero se ressuscitan?"

Not a muscle moved in her face. She kept her eyes averted. A moment of tense silence ensued. He repeated the phrase slowly, carefully enunciating every word. When she finally looked at him, her expression was one of complete incomprehension.

"Well, it was only a fancy. For some reason I thought somebody who is called La Fauvette would know the words of this Spanish song. It was silly of me."

He threw a handful of coins into her basket and, nodding, turned away. But something still held him back. For a moment he hesitated. Then he shook his wig mane, banishing whatever thought it was that had sprung to his mind. With a shrug of the shoulders, he turned and quickly marched with imperious stride through the crowd of bystanders who needed no prompting to make way.

La Fauvette was on the verge of mental and physical collapse when she reached the squat, dingy structure that was their home now. It was in better repair and more spacious—she even occupied a small enclosed space she called her room—than the one-room hut at the Court of Miracles, and was not as cramped and squalid, but the abode could hardly be described as comfortable.

She evaded the questions hurtling at her as she entered the common room. Not even Chantal would get an explanation for her tardiness that evening. She directed her steps straight to her private little space and stopped only briefly to kiss the child on the cheek, mumbling something about having to be by herself for a while.

Alone inside the sparsely furnished chamber, she sank onto a rickety chair. A wood pallet with a sack of straw and a coarse blanket serving as her bed—the featherbed did not survived La Salpêtrière—and a three-legged table above which hung the shard of a looking glass were the only furnishings in the windowless cell.

Her attention was suddenly drawn to the dimming glass on the wall. She had long fallen out of the habit of preening in front of a mirror, but that evening, by the flicker of a candle, something drew her to undertake a long, ponderous examination of her reflection.

In the cracked, fragmented image the mirror reflected, she discerned a face, morose and wasted, that made her shrink in dismay. Would Guibert still love such a haggard figure? And Antoine?

In the last few months, since those endless days and nights of brooding at La Salpêtrière, her thoughts of Guibert had begun to mingle with thoughts of Antoine. It was a curious turn of mind. Sometimes the two merged into one and she no longer distinguished between them. Her anger against Antoine had softened. She often wondered where he might be, and her heart ached at the thought of the ordeal he had to endure. The pain she felt for him was all the greater for, at long last, she had come to realize that it was his love for her, however misguided, that had been his undoing.

Suddenly she recoiled. If her face was that of a hag, what did the rest of her body look like? With trembling fingers, she peeled off the layers of rags. She turned and twisted, but no matter how she tried, the mirror was too small to reflect her whole figure. All she could do was look down on herself.

"Like a scarecrow!" she muttered several times over, each time with heightened disgust. Without her beauty, what was she worth? Who would love her? Who would even care what became of her? Maybe that was why Guibert had abandoned her, why he had left her in this hole to rot. What if he no longer found her desirable? And Antoine? He with his obsession, his fancy about the ideal woman, his fetish of alabaster firm breasts. Were he to see her now—a skeleton of loose skin and bones, her breasts sagging pouches—he would not likely waste a second look on her.

The idea that she was no longer a desirable woman began to torment her. Even as her rational self tried to disperse her abysmal self-image as a woman no man would want, that image etched itself deeper and deeper into her soul.

Although her singing had arrested his attention, the Duke de Rochemouton certainly did not recognized the once radiant hostess of the Hôtel de Valinquette behind the ugly mask poverty and privation had carved in her face. She was quite sure of that. He was plainly incredulous, unable to make the leap. Even though for a moment he had glimpsed something of her former self, her voice, he had quickly scoffed at the idea that this beggar in the street and the Marquise de Valinquette could be one and the same.

Marquise, indeed! she muttered scornfully. She grabbed the looking glass and flung it down. This here, the underbelly of Paris, was her abode, this her proper place, this, the lot to which she was born! What pretense! What impudence! What overweening pride had possessed her to defy the divine design, to challenge the eternal, natural order of the world?

So lost was she in her misery, in bouts of self-recrimination and self-pity, she did not hear the timid rapping until the door was opened under whimpering entreaties of "Maman! Maman!" The sight of the child, the one bright star in her life, made her instantly cast aside all baleful ruminations. She rushed up and pulled her inside, enclosing her in her arms with such fervor as if she never wanted to let her go.

"Are you hurt, Maman?" the child sounded frightened.

"No, no, Mignonne. Maman is not hurt, just tired and sad."

"What makes you so sad?"

"That my little princess has to live in such a bleak place. Sometimes I blame myself for not making things nicer for you."

"But I'm happy, I don't want anything else. I have you and Grandmère and Uncle Prosper, and all the others. I didn't like it at the hospital with all those strange people, they frightened me. But I like it here very much. And Uncle Lucien is the nicest and most wonderful person."

"Yes, you are right, we must be grateful to have such a good friend." She kissed the little girl on the forehead and couldn't stop hugging her, so grateful was she for the words from the mouth of one wise beyond her years.

"But I'm afraid for you sometimes," said Chantal. "Sometimes I have a dream that bad men will come and take you away from me like they did at the hospital. That scares me."

La Fauvette pressed the girl closer to her bosom, trying to soothe her fears, and perhaps hers as well, with assurances that nothing, but nothing in this world would ever, ever part them.

The incident that seemed to have etched itself into the little girl's mind and caused her so much anguish occurred several months before, while they were still quartered at La Salpêtrière. The ever resourceful Lucien had persuaded Monsieur de La Reynie that his chosen Fabrisse—the union had not been consecrated, but that was a formality that could be remedied in due course—and her brood would be more suitably housed at his own lodging. The arrangements had hardly been completed when Lucien approached the police lieutenant, telling him of Fabrisse's nightmares and insomnia caused by the uncertainty of the fate of her sons, Gaston and Rémy, who had been sent to Bicêtre in the company of their uncle, the hunchback Prosper.

Although he had some misgivings about Prosper, Monsieur de La Reynie conceded that the safety of the streets of Paris would hardly be endangered by the release of these boys. He warned his deputy, however, that locating anybody at Bicêtre, even more so than at La Salpêtrière, was like turning up a coin in a mountain of refuse. But Lucien's determination, impelled by love and stamina bordering on the inhuman, could not be thwarted by the wrenching groans of pestilence, insanity, and every woe known to man that reigned at the men's shelter just as at the women's of what was called Hôpital Général. In the end Lucien's dauntless quest produced the three lost souls. They were infected with lice and vermin, but otherwise in good condition.

Monsieur de La Reynie's patience started to betray some strain when he was asked a short time later for the release of the Widow

Caillart and the rest of her entourage. He relented on the old matriarch and the little girl, but under no circumstances would he set the Marquise and her harlots free to corrupt the morals of the city, as he put it. Later he even let the harlots go, but on the Marquise he remained obdurate.

The scene that had made such an indelible impression on the little girl took place on the day Lucien came to take her and her grandmother Gervaise away from the terrible hospital. Her mother, unwilling to be separated from her child, kicked and cursed. She was only restrained when two overseers slapped her into submission.

The separation of mother and daughter ended only when a virulent typhoid fever broke out among the ravaged inhabitants of La Salpêtrière. Dead, the Marquise would be of no use whatsoever to Monsieur de La Reynie. The fox never gave up hope: one day his prey would come home, he was sure of it.

No prostitution and under no circumstances would the Marquise be allowed to leave the city. Those were the police lieutenant's stipulations.

"Where could she possibly go?" Lucien asked.

"I'm in receipt of intelligence concerning certain movements in Brittany, near Saint-Malo. The Count de Mallac and a host of criminals from every corner of the Kingdom seem to have converged on that area. That scoundrel is obviously shrewder than even we expected. But he will hang by his own cunning. By God, I won't leave anything to chance." Monsieur de La Reynie slammed his fist on his desk so no one would doubt his words.

"This source, it is reliable?" Lucien hid his alarm under a facade of officiousness.

"Oh, yes. The man barely escaped with his life from the thieves' lair in the forest near Saint-Malo. And there is no doubt that Mallac is the leader of the murderous outfit."

"How did he gain entrance into such company?" At the risk of arousing the police lieutenant's ire, Lucien pushed the limits of caution to learn the identity of the informer.

As luck, or providence, would have it, Monsieur de La Reynie proved to be in a voluble mood that day, and unable to resist the opportunity to instruct an inferior in the tricks of the police trade, with Lucien, on this occasion, a willing student.

"Of course, he's a thief and worse, most of our best sources are. You do them a favor and they will often repay you with their gratitude. There is a certain code of honor even among thieves that can often benefit a police investigation. You should remember that, my dear Lefèvre, for the future."

Unfortunately, the police lieutenant could not be induced to divulge the name of his informant. Only much later, on the day after the Duke de Rochemouton came looking for a blind beggar woman with a voice uncannily like that of the Marquise de Valinquette, did the visit of two other men to the lodging of the Widow Caillart in the rue Saint Honoré shed some light on this mystery, and much else.

When La Fauvette at long last emerged from the darkness of La Salpêtrière, the shadowy tomb that served as women's prison, hospital, insane asylum, and shelter for the dispossessed of every description, she almost threw herself into the open air, giddy with sunlight, inebriated with a sense of freedom. She sallied along the quais and crossed to the other side of the river, cutting a path between the mendicant cripples on the crowded Pont Neuf. What were they to her, the beggars, the street vendors, the loiterers, who milled around soliciting alms, hawked their wares, or plied some sinister trade, as they had done since anybody could remember.

She lingered for a moment at the foot of the bridge where the song of a blind and lame child once, so long ago in another life almost, had touched the heart of a melancholy aristocrat with high-flown artistic ideals and dreams. She remembered his tread on the pavement as he approached her. She could sense his approach from far away. Every day he came by to speak to her and never went away without leaving a generous reward. He was so kind then, she thought. How handsome he was with his long shiny black hair tied at the nape of his neck, his dark eyes, dreamy and filled with a secret passionate yearning. But that was only one side of him, she reminded herself. Besides, she had repaid him many times over. She owed him nothing.

With new resolve she went on her way. What good was it to dwell on the past? What was gone was gone. She tossed back her head, shrugging it all off. She had better prepare for the real world, for the struggle to escape this vale of tears. Her child would not sit at a corner feigning infirmity for a few sous. No, a thousand times no! As long as she had a breath left in her body, her child would never be subject to abuse and humiliation. Chantal had seen too much of it already in her short life.

Despite her intentions, however, the real world and its struggles, in the form of petty backbiting, came crashing down on her the moment she turned into the rue Saint Honoré, searching for her mother's dwelling among the ramshackle tenements. She was still several paces away, when the foulest screams of women reached her ear. This was in and of itself nothing unusual in any of the poorer quarters of town, and so she gave little thought to the screeches as she approached the house to which she had been directed.

On crossing the threshold, she landed in the midst of a dispute, if one could dignify the wild gush of crudest epithets that way. Arlette and Ondine were having it out, and Fabrisse and Prosper stood helplessly by. Fabrisse's brood and Chantal were cheering on the hyenas, one and then the other. Gervaise was muttering to herself by the stove without taking her eyes from her pots. The verbal bout was just turning into a hair-pulling circus and might have ended with the two amazons scratching out each other's eyes, had the appearance of the Marquise not abruptly halted the altercation.

It was all so familiar, as if she had left her mother's hut at the Court of Miracles only the day before. The low ceiling, the walls daubed in soot; the sparse, crudely fashioned furnishings; the stench of poverty, thickened by the sweltering heat that attached to everything and everybody like a mangy dog—it was just like home.

But after the long, dreary months of confinement at La Salpêtrière, how could she complain? This was a palace by comparison! And as she found out, this place was more spacious than the house at the Court of Miracles, with separate sleeping quarters and a space she could call her own.

The altercation and its cause were quickly forgotten as the women and children—except for Gervaise, who stuck by her pots and merely muttered a greeting—all flocked around to embrace La Fauvette, whom they had almost given up for lost. The women took turns explaining that Lucien was determined to make honest women of them all. To that end the constable had used his connections with the owners of various factories to arrange for piecework to be brought in which would make it unnecessary for the ladies to walk the streets. The loom on which they did their work occupied the center of the room.

La Fauvette tried to operate the loom according to the women's instructions, but it soon became clear that this sort of labor was not for her. It was not the tediousness of the task, the repetitive motions of warping and weaving, nor the strain on the hands and the entire body that turned her away. It rather was that the stay at La Salpêtrière had left her with a horror of being confined for too long in closed, poorly lit spaces. A horrifying fear of walls caving in, of being buried alive, pushed her into the open air.

Lucien at first would not hear of it. But what else could she do to earn her keep? She could still pretend to be blind and lame, and she could sing. They finally settled on blindness alone. All went well for a while. Her heavenly singing enticed the good citizens of Paris to dig deeper into their pockets than they might have been inclined to do ordinarily. Prosper and Chantal collected the coins tumbling to her feet. Prosper had become apprenticed to a tanner, but the resulting odor that clung to him was more than La Fauvette could bear, and she insisted that he leave this employ.

Then one day she noticed from the corner of her upturned eyes the stout figure of an aristocrat, standing at a distance. He came closer only to deposit a handful of coins, and then disappeared among the crowd. He was back again the next day, and the following day, and so for a week or maybe even two. She did not know how long he had been doing this before she first became aware of this daily ritual. Unable to look directly at him, she could not make out immediately who he was. But when she finally did steal a glimpse, she recognized the Duke de Rochemouton.

The only explanation she could find for the Duke's seeming interest was that he wanted to assure himself of her identity before reporting her to the police lieutenant for panhandling and simulating infirmity.

Monsieur de La Reynie had posted strict directives against such scams and nothing was more frightening to her than the possibility of being tossed back into La Salpêtrière.

This was how she came to abandon her post at the Pont Neuf and take on the backbreaking work of a washerwoman, which at least permitted her to remain outdoors. However, it had not occurred to her that this aristocrat, with a pedigree as long as the history of France and whose primary pursuits had always been of a frivolous, self-indulgent nature, would feel compelled, once he could no longer find her singing on the bridge, to search for her in this decidedly unfashionable part of town.

Chapter 2

ON THE MORNING after the encounter with the Duke de Rochemouton, which had precipitated her nocturnal bout of self-pity, self-reproach, despondency, and again revived hope, La Fauvette, all energy spent, slept a dreamless sleep into the blue of the day.

Even then she might not have stirred from her slumber had she not been alerted by men's voices. She recognized Lucien's nasal tone, but the others were definitely strangers. At first it was difficult to tell whether they were animated or agitated, but she soon concluded from the shreds of words and phrases reaching her ears that the exchange was of a cordial nature.

Whoever these men were, she still had too much pride left in her to present herself as an unkempt slattern. With the help of a crude comb in front of a piece of the shattered mirror, a sprinkling of water, a bit of rouge and some straightening of her garments, a not totally unpleasing veneer was restored to her appearance, though only the spark of her violet eyes and the dignity of her gait betrayed any signs of her former status.

Silence fell over the room as she entered like a queen a throne room filled with audience seekers. The two strangers standing next to Lucien turned a curious eye toward her, and even Arlette and Ondine, aroused by the masculine presence like two bitches in heat, turned their attention away from the men for a moment. Chantal ran up to her mother and flung her arms around her.

The gentlemen, Lucien uttered that word in a dubious tone as he introduced them, had come with a message from the Count de Mallac. The sinister one with the dark beard and rolling eyes, ample girth and stentorian voice, he presented as Mathurin of Clermont. The other, who was the exact opposite in every aspect—short, thin, and fair—was one Jacques Brunat of Poitou. Both counted it their good fortune, so they said, to be business associates of a gentleman as gracious as the Count de Mallac.

To La Fauvette these characters looked suspiciously more like cronies of Pélégrin than confidants of her beloved Guibert. They began by spouting some flattering phrases, but she cut them short with a sharp demand for the message.

"Can we speak privately?" asked Jacques Brunat, who had considered it wiser not to introduce himself by his more infamous moniker, Coupe-Cheveux.

"Whatever concerns me, concerns all of us. So go right ahead. What is the message?"

"But Monsieur the Count gave express instruction . . ."

"All right, Lucien, please lead the gentlemen into my parlor!" she conceded sarcastically, and with a grandiose gesture pointed to the dingy chamber in the corner.

The one who called himself Jacques Brunat delivered Guibert's message to Madame.

"Monsieur the Count regrets not being able to come to Paris himself but he requests Madame and everyone with her to leave the city at once."

"So that is the entire message?" she asked.

"Yes, this is exactly what he asked us—Mathurin here and me—to tell Madame."

"Well, I presume you gentlemen know where it is Monsieur the Count wants us to go and you will lead us to his residence in Brittany this night," she said, barely concealing her excitement. Deliverance was here at last!

However, Lucien thought the idea imprudent.

"Tonight may be a bit too soon, after all we have to make preparations. Monsieur de La Reynie's suspicions will certainly be aroused if he hears of a sudden departure."

Mathurin hastened to correct the Marquise's misimpression. "My friend here has misled you, Madame." He cuffed Coupe-Cheveux on the head for emphasis. "Monsieur the Count is no longer in Brittany. Certain circumstances, a series of events beyond his control, I should say, compelled him to absent himself from the Kingdom of France until . . . well, until things quiet down."

"But didn't this dimwit just say the Count is waiting for me?"

"That indeed is so, Madame. But not in Brittany or anywhere in France for that matter. As I indicated, pressing matters forced him to . . . Monsieur the Count hopes Madame will be able to join him across the Spanish border in Catalonia. He said Madame is familiar with the region."

"In Catalonia? What in heaven's name is he doing in Catalonia?"

"Monsieur the Marquis suggested they retire to his estate there, as a safe haven from the French police and the Royal Musketeers. Under the circumstances, believe me Madame, it was the wisest thing to do. The King's Musketeers are a persistent lot and it was not easy to escape their reach."

"The Marquis, did you say?" she asked sharply, as this most interesting detail emerged.

"Yes, Madame, the Marquis de Valinquette. The Count and the Marquis booked passage on a Portuguese trading vessel and set sail from Brest about two weeks ago. Assuming all went well, they should be in Barcelona by now."

"I rescued the Marquis myself," Coupe-Cheveux added, seeking her approval for so brave a deed. "Well, not myself alone, of course, but I assisted the Count in every way I could. It was because of the Marquis that our grand scheme to cash in on that fleet from the West Indies, the scheme the Count had so carefully prepared, went to naught. The moment he saw the Marquis standing on the docks at Saint-Malo, he couldn't think of anything else but to get him away from the galley. Of course, I had to help him carry it out. He couldn't have done it alone. But, of course, I was glad to be of help. Monsieur the Count and I have been friends for a long time. We've stood shoulder to shoulder against our enemies . . ."

"Can't you see you're trying the lady's patience with your babbling?" Mathurin cut in.

"Let me see if I understand this right," the Marquise said with all the calm she could muster. "The Count de Mallac was at Saint-Malo, where he chanced to meet the Marquis de Valinquette."

"That's right. The galley had a hole in its bowel and the convicts were brought ashore while the ship was being repaired."

"So the Count decided to rescue the Marquis and now they are on their way to Spain together. They are expecting us to follow them there. Do you find this story a bit fantastic, Lucien?"

"Fantastic, yes. But how could they have made it all up? They know too many details no outsider could know. And what would they have to gain by making up such a story?"

"Then why is there no personal letter?"

"The Count did not want anything to fall into the hands of the police, for the sake of Madame's safety," said Mathurin.

"If we are to travel beyond the borders of the Kingdom, I'm sure Monsieur the Count did not forget that travel requires certain means. I'm sure he is also aware of my family's circumstances. Surely he must have made provisions for that."

She addressed herself primarily to Mathurin, who seemed the more articulate and sharper of the two.

"Oh, yes, of course, Madame is quite right," Mathurin replied, raising his bushy eyebrows with a glance at his companion. "Didn't Monsieur the Count provide generously for Madame's journey, Monsieur Brunat?"

"Why yes, but I thought . . ."

"The fact is Monsieur the Count entrusted this cretin here with 100 écus. But Coupe-Cheveux here lost it."

"He lost it?" the Marquise and Lucien exclaimed as one.

"I was robbed in Rennes!" Coupe-Cheveux protested.

"In a whorehouse! He lost it in a whorehouse. The imbecile bragged about the loot he was carrying." Satisfaction with being able to get one up on Coupe-Cheveux rang in Mathurin's voice. "I knew Monsieur the Count should not have trusted him."

"One moment of weakness," Coupe-Cheveux whined, "and you think you're better than me. You show me somebody who doesn't have a moment of weakness every now and then, even you, Monsieur Preacher!"

"That's enough!" the Marquise exploded. "You worthless thug, you squandered the money in a whorehouse! The money that was to liberate us from this miserable life! And you dare come to me empty-handed? What good is your message to me now? How dare you even deliver the message without the means!"

Her voice gained in volume, culminating in a mad burst of curses at both messengers—her anger did not distinguish between them—that shook the walls of the Widow Caillart's abode. Her violent outburst sent the visitors scramming for the door. They would have fled, maybe never to return, had Lucien not blocked their way and threatened them with arrest if they tried to go even one step further.

"If you don't shoot these blasted cowards, Lucien, I'll strangle them myself," she screamed. Chantal ran for cover under her grandmother's apron.

"Let's all calm down, if you please," Lucien said nervously. "The whole neighborhood can hear us and soon the news will travel to the Châtelet."

Lucien took the Marquise aside, whispering to her insistently. Realizing that the damage done would have to be dealt with somehow, she finally became more amenable to discuss the matter further with the visitors. With an air of injured dignity, she sat down across from the pair, being fawned over by the prostitutes.

A throng of conflicting emotions still stirred La Fauvette's soul. Despair and rage that fate seemed bent on perpetuating her mistfortune overwhelmed her after the hope that deliverance was finally at hand had once again been dashed. Yet she also felt a sense of exhilaration mixed with apprehension caused by the strange story of Antoine's rescue from the galleys, a rescue undertaken by none other than Guibert. The uproar over the missing money had distracted her for a moment and she did not immediately grasp the profound consequences of this turn of events for her life. When she finally gained a clearer mind and realized that no matter how much she might rage, the money was still lost, she asked Coupe-Cheveux to relate the details of the entire incredible story.

Coupe-Cheveux, who saw an opportunity for redeeming himself, complied only too eagerly. He recounted the particulars of the rescue, embellishing a little here and there where it might shed a heroic light on himself. The Marquise hung on his every word.

If she understood the story correctly, Guibert had risked everything to rescue a man with whom he had previously been engaged in mortal combat. She remembered her last conversation with Guibert at the Court of Miracles and the warm sentiments he expressed about Antoine, his faith in the basic decency of his character, despite everything that had happened. She remembered how excluded she felt from the elemental bond that existed between them. That Guibert should rescue Antoine when the opportunity presented itself, even at the risk of his own life, was, therefore, entirely plausible to her.

Perhaps the most amazing part of the story was Antoine's insistence that, when faced with the royal guns, he and Guibert had to stay alive for her sake, that nothing would be served by making her, Madame the Marquise, doubly a widow. Thus they had abandoned the battlements and beat a retreat along the Breton coastline to the seaport of Brest, where they embarked for Barcelona—but not before dispatching the two thugs turned loyal retainers, Coupe-Cheveux emphasized, on their mission to Paris.

"But how will we get out of this city with the eyes of the police ever upon us?" she wondered aloud. "And even if we could get past the city walls, without money it is hopeless to think that we could reach the border."

"Maybe this will help." Mathurin rummaged through the scrip he carried tightly girded over his jerkin. He reached deep inside and, as he drew out an object, his face glowed with triumphant satisfaction.

"Ah, here it is!" he exclaimed proudly and flung a necklace studded with emeralds and rubies, fashioned in the rare design of Mayan craftsmanship, on the table. All eyes were pinned on the gems. An awed silence ensued, as if the beauty of the jewels had rendered them speechless.

Ondine broke the silence. "This is my necklace!" She made a grab for it but was blocked by the Marquise.

"Not so fast, my dear!" she said, holding the greedy hand of the Babylonian whore. "This necklace is a unique, unmistakable piece I would recognize anywhere."

She picked it up and held it up to the light, gazing at it as though she had been reunited with a lost lover.

"You may have worn it at one time, when you got it from your pimp Pélégrin. But I'm the rightful owner. It was a present the Marquis brought back for me from the New World. How did it get into your hands, Monsieur Mathurin?"

"Madame just mentioned a certain Pélégrin," he answered with some embarrassment. "This necklace was given to me by a man called Pélégrin, a despicable swine, may he perish a thousand painful deaths and burn in hell through all eternity."

Coupe-Cheveux's ears had pricked up. "Why would Pélégrin give you such a precious piece? You were entrusted with guarding the bastard while Monsieur the Count and I went to Saint-Malo. You must have taken it when he was asleep."

"No, no!" Mathurin protested. "He offered it to me in return . . . for his freedom."

"You mean he bribed you to let him go?"

"One might look at it that way. Name anybody who could resist being tempted by a piece as beautiful and precious as this. You certainly would not." Mathurin's meek attempt to justify himself only provoked Coupe-Cheveux to continue.

"But you know what happened as a result of your letting the bastard get away."

"I need no reminder and I shall have to live with it on my conscience for the rest of my earthly existence. But now that the jewelry has been restored to its rightful owner, maybe I shall find peace of mind."

"Your peace of mind concerns me very little," grunted Coupe-Cheveux. "If the Count finds out about this . . ."

"The Count would no doubt be delighted to learn," Mathurin continued confidently, "that this piece can now be put to good use and allow these good people to make their journey to freedom, which your dissipate nature had almost brought to failure before it began." Mathurin was back in the saddle.

The Marquise, for her part, was only too eager to set aside the tortuous history of the necklace and to concentrate on finding a way to turn it into cash without Monsieur de La Reynie getting wind of it.

The two men, who in the end had indeed brought good tidings, were invited to share a meal with the Marquise and her household and were allowed to spend the night on the floor of the common room. However, the Marquise was very anxious to be rid of these jail birds early the next morning. She instructed them in the simple return message they were to take to the Count: She would join him and the Marquis as soon as circumstances permitted. Meanwhile no further communication must pass between them. The wily designs of the one intent on crossing their plans must not be underestimated.

At the crack of dawn, upon finishing her instructions, she guided them out into the street. Hopefully, no one saw them leave, at least no one who might be inclined to tattle at police headquarters. The pair was only too happy to put a distance between themselves and the city, where, by their lights, far too many gendarmes and armed officers of the King made their presence felt.

Later La Fauvette closeted herself in her room. A plan had formed in her mind and she rehearsed the scenario with painstaking care. There was some risk of failure, even of complete reversal. But it was her only chance. She spent considerable time preparing and grooming herself, smoothing her garments, sewing a tear here and there, and making herself up in the best manner possible. Then she slipped out without letting anyone know where she was going.

She walked along the familiar pavement with firm, determined steps, directing them without wavering toward the prefecture of the police. The time had finally come for the long delayed rendezvous with the police chief of Paris.

Monsieur de La Reynie immediately interrupted all activity when the Marquise de Valinquette was announced. In all the years of the war of nerves between them, he had never given up hope that someday she would come to her senses, as he saw it, and accede to his demand to aid him in the capture of the Count de Mallac. So when he was told that she requested to see him with some urgency, the embers of hope flared up for a brief moment that the day had finally come, that she had come to surrender. It had been only a matter of time before she would break, he thought, satisfied with himself.

But what he encountered was not a meek woman ready to lay down arms. Haughty, defiant, even accusatory, she stood before him. Without a word she flung the necklace on his desk like a gauntlet, a challenge for a final face-off. He gazed at the hypnotic gleam radiating from the rubies and emeralds.

"Never mind how these gems were returned to me," she fended off his question before he had a chance to ask. "It is of no import. The question is how did they get from Monsieur's possession into some rather unsavory hands?"

At any other time, the police lieutenant would not have tolerated this kind of arrogance toward him, the arm of the King's law. But the sudden appearance of the necklace in her hands paralyzed his thoughts. He had put the murder of Gaston Caillart out of his mind. By the time he heard about it from his deputy, it had been too late anyway to do anything, though a gnawing sense that he somehow was responsible, or should have done something had never quite left him. But what would an investigation have accomplished? Every day, at any hour, somewhere in some tavern, in some alley of the city, a thug gets himself killed in a brawl, usually a drunken brawl. A man like Gaston should have known not to enter a tavern with a pouch of precious stones in his possession. The bloodhounds can sniff such stuff right through the leather.

"Last time I saw this particular necklace it graced the bosom of Pélégrin's whore. Of course, I was not in a position then to claim it as my own without risk of having my throat cut," she said after a long silence, which the police lieutenant showed no inclination of breaking. "The question that poses itself is, how did the necklace get there? How did my jewelry, confiscated by the police, get into the hands of that lowlife who called himself king of the Court of Miracles? The same king who got away safely, with his contraband, before the Court of Miracles was demolished, burnt to the ground, while lesser inhabitants were tossed into the street, or into the hell of La Salpêtrière and Bicêtre."

"Is Madame aware that she is making grave accusations against an officer and servant of His Majesty the King?" La Reynie finally managed to say. He spoke calmly, but an undertone of irritation should have warned her not to push the limits. She should have treaded more carefully, but the impetuous side of her nature, especially when her ire was aroused, was gaining the upperhand.

"The servant of the King of France or of the king of Saint-Médard?" The arrow hit its mark and quivered there. Never, but never, had any aspersions been cast on the honor and moral integrity of the lieutenant of police.

"You scurrilous little guttersnipe!" he burst out. His face glowed as red as the rubies on the desk. Hurt pride, outrage, and shame mingled in his demeanor. "Not even Lucien Lefèvre, that befuddled, misguided clown, will save you from your just punishment for defaming the name of a public official!"

The virulence of his reaction made her take a few steps backward for fear he might lash out at her.

"How does Monsieur explain the strange transfer of the jewels from this office to the hands of Pélégrin?" she persisted, but less truculent.

"The police lieutenant does not have to explain anything to one such as you! He is answerable only to His Majesty King Louis XIV of France." He took obvious satisfaction from the fact that he had succeeded in intimidating this queen of the gutter, who gave herself airs as if she hailed from the best society.

"This," he picked up the necklace with two fingers as if it was a poisonous snake. "This is obviously contraband and will have to be requisitioned until proof of ownership can be established. I don't presume Madame has such proof. Unfortunately, the one person who could provide proof, the Marquis de Valinquette, has become a fugitive from the law. It seems he joined his fortunes to those of the other infamous fugitive, the Count de Mallac. I don't suppose either of the gentlemen will visit our fair city in the near future. Or am I wrong?"

She understood his insinuation that she should understand the reconciliation between Guibert and Antoine was somehow a conspiracy against her, but she hardly paid attention to his words. All she could think of was that she had to get the necklace back. Her mind was working feverishly. Her eyes surveyed the man in front of her from head to toe. He was a man in his middle years, small of stature and rotund. They were alone in the room. If she moved quickly she might be able to overpower him with a blow to the head. But she would never reach the street. No, she rejected the idea as soon as it was born. She had to use cunning, distract him, even seduce him. He was a man, wasn't he?. But she no longer possessed a face or figure that turned men's heads and clouded their judgment, the charm she once possessed in such abundance was gone, due in part, at least, to the machinations of this little worm in front of her.

As she racked her brain what to do, La Reynie went on. "No, I won't send you back to La Salpêtrière, although I certainly could keep you there for the rest of your days and nobody would know. Though justice must be done, I am not a vindictive man. Justice above all else! So I will let you go. And when the Count or the Marquis, or even both, should get near you, I'll be ready to snap up all three of you. Of course, you are no longer in the flower of your youth and beauty, and the bees may be feasting on other nectar."

In his anger he had carelessly laid bare his designs. So he was still intent on using her to catch Guibert, and now he was also after Antoine. No, she would not fall into his trap. She would not be provoked by his insults. She would rather relinquish the necklace than counter his insults by boasting of the message she had received only the day before.

The only way to reclaim the necklace was now quite clear to her.

"Monsieur, I declare myself defeated. My fate is once again in your hands," she said humbly, almost meekly, "but what possible satisfaction could a man like you gain from keeping a wretched woman like me and her loved ones in such insufferable conditions. All this would not have happened—I mean all the hardship, deprivation—if what was rightfully mine had not been taken away. What would you have thought in my position, Monsieur, if you were certain the jewels were in the hands of a police lieutenant, for safekeeping to be sure, and then you saw, with your own eyes, the same jewels adorning the neck of the trollop of a vicious criminal, who was terrorizing you with death threats? What would you have thought, what conclusions would you have drawn? Especially given the common knowledge that the police were loath to enter the domain of this criminal, who even boasted of his good connection with the police."

"The police of this city fears no one, and I can assure you that we do not regard vermin like this Pélégrin as anything but useful on occasion," the police lieutenant declared. "We know him to be the worst of his kind. But he has indeed served our purposes from time to time. The police must resort on occasion to distasteful methods to fight crime. As for the necklace, how Pélégrin knew that Gaston was carrying the jewels, I do not know. But spies and informants are everywhere."

"Monsieur, please help me understand. Must I conclude that you entrusted the jewels to my brother Gaston?"

"Of course, I did. Monsieur the Marquis, unfortunate man that he is or was, before they took him away to the galleys charged me expressly with the mission of returning the jewels to you. I must admit that I failed. For all we know, Gaston might have sold them."

"That is impossible!" she protested. "Gaston may have been a thief, but he would not betray his family."

"Your faith is very touching, especially in a man who forced a child to beg in the streets by feigning blindness and lameness. Had it not been for the generosity of the Marquis de Valinquette, Gaston would certainly have continued to profit off your earnings from prostitution, as he did with your sister, who ended up in the river, the victim of a brutal murder. You see, the police is well informed."

"Stop, Monsieur! For the mercy of God, stop!" She placed her hands over her ears and shook her head frantically as if to bar the words from penetrating.

"All I am saying, Madame, is that we don't know how Gaston came to such a bad end, and we probably never will."

"I prefer to think that Pélégrin's ruffians murdered him and stole the jewels for Pélégrin," she said. "Gaston would never betray his mother."

La Fauvette noticed that Monsieur de La Reynie showed signs of tiring of the discussion. The time to strike a bargain with him was now, or never.

"Perhaps it would be better not to linger on what's past. Gaston, may his soul rest in peace, won't be brought back to his grieving wife and children. But Monsieur might be kind enough to consider that he still has an opportunity to make good on the promise he made to the Marquis de Valinquette."

"As much as I enjoy our little battle of wits, I am sorry, Madame, I cannot grant you that wish. I no longer feel bound by a promise to a man who has now become a fugitive from the law and is keeping company with the enemies of the King."

"If Monsieur means the Count de Mallac, I can assure you that you are mistaken. The Count is no enemy of His Majesty."

"The day will come when Madame will recognize that she has squandered her affections on a scoundrel and thief. Yes, one day Madame will see that she would have been much better off had she cooperated with the law. As for the necklace," he said, picking up the shiny piece and holding it up to her like a loaf of bread to a famished supplicant, "I suppose we begin with how the necklace got into your hands."

"Things have a way of returning to their rightful owners, as I'm sure Monsieur has observed," she rejoined. How rash she had been to toss the necklace on his desk, out of her reach! He was not about to yield this advantage. She had to find another way. Maybe Lucien could help.

She rose, throwing back her head, outwardly still haughty and undaunted. "I have nothing further to say. If it pleases Monsieur I should like to return home. I have a child in need of her mother's attention."

"I am aware of that. I also believe that the child deserves better. Perhaps tomorrow we can come to an agreement."

"On what, the betrayal of the father of my child?"

"I see Madame is adamant. Very imprudent. Too bad, too bad for everybody, especially the child."

She prepared to leave the room. When she reached the door, he called her back.

"Madame is advised to come back tomorrow morning with the answer to my question. How did the necklace get into your hands? Then we can talk about other things. If Madame, however, should decide to persist on a recalcitrant course, then the offense of insulting an officer of the King is not something easily dismissed."

As she hurried down the steps of the Châtelet, her heart was once again in the grip of terror, again she felt trapped without hope, with no way out. She fled through the streets, cutting a trail with her elbows and shoulders pushing aside beggars, vendors, loiterers, ignoring the shouts and curses hurling after her. She had to get out of this city, she had to get out of this city. Now. Before the morning. She, Chantal, they all had to leave this city.

Lucien met her at the door. "What in heaven's name is going on? Every gendarme has been put on the alert for you, as if you were the worst criminal in this city."

"That just shows you what a fine gentleman your Monsieur de La Reynie is!" she raged. "We are getting away from here tonight."

Breathless, she pulled him inside. "La Reynie is apparently convinced that Guibert, maybe even Antoine, will sooner or later come to Paris in search of me. He only let me go because he hopes to entrap them."

"But how can we leave with every policeman watching? Besides, it will take a while to sell the necklace."

"Forget about the necklace. La Reynie confiscated it. I gambled and I lost. We have to find some other way."

"Without money or other resources? With all due respect, Madame, I don't understand what purpose you had in mind when you went to La Reynie, and without first speaking with me."

"I'm sorry, I miscalculated. I thought I had a trump card, but somehow I didn't play it right. No time for regrets now. Let's gather everyone together."

"What means of transportation are we going to use? With the children in tow, the frontier is weeks away. The King's forces will catch up with us before we get to Chartres."

"That is if they know we are gone and where we are going."

Everybody was talking at once, bombarding her with questions, accusing her of imprudence. The whole world seemed to be turning against her that day. She did her best to calm them, reassure them. The children started to fight amongst each other. Chantal began to cry and held on tight to her grandmother's apron. La Fauvette knelt down next to her, speaking softly, soothingly. They would leave this place and never come back, she promised her. They would go somewhere where it was warm with plenty to eat and they would have comfortable beds to sleep in, and where people were friendly and loving. But Chantal only buried her face deeper in her grandmother's apron.

"And how do you propose to accomplish this miracle?" Gervaise Caillart made one of her rare inquiries. She did not wait for the answer, however, and retreated with the child into the corner, rocking and holding her.

"I shall find a way. You'll see. Just have a little faith in me, this once. There is one last possibility."

She wrapped herself in a thin shawl, covered her face, and headed for the door.

"I want you all ready by nine o'clock tonight. Nobody leaves the house and don't talk to anybody. It may take a miracle, but miracles do happen. Trust me, I shall make it happen."

"Let me go with you, wherever it is you are going," Lucien pleaded. "Remember the eyes of the police are everywhere."

"No, I must do this alone. I'll be back, so be ready." And with that she was gone.

Hugging the shadows and melting with the crowd, she turned the corners and cut a meandering path through alleys and passageways, apparently without aim, but all the while set on one goal, a certain mansion in the quarter of the beau monde, the fashionable Marais.

Chapter 3

THE DUKE DE Rochemouton fussed nervously with his toilet in front of the mirror. Once again, he was late for his rendezvous with the fair Angélique and now he could not find anything fitting to wear. The first maxim of a true gentleman was never to keep a kept woman waiting, especially not a beautiful one. Now it had happened a second time. Until recently, the Duke de Rochemouton was always on time at the demimonde salon of the beautiful Angélique. Most courtesans, of course, were beautiful, beauty being the prerequisite for such a career. Wit was also often cited as a desirable attribute, but its lack could be easily overlooked or could be dressed up as a certain innocent charm. Angélique's reputation of beguiling charm and disarming wit rested on her enigmatic silence and inscrutable smile.

On this evening he had been detained by trivial domestic duties. Another one of those irksome discussions on the pervasiveness of pauperism had prolonged the supper hour with the Duchess and their daughter, La Belle Hélène. The Duchess, as always, had spouted lofty notions of the aristocracy's responsibility to dispense charity to the destitute among His Majesty's subjects, a tradition going back to the beginning of time, she said with an air of superior wisdom. He was never quite sure whether she propounded such radical views to spite him—he had never really seen her descend into the squalid precincts of the city to distribute alms among the poor—or she really believed this drivel.

Not that he was by nature uncharitable or callous toward human misery. But he put his trust in his King. The King's ministers would know how to attack the ugly fungus of poverty and contain its growth. He had other things to worry about like finding a doublet that did not split in the seams when he was breathing. Several times the table debate had come dangerously close to the boiling point, accomplishing nothing but making him late for his evening outing—which may have been the real point of it all, he thought, ever suspicious of his wife's motives.

Not even the insults heaped on his valet made it any easier to tie the garments over his ever expanding girth. Drawing in his breath no longer did the trick. His forehead oozed with sweat of frustration and streaked his carefully applied make-up. He shouted at his valet to open the window.

As he rummaged once more through piles of doublets and shirts he had already given up on, his hands suddenly dropped and he ceased his frantic activity. He lifted his head; paralyzed, he listened to the sound coming from outside. Through the open window drifted a woman's voice in Moorish cadence "Qu'importa que muero se ressuscitan?" carried at first on a lilting ripple, then burst in a sudden surge of sensuous yearning and provocation, straight to the Duke's heart. Only one voice on this earth soared with such unearthliness.

"Fernand, go tell that woman in the street that I want to speak to her," the Duke commanded after listening enthralled for several minutes. "Bring her to the gatehouse, or better yet the kitchen, but send away the servants and maids."

"Better yet," the Duke called after the departing valet, "better yet, bring her into the library."

The Duke decided on a loose-fitting housecoat. He then sat down at his writing table, composed a brief note, sealed it carefully, and dispatched a messenger to Angélique's house.

On his way to the library, the Duke almost collided in the hallway with the Duchess, his daughter and her paramour, the Count de Launay, all of whom had been drawn out of the drawing room by that selfsame siren call that evoked such memories of an Anjou summer idyll.

"Since you are here, you might as well join in," said the Duke. "I am sure you are as eager as I am to find out what brings the Marquise de Valinquette back to the Marais."

While she was waiting in the library, La Fauvette, the song bird from the gutter of Paris, was very pleased with the progress of her plan so far. She remained standing, rehearsing a few more times the gestures, the demeanor that would make an effective accompaniment to her plea—the wording, the inflection, the dramatic coloring, she had all carefully composed in her mind.

She curtsied in the best manner of the subservient in the presence of her social betters when the ducal party entered the room, eager to hear her purpose.

The Marquise proceeded to reprise the exuberant, heady summer of love and games on the Rochemouton estate in Anjou, which no doubt everybody present still remembered as fondly as she did. Her account was especially accurate as to the night she had entertained the company with the Spanish ballad to the accompaniment of a fiery dance executed on the table in the chateau's drawing room, and how that performance had been interrupted by the sudden appearance of the Marquis de Valinquette, come back from the field of battle. Although it was difficult to see in the haggard form before them the ravishing beauty they had once known, her listeners, who remembered the interlude well, were convinced that only the Marquise herself would be able to supply the details and flourishes with which this woman presented her story.

The Duke, as perplexed as was his wife, the Duchess, and his daughter and her companion, asked the inevitable question. If Madame, they said, is indeed who she says she is, if she is the long lost Marquise de Valinquette, and who could doubt it after all that she just related—and then, of course there is that voice, that inimitable voice of which there can be only one in this world—how then did she come to be in such a deplorable, destitute state?

"You may kindly remember the unfortunate circumstances that led to the Marquis de Valinquette's trial and subsequent sentence to servitude on His Majesty's galleys?"

"Yes, yes, certainly. A most unfortunate turn of events, pitiful, and such a fine gentleman too, of best lineage," said the Duke.

"Well, I too was touched by tragedy and did not remain unscathed, as you can see," she said, pointing to her tattered rags.

"But we presumed that Madame had returned to her Spanish homeland," puzzled the Duchess.

"My homeland was never in Spain, Madame. It is true that from the time I was twelve years old I was raised in Catalonia in the household of that most gracious lady Doña Elvira Barca y Alarcon, the Marquise de Valinquette, the mother of the present Marquis. She raised me like a daughter. But I am as Parisian as the little birds you see hopping around on the Parvis de Notre Dame. My cradle did not stand at any royal or ducal court, it stood in a hovel at what was once the Court of Miracles at Saint-Médard."

A hushed sound of horror escaped from the ladies' lips.

"You mean to say that the Marquise de Valinquette, the woman at whose feet worshiped the most illustrious and august members of the Parisian nobility, did not have an ounce of noble blood in her veins? Are we to believe her pedigree was a trail out of the gutter?" The Duchess's ample chest heaved heavily with indignation. "I don't understand the point of these disclosures after all this time Why have you come here now with such revelations? To set us all up to ridicule?"

"It is true there is not a trace of noble blood in these veins," La Fauvette replied, "but I never meant to ridicule Madame or Monsieur. You have been very kind to me in the past."

"Not a drop of noble blood!" the Duchess shook her head. "I'm afraid, my dear, I must ask you to leave. If word of this leaks out we'll become the laughing stock of polite society. Louis, have this woman escorted out at once."

"Dear Maman, how can you be so unkind?" La Belle Hélène, who was getting precariously close to a certain age when the epithet attached to her name would become a mere reminder of past glory, scolded her mother. "We all benefited from the deception, did we not? Did the Marquise not enchant us with her beauty, her wit, and not least with her singing? What a magnificent impostress, who not only imitated the ways of the nobility but made them her own! She deserves our admiration, not our disapproval and indignation."

"But the audacity, the effrontery of it all!" The Duchess shook her head in distress over what the world was coming to. Her belief in the divine scheme of natural divisions among men were turned upside down, and she felt dangerously unsteady.

The Duke, still somewhat bewildered, meanwhile pressed La Fauvette to give as full an account as possible of how she came to be in her present condition. She spoke of her return to the Court of Miracles and her subsequent encounters with Monsieur de La Reynie, who was bent on using her as bait to trap the Count de Mallac.

"Ah, the Count de Mallac!" The Duchess perked up at the mention of this name. "There is a fine gentleman, a scion of a proud and ancient Breton race."

The Duke swallowed his desire to enlighten her that this fine gentleman was a notorious thief and smuggler with a price on his head by order of His Majesty the King of France. But realizing that nothing would be gained from it, he turned again to this wretched woman who had such a wondrous tale to tell. There was plenty of material here for the amusement of the guests assembled at Angélique's house. What a marvelous opportunity to make himself an admired raconteur, the center of attention of the young women in his mistress's entourage!

Monsieur de La Reynie, she explained, seems convinced that the Count and the Marquis, who he says has escaped from the galleys, will sooner or later come to Paris, and that she will lead him to them. He threatens her with La Salpêtrière if she does not comply. Since neither the Count nor the Marquis are anywhere near the capital, in fact they are far beyond the borders of the Kingdom of France, her fate is practically sealed. So is that of her child. Her only hope was to leave the city that very night.

The kind interest Monsieur the Duke expressed in a beggar woman recently has nurtured in her the hope that the plea of a woman in fear for her life—La Salpêtrière is as good as being buried alive—would not fall on deaf ears.

"La Salpêtrière? Is it really such a bad place? It was His Majesty's benevolent concern for the poor and destitute, the infirm among his subjects, that prompted the establishment of this hospice," the Duke mused.

"Believe me, Monsieur, the place is hell on earth," La Fauvette said heatedly.

"Well, however that may be," said the Duke, taken aback by her directness, "my dear woman, as much as your story touches my heart, and I am sure that of the Duchess as well, we have a reputation to consider, social responsibilities, a rank and station in life. I would place myself in an untenable position were I to aid and abet someone who has been marked by as upright and loyal a servant of the King as is our dear police lieutenant. I hope nobody was following you here."

La Fauvette's heart sank. She should have known. This coward had neither the nerve nor the charity his protestations of concern were so much empty posturing.

But she still had her pride, she would not beg. She had decided on a course of absolute honesty and truth as the best way to win their hearts and support. This was all she could do. If it must be La Salpêtrière, so be it. She would not grovel.

She thanked the Duke and Duchess and with a nod in the direction of La Belle Hélène, she turned toward the door with the measured stride of a true Marquise, leaving behind a very perplexed ducal pair whose view of the world had been severely shaken.

From the marble hallway, she directed her uncertain steps toward the servants' exit. What was she to do now? Everything was turning against her. This had been her last resort. Her greatest hopes had all turned to dust.

Just as she was about to open the door, the voice of a man, decidedly not the Duke's, called out to her, asking her to wait. She turned around and came face to face with the Count de Launay.

"Please, Madame, if you please, don't go yet. The Duke may not be able to fulfill your request for help, but perhaps you will consider accepting my assistance." His courteous, almost pleading manner aroused in her a peculiar feeling of wariness. He addressed her with a deference she once commanded from nobles even more powerful than he was, but which under the circumstances seemed comic.

She remembered well the Count de Launay, scion of ancient stock, heir to vast holdings, numerous fiefs in the southwestern provinces and in the province of Poitou. Despite all that was his, he was condemned to be the eternal suitor of La Belle Hélène, with no prospect of winning her hand in marriage because of his Huguenot faith, she remembered the philosopher Desmoulin explain to her. Abjuring the religion of his forebears, which in reality meant nothing to him, he had told her, was impossible, for he would lose his inheritance, leaving him penniless and even a less desirable suitor.

La Fauvette had been only vaguely aware of his presence in the library. The glances exchanged between the ill-starred lovers, whose long association had bred a tacit way of communicating by means of glances, nods, and winks, had escaped her usually keen sense of observation. Had she observed them as a disinterested party, she might have noticed how her story had moved them both, and the resolve that seemed to form in their minds as they listened to her plight.

"Monsieur is very kind, but I am afraid it was preposterous of me to impose on the Duke and Duchess in this way and to expect them to show mercy for someone whose very existence must be an insult to their sensibilities. I certainly would not want to imperil your prospects for the future."

"What prospects should a Huguenot have in this world where the Apostolic Faith asserts itself more forcefully every day? His Majesty the King has turned a favorable ear toward those who wish to declare the Edict of Tolerance his grandfather, King Henri IV, issued at Nantes, null and void. And he himself seems very ill disposed toward the faith that once counted the House of Bourbon among its staunchest defenders. But I guess that is of little consequence to Madame. I only mean to explain that I do not expect to be received at the Royal Court, and consequently I have no social pretense to uphold. But I do have considerable means at my disposal which I will gladly put at the disposal of Madame's cause."

She needed no further convincing. Here was the divine intervention she had been praying for and she would not pass it up.

"I shall need transportation for seven adults and six children," she stated plainly.

"Oh, I was not aware there were so many." He paused for a moment, but then he quickly reassured her that he was not faltering in his resolve to be of help. "In that case we shall need more than one coach."

They decided on a meeting place and discussed some logistical aspects. He surprised her with a clear-headedness and perspicacity that contrasted with the image she had of him as a lethargic slave of love, rather foppish and degenerate. She had, of course, never seen him on the battlefield, where he had on many occasions comported himself with great courage and presence of mind. They decided on departing via the Louvre gate, the passage out of the city used by the aristocracy. The sentries there were likely to be less inclined to make a thorough search of the passengers and goods in the conveyance that bore the emblem of a noble house. They would leave at dawn when the gate first opens.

Darkness had already fallen when she arrived back at the rue Saint Honoré. She was received by an anxiously waiting crew. The barrage of questions and reproaches they hurled at her when she entered subsided when they saw her bristling with the confidence of a general who has just achieved a major victory.

"As promised, we are leaving Paris tonight. We leave when the gates open at the crack of dawn!" she declared. "We must all work together. Timing is essential. And Fabrisse, you must keep the children quiet. Our lives depend on it. Anybody who would rather not be of the party and would prefer to stay, let me know now."

The motley band gathered around the table with flushed faces, for what was to be the last time, in hushed anticipation of a new life away from the squalor and misery but also with silent dread of the unknown that lay ahead. As they were eagerly packing their bundles, La Fauvette was reminded of the Israelites on the eve of their departure from Egypt. They too were fleeing from a Pharaoh who was seeking to oppress them, Pharaoh de La Reynie. She was also aware of the long journey to the land of freedom, the promised land of Spain, and that much could still happen that would thwart their goal. The Israelites had God on their side. She could not be sure of such divine benevolence for her cause. But she had renewed confidence that all would be well.

She laid out the plan, named the place of rendezvous where the coaches would be waiting to take them beyond the walls of the city, but she did not reveal the name of her benefactor. Obviously they could not all be wandering through the streets together at the crack of dawn without attracting attention. They would have to split up into three groups—Lucien with Fabrisse and the children, Prosper with Arlette and Ondine, and she herself would follow with Chantal and Gervaise. Anybody who was not at the appointed place at the appointed time would be left behind. The carriages would leave as soon as the city gates opened. Commanding the motley crew in what to do made her keep up her own courage and project confidence that would inspire the others. As long as she gave orders, she was in control. What she needed most on this night was a sense that she had her destiny in her hand, that she could mold the future.

All arrangements completed, they settled down and waited for the dawn. The children slept in the corner, but none of the adults closed an eye for long, except for Ondine, who stretched out lazily on her pallet. Everybody else sat in quiet suspension, waiting through night's endless, dark shroud for the first gleam of light.

In her mind, La Fauvette went through every possibility of what might go wrong. La Reynie's men might be watching the house on the rue de Saint-Honoré even now. Anything could happen on their walk to the Place du Palais Royal where the carriages were to receive them. Even if they got that far, the carriages might not be there. The

Count might change his mind. La Belle Hélène might succumb to the influence of her parents and try to dissuade her lover from his whim.

She tried to chase these thoughts from her mind, but the harder she tried, the more tenaciously they haunted her. She wanted to turn her thoughts to the future. But even there, worrisome questions tormented her. Whose wife would she be? Obviously she was still married to Antoine. Would he tolerate Guibert as her lover? She realized that her husband was still a puzzle to her. What were his true desires? She knew him as unpredictable, a captive of his moods. And Guibert, he was an even greater riddle. Since the two strangers had appeared with Guibert's message, she had not had a moment to contemplate and sort out all that she had learned. The incident at Saint-Malo—Guibert risking every thing in a heroic rescue of Antoine! It was almost too fantastic and yet apparently true. Then again, it was not completely implausible.

The bond between the two men of her life alternately chilled and warmed her heart. What would her place be? Where would she fit in? Somehow it would all work out, she tried to calm herself. Maybe she would spend the remainder of her life in celibacy. After all, except for the brief interlude of Guibert's visit to the Court of Miracles, she had been living that way for many years.

Besides, of what import were her comfort and desires in the grand scheme of this human drama? A step backward for a larger view, away from all petty concerns and squabbles, revealed the whole affair to her as a comedy, a farce of human foibles. A phrase flew into her mind from a distant shore, a phrase she had once heard or maybe read somewhere, she could not remember which or where—life is a striving for wind. What a treasure of wisdom this simple phrase contained!

Her thoughts turned to Antoine, to his obsession with the perfect female form, his desire for recognition, his ambition to be received at the Royal Court. What did it all bring him? Wouldn't life have been better had he been content to stay among the Barcas in Catalonia? It certainly would have been different. But what's the use of wallowing in regret and wondering what might have been? Could it really have been otherwise? Is it not all in the hand that guides human destiny?

Fate. It seemed to her that human beings have very little control over their own destinies.

A striving for wind! But if that was all that life amounted to, why go on, why break one's back, why endure? Chantal. Here was the answer. Her child. She peered through the darkened room to the corner where she knew Chantal was sleeping. She made out the blurred figure of Fabrisse, crouching near her children, a simple, passive woman, not given to tortuous ruminating, but who would turn into a lioness to defend her brood. Fabrisse's dark figure slowly took on a more distinct form, illuminated by a grayish light that rose behind her.

La Fauvette jumped up.

"It's time, it's time to go!" she proclaimed with urgent but muted voice. "Lucien, Fabrisse, it's time! You go first."

They roused the children and lined them up at the door. La Fauvette did something she had done only once before. She kissed the children one by one as if they were going to be separated for a long time. She hugged Fabrisse and gave her arm a squeeze of encouragement.

Prosper and the cocottes were dispatched next. They were to take a different route but with the admonishment not to tarry and to go straight to the Place du Palais Royal.

When they were gone, she let out a sigh of relief and turned to Chantal and Gervaise, waiting in the corner by Gervaise's stove. The pots were cold and empty on this morning. The child sat on her grandmother's lap talking to her softly in tones that seemed to La Fauvette alternately gentle and insistent.

"Maman! Chantal! We must go!"

"Grand-mère is sad," said Chantal, "but she won't tell me why."

"The sun will be up in half an hour, we must go!" La Fauvette insisted. She had seen her mother weep only twice and each time it was on the occasion of the death of one of her children. There had been other deaths but those were before she was born. What could be the matter now?

"Maman, please, any delay may bring disaster," she pleaded.

"You go, just leave me here," Gervaise said, grunting as she lifted Chantal from her lap and guided her toward her mother. "I'll be all right."

"I don't want to go without Grand-mère," Chantal whimpered, torn by a desire to return to her grandmother's lap and her mother's now sharp demand that they leave at once.

"Must you spoil everything with your obstinacy? Do you want to go back to La Salpêtrière? Must you be so selfish just when we have everything to gain or lose?"

"I told you to go. I don't want to die in a foreign land, far from Paris. This is where I'm at home. This is where I have lived my life, and this is where I want to die."

"This is ridiculous!" La Fauvette's despair burst into anger. "Look how late it is getting! This is no life, for us or for you! My God, stop this nonsense, for your granddaughter's sake if nothing else."

"Please, Grand-mère, please!" Chantal pulled the old woman's skirt. Gervaise looked even more haggard than usual. She confessed her dread of the uncertain, of being uprooted, of the vast unknown world out there.

La Fauvette spoke calmly now as she tied a small cloak around Chantal.

"Look, we are all frightened. Nobody knows what the future holds, whether we'll ever make it beyond the border, but it's worth a try. There's nothing here, nothing but misery and the hell of La Salpêtrière."

She picked the child up and started for the door. The little girl's hands reached beyond her mother's shoulders still entreating her grandmother: "Please, Grand-mère, please! I don't want to go without you."

They had crossed the threshold when they heard the old woman shuttling along behind them.

A thin layer of snow covered the rooftops of the city. On the cobblestones the white was already turning to gray slush. The track of little feet and bigger feet could easily be followed. Under a sky thick with low-hanging snow clouds, the city was coming to life. The victual vendors of Les Halles were unloading their wares and setting them up in the open-air stalls. The aroma of fresh bread mingled in the alleys with the miasma of the contents of chamberpots pouring from the windows into the fetid rivulets running in the gutter.

A twinge in the stomach reminded La Fauvette that they had not eaten. There had been no time for Gervaise to start up her pots with breakfast gruel. Maybe that's why she was so grumpy. She had to leave her pots behind. She will have new pots and better pots and maybe even something good to stir, La Fauvette said to herself. At any rate, she had packed a few pieces of stale bread that could be shared once they were beyond the city walls.

At the Place du Palais Royal, three coaches were waiting, each harnessing six horses and rivaling each other in magnificence. The horses pawed the pavement, neighing impatiently. The coachmen's curses cut through the morning air. La Fauvette was sure the whole town would turn out the very next moment to find out what was going on. Something a little less ostentatious would have done just fine, she thought.

In the window of the larger of the three coaches, the one emblazoned with the seal of the House of Rochemouton, appeared the head of La Belle Hélène who waved vigorously at La Fauvette.

"No explanations now! I have decided to accompany you. Now, everybody quickly get in. We have no time to lose."

Fabrisse and the children, guided by Lucien, had arrived as instructed. While the party waited for Prosper and the girls, the children were herded into a carriage they would share with several coffers as well as ladies-in-waiting and chambermaids. Fabrisse was about to climb in after them, when Lucien spoke to her and planted a passionate kiss on her mouth. She froze, one foot on the pavement, one foot on the tread of the carriage.

"I shall join you in a few months," La Fauvette heard Lucien say, "I just cannot leave this city like a fugitive."

"But will you be safe here? What will Monsieur de La Reynie do when he finds out?" Fabrisse asked in a panic.

"Yes, what will he do? You could end up on the galleys or even worse, the gallows," said La Fauvette.

"No, don't worry about me. You just take care to reach your destination and I'll be with you soon, I promise. I cannot take leave without resigning my position in an orderly manner. Look, I have committed no crime. You have committed no crime. What could I be accused of? Helping honest citizens of Paris embark on a journey? There is no law against that."

"I hope Monsieur de La Reynie sees it that way. It's better if Lucien follows his conscience," La Fauvette said to Fabrisse.

Lucien gave Fabrisse a light push that made her pull up her foot. They waved, the door closed, and the carriage pulled out of the square toward the Louvre gate.

Lucien walked with La Fauvette to the other coach, where the Count de Launay had descended from his mount. Lucien sent a sigh of relief after the departing calèche that would carry his love to a better life. He bowed gallantly in the direction of La Fauvette. Chantal and Gervaise were already inside the other carriage and La Fauvette was prepared to follow, but was casting worried glances around the square, hoping to catch sight of the stragglers. She turned to say good-bye to Lucien, calling him her guardian angel and other endearing things. What would have happened to them all without his devoted friendship?

At this moment shouts arose from the other side of the square. It was Arlette, running through the slush and waving her arms. She was breathless but with a little coaxing they learned that Ondine had slipped away. Arlette and Prosper followed her and until they saw her disappearing inside a house she seemed familiar with. It turned out to be the place where Pélégrin lived. How she knew where to find him was a riddle time did not allow them to ponder. She roused the dethroned kind of beggars and thieves, told him the rendezvous in which Monsieur de La Reynie would surely be interested.

"Prosper says he will waylay them to keep them from going to the police, but I'm afraid he's not strong enough alone," Arlette wailed.

"We'll see about that!" Lucien helped the women into the carriage. He turned to the Count de Launay. "Please wait a few leagues out on the Orléans highway for half an hour, no longer. If Prosper has not caught up with you then, you must drive on."

"I'll leave the steed hitched here and ride in the carriage," said the Count. "I presume this Prosper knows how to ride a horse."

"He will, he will!" Lucien assured him, turned and was gone down the alley Arlette had pointed to.

Meanwhile as the team of six horses bolted into motion, the occupants hardly dared to breathe, so great was their apprehension. La Fauvette looked at her mother's inscrutable face. Was she aware of the danger Prosper, her last son, found himself in?

The passage through the Louvre gate went without incident. If there was something strange about three stately carriages exiting the city in a hurry in the small hours of the day, the keeper of the Louvre gate probably passed it off as aristocratic eccentricity of which he saw plenty every day. He certainly had no reason to inspect the passengers, and even if he had done so, he would hardly have believed his eyes and would have kept quiet about it—riffraff traveling in luxury and style—for fear of being hauled off to Bicêtre.

The Count de Launay's carriage picked up a good clip once it gained the Orléans highway. Several leagues down the road, out of sight of the sentries, the horses slowed their pace and pulled over to the side and came to a halt. The carriage of Hélène d'Alembert and that of her servants which also held Fabrisse had already gone ahead.

"Won't those in the other carriage wonder what has become of us?" La Fauvette asked, to break the unbearable silence.

"For the eventuality that the carriages should become separated," said the Count, "we have arranged to rendezvous at one of my estates just south of Orléans. We can rest there before journeying on. I am sure Madame will find the accommodations to her satisfaction."

"Oh, I am sure I shall, indeed. Monsieur's kindness is beyond anything we deserve, and certainly beyond all expectations."

"The reason is very simple, and you will see it is not entirely altruistic. While we were listening to Madame telling her story last evening, I saw something in the demeanor of my beloved Hélène, a sudden surge of courage to break with the parental tyranny that has stood in the way of our happiness for so long. For ten years, parental whim—bigotry is more accurate—has kept us from being united in Holy Matrimony. The lineage of the Launays and Montaubans is as ancient and as proud as that of the Rochemoutons. In fact my grandmother was a Bourbon, a cousin of the beloved King Henri, and when it comes to adding up the number of estates, fiefs, and general wealth, we can probably outdo the Rochemoutons and d'Alemberts together. Only the difference in religion has stood in the way. You, Madame, gave us the courage to jettison everything and embark on this flight to freedom. Neither of one us is impecunious and only our sense of duty and devotion to family tradition has so far prevented us from taking a step that we know our families will find unacceptable, even odious."

La Fauvette was left speechless by this confession. Of course, in her days in the Marais, she had known that this Count was La Belle Hélène's ardent suitor. But she had assumed his display of devoted affection was nothing more than the usual parlor game and that he had a serious mistress or even a wife somewhere else. Hélène d'Alembert seemed to her the perfect frigid beauty whose flirting simply followed the rules of the game. The whole story of the Rochemoutons' objections to him as a Huguenot she thought had been a part of the plot, to add spice to the drama. The revelation that the pair had been ill-starred lovers, yearning for fulfillment of their love for so many years, made her think how difficult it was to see behind the masks people wear, how rarely one could catch a glimpse of their true character.

"You are planning to cross the Pyrenees with us then?" she asked.

"Yes, I have an estate near Manresa, not far from the Barca estate. We shall be neighbors. And no more games of shepherds and nymphs," he laughed.

La Fauvette had been keeping her eyes trained on the road through the rear window and was anxiously scanning the horizon. The time Lucien had set had almost expired.

Then Chantal suddenly called out: "Look! There, a black horse!"

As the horse, galloping at breakneck speed, came closer, Lucien became visible in the saddle.

"Where is Prosper?" The anxious call came from Arlette. "Can you see Prosper?"

"Yes," said Chantal, "there's another person behind the man in the front. It must be Uncle Prosper!"

No sooner had she uttered the words than Lucien jumped from the steed almost before it came to a halt, with Prosper tumbling down right after him.

"Pélégrin has been silenced, he will no longer threaten anybody," Lucien said gasping as he pushed Prosper into the carriage, and then climbed in behind him. "But Ondine slipped away. She may be talking to La Reynie this very moment."

"Let's go then! And Godspeed! We must pass Orléans before nightfall," the Count de Launay shouted to the coachman.

The carriage rattled down the highway, farther and farther away from the arm of the police lieutenant of Paris who thought he was doing his duty and serving his King by threatening the poorest of the poor in the city. As the distance from the city of gloom grew, an exhilarated glow brightened the faces of the fugitives. The sudden awareness of being free made them burst into a mad, jubilant, uncontrollable fit of laughter. Even Gervaise smiled and kissed Chantal.

The Count's valet unpacked provisions of dainty goose liver sandwiches, which the ravenous company devoured instantly. Roasted chicken legs followed and the finest vintage from the slopes of the Launay estates near Bordeaux.

After the meal, they all withdrew into a sweet silence. The exertion and excitement of the day began to take its toll. Chantal fell asleep in the lap of her grandmother, whose eyes closed and whose thoughts and dreams, if she had any, remained as hidden as those of a sphinx. Arlette gathered Prosper to herself and tended to a slash across his brow. Only Lucien could find no rest. He sat staring in front of him, brooding.

La Fauvette touched his arm. "The world can breathe easier now that Pélégrin no longer plies his evil trade."

"You are right in that. I don't regret Pélégrin's demise, and I don't regret having been the one to dispatch him into the nether world. But this is not how I wanted to leave the city. Now I'm a fugitive from the law. If I had remained after killing Pélégrin, La Reynie could have pressed all kinds of charges against me as an accomplice in your escape. With blood on my hands, what chance would I have had to clear myself? So I had no choice but to flee. And that is what disturbs me—to have my hand forced like that, by something so unforeseen."

"Isn't that how it goes in life?" she sought to console him. "Doesn't fate always seem to have a way of forcing the hand of her hapless victims, tossing the unforeseen in our way? We can only make the best of it all and somehow hope for the best."

With that La Fauvette leaned back. She closed her eyes, savoring the caressing, sweet fragrance of the satin cushions. Memories of luxury and comfort came back from far-off recesses where they had been stashed away so they would not embitter her daily existence. But now, now they were allowed to emerge again. She could get used to such amenities again, she said to herself, yes she surely could, and why not? Within a few minutes, she drifted into a deep, dreamless sleep without consciousness of either past, present, or future.

Chapter 4

THE CARAVAN OF carriages rumbled over the rock-strewn road on its arduous climb of the Col d'Arès in the Pyrenees. Like a column of ants scaling an enormous hill, the horse-drawn train tackled the formidable barrier that separated the Kingdom of France from the Kingdom of Spain.

In the vanguard fluttered the yellow butterflies of the House of Montauban chased by the demi-ram of the House of Rochemouton. The two conveyances, rivals in magnificence of decor and comfort, were trailed by more modestly appointed coaches, transporting a battalion of servants as well as a wealth of household goods and other necessities. Four coaches, containing Hélène d'Alembert's wardrobe and fashion accessories, creaked precariously under the weight of coffers, chests, boxes of every size and description.

The spring rains had washed out the roadway in many parts. Torrents of melting ice and snow had gouged meandering patterns of deep furrows into the side of the mountains. Every so often the train was brought to a halt to repair a broken axel or wheel on one or the other of the carriages. At other times deposits of boulders and rocks had to be cleared from the roadway for the cortège to proceed.

The passengers' mood was heightened with every step that took them farther away from the realm of the Sun King and closer to the Promised Land of Spain. To while away the long hours during the crossing, the Count de Launay amused the company with the story of the origins of the yellow butterfly in his family's emblem. Although the Count's grandmother, a cousin of the good King Henri IV and, if his narration could be trusted, one of the most extraordinary women of her day, was by then familiar to everyone, they did not tire of hearing of her exploits during the wars of religion. From a standard bearer of the Huguenots, she became a renowned libertine in the reign of Louis XIII, and she never ceased to denounce the tyrannies of her cousin Henri's successors and their ministers until the day she died, at the age of eighty-nine.

La Fauvette's imagination was particularly fired by the vicissitudes of this woman's life, from impoverished orphan to scintilating lady at the court of Henri IV—her fierce, abiding love, as her grandson put it, for a Catholic nobleman, a brief marriage, ordered by the King for reasons of state, to the Count's grandfather, a devout Huguenot who was killed defending the Kingdom of France against the Spaniards. She had first heard the Count relate the story during the long winter months they were stranded on the Launay provincial estate in Périgord waiting for the ice and snow to thaw before they could attempt the crossing of the mountains. The inimitable Marguerite de Montauban became the subject of fascinating conversation on many a wind-battered night. Reciting the lady's exploits, as faithfully as the daily breviary, in great detail and complete with myriad narrative variations, had become a cherished tradition among her progeny. La Fauvette wished she had the talent to write a ballad about her.

Except for this pleasant distraction, the protracted layover in Périgord had set her nerves on edge. She found it almost impossible to maintain the amiability which polite etiquette dictated. She tired of having to gush with gratitude and in her darkest moments she resented the host's generosity, which burdened her with an irksome sense of obligation. Her dreams were haunted with forebodings of disasters and failures, of forced returns to Paris, La Salpêtrière, Monsieur de

La Reynie. As long as they remained on French soil, she was unable to rest and breathe easy.

Lucien's transports of fear and remorse didn't help matters either. The sound of hoofbeats startled him into terror as if the Royal Musketeers had no more urgent mission than to scour the Kingdom for the killer of a criminal parasite. At times, his wallowing in remorse for having deserted his post, for having betrayed his benefactor, took such violent hold of him that nobody, not even Fabrisse, could bear to be near him. It then took all of the Marquise's power of persuasion to restrain him from beating his way back to the capital.

Had they been privy to the scene that took place at the police prefecture on the morning of their flight from the city, their fears and anguish would have dissipated and they could have enjoyed the Count de Launay's hospitality with much more equanimity. But how could they have known what transpired that morning in the police lieutenant's office? Perhaps they should have guessed. Monsieur de La Reynie after all had a reputation for being as fair-minded and good-hearted as he was rigid in enforcing the law. In fact, he regarded the canaille who sat in front of him, ratting on those who had saved her life, with an honest citizen's revulsion. Ondine held his interest only long enough to assure himself that neither the Count de Mallac nor the Marquis de Valinquette had been in Paris. He decided then to close this chapter and that it would remain closed for him for as long as neither of these two gentlemen set foot on his turf. He saw no further reason to stand in the way of the Marquise's escape from the squalor of a life he had always considered unseemly for a woman of her quality.

And if Lucien Lefèvre really squeezed the life out of that vermin Pélégrin, so much the better for the world. He regretted losing a deputy of Lucien's upright character and sense of duty. But he conceded that he had to follow his heart, and Monsieur de La Reynie wished him well. He wished them all well. The case was closed for him.

The fugitives—for, ignorant of the outcome, that is how they still saw themselves—endured the months of waiting for the ice on the mountains to melt as a time in purgatory. But as purgatories are meant to be, it was not without its pleasurable side. The Count's plentiful larders supplied many a feast, adding flesh to the bones of the marasmic band and putting a healthy glow in the children's sallow cheeks.

Soon after their arrival at the estate, the household staff, the seamstresses, and chambermaids, became engaged in a flurry of activity to outfit the entire crew, men, women, and children, with new clothes, simple but warm, to replace the tattered rags that were a meager shield against the bite of winter. Before they donned the new garments, they each—Gervaise was persuaded after some resistance—partook of a rite of purification of body and spirit. The soot and grime that had formed a thick coating on the skin like a tight-fitting glove and from which exuded the ghastly fumes of poverty were scrubbed away, sloughed off. The children squealed with delight as they took proper baths what was probably for the first time in their lives.

The three graces—La Fauvette, Fabrisse, and Arlette—took turns scrubbing each other and washing each other's hair. With prolonged lathering, La Fauvette's chestnut curls once again sparkled in their former softness. They luxuriated in toweling and embalmed each other with sweetly fragrant Spanish musk and amber.

One day, having emerged from her bath, La Fauvette discarded all trepidations and stepped in front of a full-size mirror to inspect the results, or, as she feared, to assess the damage. Well, a foam-born Venus she was not, that much was clear, she told herself with a touch of self-mockery. The years of privation had taken their toll, probably irreparably so. The thought of Antoine made her laugh. What would he say if he could see her now? Her skin no longer taut and supple, her breasts empty and sagging, crows' feet around her eyes and furrows on her brow. But then why should he have anything to say? Why should he even see her in her natural state?

But the thought of her husband—yes, he was still her husband and that he might insist on conjugal rights was not out of the realm of possibility—preoccupied her more and more. Like swirling shreds of an old, long-forgotten song, fragments of images of their early days in Catalonia assailed her mind with greater frequency. Nor were these memories, she had to admit to herself, entirely displeasing.

Wintertime always seems to drag on endlessly, but this one tried even the patience of a man as unruffled as the Count de Launay, who was by then quite avid to be joined in Holy Matrimony, at long last, with his beloved Hélène. So the decision was finally made to continue the journey even before the first flowering of spring with the goal of reaching Perpignan by winter's end. From there, they would take the road south to the lower-lying passes near the area where the mountainous range made its descent toward the sea.

A courier was sent ahead to the Barca estate in Catalonia with a message of the imminent arrival—that is, in two to three weeks—of the Marquise de Valinquette and her entourage.

The reunion took place on the road near Ripoll, just on the Spanish side. Guibert and Antoine came riding out on horseback to meet them. The actual meeting resembled little the scene the Marquise had rehearsed in her mind over and over in the preceding months and weeks and days.

The cortège had pulled up at a roadside inn. Several wheels had been damaged by the rough ride over the mountains and the horses were close to exhaustion. They all disembarked. It felt good to stretch and take a deep breath of the Catalan air that was deemed as sweet as a breeze of the land of milk and honey

The Marquise had walked to the edge of a field, staring in wonder at the Catalan countryside. She still found it hard to believe that she was not dreaming, that they were only a few days' journey from their destination. Her head was as light as air and her cheeks were flushed. It must be the excitement, she thought, wiping the moisture from her brow. Had she followed her impulse, she would have fallen on her knees and kissed the earth, but she reminded herself that such demonstrativeness was unbecoming a lady, which is what she soon would be again.

She was so lost in thought that she remained unaware of the party of horsemen who came charging toward the inn from the south. So when she returned to the inn and was suddenly confronted with the two men who had been, each in his way, the joy and sorrow of her life, she was at a total loss what to say or do. There was Guibert flashing his familiar grin, exuding life as if the years had left him untouched. She wanted to fling her arms around him. But something held her back and she was barely able to smile.

And there was Antoine, a few feet to the side of Guibert, reticent and melancholy. The years of hardship and grief had not been good to him. He seemed gaunt, his elongated features even more drawn. His beard was streaked with silver threads, his skin pallid. Only his eyes, those dark eyes, were as she remembered them, wide open, direct, penetrating to the soul, filled with a sadness that seemed to have deepened still more.

Inadvertently, she took a step backward. Had rebuke spoken from Antoine's eyes, had his gaze been accusing, castigating, had he spit her in the face, she could have tolerated it better than this dejected demeanor, this seeming submission, acquiescence in an unalterable fate, this display of a permanently wounded soul. So she stood, immobile, a statue of stone, held in the grip of Antoine's melancholy, yet unable to avert her eyes.

How long this all lasted she could not tell. It could have been seconds, minutes, or hours. Guibert finally broke the silence. He realized the awkwardness of the situation and instead of gathering his beloved into his arms, he greeted her with a cordial bow and went on greeting everyone else with boisterous good cheer. Antoine followed Guibert's example, bowing respectfully before her and went on to welcome her fellow travelers, especially the Count de Launay and Countess d'Alembert, to Catalonia. Soon, without yet having spoken to La Fauvette, he was engaged in a discussion of the best course to follow for the remainder of their journey.

The entire party, led by Guibert and his two right-hand men, Mathurin and Coupe-Cheveux, went inside the inn for a meal. Guibert lavished his attention on Chantal while they all dined with great pleasure. La Fauvette observed what was going on around her as if she was watching a theatrical spectacle and touched little of the food. She was touched to see that Antoine too seemed to take little interest in the repast. Although she was unable to catch a glance from his eyes, she began to feel an undefined bond forming between them, a bond maybe that went back to a common past and memories linked to the familiar surroundings they would soon enter. A longing for a private exchange with him made itself felt. There was so much to explain, clarify, to forgive. But what was she thinking? It was much more likely that he hated her. What made her think that he would ever forgive her, that it wasn't for Guibert's sake alone that he had gone along with the scheme of bringing her to Spain? And what was the matter with her anyway? Silly that her thoughts should be fixed on Antoine. Guibert was the man she loved. He was the father of her child. Once they had reached their destination, everything would fall into place. Antoine would be reasonable and agree to an annulment of their marriage, she reassured herself. She would leave it all up to them to arrange. Right now, she had to put these thoughts out of her mind or she would go mad.Following the meal, Guibert decreed that they had better spend the night at the inn and get a fresh start early in the morning. His voice was heard everywhere, directing, advising, arranging. The Parisians had come a thousand leagues on their own power, had overcome every obstacle, road and weather conditions, and now the last leg of the journey apparently could not run a smooth course without the organizational genius of the Count de Mallac.

As the night descended and they were readying to turn in, she was pleased to see Antoine finally coming up to her.

"Guibert is still the same Guibert," he said with a good-natured smile as he accompanied her to the chamber she was to share with the other women.

"Yes, it seems so," she rejoined softly with downcast eyes.

"But I don't mind it anymore," he continued, "I now know that there could not be a truer friend."

The remark struck her as odd. She was unsure what it was he was trying to convey at that moment.

When they arrived in front of the chamber door, he bent gallantly over her hand. "Welcome home, Madame!" Then he was gone, leaving her breathless. Unaware of what she was doing, she pressed the spot where his lips had touched her hand to her lips. The skin was burning hot, his scent still clung to it. She closed the door behind her just in time. Her knees gave way, she gasped and fainted.

For the rest of the journey, she cowered in the corner of the carriage, wrapped in a warm blanket and pretending to be asleep. She hid her face from the world around her, not even peering through the window at the magnificent landscape that had earlier made her heart beat faster. Outside, Guibert's shouts were heard above all other voices, giving orders and advice, issuing warnings. He had taken full control. Trepidation seized her heart and all she could do was succumb to the mental and physical exhaustion that finally overwhelmed her.

Chapter 5

HOW LONG SHE had been hovering between being and not being she could not tell. Every time she regained consciousness, she saw two faces near her, one long, oval, and pallid, with dark, Iberian, melancholy eyes, and the other round, glowing, and ruddy, with grayish, Breton, twinkling eyes and a broad smile. As unlike as they were in appearance and disposition, in La Fauvette's mind the two began to blend into twin shapes, always together, falling over each other with polite consideration. This brotherhood was a living nightmare, a reminder, it seemed to her, of her past transgressions and the impossibility of the future. Her only escape was flight into unconsciousness.

Her awakening, followed by fright and retreat, was repeated several times. She had no idea where she was and had no inclination to raise her head far enough above the feather bedding to find out. Ah, the feather bedding! This much she was able to ascertain, they were all at the Barca estate where their new life was set to begin. A new life! The thought frightened her and she had just one desire—to delay this beginning for as long as possible. She had not heard anything from Doña Elvira, and that was just as well. How could she face this kind lady, who worshiped the ground her son walked on, how face her after what she had done to her Antonio? She would never understand that what her Antonio had done to her was an insult to her womanhood.

But the day came, as it had to come, when she opened her eyes and said to herself, enough of this, enough of hiding and turning away from the world. Nobody wished her evil. It was only from her own herself that she was seeking to hide. She sat up, determined to face whatever may come. Besides, there was Chantal. God in heaven, how could she have been so selfish to neglect her child?

Facing reality was still easier decided than done. Slightly enfeebled from the long bed rest, she rose, assisted not by a maid but by her two unsuspecting tormentors, who expressed immense delight in seeing her finally willing to face the world. Her first meal was almost spoon fed to her. And it was these two gentlemen who supported her, one on each side, as she took her first walk in the garden.

The Catalan spring was in full bloom and the estate, the first home she and Antoine had shared, was bustling with life. The sounds of children filled the yard. Chantal left her playmates when she saw her mother and flew into her arms. Life, wonderful life abounded all around. As she looked around, she realized they must have been here for a good while already.

The other fugitives from France had apparently long settled in by then. They all had a place and a task to fulfill. There was so much to be done around the house, the fields, and the vineyards that nobody was idle. A place had been set up for Gervaise in the kitchen. The pots she was now stirring brimmed with a thick hearty stew or potage. She had to bear the company of the head cook and a staff of kitchen helpers, but as long as she did not have to converse with them, which, given the language barrier was impossible anyway, she gruntingly acquiesced in the circumstances.

Only for the Marquise, there was little to do, even after she had recovered and was able to go about unassisted. She was the lady of the manor and therefore entitled to a life of leisure. But idleness leaves the mind to wander and to get lost in a maze of tortuous thoughts. She tried to cultivate the lost habit of reading, but the dimness of her eyesight made it a difficult chore and so was needlepoint, which she had always abhorred in any case.

She wandered about aimlessly for long hours in the vineyards and meadows. The exhilarating sense of freedom, she had savored at first, was dampened by a sense of futility and profound loneliness. Guibert was now frequently away in Barcelona, or somewhere—she knew not where—for long periods of time. Antoine too seemed preoccupied and kept his distance, now that she no longer needed any special care. She saw him only in the evenings, a dark, quiet figure across the common dinner table. He disappeared as soon as the meal was finished, as if he had some important business to attend to elsewhere at an appointed time. His evening forays from the Hôtel de Valinquette in the Marais revived in her mind, when not even her most alluring charm would keep him from the courtesans. Back then she did not permit herself to dwell on jealous thoughts no matter how much the hurt she felt. Jealousy was an emotion much disdained among the beau monde. But that was in another life. The beau monde and its foibles were far, far away in a world she barely remembered. The rules of the games the beau monde played had long lost their validity. Although she had forfeited any right to Antoine, the bitter poison of jealousy crept into her heart and at times drove her almost to distraction.

Confusion overwhelmed her. She paid frequent visits to the neighboring estate of the Barcas, and she extended her stays for longer and longer periods. Doña Elvira was always glad to see her. She had aged and was nearly blind, but when it came to matters of the human heart her perception had not dimmed. She was happy to have back the girl who had been like a daughter to her, even though she never considered her socially worthy of being her daughter-in-law. Her daughters were still unmarried, due to their brother's neglect of his duty to find suitable matches for them, she would say.

On days when the furies plagued her with such intense remorse that she could not face the kind old lady, she drove the greater distance to Manresa. La Belle Hélène felt lost and lonely in this foreign land and was happy to have somebody with whom she could converse in

French. The wedding preparations dragged out mainly because Hélène found myriad ways of delaying the moment when she would be permanently severed from her parents, from the world of the Parisian salons, the balls, the theaters, the summer parties in the country, and the flock of suitors, professing their willingness to fall on their swords if she said the word. She never put these effusions to the test, but then that was not the point anyway.

Hélène reminisced much about the past. The fleshpots of Paris were beckoning her, the lavish balls and feasts, life without a care. One day Hélène was gone, without a word, leaving behind a very distraught lover.

Guibert's travels in the company of Mathurin and Coupe-Cheveux became more frequent and more prolonged. His secretiveness, or perhaps it was just his lack of inclination to explain, aroused in her the fear that they may have returned to their former trade. Guibert was evasive, referring to his activities as "business" or, at other times, "important business." That was as specific as he would get. She had heard this explanation too often before not to know that it covered a multitude of doings, not excluding commerce conducted in houses of ill repute. The only person who was likely to know whether Guibert was engaged in something that might get him into conflict with the law was Antoine. She had observed that he spent a good deal of time at an old mill near the brook, and one afternoon she decided to pay a visit. As she came closer, she noticed that the mill had been refurbished for a different purpose. Was he still pursuing his artistic ambitions? Perhaps he had found another model and her intrusion would be awkward. Curiosity drove her on. She walked up to the window and peered inside. What she saw was quite astounding.

Her entire family, it seemed, was gathered there, engaged in some activity, the nature of which she could not determine at first. She made out Lucien standing over a copper vessel, huge as a cauldron. Gaston and Rémy, Fabrisse's oldest boys, sat at a table, contemplating some object in front of them. Antoine was speaking to them intently, pointing at the object. In the rear of the room were Arlette and Prosper. Their attention was also fixed on some object she could not make out.

Feeling like a spy who had stumbled upon some secret, perhaps illegal activity, she nevertheless wiped the pane to get a clearer view. This attracted Antoine's attention and he came immediately out to greet her.

"What a pleasure! Won't you come in, Madame!" he said, holding the door. It irked her that he addressed her so formally and wondered whether he meant to mock her. But she let it go. One day they would have to talk about the past and the future.

What she saw inside the mill made her head spin and almost took her breath away. Where ever the eye turned, there were carved wooden statues in the likeness of the Holy Virgin. They were everywhere, in every size, crowding shelves along the walls, stacked on tables, in various stages of completion on one side of the room; others, with bodies of gold and faces of lacquered black, were sitting in crates or ready to be put away. Now she saw what Lucien was doing at the cauldron. With the help of an elaborate pulley, he lowered the statues into the vessel, one at a time, dipping them into a bath of molten gold. Gaston and Rémy tried their hand at carving and painting. Prosper and Arlette were packing the finished products into the wooden crates.

Antoine was delighted to see her and proudly offered to show her around. Arlette and Prosper had been doing good business at the steps of the monastery at Montserrat, he explained. The monks made several attempts to have their stall shut down, but the popularity of the statues among the peasants forced them to back down.

"This is the Virgin of Montserrat, many times over!" La Fauvette marveled.

"Yes, it is an exact replica. Now every peasant, every bourgeois, every noble household can be a home for the Holy Virgin. Different sizes make it possible for everybody, even the poorest, to afford one." Antoine spoke with the pride of a successful entrepreneur.

"Here," he urged her, "why don't you choose one of these? See for yourself. Wood is, of course, a much more malleable material than marble or alabaster, quite satisfying to work with. Also not as heavy, and the results are rather pleasing."

She picked up one from among the statues that were ready for packing. Her fingers traced the fine lines of the Virgin's blackened face. There was something sad, something unearthly in her expression that reminded her of Antoine. Her pilgrimage to Montserrat in Barcelona so many years ago came to her mind. She had prayed for a child in the hope of keeping Antoine from all thoughts of Paris. How naïve she was then. The first part of her wish was fulfilled, only to be dashed in disaster. The second went unheard. But she had promised herself that she would not dwell on the past. It could not be changed. She had to look toward the future.

"You are a true artist, Antoine," she said softly, putting the statue back in its place. "This is an object of absolute beauty."

"Although they all look very much alike, to me they are individuals, and some of them one comes to love more than others." He picked up one of the medium-size statues and held it out to her. "This is one of my favorites. Please take it, it is yours."

"I should be very pleased." She took the figure from his hand, examined it from all sides, and stroked its smooth surface. On the bottom was an inscription. She could not make it out because she had come without the spectacles Guibert had brought for her from Barcelona.

"What does it say?" she asked.

"Oh, it's the name of the artist and his workshop."

"So what does it say?" she insisted.

"It says, Workshop of Antonio Barca."

"Antonio!" It sounded more sensuous than Antoine. "I used to call you Antonio—remember?—a long time ago."

"Yes," he nodded, "that was a long time ago."

"And what does it say underneath? There is another line."

"It says La Corte de los Milagros—that's the name of this workshop and of the estate."

She looked at him for a moment; then the meaning sank in. She raised herself up on her toes, drew his head down toward her with both hands, and covered his face with kisses.

"You wonderful, wonderful man! You named this place Court of Miracles? A much more apt application for this place than for the other one that went by that name."

"Didn't you know?" he said, gently releasing himself from her embrace. "You can see the inscription wrought in iron, in big letters, at the entrance gate to the estate—La Corte de los Milagros."

"I must have been too distracted to notice." She laughed a bit nervously, almost giddy, and turned toward the companions of her former trials. They had apparently had a much easier time getting used to the new circumstances. They greeted her but indicated that too much work was to be done to leave time for conversation.

She said good-bye and cradled Antoine's gift in her arms. Suddenly she remembered the reason why she had come to the mill in the first place and turned back toward Antoine.

"I don't want to disturb your work any further, but could I have a private word with you, just a brief word?" she whispered.

He showed her into a small room that looked like an accounting office with stacks of parchments piled on a desk and shelves.

"I am worried about Guibert," she began. Maybe she imagined it, but it seemed that Antoine's face darkened at the mention of the name. "It's his travels," she continued almost regretting that she had brought it up, but she had to go on now. "His travels give me cause for concern, especially in the company he keeps with criminals. I don't know how to say this . . ."

"You think Guibert might be engaged in something that will get him into trouble with the law," Antoine finished the sentence for her in the sanctimonious tone of a father confessor. "Well, fortunately I can put your mind at ease. The two criminals, as you call them, though driven to a life of crime in the past, are fully . . . but never mind that now. As for Guibert, he is my business partner. Yes, he handles the import and export side of the business. He obtains the raw material—gold, wood, dyes, whatever else. He also ships our products to markets in other parts of Spain and elsewhere. Right now he is in Barcelona to hire a cargo ship for a voyage to the New World." He was all businesslike, a manner she had never seen in him.

"Imagine what a demand for the Virgin of La Corte de los Milagros there will be!" he marveled. "The prospects are spectacular—millions of new Catholics willing to trade their gold for statues of the Holy Virgin. Gold is abundant in those regions and it has little value to these people. Every household can become a shrine, and we will profit handsomely in the bargain! Everybody will benefit!"

"It's very strange to hear you talk this way. Don't take me wrong, but it's so—how should I say?—bourgeois. But at least all this is not against the law, I presume."

Although her concerns had been put to rest and what she had discovered was truly exciting, the Marquise could not suppress a vague sense of sadness as she walked along the path that took her back to the manor house. It was not so much that Guibert was preparing for a voyage to the New World without taking the trouble of telling her about it—although that too irked her somewhat and she did not know what to make of Guibert's behavior toward her—but what saddened her most was that Antoine sounded so much like Guibert, like a profiteer. In Guibert this was part of his charm, the image that he could set the world on fire; in Antoine it sounded shallow and affected. Where was the idealist, the artist, the soul of the poet? Did he ever exist, or was he too a figment of her imagination? She totally seemed to forget that Antoine had been the man who in his younger years made a fortune in the New World which had permitted him to regain his title and possessions from the French Crown and to engage in a lavish lifestyle among the beau monde of Paris. Somehow in the time since their reunion in Catalonia, she had formed an idealistic image of him that excluded much of the reality of the past.

That afternoon she rambled aimlessly among the vineyards, thinking about what Antoine had said, about the activities at the mill, about Guibert's travels. Where was her place in all this? Utter dejection and worthlessness chilled her soul. Her imaginings that Antoine was heartbroken, that he avoided her because her presence was too much for him to bear, that he felt betrayed and hurt, none of this came to the surface during their conversation at the mill. His perfectly polite but cool manner singed her heart. She thought about his insistence on calling her Madame, never the old Galatée or La Fauvette. One thing was clear. She could not go on like this.

There had to be some stripping away of the polite pretense, some sorting out of who she was, of what her place was in the general scheme of this Corte de los Milagros. Was she the Marquise de Valinquette? Or was she the common-law wife of the Count de Mallac and committing adultery in her heart by desiring the Marquis de Valinquette? For this much had become clear to her, she was consumed with longing for Antoine.

Guibert's irregular comings and goings continued. Of Antoine she still saw very little. He was apparently taking dinner elsewhere more and more often and was otherwise busy down at the mill. They shared the same house, but lived in parallel worlds that rarely overlapped. Guibert made up for his absences by lavishing attention on her and Chantal when he was around. But they were never alone long enough for a serious talk. She was sure he was evading a direct confrontation.

Meanwhile preparations for his journey to the New World continued apace. The bustle at the mill intensified. Crates upon crates packed with Holy Virgins were transported to the docks in Barcelona. Mathurin and Coupe-Cheveux sat around the yard cleaning their pistols and muskets; they sharpened their knives and swords with the loving care of those who appreciate the peace of mind that comes from being prepared for eventualities. Since they had been entrusted with the protection of the Virgins, they used a little extra spit and polish on their weapons, just to be sure.

The wheel of life spun on in its relentless, eternal rhythm. The grim reaper gathered up Gervaise, abruptly and unannounced. She simply sank into herself one day while she was standing at the stove, still stirring her pots. A gentle parting from a life daubed in violence and grief. That she was buried in foreign soil mattered no more.

A short while later, wedding preparations sent a spark of excitement from the Barca estate to La Corte de los Milagros. The

Count de Launay had finally risen from mourning the loss of La Belle Hélène and had appeared at the Barca estate to ask for the hand of Camila, the older of Antoine's sisters. Gabriela, the younger one, tired of waiting for her brother to find her a husband, had run off with an itinerant guitar player and was never heard from again. That scandal, a wound in Doña Elvira's heart, one did not dare mention in the presence of any of the Barca clan. As for the Count de Launay's petition, one had certain reservations about his Protestantism, but after some consideration one was willing to overlook that shortcoming. There were after all not many competitors, and besides, his lineage was impeccable, one might even say of royal blood. A grand noble name and tremendous wealth made religion in this case a trifling matter.The festivities brought a lavish, extravagant French feast to the more rustic fare of the Catalans. The guests included every living soul on the Barca and Launay estates. They interrupted their drinking and gorging only to engage in wild, boisterous singing and dancing in honor of the bride and groom.

The Marquise sat quietly among the guests. Her wedding to Antoine, years before, had been a much more subdued affair. She decided that she liked that better. Her gaze fell on the bride, a virgin bordering on middle age, waxen with fright of what these raucous nuptials might portend. She had come precariously close to having to reconcile herself to spinsterhood. The sudden, unexpected rescue from a fate worse than death, as Doña Elvira saw it, was therefore quite overwhelming, especially given that she had met the groom only two weeks before the wedding and had never been alone with him to find out what kind of man he was.

Sisterly pity filled the Marquise's heart for the girl who, having never strayed from Doña Elvira's watchful eye, knew little of the world. She was looking for an opportunity to assure her that the Count de Launay was a kind, generous gentleman and that she could not wish for a better man, but just then, a sudden hush fell over the gathering. The musicians had abruptly stopped playing. All eyes turned toward the far end of the hall. The crowd parted, forming an espalier. At the far end of the aisle appeared the Count de Launay and the Marquis de Valinquette, side by side, each decked out in raiments more splendid than a peacock's plumage. The musicians started up again, the baleful voice of a lone flute gradually diffused into a solemn, sweet melody.

One by one, the tremulous, vibrant strings joined in a haunting dialogue. Just as slowly, the two gentlemen began to move down the aisle, their steps measured in mannered rhythm. They bowed gracefully from side to side with sombre expression, then strutted erect and graceful, one arm raised with the hand resting against the nape of the neck, the other on the hip, to the gently throbbing lilt of a pavane. As though initiating an exotic mating dance, they glided toward the dais—the Count toward his bride and the Marquis toward his wife.

The Marquise suppressed an inadvertent giggle that seized her at the sight of this bizarre display. Her bemusement soon gave way to flustered embarrassment. Antoine's serious, dark eyes held hers locked in his gaze. She distinctly felt that he was making love to her. Fear seized her that at any moment he might scoop her up into his arms. But she shouldn't have worried, he held strictly to the etiquette of the dance. He performed the prescribed pattern of elegant bows and curtsies in front of her and then turned and moved in perfect synchrony with the Count back down the aisle in an excruciatingly slow procession. A choreography executed to perfection!

From that day forward she secretly called him "mi pavo." Whenever they met, there was a slight embarrassment between them as between two secret lovers. He became more attentive, and she noticed that he stayed near her much more than in the months past. He accompanied her on early morning walks in the vineyards, on visits to Doña Elvira or to Manresa and the new Countess de Launay. He helped her in and out of the carriage, extended his arm for her to lean on. But he was always what might be called correct.

In the evenings, after she had put Chantal to bed, they sat together in the drawing room by the fire. He would read to her. As in the old days, she thought. Or he would stretch out in front of the fireplace, close his eyes and listen to her sing the doleful Spanish and Catalan songs he loved so much. But she never sang the one of the rising dead.

Sometimes he would ask her to sing something in French, although France, once his holy grail, had become a remote place that held few pleasant memories.

Outwardly they gave the appearance of an ordinary married couple, except that they parted at night at her chamber door. One evening when they were saying good night, he touched his lips gently to hers and she fought the impulse to pull him into her arms. After that they said good night in the drawing room or library and she mounted the stairs alone. But even without turning her head, she felt his gaze following her every step until she closed the door behind her.

Thoughts of Guibert faded more and more with each passing month of his absence. Few messages from him reached the estate at La Corte de los Milagros and those that did were almost exclusively assurances that business was going well. The Virgins were a great success in the New World and he admonished Antoine to keep up production. His pledge of love for La Fauvette and Chantal seemed added as a polite afterthought.

Wherever she turned, Antoine was there.

"You are neglecting your work, Antonio. What is going to happen to the Virgins?" she scolded.

"I have very talented assistants. Before long Gaston and Rémy will take my place."

They continued their reading together in the evenings by the light of the fire. One evening he brought something special, a worn copy of *L'Astrée*. He began to read the passage of the presumed suicide of Céladon, who jumped into the river because Astrée would not reciprocate his love. She listened and said nothing.

That night he accompanied her again to her chamber door. He leaned forward to kiss her good night, a light chaste grazing of the lips, but the kiss she returned was not meant for a mere friend. He suddenly found himself showered with such passion, he retreated a step to gasp for air. She firmly took him by the hand, pulled him inside, and bolted the chamber door. She guided his hands to loosen her garments while she reached for the single burning candle. But before she could extinguish the flame, he held back her hand.

"I want to see you," he muttered. His eyes gleaming with desire, he gently stroked her breasts, no longer alabaster, firm, and youthful. Still his eyes feasted on every part of her body, which had none of the perfection of the one he had placed on a pedestal but would not touch.

"Are you very disappointed? I'm afraid Galatée has ceased to exist, if she ever was real."

"Don't worry. I've long given her up for lost," he whispered. "And as you say, she was more a figment of my imagination than a real woman. You are to me the most beautiful woman in the world, just as you are. What a fool I was! How much pain I brought on both of us with my fancy! It took a long time, but I have finally come to realize that my love always belonged to the little songbird on the Pont Neuf that first moved my heart, La Fauvette from the Court of Miracles at Saint-Médard."

Edwards Brothers Malloy
Thorofare, NJ USA
January 16, 2013